SILENT CRICKETS

The Shallow End Gals Trilogy

Book Three

TERESA DUNCAN

VICKI GRAYBOSCH

MARY HALE

LINDA MCGREGOR

KIMBERLY TROUTMAN

BOOK ONE: ALCOHOL WAS NOT INVOLVED

BOOK TWO: EXTREME HEAT WARNING

BOOK THREE: SILENT CRICKETS

A VERY SPECIAL THANKS TO:

ERIKA CANTER

BOB SMITH

MICHAEL SUTHERLAND

SUSAN WEAVER

SADIE CORBIN

JOCELYN SCHULTZ

CAROLYN GALE

CINDY ROY

VALETA COVINGTON

DEBBIE JASINSKI

JENNIFER DUNCAN

JUDY LUKASIEWICZ

Copyright © Vicki Graybosch 2013
All rights reserved
Printed in the United States of America
Copyrighted Material

ISBN-1484034155

ISBN-9781484034156

Editorial Services: Erika Canter

List of characters at end of book

SILENT CRICKETS

CHAPTER ONE

Mambo stood at the edge of the swamp and focused her large dark eyes across the black bayou inlet. She had tried for many months to lure the child spirit to her. She could see the slight blue glow of his small frame squatting in the tall marsh grasses. He was looking at her, peeking through the reeds. He was closer this time. Mambo could sense his fear. She closed her eyes, rubbed her amulet and asked the spirits to assure him she could help. Like all of the times before, when she looked back to him, he was gone.

Jeanne called out again for Lisa. Why wasn't she answering? Jeanne walked half the length of the damp tunnel when she heard footsteps running toward her. She held her gun behind her back. If it were Lisa and Jamie she didn't want to scare them. In the dim light from the wall lantern Jeanne could see the small form of Jamie moving toward her. Lisa was directly behind her, "Mathew was just here. He told us to stay with you. He said he needed to make some things right."

Tears streamed down Lisa's cheeks. She was noticeably frightened. She looked at Jeanne and asked, "Who are those men? Why are they trying to harm us?" Jamie sucked on her thumb, her eyes wide as she leaned into Lisa and hung onto her shirttail. Jamie was six years old, and Jeanne was quite sure she had stopped sucking her thumb years ago. Lisa and Jamie were in an impossible situation now.

Jeanne answered, "I'm having you both taken to our field office for safety. An agent there will explain to you what is happening." Jeanne knelt down and looked into Jamie's eyes, "The bad guys will not hurt you now. There are two more agents here, and one of them has been injured. He's my brother. We need to get him to the hospital. I'd like to meet up with you later. Is that okay Jamie?"

Jamie nodded and took her thumb out of her mouth. "Is your brother an FBI person too?"

"Yes."

Jamie exhaled and looked at Lisa, "Mom, we have a lot of thinking to do. You should stop crying

2

now and try to think of something happy. There is always something happy, remember?" Lisa wiped her eyes and smiled at Jamie. Jeanne's heart was breaking for them both. Life was never going to be the same for them.

Supervisory Special Agent Dan Thor called the New Orleans field office. He told them to send an ambulance for Pablo, and an agent to provide protection for Mathew Core's wife and kid. Thor added, "Send a cleanup crew. We have three dead guys in the swamp grasses out here."

Thor was on the ground. Pablo's head rested on his lap. Thor applied pressure to the shoulder wound and prayed help would get there soon. Pablo was showing signs of shock and had lost a lot of blood. Thor watched the ambulance pull in and waved them over. Special Agent Nelson's SUV spun into the drive. Thor pointed to Jeremiah's house where Nelson would find Lisa and Jamie.

Jeanne ran over and helped the EMTs get Pablo on a stretcher. She kissed his forehead and said, "You're going to be okay. I know it." Pablo blinked his eyes as the EMTs put an oxygen mask on him and hoisted the gurney into the back of the ambulance. Jeanne watched as they left, sirens blaring. Her mind was racing. Jeremiah would come home to this chaos and be afraid. She knew she should stay at the site and give her report to the field agents who were now arriving. She could feel Pablo's pain and fear. They were twins. She wanted to be near him.

Jeanne looked at Thor. He was covered in Pablo's blood. His eyes locked with hers, and he knew exactly what was racing through her mind. He pulled a handkerchief from his pocket and wiped Pablo's blood from his hands. "Come on. I'll drive."

Jackson didn't pay much attention to the guard who said, "Get up. You're outa here." Sadistic son of bitches would say anything to get you goin'. The guard unlocked the door and mumbled, "You one lucky fool."

Jackson looked at the guard's facial expression and realized he was serious. "What you talkin' 'bout?" Jackson moved to a sitting position on his cot. This had been home for five years, and there was still another dime left on his sentence.

The guard motioned with his arm, "Quit askin' stupid questions, and just move it. Seems someone got your ass a sentence revoke order. You got a ride waitin' on ya. Best move it." The guard chuckled as he jingled the keys, "Lessin' you want to stay?"

Jackson threw his shirt on and slipped into his shoes. He put his hands out for the cuffs and the guard laughed, "You deaf boy? You be a free man! I ain't cuffin' your ass. I'm walkin' you to the gate."

If this was some kind of mistake, Jackson wasn't going to be the one to mention it. He quickly shuffled down the hall with the guard and barely heard the deafening jeers of the other inmates. The guard buzzed through several corridor gates and pointed to a large steel double door. "We're going out this way." Jackson followed. He had never been in this part of the prison before.

Soon they were outdoors. Even though the heat was oppressive, the breeze felt like magic. They walked over to the tall chain link gate used primarily for delivery trucks. An old, gold Chevy Impala sat idling. A man about Jackson's age got out and walked over. He had something cupped in his hand as he shook hands with the guard.

He winked and said, "Rest of yours been taken care of." He looked at Jackson, "Let's go. You're already late for work."

Abram put the car in gear and pulled away from the prison yard. He looked over at Jackson. "My name is Abram. I guess you could say I'm your new boss. Old boss got shot this morning. 'Bout thirty times!" Abram laughed out loud then turned to Jackson, "You heard what's been goin' on in the city?"

Jackson shook his head. Abram looked in the rearview mirror, used his turn signal and slowly pulled into the traffic on the highway. He looked at Jackson. "You got to watch yourself real close right now. Feds had some big weapon/drug seizure at the docks last night. Streets are dry. Nobody got much product. You can't get your hands on nothin'! Lot of folks startin' to panic, ya know?"

Abram used his turn signal to change lanes and glanced down to make sure he wasn't speeding. "Heard it was FBI, but they got Navy, Coast Guard and National Guard involved too. Said Nawlens under martial law or some damn shit. This morning they blasted the four main hoods. Killed people, took our drugs and guns. Left military jeeps rollin' through the streets. We figure we lost a couple dozen guys at least. Dead. Whole bunch of 'em in the Navy jail. Hear tell, if the government declares martial law, it ain't like a regular arrest where ya go to jail. *Them* boys lookin' at court martials." Abram looked at Jackson's shocked expression and continued. "Manio Cartel lost some people this afternoon in some kind of abduction thing. FBI not only killed 'em all but knew they were comin'. Nasty shit goin' down."

Jackson wondered if he hadn't been safer in the prison. "So what do you want with me?"

Abram glanced quickly over at Jackson. "I always heard you be a standup guy. Took the jail time and didn't squeal none. Hell, didn't really have nothin' to do with nothin'. I need to replace a guy we lost this mornin'. Fast. Need somebody trustin'. Good money to be had, and I figured we owed ya. Falled on me to make a couple of calls and here you are. We got us a judge we use."

Abram rubbed his chin and quickly glanced over. "You got a problem snatchin' kids?"

Jackson surprised himself when he answered, "No." His mind screamed, *Hell yes!*

✳ ✳ ✳

Mathew Core knocked on the door of his rental unit over the jewelry store next to Mickey's Bar. Duane came to the door and said, "Hey man. Rent not due yet."

Mathew smiled and said, "I got twenty grand cash says you just decided to move. Now." Mathew held out the fat envelope. Duane peeked inside.

Duane grasped the envelope and said, "Just let me grab my car keys."

✳ ✳ ✳

Alan was driving down the highway toward Slidell when he saw an ambulance tear out of Uncle Jeremiah's driveway and head towards New Orleans. What the hell? He abruptly turned his truck onto Jeremiah's drive and almost collided head on with an SUV driven by Agent Todd Nelson. Nelson lowered the driver's window and stuck his hand out for Alan to stop. Alan yelled over, "Is Uncle Jeremiah okay?"

Nelson nodded. "He's out on his boat. There was a shooting here. Pablo was hit in the shoulder. Can you stay and explain it all to Jeremiah? The guys back there will bring you up to speed."

Alan noticed a woman and child in the backseat. He answered "Sure," and continued to drive back into the property. Two NOPD patrol cars, a coroner wagon, and two black FBI SUVs sat in Jeremiah's drive. Agents and officers walked around Jeremiah's yard pointing and writing in notebooks. Alan could see Jeremiah pushing his boat to shore and looking around at the chaos. Alan parked his truck and ran over to the edge of the swamp to meet him.

"Uncle Jeremiah, everything is fine. There was some kind of situation here, but it is over now." Jeremiah looked tired. Worried. His skin was sweaty from the oppressive afternoon heat. Alan held out his arm to help Jeremiah off the boat. Jeremiah wrapped a rope around a large cypress root and slowly lowered his old bent body to sit on his favorite stump.

He looked at Alan, "Is Jeanne okay?" To be out at his place, he knew whatever happened must have involved her.

"Think so. I only know her brother, Pablo, was shot and the ambulance has already taken him away." Alan and Jeremiah watched the coroner's team carry a body out of the tall marsh grasses, load it in the coroner's wagon, and return back to the grasses with the body board.

Jeremiah swatted a mosquito on the side of his neck and adjusted his eye patch. He looked at Alan, "I 'spect somebody pissed her off."

* * *

SSA Roger Dance dropped his briefcase on the hotel bed and hung his suit jacket on a chair. On the jet, the FBI Director had given him twenty pages of transcripts from last night's communication sting. He carried the stack of pages over to the small table near the window. Roger had asked Paul and John to give him about thirty minutes to think things out. Thor had called to tell Roger he was driving Jeanne to the hospital to be with Pablo. Nelson had Mathew Core's wife and daughter in protective custody at the FBI field office.

Roger was grateful Jeanne had survived the abduction attempt of the Manio cartel against Mathew Core's wife and daughter. His team had been pushed to their limits after the raid last night at the dock, the neighborhood sweeps this morning, and the shoot-outs at Core's house and Jeremiah's a few hours ago. It had already been an extraordinary last couple of days.

Roger's plan to capture all communications in conjunction with last night's martial law raid had revealed through the transcripts, his team faced even larger threats than he had suspected.

Roger ran his fingers through his hair and stretched his neck. The sunlight coming through the window blared across his pages and reminded him how oppressive the New Orleans heat was outside. He caught a glimpse of his reflection in the window glass. The Director wasn't the only one this case was aging. Roger shuffled the transcript pages until he found the call where Mathew Core was warned of the FBI raid, precisely when it started. Later, Core had called the Deputy Director of the FBI, William C. Thornton. Thornton had then called Thomas Fenley.

John Barry and the FBI Director were quite alarmed to see Fenley's name in these transcripts. Roger had to assume Fenley represented a new threat.

Roger knew the sting cover could be blown any minute. Thomas Fenley and FBI Deputy Director William C. Thornton had any number of ears that would soon be alerting them that all communications were being monitored, including secure government lines, until midnight Friday. Tomorrow. Roger could only hope they would capture a few more meaningful transmissions before then.

Roger's eyes moved down the pages to the call that Thomas Fenley had placed to Jesse Manio, head of the Manio Cartel. It was obvious now. The Manio Cartel was the intended recipient of the sixty tons of weapons diverted to the port storage building from the ship. The remaining thirty tons on the ship had been a decoy transaction the Deputy Director of the FBI, William C. Thornton, had arranged to entrap the Zelez Cartel. Mathew Core had brokered the deal. Bringing ninety tons of weapons into the United States by ship from Algiers, under FBI protection, for some scheme with two major cartels was astounding and arrogant. These men were confident they could do anything they wanted and probably had been doing so for quite some time.

He read again the passage where Manio ordered the abduction of Mathew Core's wife and daughter, and threatened blood baths in fifteen U.S. cities. Roger rubbed his temples and closed his eyes. When he had first read this, it scared the crap out of him. Now, an hour later, this sounded like a spoiled child's rant. Manio hadn't kept his position of power by acting on non-productive threats. Manio would be looking for a better resolution.

Roger paced around the small room. He could actually taste his contempt for Manio, Thornton, and Fenley. Roger needed them to feel like they were still in control if he was going to win this thing.

The one piece he couldn't connect was Jason Sims, Mathew Core's computer guy. What was he trying to do with the CIA super-frame? Was he protecting his own interests or was there a larger picture? Mathew Core was connected to all of these players in some way. A decorated Marine turned black op. He was apparently, both a valued asset of the government, and a dangerous threat at the same time. Whatever Core was, he was in a bad spot, and he was asking for Roger's help.

Stopping the sicko club was in the front of Roger's mind too. If they acted quickly, they would be able to save any number of children from this group. He had John Barry's guy, Tourey, closing in on Patterson, but there was no time to spare. Patterson still had to be caught. Thanks to Tourey they knew where Patterson was hiding. Roger sat across from his computer and started tapping his pen on his knee. Any one of these problems would normally require months of investigation and a lot of manpower. Roger didn't have either. He had to buy some time.

Roger searched his computer for his downloaded version of Ravel's Bolero and walked around the room as he listened to the steady, restrained beat of the snare drum and the almost sickeningly sweet melody that just repeated and repeated until it almost seemed like an unstoppable march. He knew percussionists hated this song. They had one cadence to play, and the tempo was unchanged from start to finish. Fifteen minutes of hell for the drummers. Some conductors appeased the drum section by letting them sit in front of the orchestra for performances and advising the audience of the difficulties of maintaining the tempo and volume for such an extended time.

He tapped his pen to the beat as he listened to the orchestra instruments enter and one by one, grab the melody and slowly twist and distort it.

About three quarters through the piece the trombones boldly enter with what sounds like a taunting brash assault on the melody and the power of the piece shifts to the strings, double reeds, and saxophones. The brass instruments mimic the drum cadence and quickly take over with sheer volume and attitude. The once fluid melody is now staccato and brazenly altered. The buildup to the ending has every orchestra instrument adding their taunting twists, attacking the melody, and completely drowning out the once unchallenged snare drums. Then the choir voices join in, the voices of the people. The last sixteen bars of the piece sounds as if the orchestra has gone mad and is laughing at the ruin of the original melody. As a listener, he had always felt the piece should have been entitled, 'The Orchestra's Revenge'.

Roger liked the comparison of Fenley and friends to the snare drums. They had been steadily tapping along, marching their sickening melody onward with no intervention. Roger decided his plan needed to be subtle. He needed time to organize the rest of the orchestra, quietly introduce his players, and methodically twist the tune.

Paul and John arrived outside Roger's hotel room and heard the music coming from inside. John looked at Paul, "You hear what I hear?"

"Yep, sounds like Roger's got a plan."

Retired Senator Rolland Kenney tried again to reach Patterson by phone. No answer. Rolland had told him not to leave the country house. With the FBI and that crazy spook-type guy looking for him, you would think he would have listened. Ever since Bernard Jacobs confessed his true identity, William Patterson escaped pedophile and murderer, Rolland had been torn between feelings of pure admiration and fear. Patterson was famous. The ten million dollars Patterson had paid him had been confirmed by Rolland's bank as received. All of this drama was actually very exciting. The other club members had to be kept in the dark about this though. Hell, one of them was a sitting judge.

Rolland looked at his appointment calendar, then his watch. It was two-thirty now, and he had a three o'clock he needed to attend. If Patterson didn't answer after that, he would just drive out to the country house. Rolland smiled. Their deliveries would start arriving Monday. He got goose bumps from his excitement. He turned to his computer and replayed the DVD of the Los Angeles Children's Art Contest again. He wiggled in his chair and clapped his hands when his 'winner' appeared on the screen describing his art piece. Oh my, he was precious!

CHAPTER TWO

SSA Simon Frost finished up at the crime scene at Mathew Core's house. Special Agent Todd Nelson told Simon that he was with Core's wife and kid at the FBI field office. Simon arrived and found Nelson in SSA Frank Mass's office. Simon knocked on the open door and walked in. "Somebody want to bring me up to speed?"

Nelson pushed his chair back, so Simon could take the other seat across from Mass's desk. Nelson looked at Simon, "When I got to Jeremiah's, they were putting Pablo in an ambulance. Thor was covered in blood. Pablo's. Pablo took one in the shoulder. He's in surgery now." Simon's eyebrows went up. Nelson continued, "Jeanne and Thor are at the hospital. We found three more dead guys at Jeremiah's. We're running IDs on them now. Roger told Thor they're probably part of the Manio Cartel. They sent eight guys out to get Core's wife and kid to use as insurance on that weapons deal. Roger said the sixty tons on shore was for Manio."

Simon whistled, "Well, if you're going to piss somebody off, might as well start at the top. We killed all eight? That ought to make Manio happy. Shit. That is the largest cartel in the Americas." Simon rested his left ankle on his right knee and leaned his chair back. "If Manio had eight guys to get Core's family that fast, they have a heavy presence in New Orleans."

Mass looked at Simon, "They do. Look at a map. Whoever controls the ports of New Orleans owns the U.S. The numbers on last night are worse than we thought. My sources say last night we confiscated four times the amount of drugs than we thought came into this port in a year. Obviously a lot of crap's flyin' under the radar. I'm surprised the Zelez Cartel is trying to squeeze in. Everyone knows Manio runs New Orleans."

Mass leaned forward, "I'm worried. Roger wants Core's wife and kid safe. They are resting in a small apartment here at the office under guard. I can kick in witness protection or handle this in house. What's your gut?"

Simon shook his head slowly, "This has to be Roger's call. He's getting information from last night's communication sting that we don't even know yet. All we know is the Manio Cartel want these two. That sure as hell isn't good. Our most vulnerable window is right now, before we decide what to do."

Simon looked at Nelson, "Jeanne obviously killed five guys at Core's house, you said three more were dead at Jeremiah's, and she shot Devon yesterday. This chic needs some down time. Pablo is having surgery, so he's out. Ray's a geek and isn't field trained. I think we have a manpower issue, especially if this office is the only thing keeping Lisa and Jamie safe from Manio."

Mass nodded his head, "I only have myself and two other field guys here. Phillips is worthless in the field. Local PD is calling us every hour for some kind of help. This martial law operation has had a few downsides to it. I suppose we could tap the National Guard."

Just then Mass's phone rang. He listened for a while, said thanks, and hung up. He looked at Simon and said, "Can you believe a gang of punks tried to break into the secured naval yard and steal back some drugs? Streets are close to dry today, might make for some tense moments."

Simon stabbed a toothpick into the corner of his mouth, "Get some Guard here to secure the perimeter of this building. This is probably just the beginning. Desperate people do desperate things."

We were all still riding around town with the National Guard dudes. I kind of thought hangin'

out with the guys I would hear some good jokes or *something*. Nope. These guys were all business. I was actually happy when Ellen called and said to meet Betty in the park at Transition College. We haven't seen Betty for a long time. She not only looked like Betty White, because heaven wanted us to feel comfortable, but she seemed to have her personality. Ellen had said this case of Roger's was too fast paced for Betty. She preferred to stay on the education side of our training. The bad thing is, that probably means we are supposed to learn something new. I'm still on shaky ground from the last batch of classes. I got to the park and Linda, Mary and Teresa were already there.

We heard a motor revving up behind us and saw Betty riding a pink motorcycle with a sidecar off to each side. Cool! She had on the cutest pink helmet and little pink leather jacket and boots. There was room for two of us in each sidecar and Betty waved us over, "Come on gals! Let's take a spin to the zoo!"

Alright! I bet we are being rewarded for a good job!

Teresa yelled to be heard over the motor, "We thought we had to take another class!"

Betty smiled, "You have to take three classes: one to turn into animals, one to implant memory gaps, and one to freeze mortals."

I looked at Mary, "Did she say we have to turn into animals to implant flaps to please mortals?" I was getting a very bizarre vision. Seemed kind of kinky for angels.

Mary looked at me, "What is wrong with you?"

I'm wondering why we would have to be animals to implant flaps. Couldn't we just look like doctors? Monkeys could probably do it. They would look cute in the doctor outfits. I'm going to get a head start on this. Where would be the best places for flaps? Hmmmm.

Betty stopped the motorcycle and closed her eyes. "How does Ellen do it?" Then she tilted her head, put on that big Betty White smile, and looked at me, "Watch my lips. You are going to learn how to turn into animals, implant memory GAPS, and FREEZE time around mortals." Ohhhhh. Huh. I'm not sure that makes any more sense than my version.

We arrived at the zoo and followed Betty into a large caged area. Linda smiled at me, "You crack me up." Goody. Wait 'til their hearing starts to go. Just then a large polar bear slowly sauntered out from a huge black hole in the hillside. EEE GADS!

We all jumped behind Betty and the polar bear said, "I'll take it from here."

Betty turned and smiled at us, "Have fun gals. When your instructors say you're done, go find Ellen." Betty patted my shoulder, "You'll do just fine dear." And she was gone.

Thor and Jeanne arrived at the hospital and were ushered into a small, dark, surgical waiting room. They were the only people in the room. The blinds were closed on all but one of the glass windows facing the busy hallway. The nurse told them Pablo's surgery would probably take an hour or so. Thor took a seat at one end of a small couch, and Jeanne sat at the other.

Jeanne closed her eyes and raised her chin to rest the back of her head against the wall. "It's true what they say about twins, you know. I can tell Pablo is going under." She rolled her head in his direction and barely opened her eyes, "Thank you for letting me be here." Thor nodded. Jeanne kept looking at him. There was something about him, she sensed his raw strength, and a hungry soul. "I hope I'm not out of line, I just….it's almost spooky. I feel like I've known you forever. Sometimes, it seems like I know what you're thinking."

Thor's mind screamed, *Damn, I hope not!* He heard himself say, "Yeah. Whatever. You're just tired." He walked outside of the room and came back with a pillow. He held it out to her. "Here, close your eyes for a few."

Jeanne looked around the room and asked, "Can I use your lap?" Thor sat back down, his mind screaming, *Holy Crap!* Jeanne looked at his blood soaked pants. She saw they were dry and placed the pillow on his lap. She closed her eyes and was breathing deep in minutes. Thor knew she was exhausted, so was he. He tried to rest his arm along the top of the narrow couch, but it wasn't comfortable. He let his arm rest along her side, put his head back against the wall, and closed his eyes. He fought the temptation to watch her sleep. It felt like electrical currents were charging through his body. He was in trouble. Damn, deep trouble. He knew it the first moment he saw her.

* * *

Paul glanced over at John as he knocked on Roger's hotel room door. "Did you come up with any grand plan?" John shook his head.

Roger opened the door to let them both in and smiled. "Thanks for giving me a few." He walked over to the small table now pulled into the center of the room and gestured for the others to join him. John Barry stood by the window, and Paul sat with Roger at the table. Roger had his papers from the Director neatly stacked. He looked at them both. "Where are we?"

John looked very serious as he turned from the window, "I need to tell you both about a case OSI and CIA have been working on that might end up part of all of this." John waved his copies of the transcripts in the air. "Some of these phone conversations seem to tie in."

Roger leaned back in his chair and started clicking his pen, "Okay, John."

John shook his head slightly. "About five years ago Tourey and I were part of a black op to expose a global computer terrorism plot. The masterminds of this plan represent oil and diamonds in London, money in the U.S. and Caymans, and manpower and guns in Yemen. The CIA used the first letter of each: London, U.S., Cayman and Yemen to nickname this group LUCY. I would say LUCY is one of the most serious threats the United States faces. LUCY has the will and assets to get what they want, and the ability to implement their plans."

"The goal of LUCY is to use their codes to infiltrate critical computer systems. The utility grids and security programs of every developed country in the world are at risk. LUCY's goal is to be in a position to threaten those triggers. What LUCY wants is for all monetary agencies to ignore the movement of their money."

Roger said, "So the deal is, you leave our money alone, and we leave your utility grids and security systems alone."

John answered, "Precisely. There is a difference between staying ahead of the law, buying off the law, and owning the law. It costs LUCY trillions of dollars to work through shell corporations, shell banks, and ghost entities. Our entire legitimate banking system is involved and, to no small degree corrupted. We slap sanctions on them, fine them, they fire a few people and start again. We don't stop them, but we are very annoying ticks in their fur. We are everywhere since the Vienna and Palermo Conventions."

This was sounding familiar to Roger. "I've heard of LUCY through agency briefs, but I thought the CIA spooks had this under control." Roger leafed through the papers the Director had given them from the communication sting. "We have Thomas Fenley calling Manio, and then Manio calling someone in London. That person then called someone in Yemen." Roger focused on John, "This does sound like your LUCY." John nodded. Roger continued, "Makes me wonder what Jason Sims was trying to do in the CIA super-frame if LUCY is ultimately a cyber-terrorism threat."

John answered, "I just spent thirty minutes on the phone with my Director on that very topic. We were able to stop them in London five years ago largely through information obtained by one of our outside contractors."

Paul asked, "Core?"

"Yes. People way above me know the details. We released our first solid evidence in February 2004. The U.S. –Canada Power System Outage Task Force released their final report on the US eastern blackout. It had been scrubbed, but it did mention, on purpose, the identity of a software bug known as a race condition. This bug existed in General Electric Energy's Unix-based XA/21 energy management system. Once triggered, the bug *allowed* an entire chain of events by not acti-vating the alarm system for the event. Few people connected the dots that after the grid came back up, over a hundred oil drilling permits were issued that had been tabled. We wanted LUCY to know that we knew what they had done. That's why that line was left in the report. Even though we publically blame the Russians and Chinese for most cyber threats, LUCY is all about oil."

"That access 'hole' in the software program Ray discovered is now being called the rabbit hole. For the first time, ever, we have direct evidence of who is pulling the strings, and more importantly, how. That is really why we were able to get this 'sting' of yours classified a martial law operation. Frankly, the United States is the only hope left for stopping this."

Roger asked, "Then what do we have here with Core? Is he a good guy, rogue, what?"

John answered, "I honestly don't know. Decorated marine, one of our best. His connection to Jason Sims is certainly suspect, and he obviously takes jobs from Fenley and Thornton. He also seems to be of the mindset that he is above the law. I suspect by now he is a little of everything."

John started pacing, "One of the names Ellen told me not to trust is the CIA's task force leader on the LUCY project. This task force is supposed to protect us from LUCY. They got to him. He's a mole."

Paul leaned his chair back and caught himself from tipping at the last minute. "Whoa! How did you explain knowing that and the rabbit hole?"

John smiled at Roger, "I reported this was discovered by the FBI. I think your Director came up with a cover story. This is really tricky working with information from Ellen that we can't prove. We can only strongly suggest our suspicion about the task force leader, and hope the bureaucracy paranoids take over. The rest of the task force are all good people. Believe me, they are all over this. Ray's rabbit hole is the break they needed." John sat back on the couch, "For right now I think we can concentrate on our more local issues and leave LUCY to the big boys. It does help knowing these agendas though."

Roger leaned forward in his chair. "John, are you going to be tied up in this LUCY deal or are you available for this local stuff?"

John shrugged, "For now, I think I can help you with the local stuff. Fair warning, OSI expects these cases to collide."

Roger loosened his tie and walked toward the window to look out at the street traffic. "Okay. Let's move on. Manio needs his guns to ward off competing cartels like Friday's buyer Zelez, right?" John nodded. "What if we offer Manio something better than the guns? Some kind of evidence that our focus is to destroy the entire Zelez Cartel? Wouldn't he play along to see if it works? It would certainly make his life easier to eliminate the competition. It might buy us some time to form a real plan."

"It might also cause Fenley to call off the hit on you and Paul if he thinks you are actually helping him."

Roger started clicking his pen. "The Manio and Zelez Cartels are the big worry right now. I can only think of one way to get our information to both Manio and Zelez."

John and Paul answered in unison, "Core."

Roger looked at John, "I'll have my Director convince Thornton we are hell bent on taking down the entire Zelez Cartel. I'll promise specifics later. If we are right about these transcripts, we have stumbled into a LUCY operation. I see a huge opportunity. LUCY's goals are the accumulation of money from illegal activities, and having a 'safe haven' from law enforcement. If we create a safe haven, would they use it?"

John and Paul looked at each other. John asked, "How are you going to do that convincingly? That's been tried a dozen times and they always sniff out a sting."

Roger smiled, "They didn't have martial law rules to play by. We can pick our players. No leaks. I want Thornton to think I have botched a couple of things. Big things, like the French Quarter Bank accounts. I need to think this out more. If it works, LUCY will just hand over their precious money. Thornton and Fenley need to keep feeling superior and in control. This might buy us a little time."

Roger's thoughts jumped back to Patterson and the sicko club. "John, can you check with Tourey, see if anything has happened on the Patterson front, and let me know?"

John nodded, "Tourey isn't thrilled I volunteered him to the FBI, but if anybody can connect the dots, it's him. I don't know how long we can keep him on the Patterson case though. He has a history fighting LUCY, and it wouldn't surprise me if the CIA doesn't pull him back in the case, too."

Paul stood and stretched his back, "Normally we would need a couple of months to sort through all of this. I'd be happy with three days."

John headed toward the door, "These kids don't have three days. If this pedophile club is expecting a delivery from Los Angeles on Monday, some kids are going to come up missing sometime today or tomorrow. That's just the delivery we know about."

John left and Roger looked at Paul, "I'm going to call Core. Core wants his family. He'll work with us. We can't secure Core's family at the field office, and I need what's left of our team on this sicko club. Call Mass and see how fast we can get Core's wife and daughter in Witness Protection."

Mass said he would start the process of getting Lisa and Jamie into the program. Paul asked Mass to send Simon Frost and Nelson back to the Star Ship to focus on Patterson. Paul's phone rang.

It was Ray. "By the way, our dead guy, Devon, has been moving his money into Core's corporate account over the last half hour. Got a bunch coming in from Patterson, too. All from the Caymans. I'm up to over 300 million and growing."

Paul whistled and looked at Roger, "Core has been moving Devon and Patterson's money to his corporate account. He has over 300 million there now, and it's still coming."

Roger had just hung up from talking to Core, "Core will be here in half an hour. Ellen will be here to help."

CHAPTER THREE

Tourey hit print and pushed his chair away from his desk. He rolled across the room to grab a binder from his bookshelf and started flipping through it. Somewhere he had a code for the secure FBI database on missing children. He had hidden the code on the back of a photo of a missing child in what looked like a family photo album. He replaced the binder after searching about ten minutes and pulled another down. There. He found it. He rolled back to his computer, entered the FBI National Crime Information Center website, and entered his code. The site reported that in 2011 alone there were 780,000 children reported missing. An increase of 480 *percent* over 2009.

He filtered his search for missing children, last five years, and in the cities where the sicko club had branches. Tourey watched the revolving curser spin. Finally the search revealed 497,000 children still listed as missing. He filtered this data with the tag words 'art contest'. This would only sort out those children missing where the investigating officers had entered the words 'art contest', but at least it was something. The cursor spun again. Three thousand six hundred and twenty. Shit.

Tourey searched for unidentified murdered children in the same cities. Twenty two thousand and ten. He moaned and rubbed his temples in frustration. Normally his CIA undercover position didn't put him in contact with these statistics. It was a staggering growth in abduction numbers. What was happening? Now to figure out how to match a body found in one city to the missing kids of another. Unfortunately less than five percent of the missing children had DNA registered in the national database. Tourey shook his head. Certainly with today's technology we could implement a better system. It was easier to find our pets with implanted chips, and an established, accessible national ID base.

Tourey's cell phone rang. He leaned back in his chair, and welcomed the distraction from his computer. He looked at his caller ID and put on his Nawlens voice.

"Hey Spicey. What can I do for ya?"

Spicey answered, " 'Member you asked me if I knew anyone worked around that retired Senator Rolland Kenny or Judge Williams?"

Tourey answered, "Yeah."

Spicy continued, "The lady that used to clean for Bernard Jacobs? 'Member he torched his place over on Burgundy Street? She just got a job cleanin' for Senator Kenny. Both his city place and country house. I'm thinkin' she can do some spyin' for ya as long as she don't realize she's doin' it."

Tourey liked the sound of that, but he was sure her access to the country house would be pretty limited. With what the sicko club planned on doing at the country house, they wouldn't have people coming and going. Tourey asked, "When is she supposed to start workin' at the country house?"

"Wilma said the Senator told her it would be a few weeks yet on that country house. Meantime, he paid her two weeks in advance, and she starts at the house in town next Monday. He's havin' his driver pick her up and take her home. Only has to do that country place once a week. City house'll be most every day. We were thinkin' bout taking a little ride out to that country place to just check it out some."

Tourey sat up straight. William Patterson was hiding at the country house. "That's a bad idea. Trust me. You stay away from there for now. I'll tell you when it's okay."

Spicey was quiet a minute, then said, "I don't see what harm there be in drivin' by." She waited for a response and then realized Tourey had hung up.

Spicey looked at Sasha, "Must still be trouble with some phones. I'll put a call to Willie and see if he be willin' to drive us out by that country house.

Just a nice little motor ride. You call Wilma and tell her we gonna pick her up shortly. Ain't doing much business today anyhow with all the police drivin' around." Sasha clapped her hands in excitement. Spicey walked over to the door, flipped the sign to closed, and turned off the neon light that said 'House of Voodoo'. Ain't no man gonna be tellin' her where she can and can't go.

Ellen asked us to meet her at the secured Navy yard where the confiscated boat was docked. When we arrived, she was sitting on a deck chair, sipping lemonade. She had the cutest short set on and a red sweat band around her forehead. "Well, your instructors said your mortal minds are messing with their equipment. They hope you guys are ready, but nobody is making any bets. The way I see it, we have a couple of things on our side. Most mortals have experienced dejavu." Ellen chuckled, "I've caused my fair share of that! All that means is if you mess something up, freeze time and go back and fix what you can. Mortals will have a vague sense of familiarity to a situation but there's no real harm." We were all nodding like we totally got it. I was thinking, *there are going to be a lot of frozen people in New Orleans.* She was actually talking like we knew what she meant!

Ellen frowned at me and continued, "Also, most mortals believe that animals can sense things humans can't. You may need to present yourself to a mortal for any number of reasons. The use of animal images may help you." Ellen looked at me, "*You* have to be very aware that your imagination may affect the others. Especially when deciding to turn into animals. At least try to keep your animal choices limited to animals that make sense to the mortal's current environment."

Ellen smiled, "If you HAVE to communicate with a mortal you must go through Kim but you can show yourself as an animal. Like I talk to Roger as a cat. I'm not sure you are going to need this skill, but Granny thought you might. The memory gaps are the most serious skill you were given, and I want you to think very hard before you use them. If you point your watch at a human and touch that top gold button, they are going to forget the most recent three thoughts they had. It would help if you tried to read their minds before just zapping them."

Ellen leaned in to talk to us, "You guys are going to be on your own for a while. Even Betty questions her skills being of any help from here on. I will be very busy with Roger and the Director. I'm thinking that if I run into a problem I don't have time for, I'll just call on all of you."

I didn't like the sound of this.

Mary had a very thoughtful look on her face and was twiddling her thumbs. Finally she said, "I can't think of any reason we would ever need to turn into animals."

Teresa offered, "Maybe we would need to scare a mortal away from danger or something."

Ellen looked surprised, "You know, I can see that being useful! Just be sure your animal choice is appropriate." Dang. I was starting to think this was the skill I would have the most fun with. Maybe I could pop into Kim's house as a giraffe. That would crack her up! Everyone was staring at me. Oops.

Linda asked, "What do you want us to do now?"

Ellen answered, "Other than Patterson, re-tired Senator Rolland Kenny, the gallery own-er Theodore Chain, Andre Baton from Loyola University, and Judge Harold Williams are the re-maining members of this pedophile club in New Orleans. Roger needs a lot of information fast if he is going to capture them before any children are harmed. They have already arranged for five chil-dren to be kidnapped and delivered by Monday."

We were all shaking our heads at how sick some mortals could be. Ellen continued, "Remember the cameras you wore on your heads to record the guns and ammunition at the docks?" We all nod-ded. "Now I want you to wear them all the time in case there is something you need to record for Roger." Great. Now we are going to look like a bunch of flying miners.

Ellen frowned, "I need you to search their computers for where they store their club infor-mation. You can download to your watches and get that info to Roger. These guys communicate with the other branches of this club somehow. Maybe we can get those names to Roger too. We actually need the network of people who are taking these kids. A list of the kidnappers." Ellen stood and stretched, "I really need to get going, but I also want you to visit the country house where Senator Kenny told Patterson he could hide. Remember?" We all nodded.

Ellen smiled, "I can't believe I'm saying this, but I trust your judgment. Call me after you have all the information. Then we will get it to Roger." Ellen disappeared. We stood looking at each other.

I had a thought, "I don't know about the rest of you, but I don't want to go off snooping on my own."

Linda smiled when she said, "You're just worried you will get lost." I started to protest and decided what the heck. She's right. I am going to get lost. Oh well. They can just spend their time trying to find me! Good luck with that. I could be a bird…a plane…a

Teresa frowned, "I think she forgot we can read her mind." I did.

Mary asked, "Why don't we break into teams? That's faster than hunting down Vicki in New Orleans." Oh crap. I'm going to be the last one picked again. They'll probably do rock, paper, scissors. Mary said, "I'll take Vicki and we'll start with the judge." Huh. Linda and Teresa said they were going to the University dude's house.

Flying to the courthouse, I asked Mary, "Why did you pick me? I thought I made you nervous?"

Mary started laughing, "You do, but you also get some good ideas. If we get in a mess, I want your devious mind on my team!" I think that was a compliment!

The Director of the FBI pulled on his face with his hands and then pressed the intercom button on his phone. He had just spoken with Roger and was now ready to meet with Thornton. "William? Sorry it has taken me so long to respond to your call. I can meet with you now."

Less than five minutes passed. Thornton tapped on the Director's door and sat down heavily in the visitor chair. The Director looked up from his papers and offered up a forced smile. It took all of his control to keep from leaping across the desk and punching Thornton in the face. The day he would be able to tell Thornton he had proof he had poisoned him, arranged the delivery of ninety tons of weapons shipped from Algiers in an FBI protected ship, and had connections with Thomas Fenley and two drug Cartels would be the best day of his career.

The Director leaned back and decided to have at least a little fun with Thornton. "I am at liberty to tell you now that martial law was declared in New Orleans last night."

The Deputy Director nodded, "I heard that. One of the reasons I wanted to meet with you was to find out why I hadn't been advised of this in advance. What brought this about anyway? Martial law? What happened?"

The Director tapped his pen on a file folder, "CIA and OSI got the martial law thing done. Roger stumbled into more stuff at the port than your little gun sting with Zelez Cartel. I guess everyone decided it was as good a time as any to expand the trap. Roger is working on a plan to not just catch whoever picks up these guns but to break the entire Zelez Cartel."

Thornton was rubbing his chin, "Really? Roger Dance is going to bring down the entire Zelez Cartel? Just how does he propose to do that?"

The Director almost started laughing, he knew how his next comment would register with Thornton. "The real reason they declared martial law was to implement a communication sting. All calls, including government bands, have been monitored since eight thirty last night. We have over one thousand communication techs from four agencies picking through captured calls based on our key word triggers. This is the most comprehensive communication sting ever initiated by the United States government."

Thornton actually went pale. The Director didn't say any more, and Thornton eventually asked, "Why include secure government bands?"

The Director continued, "Roger wanted to follow any money coming and going and needed those federal banking codes. I guess at some point these bands all go through the same security filter, and it was just faster and easier not to separate them. We thought. It appears there has been some kind of breach of some security code that directly affected the accounts at French Quarter Bank, and well....it's a mess."

Thornton was noticeably uncomfortable. He wanted to find out what the Director knew without asking too many questions. "Well, when will we know what he found out? What are we supposed to do now? Just wait for Dance to let us in on his plan?"

The Director forced himself not to chuckle. Thornton was coming unglued. Those calls he made to Fenley and Core didn't look good at all and would be impossible to explain. "Well, like I said, some of this didn't go exactly like we expected. Something interfered with the central information system (CIS), specific to the bank, and managed to corrupt a lot of account numbers. That has to be fixed. We probably lost some valuable call information from the early hours of the sting."

Thornton nodded. That explained why the Director didn't seem to know about Fenley, Manio, and himself. They certainly didn't know of their connection to LUCY. Also, it meant Dance was going to be busy working on something to take out Zelez. This could actually be good news. "I know

I didn't share the information about the weapons sting with you, but I really didn't think it would be that big a deal. We had it covered well."

The Director could feel the heat rising on his neck, "Just how did you arrange a deal with the Zelez Cartel anyway?"

Thornton answered, "We have used an outside guy for stuff like this for years. Mathew Core. Actually Dance has messed this up pretty well when you think about it. I had this all set. We would have taken out Zelez's key man in New Orleans tomorrow."

The Director cleared his throat and said, "Roger wants Zelez. Not his key men. He says he knows how to bring down the whole cartel. I don't know if he will use Core or not. Roger likes to work with a tight team. His own."

Thornton stood to leave, "I appreciate you bringing me up to speed. I don't think it is a secret that I am not as big a fan of Dance as you are. You might start re-thinking your assessment of him in light of this fiasco. Messed up sting, messed up banking numbers, an entire city under siege. For what? Because Dance didn't want someone else getting credit for a bust? Might be you're getting played, buddy."

The Director looked Thornton in the eyes, "Smart money says that's a bad idea." He knew damn well who was playing him. Thornton shook his head, gave a sneer and left the office. The Director pushed his chair from his desk and stood. He stretched his back and rubbed the back of his neck. *He couldn't wait to bring down that arrogant bastard!*

Willie pulled in front of the Voodoo shop and hit the air horn he had installed on his car. It sounded like a cruise ship. Spicey jumped from the sudden loud sound and looked out the window. She saw a long, dark burgundy 1991 Fleetwood Cadillac waiting. Willie was at the wheel wearing a wide brimmed hat, smilin' from ear to ear and wavin'. He said he had himself a new car he needed to test drive. Weren't new, but sure was shiny!

Spicey yelled to Sasha who was in the back, "Best you move it girl. We got ourselves a real fancy ride a waitin'." Spicey put her pistol in her purse and grabbed a few twenties out of the cash register.

Sasha was all smiles when she walked into the room, "This was such a good idea to take a ride in the country. 'Specially today with all this cop stuff goin' on. Wilma's all excited, said she'd be waitin' on the corner by her house. She never seen this place 'fore." Sasha looked in the small mirror on the wall and fluffed her hair some on the sides. "You think I should get my colors touched up some? This purple stripe is startin' to look like the pink one."

Spicey gave her a good look, "Yeah. Getting' so it's hard to tell them are stripes. Looks like somebody done ran past ya with a couple of snow cones."

Sasha giggled, "We don't all have behavin' hair like you. I need a little somethin' extree so people don't look at my ears."

Spicey laughed, "Ain't nothin' wrong with your ears, 'cept ya don't listen with 'em."

Willie honked the horn again and Sasha jumped. "What kind of horn he got? Sounds like a big boat!"

Spicey waved Sasha out, locked the door, and pointed to the back seat. "You and Wilma ride in the back okay? I get car sick if I don't have a front seat." Sasha rolled her eyes, crawled in the back, and said hi to Willie.

"Hot dang, this here back seat like a whole couch! This leather feelin' like a baby's butt." Sasha giggled, "You look like you sittin' a whole block ahead of me. How big is this car anyway?"

Willie chuckled and waited for Spicey to snap her seat belt before he pulled from the curb. The car gave a belch and lunged forward. Willie hung on, and Spicey had her nostrils flared. "You been eating fried chicken? I'm smellin' fried chicken." Sasha was sniffin' and lookin' around the back seat.

Willie laughed, "This here's my new 'speriment. Car runs on fryin' grease. I get free grease from Otis's place. Little tinkerin' here and there and I don't need to buy no gasoline no more."

Spicey was frowning as she looked around and heard the car burp again. "How long you been drivin' this thing on chicken fat?" Willie declared this was the maiden voyage, and Spicey turned to look at Sasha. *"Assumin'* we get back from this trip, we goin' to have to take about four showers 'fore we go anywhere. We be havin' dogs chasin' us down, we smell so good."

Sasha pointed and tapped on the window, "There's Miss Wilma. Now don't she look pretty, Willie? She all gussied up in that flower dress an' all. You need you a good woman. Ought to think hard 'bout Miss Wilma there."

Willie grunted and pulled over to the curb. He got out of the car, took his hat off and opened the back for Wilma to get in. "Miss Wilma, you lookin' mighty fine today," he gave a little bow and the sunshine bounced from his gold tooth.

Wilma giggled and seated herself in the car. She said hello to Spicey and Sasha and immediately started sniffin' and lookin' around. Sasha volunteered, "Willie is such a genius. He made this beautiful car to run on chicken fat. You get a little aroma here and there, but you save big money on gasoline." Wilma was impressed. Willie beamed with pride. Spicey looked out the window, rubbed her amulet, and prayed they would make it home again as the car burped every mile or so.

✳ ✳ ✳

William C. Thornton needed to speak to Fenley in person. Fast. First he wanted to make a couple of phone calls to find out the extent of the communication sting revelations and talk to Core. If Dance was really focused on taking out Zelez, he and Fenley might want to alter their plan. Thornton sent Fenley a fairly innocent looking email stating his recent contribution to the duck wildlife fund was appreciated, and the amount of five hundred dollars would be put to good use. The real meaning of the message was "meet me at the duck pond in Washington Park at five".

Thornton wanted to call Core. Damn. Core was in New Orleans and none of those lines were secure. The Director had said this stupid communication sting would last until tomorrow night. Thornton dialed his contact at the Federal Reserve, Franklin Morris, sitting member of the Board of Governors, Chairperson of the FOMC, Federal Open Markets Committee. Thornton wanted to find out the real situation at the French Quarter Bank. A lot of very important people used that bank. Serious money was spent to keep it open, in spite of overwhelming regulatory violations. Core ran his corporate account through there for that very reason. Core had also established accounts in Thornton and Fenley's names as insurance. Having these accounts under a microscope because of some stupid mistake of Dance's could be bad.

Thornton leaned back and pulled a slip of paper from the center drawer of his desk. The account Mathew Core had established in Thornton's name was based at that bank. Damn. There goes forty million dollars out the window. Thornton was told his call to the Federal Reserve couldn't be put through at the moment, to try later. He stood and hit the intercom to the Director. "I'm heading out. Should be in the office early morning."

The OSI surveillance team monitoring Thornton was in position to follow. The email had looped to them and the true meaning was foolishly transparent. The call to Franklin Morris had been intercepted and delayed. Thornton had just confirmed he was tied to LUCY. He was being sloppy, and he just brought in Fenley.

CHAPTER FOUR

Mathew Core knocked on Roger's hotel room door and put his hands in the air when Roger opened it. Core walked in, turned to the wall and announced he had a carry permit, a gun in his waistband, and a knife in each boot. Roger disarmed him while Paul held him at gunpoint. They knew Core could possibly take them both if he wanted to, and he had already told them he had been hired by Thornton and Fenley to do so.

Ellen was sitting on the credenza licking her paws. Core looked at her, "You bring your cat on field assignments?"

Roger answered, "She helps me think. Sit here." Roger had pulled out one of the chairs from the small table. Sitting across from Core he would be able to watch Ellen's eyes during the interview. Roger pointed at Paul, "Mathew, this is

SSA Paul Casey, and you know who I am. We need to know about you. Who is Mathew Core, really?"

Mathew had a very serious expression on his face when he answered, "That is the second time today I have been asked that. The first was my wife, Lisa. I'll tell you what I told her, I don't know anymore." Roger looked at Ellen, who winked. Mathew continued, "I plan on answering anything you ask me as honestly as I can. I will also do whatever you ask of me if it ensures the safety of my wife and daughter. If I could have some chance of getting back with them, that would be nice, too." Mathew offered a weak smile. Ellen winked.

Roger answered, "First things first. We have multiple murder warrants out on you."

Mathew raised an eyebrow and said, "Then let's get started. What murders do you think I did?"

Paul walked over to the table and sat down, "We have testimony from Daniel Warren, Devon's imposter, that six men were murdered in that escape plot. Warren saw pictures."

Mathew nodded his head, "I didn't kill them. Next?" Ellen winked.

Paul continued, "Patterson's double was shot in transport from the trial."

Mathew smiled, "I believe you have proof I was in New Orleans when that happened." Ellen winked.

Roger was clicking his pen, "I suppose you didn't shoot Mark Mills behind Mickey's bar?"

Mathew paused, "There's no proof I shot Mark Mills." Ellen winked.

Roger smiled, "You are playing with semantics here. Let me remind you that I only have to establish your likely involvement. Don't play coy. We need each other, unfortunately, and none of us has time for bullshit." Roger didn't have time for a pissing match with Core.

Core answered, "I know I can be valuable to you. I'm not being coy, I'm pointing out there may be problems prosecuting me. I'm hoping that fact will make it easier for you to accept my help. Where are my wife and daughter? What are you doing to protect them? You answer that, and we have real traction."

"They are at our field office. I've arranged to expedite their move into witness protection."

Core nodded his head, "Let me show you something. Can I borrow your laptop for a minute?" Roger nodded to Paul, who brought it over. Core entered several web addresses, numerous key entries, and proclaimed, "They are preparing to transport them here." He turned the laptop around and showed them both he had located the witness protection address just assigned for Lisa and Jamie. "I wouldn't call this *safe*."

Roger was stunned. What information was secure anymore? Roger looked at Mathew, "Okay, we'll get back to *this*. Where would you consider safe?"

Core shook his head, "That's a good question. I don't know." Mathew looked genuinely stumped. Roger looked at Ellen, she winked. Great, even Core was clueless.

Roger asked, "If I can get them to our Hawaii base, I have a personal friend who will take over security, off the grid. Does that work for you?"

Core nodded slowly, "If you trust this friend, it works for me."

Roger stood and began pacing. He looked at Mathew, "I am in the awkward position of needing you, and I don't trust you. I want to convince Fenley, Manio and Thornton that my only goal is to bring down the Zelez Cartel. I want them to think they have escaped my radar completely."

Core closed his eyes and rolled his neck. He was surprised Roger had mentioned Thornton and Fenley. He was curious how much Roger knew. Especially about Fenley. Manio's connection to New Orleans drug traffic wasn't a big secret. "You probably don't know everything you need to know about these guys. I have to deal with Manio and Zelez within hours, and you took my leverage. Was it Manio who went after Lisa and Jamie?"

Roger answered, "Yes."

Core looked very serious. "I need to buy time, I need someone to blame. What new leverage do I have? I'm assuming you won't let go of the guns or drugs."

Roger sat down across from Core, "You're right, the guns and drugs are not going anywhere. I might be able to offer up something better. Convince Manio I am only interested in taking down Zelez. Then I need Manio to believe I have screwed up bad by having the banking information of French

Quarter Bank included in our martial law sting. I want Manio, Fenley, and Thornton to believe a 'money safe haven' has been created through technical errors and is theirs for the taking."

Core answered, "Zelez will give us more time if he thinks he's getting all of the weapons. Manio will give us some time if he believes you can really bring down Zelez. I would have to lay out some heavy details for Manio of that proposed 'sting' on Zelez for this to work. Convincing Fenley there is a true 'safe haven' in an American based bank is a whole other story."

Roger knew he was on dangerous ground. He had just told Mathew Core a large part of his plan, based only on Ellen's winks. "I think I can deliver both. I have one more question for you before we proceed. Which side of the fence is Jason Sims on?"

Core sat up straight and answered, "He's one of the good guys, but he's in deep undercover." Ellen winked. Mathew looked concerned when he stated, "He may be dead. I haven't been able to reach him."

Roger smiled, "He's alive, and we have him."

Roger, Paul, and Core discussed what the two cartels would believe to stall for time. Roger looked at Core, "Manio will suspect that you know he tried to kidnap Lisa and Jamie. Why would he trust you now?"

Core answered, "He won't. He'll check with Fenley on everything I tell him. I can plant a few seeds of doubt with Fenley about Thornton. That may help down the road. Thornton is disposable at this point."

* * *

Abram drove Jackson toward the city then turned on a rural road. Jackson looked over and asked, "Uh, where you takin' me?"

Abram said, "Start paying attention to where we are. You are goin' to bring the snatched kids to this place out here in the country. You leave 'em there, come back to find me, and then you get paid. Five grand per kid. There should be five kids, but I don't have the specifics of who yet. We'll get that when we get to town." Abram jerked his neck around, "Should be a dirt road around here somewhere."

Jackson did the math. Somebody pretty important wanted these kids if that was just his cut. Jackson asked, "Who's gettin' these kids anyway?"

Abram frowned at him, "Ain't none of your business! Your job be getting' the right kids and bringin' 'em here." Abram's voice raised, "Right there. That dirt drive. See it?" Jackson nodded and Abram turned the car onto the dirt path. It could barely be called a drive it was so bumpy and overgrown. Abram cursed he'd have to wash his car again. Jackson still worried why Abram had him way out in the woods.

Abram must have sensed Jackson's fear and chuckled, "Ain't nothin' gonna happen to ya. I'm tellin' ya straight. This is where you bring those kids. There! See that big barn up there?" Jackson nodded. Abram continued, "Driveway to house comes in from that other road over there. You don't never go near the house, you understand? Just the barn." Abram pulled up behind the barn, next to a side service door.

"This here's how you get in." Abram rolled a big rock by the door to expose a key that opened the padlock. They walked inside. Jackson thought this must be the cleanest barn in the world. Over in the far corner was a row of kennels.

Jackson asked, "Where's the dogs?"

Abram scrunched his face, "How many dogs you know need a cot and a toilet?"

Jackson looked again. Each kennel was out-fitted with a cot and a toilet. Holy crap! Jackson looked at Abram, "I'm supposed to put the kids in these kennels?"

Abram looked very serious when he said, "You can't do this, we got us a problem." Abram took a gun from his waistband and waved it at Jackson, "This ain't really my style, but I be a fast learner. You in or out?"

Jackson got the message loud and clear, "I'm in. Don't mean I like it none."

Abram nodded, "Yeah, I hear ya."

Just then they heard a loud sound like a gunshot or a backfire. Abram motioned for Jackson to follow him across the barn. They peeked out of a semi-boarded up window. Abram saw a long burgundy Cadillac stopped in the driveway for the house, and people getting out. It looked to him like the woman getting out of the front seat was Spicey, the Voodoo lady. Damn. Why she always showin' up when he be on a job?

Willie had insisted that the car only smelled hot because of the chicken fat. When smoke started coming from under the hood and the car backfired, he conceded maybe he needed to tinker with it some. They hadn't been able to see anything from the road. Spicey had urged Willie to just pull in the drive enough they could see what the house looked like.

Now they were all out of the car. Willie had the hood up fanning the smoke that billowed from under the hood. Everyone started coughing and waving it away from their faces. Wilma was beside herself, "Oh Lordy! Now what we gonna do?" She had looked up the drive to the front of the house. "Oh Ms. Spicey, look how fine that house be. Uh huh!"

Spicey noticed the front door was wide open, meaning someone was probably there. Suddenly she was thinking this probably had not been her best idea. Tourey told her not to come out there.

Spicey looked at everyone and said, "I might have left off we're not supposed to be out here."

Sasha knew the look Spicey had on her face, and it wasn't good. Sasha was afraid to ask but couldn't stop herself, " *Who* be sayin' we best not be here?"

Spicey very quietly answered, "Tourey."

Sasha threw her arms up in the air and brought her fists down to rest on her hips. "Ain't Mambo tellin' you Tourey into some bad shit 'nough to have you listen? No tellin' what kind of bad shit rich people up to." Sasha gave Spicey her neck waggle and asked, "Well? You be the one with all the *IDEAS*. Now what?"

Spicey looked at Willie and asked, "What do you need to make this car go again?"

Willie pulled his head from under the hood. "We just had a hose blow underneath. Got a spare in the trunk." He scratched his head and said, "I think we let it cool down a spell, replace that hose, poor in another bucket of chicken fat, and we be gone."

Wilma looked like she was going to cry, "I be fired 'fore I ever start this job. We can't be caught sittin' in this here driveway!"

Spicey pushed her bracelets up her arm and said, "Let's push this here boat back to the road. It'll look like we broke down there. Never did come in this driveway." Spicey opened the driver's door, climbed in, and proclaimed that she would steer.

✳ ✳ ✳

William C. Thornton made one last attempt to reach his contact at the Federal Reserve. He was in his car heading for his meeting with Fenley in Washington Park. Much to his surprise, after a brief wait, Franklin Morris answered and said, "You boys are certainly causing everyone problems aren't you? A little late for an apology call, don't you think?"

William figured Franklin must be talking about the messed up accounts at French Quarter Bank. "Actually, I just found out. How bad is it?"

Franklin snorted, "As if you don't know. This is all the FBI's fault."

William pulled his car over and turned on his emergency flashers. What the hell was Franklin talking about? "You need to give me a little more here Franklin. I haven't been given the specifics on the money mess yet. As you can imagine, I have been pretty busy putting together a martial law operation in one day. I wanted to hear from you directly." Franklin wouldn't know he had nothing to do with the martial law operation, but it gave him an excuse and some added credibility. There was a pregnant pause from the other end.

William continued, "You understand there are things I can't talk about yet."

Franklin finally answered, "You might afford me the same courtesy. I can tell you this much. Friday, midnight, when this damn martial law thing ends we can START to rebuild our entire tracking system on laundering. It is going to take years! Your little FBI fiasco corrupted accounts so badly the only thing we could do was re-issue exempt clearing numbers to all established accounts there."

William asked, "So these accounts at French Quarter Bank are exempt from what?"

Franklin huffed, "Everything! They all have Federal ID numbers now. No reports, no tracing, no activity logs, nothing! That's not the bad part. Anywhere this money moves, the new exempt numbers become primary and clear all info on the old numbers. It's like a damn eraser! From last night until tomorrow midnight, there isn't a damn thing we can do."

William's mind was spinning, "How long is it going to take to sort this out?"

Franklin chuckled, "You and I will be retired if they do this the standard way. I think the best plan is to re-issue new legitimate numbers on real Fed accounts and start again from there. The Board is meeting in an hour to make this official. We actually have programmers working on it now. Real time before we can switch? Maybe two months. Every clearing house in the world will need the new numbers programmed in. Any new accounts opened after Friday will have normal numbers. I guess we can be grateful that this is a very small bank."

William had one last question, "Who knows about this?"

Franklin answered, "The whole story? Me and a handful of guys here, the National Security Council and now you. I'll bust your balls if this list grows." William assured him it would not grow from him, said goodbye, and started back down the highway. He suddenly felt a sense of glee sweep through his body. *My God, they had a safe haven in the U.S.!*

The Director listened to Thornton hang up from what had actually been a conference call. Franklin directed his next question to the Director of the FBI, "Well, how did I do?"

The Director answered, "I believe you did just fine Franklin. You will probably get a similar call from someone verifying for Fenley. Make sure the National Security Council guys know the story, too, in case the call goes there. Give the same speech, and then call me. You can hang up now." After Franklin hung up, the Director asked, "Is that what you wanted?"

Roger answered, "Yes, sir. Thank you."

SSA Simon Frost watched the National Guard van pull away from the field office garage and leave the parking lot with four armed escort vehicles. Lisa and Jamie Core were with them and heading to a location known only to Roger and the Director. Roger had requested that the National Guard remain at the field office to maintain the ruse that Lisa and Jamie were still there. Roger had requested Simon and Nelson return to the Star Ship and assist Ray in identifying all of the account owners at French Quarter Bank. Roger also wanted an update on Mathew Core's account activity.

When Simon and Nelson arrived at the Star Ship, Ray greeted them, "Hey. You guys did remember I was still here. What's happening?"

Simon answered, "I can't tell you what is happening because I don't know. I can tell you what Roger wants us to do."

After listening for a few minutes Ray rolled his eyes and said sarcastically, "That's all?"

CHAPTER FIVE

L inda and Teresa entered the home of Andre Baton to look for his computer. They heard a phone ring in the distance. A male voice said, "I'm sure it will be another four weeks at least before I can possibly even think about coming in to the office. My doctor is insistent that I not stress myself during this recovery time."

Linda and Teresa followed the voice down the hall to a big library where a wimpy looking man in a bathrobe was pretending to hit tennis balls while he spoke on the phone. Teresa pointed to a TV screen where a game of tennis was actually being played. "He's playing with a Wii! He's not sick."

Linda saw his computer on the desk and sat in his chair. She slowly started turning the computer to face her when Andre turned. "I don't care what you call it. Call it vacation if you want to, I have plenty coming to me. Don't expect to see me at the office for another month. Got it?" He hung up, grabbed the remote, and started his game over again. He was actually quite good.

Teresa snuck over to his control and kept dialing up the speed on him. He was working up quite a sweat by the time Linda had located the computer files and uploaded them to her watch. Linda asked, "Do you think we should look for an address book or anything? I don't know if the information we want is really on his computer or not."

Teresa said, "I think I can arrange a diversion to get him out of this room, so you can go through that desk."

"A diversion?"

Teresa giggled, "I bet he's afraid of mice." She had no sooner said it than Andre screamed and jumped up on a club chair. Teresa was a gray mouse, sitting on the floor, looking at him. She lunged forward, and Andre jumped from the chair and ran from the room. Linda saw Teresa chasing him out of the room. Andre's high pitched little girl screams trailed all over the house. They passed the doorway twice. Teresa ran on her hind legs with her arms in the air. Linda could hardly see she was laughing so hard. All of a sudden she heard pots and pans being thrown and a door slammed. She finished making copies of an address book she had found just as Teresa walked back into the room.

"Where did he go?"

Teresa laughed, "He's banging on the neighbor's door. That was fun!"

Mary and I arrived at the courthouse and sat in the jury box watching a trial that the Honorable Judge Harold Williams was presiding over. We kept glaring at him, but of course he couldn't see us. I couldn't help it. He looked so smug in that robe. Every time he was asked for a ruling I zapped him with a memory gap. He would open his mouth, look at the lawyers and ask, "Now what did you ask?"

The prosecutor and the defense attorney exchanged glances. Judge Williams was known to never miss a word.

Mary made me stop after five times.

We went into his chambers and checked out his desk drawers and computer. Nothing. Mary said, "You know it makes sense he wouldn't have this stuff here. I bet we have to go to his house. Find his home address on something."

Just then he walked into his chambers and sat in his chair. Mary and I moved up by the ceiling. He called his bailiff to come in. "Ron, I think I need to reschedule these last two cases. I didn't sleep well last night and I seem to be having some issues."

The bailiff pretended concern, "Do you want a doctor or something?" He was thrilled at the prospect of leaving early and figured Harold's real problem was probably too much bourbon last night.

Judge Williams waved him away, "Nah, I'm just going to go home." Cool. We can just follow him. Judge Williams took off his robe and grabbed some keys from his desk drawer. We followed him through the parking garage to a little red Corvette convertible.

Mary yelled, "I got shotgun!" Shoot. Riding in the convertible was fun, and a lot of people waved at us as we passed. We waved back. Seemed the Judge knew a lot of people. Being an angel does have its perks. We finally arrived at Judge Williams's house and followed him into the kitchen from the garage. He stuck his head in the refrigerator and came out with an apple and some Colby cheese. I sniffed my wrist. That looked pretty good.

Mary yelled from down the hall, "I found the computer. Keep him busy out there." Hmmm. He started to walk out of the kitchen so I smacked his plate of cheese. It fell on the floor. He cursed, bent down, picked it up, and decided to eat it anyway. Then he started walking again. This time I knocked his apple from the bend of his elbow. He stood and watched it roll across the floor. "Well, I must have the dropsies today." Dropsies?

He walked over to the front door, opened it, and retrieved his newspaper from the mail box. Then he sat in a big overstuffed chair and began reading. He pulled the recliner back a little and was snoring in five minutes. I went down the hall to see how Mary was doing.

Mary was going through a rolodex and making copies with her camera. I forgot we even had them on. I kept sniffing my wrist as I watched her, She finally asked me, "What are you eating?"

"Apples and cheese. I'm starting a diet." Mary shook her head.

"Don't you want to know why?"

"No. But I am sure you are going to tell me." Mary chuckled, "No, let me guess. If you lose weight you can fly faster."

I was shocked!

"Wow, you are good! I also could have you make me some of those cute outfits you have been wearing."

Mary kept smiling and taking pictures of address books and finally said, "For someone who is supposed to be smart, why do you keep forgetting we can read each other's minds?"

Oh. That is a good point. Probably because I don't try to read theirs. Maybe I should.

Mary pushed her chair back and said, "I'm done. I didn't see anything important though. Should we call Linda and Teresa and see if they are ready to go to the Senator's house?" I kept eating and just nodded my head. Teresa and Linda had already been to University guy's house and were just finishing at Theodore Chain's. They said they would meet us at the Senator's city house.

Mary looked nervous, "You know this has been going pretty smoothly so far. I hope we don't have any surprises."

"You worry too much."

A nurse poked her head into the surgical waiting room and cleared her throat to wake Thor and Jeanne. It had been two hours but had seemed like only minutes. Thor took a minute to get his bearings back. The nurse looked at them and said, "He's in the recovery room now. You can visit for a minute, but he is still very drowsy."

Thor and Jeanne followed the nurse down the hall to where Pablo appeared to be sleeping. He had bandages across his shoulder and IV's in each arm. Jeanne sat next to him and cradled his hand in hers. Pablo opened his eyes and blinked at her, "I killed a kid today. He was just a *kid.*" Jeanne looked at Thor, she didn't know what Pablo was talking about.

Thor stepped over to be in Pablo's line of sight. "Yeah you did. A kid with an AK47 aimed at you. Seems I remember you saved my life on that porch too. You've had a busy day, managed to get shot at the swamp to top it off."

Pablo frowned and looked at his shoulder. Then he looked at Jeanne, "Are you okay? There were dead guys every place we followed you."

Jeanne smiled, "I'm fine, not a scratch. I even had a nap with Thor."

Pablo looked at Thor, "What?" Thor shook his head. *Ah shit.* Thor hoped he didn't have to listen to this all day. Thor told Jeanne to visit a few minutes and meet him at the car.

When Thor left, Pablo stared at Jeanne, "You like him, don't you?"

Jeanne didn't answer.

When he got to the car, Thor called Roger to tell him they were done at the hospital. Roger asked him to meet at Core's building that everyone now called the Star Ship. He hoped to brief everyone shortly about the findings from the sting transcripts. Thor rested his head against his window. Whatever he was thinking about Jeanne had to stop. They barely knew each other and she had just been through hell. It must be he was feeling the tension of this case. He barely spoke when she opened the passenger door and got in.

Jeanne looked at him for a moment then turned to look straight ahead. "What do we do now?"

Thor put the car in gear and answered, "Roger wants us at the Star Ship."

✳ ✳ ✳

65

Tourey met John Barry in the common park in front of the Law Library at Loyola University. Tourey had his eyebrows raised and was shaking his head. "I know that facial expression of yours, and I have a feeling I'm going to regret this meeting."

John answered, "I'm sure you are. Your Mambo was right. LUCY is alive and well."

"Ah shit!"

A couple of students walked past them and sat in the grass too close for comfort. Tourey tilted his head, and they both walked away. John spoke first, "Regardless, I really need you to stay on Patterson until they call you in on LUCY. We are out of time with this sicko club, and we are short on manpower." John brought Tourey up to date on Jeanne's encounter with the Manio cartel and Pablo getting shot.

Tourey stopped and leaned against a tree. He swatted a fly from his arm, "This club has branches and members all over the country. They've been doing this awhile. The key here is to figure out who they get to snatch the kids, where they stash 'em, and what they do with them when they are done. The statistics on this are sickening, I've been doing some research. I hate to say it, but short of a miracle, we may have to wait 'til they snatch another kid to figure this out."

John was shaking his head, "We have Patterson who we can pick up now. Maybe he knows something about the structure of the club. Do you think he is still at the country house?"

Tourey was nodding, "Yeah, but if we move on Patterson now we lose our chance to catch the rest of 'em. We don't have anything on these other guys yet. I might be able to get Patterson to tell me how they move the kids, if he even knows. He's new to this bunch." Tourey reached in his pocket, "Here's a flash drive with what I have found out about the club, missing kids and dead kids. I think at least we have an up to date list of all the members of this club."

John put the flash drive in his pocket and said, "Try to get something out of Patterson. If he isn't willing to talk to you casually, call Roger about arresting him. We have to do something. We're out of time."

Tourey pulled an amulet from under his shirt and dangled it for John to see. "I got this here present from Mambo that she said I should wear. Message seems to be we're lookin' at facin' trouble." Tourey winked and walked away.

John walked back to his car with a heavy heart. It never ends. He sat listening to the cool air escape from the vents, closed his eyes, and said a prayer. Tourey was right. They needed a miracle. He looked up to his rearview mirror to back out of his parking space and saw Ellen's face looking back at him. "Workin' on it!" She gave a big smile and disappeared. John exhaled after a couple of moments and headed toward the Star Ship.

✳ ✳ ✳

Mathew Core watched Tourey leave his house. As soon as it was clear, he entered Tourey's library and copied the latest files on the sicko club to a flash drive. Perfect. One of the files was a list of members' names at all of the branches of the club. One hundred and thirty- two names.

He then went to his apartment above the jewelry store. Core could still feel the heart wrenching fear he had felt when he thought Patterson's sick group had kidnapped Jamie. His guilt at orchestrating Patterson's escape was driving his decision now. He didn't trust this club could be stopped by law enforcement. Not soon enough. He knew a few guys that could get the job done clean if they chose to do it. It meant that Core would be breaking the law, again.

Core picked up his phone and made a conference call to three men. He told them fifty million dollars had been transferred to each of their accounts. Have a nice life. Core told them he was officially retired. He mentioned he was transferring information to each of their computers. He warned them the FBI was working it, hard. Perhaps there was some hope for justice. He suspected they would be cynical. He knew if they chose to participate, they would be efficient. Core couldn't think of a better way to spend Devon and Patterson's money.

Now to call Manio and Zelez. He hoped Roger knew what he was doing.

✳ ✳ ✳

Alan had stayed with Jeremiah long enough for all of the cops to leave and to help Jeremiah remove minks from traps. He could tell Jeremiah was tired, but at least he wasn't worried about Jeanne anymore. One of the cops told them Jeanne saved this lady and her kid from a drug cartel. Shot five of them in town and killed three more out at Jeremiah's place.

Alan could tell Jeremiah was proud. When everyone had left, he looked at Alan and said, "There are some people you come across got that somethin' special, ya know? Mambo done named her Heeshia, means 'chosen óne'. You know why?" Alan shook his head.

Jeremiah continued, "You see them special blue eyes of hers? That means somethin' boy. Mambo never wrong. You look it up on your 'puter when you get home. Black Madonna. Jeanne's what they call a *messenger* of Black Madonna. A warrior spirit, protector of women and children. Yup. You check it out. Blue eyed Haitian that one is."

Alan tried to make sense of what Jeremiah was rambling about. Alan was getting anxious to get to the city. He had an air conditioning job to do and the customer waitin' on him had a bad temperament even when he was cool. Jeremiah told Alan to be on his way but asked him if he could bring some fruit loops back next time he came around. Mambo had liked them.

Alan went to town, did his job, and went into Mickey's Bar to grab a sandwich and a beer. It was only four o'clock but he was already hungry. Alan saw Dusty sitting at the end of the bar and joined him, "Hey there. See you survived the martial law sweep they had in town this mornin'. Man, traffic is a bitch."

Dusty tilted his head back as he swallowed the last of his beer. "Those FBI guys are *crazy!* I had six dudes at my house this mornin' dressed in SWAT gear, screamin' through my walls with one of them loudspeakers. Damn! I moved to town to get away from them stupid *roosters*! Now I got SWAT dudes? Shit. I haven't had a good night's sleep since FBI got to town. Worse, now I know 'em all!"

Alan laughed and ordered Dusty another beer. "There was some kind of shoot-out at Jeremiah's place a couple of hours ago. Drug cartel."

Dusty's eyes opened wide, "Jeremiah messin' with drug cartels? What the hell?"

"No, no….drug cartel and FBI ended up there. Guess that FBI chic helped some lady and kid escape 'em or somethin'. Pablo got shot."

Dusty hung his head, "Damn. I liked that Pablo." Dusty raised his beer mug, "To Pablo."

Alan shook his head, "He ain't dead, just got shot in the shoulder."

Dusty smiled wide, "Well that's the first good thing you said since you got here."

"Where's your easel and stuff? You're not workin' today?"

"Ain't no customers. Got the National Guard drivin' all over, makes the tourists think Nawlens ain't safe."

"It's not!"

Scotty, the bartender, walked down to the end of the bar and leaned in close, "You know that guy I told you was asking me about Tourey? He moved into the apartment over the jewelry store next door. He owns that building too. Guy that was rentin' from him, Duane, says he showed up this morning with twenty grand cash. Asked him to move."

Dusty laughed, "Damn, I'd move for twenty grand cash and I *own* my house! Piece of shit, fallin' down anyway."

Alan lowered his voice, "Must be somethin' pretty special 'bout this neighborhood."

Scotty sneered, "You got that right. FBI across the street!" Scotty wiped the bar, took Alan's empty sandwich basket, and said, "I don't think these guys are done with Nawlens. I'm thinkin' we got more trouble comin'. Mark my words, it's gonna start right over there." He walked away waving his bar rag to point across the street.

The juke box started playing Creedence Clearwater Revival, Bad Moon Rising.

Dusty looked at Alan, "You thinkin' what I'm thinkin'?"

"We need a new bar."

CHAPTER SIX

Abram thumped his temple with the barrel of his pistol and moaned. "I don't like Ms. Spicey being out here! Not good. No way this be good."

Jackson backed up a little and maneuvered to get out of line of fire in case Abram's gun went off. "Who is she anyway?"

Abram stuck the gun back in his waistband and scowled, "She be a Voodoo lady." Abram looked at Jackson, "Just yesterday she showed up at a house I was 'sposed to torch. Mind you, only ten minutes after I get the call to do it! She knew why I was there, man! Told me I ain't getting' away with nothin'. Made me help move the furniture out first!" Abram was pointing up to the heavens. "She's spooky."

Jackson glanced out the window again, "I think they might be at the wrong place. They be pushin' that car back to the road. See?"

Abram pushed Jackson to the side and said, "We best be leavin' now, and just hope they don't see us. You clear what you need to do out here?" Jackson nodded, and Abram gave him the key. "Don't be losing that." Jackson noticed Abram didn't lock the door back up. Jackson slipped the key into his pocket and slid into the passenger seat of the car. As far as he was concerned, they couldn't get out of there fast enough. A visit from a Voodoo lady didn't make him feel any better.

The old Impala crawled away from the barn, back down the dirt path toward the road. The main driveway headed off to the right and was not visible, but Abram didn't want to make a dust cloud or any noise that would draw attention to his car. When they reached the end of the dirt drive and edge of the road he stretched his neck as far forward as he could. He didn't see the burgundy Cadillac. "They must have got it runnin' again. We lucked out!"

Abram gave the car some gas and headed back toward town. Willie, Wilma and Sasha had stopped pushing the Cadillac to rest in the shade of a big tree for a minute. Their car wasn't visible from the road because of undergrowth, but Spicey had been steering and saw Abram drive by. Some guy was with him. They had come out of the woods just a hundred yards down the road. Somethin' real fishy goin' on.

Spicey got out of the car and walked back to Sasha. "You be willin' to take a little walk with me? We give Willie and Wilma a chance to get to know each other, and we'll see if we can find us some wild berries down here."

Sasha looked puzzled, "Wild berries in the fall?" Spicey frowned at her and Sasha figured Spicey had some sort of plan. It probably didn't have a dang thing to do with berries either. "How 'little' a walk you talkin'? I ain't exactly dressed for hikin' around in the woods."

Sasha caught up with Spicey who was now already on the road and starting to head for where she saw Abram's car came out of the tree line. "Come on girlfriend. Won't hurt us to get a little exercise in today." Sasha couldn't believe Spicey had said that. Spicey would use her cell phone to call the store answering machine for messages when she was in the next room. Exercise!

When they had walked a ways down the road, they saw the dirt drive heading back to a barn. Spicey started walking down the drive. Sasha asked, "We walkin' all the way to that barn over there?" Sasha sidestepped a briar bush trying to grow in the middle of the drive. "Thought we not 'sposed to be here."

Spicey whispered, "I just saw Abram Davis and some dude pull out of here in that big ol' Impala of his. Why you think Abram be out here?" Sasha was shaking her head but still walking with Spicey. "I bet he be up to no good for sure, and I know Tourey got somethin' goin' out here. I think we owe Tourey to check this out. You know, spy a little."

Sasha liked the idea she was a spy. Especially since it looked like the bad guys were probably gone. Sasha started humming 'Goldfinger', and Spicey started laughing. They made their way around the back of the barn and saw the service door. Spicey held out the open padlock for Sasha to see. "If there was somethin' bad here you'd think they'd have locked up." Spicey slowly opened the door, and they walked in.

Sasha whistled, "This be the biggest, cleanest barn I ever did see." Both their eyes floated around the walls to land on the row of kennels. Spicey started walking toward them. Her walk became slower, and she stopped.

Spicey looked at Sasha, "Why would there be toilets and beds in kennels? No dogs nowhere. This looks more like little prison cells."

Sasha looked puzzled then said, "Uh oh." She held up a stack of coloring books and crayons that sat in a pile on a table. "Maybe for little prisoners?"

Spicey's mouth flew open, and she clutched her amulet. "Somethin' be real wrong here."

Spicey looked at Sasha very seriously, "You don't have to come with me, but that front door be open. I want to see if somebody's home. I'll tell them our car broke down, and we need a phone." Sasha didn't like the sound of going up to the house, but she also felt a strong desire to find out what was going on. If somebody was holdin' children prisoner, she wanted to help Spicey get 'em caught. She looked at Spicey and gave her a big nod. As they crossed the lawn to the front door, they were both humming 'Jesus Loves Me' for courage.

Spicey knocked loudly on the open front door, "Yoo hoo! Anybody home? Yoo hoo." They looked at each other, and Spicey took a couple of steps into the foyer. "We be needin' to use a phone. Anyone here?" Silence.

Sasha stepped up close behind Spicey and whispered, "We best shut the door, look at all the flies in here."

Spicey looked around and saw that most of the flies seemed to be comin' from a room on the right. She slowly started walking toward the room when Sasha grabbed the back of her skirt and startled her.

"Don't be grabbin' on me! Scare the pee outa me!" They walked further into the room and saw feet protruding from a recliner chair. There was a black liquid all around on the rug and the buzzing of the flies was so loud Spicey raised her voice. "Excuse me but we need a phone." The feet didn't move. They inched closer. Spicey was now hanging on to Sasha, too, as they sidestepped closer to the front of the chair.

They saw him at the same time. Blood everywhere. Bullet holes, flies. They looked at each other, screamed, and ran for the front door. Spicey yelled, "Stop!" Sasha kept going. Spicey took a deep breath, leaned against the open door, and then turned to go back in. There might be some kid in there needin' her. Damn it all anyway! She slowly started walking through the mansion. She peeked in every room but didn't see signs of any other people. An icy chill suddenly shot through her spine. She bolted down the center hall to the foyer. She slammed the door on her way out and ran down the driveway screaming the song 'Jesus Loves Me' in a warbling voice.

When she got to the car, the motor was running, and Willie, Wilma and Sasha were all inside. Spicey got in, her chest heaving, and looked to the back seat at Sasha who had her knees up to her dropped head, and her hands covering her face. Wilma volunteered, "Sasha not feelin' so good. Got them bad hiccups, too. Best we get her home." Spicey saw one of Sasha's eyes peek through her fingers. Then a loud, "Hic!" Looked like her eyeball was ready to jump from its socket.

Spicey dabbed her cheeks with a hankie, "We probably got a little more exercise than we be ready for." She rubbed her amulet all the way back to the city, humming 'Jesus Loves Me' while Sasha hiccupped and the car burped.

Tourey headed out to the country house of Senator Kenny's. He wasn't sure how to get Patterson to tell him what he needed to know, but he had to try.

Hopefully, none of the other club members would show up while he was there. Tourey had reviewed his notes on the human trafficking case the CIA had worked on last year. They had made some arrests and saved some people, but they knew the organization still existed. Judge Harold Williams's name had kept popping up in that investigation. He was a member of this sicko club.

Could be it was time to dig into the judge some more too. Roger had his hands full. Tourey knew everyone was counting on him. Tourey arrived at the country house, parked out front, and knocked loudly on the door. He waited a few minutes and knocked again. There was a wrap-around porch, so Tourey walked around to peek in the windows.

Damn. William Patterson laid sprawled out on a recliner obviously dead.

Tourey walked back to the front door. It was unlocked, so he went in. He stood facing Patterson as he called John. "Got a problem gettin' much info from Patterson. Been shot about five times from what I can see. Based on insect activity, probably about six hours ago. Now what?"

John arrived at the Star Ship and gave Ray the flash drive from Tourey. Thor and Jeanne had been the last to arrive. Roger asked Jeanne to bring them up to date on what had happened at Mathew Core's house when she went to warn Lisa about the sicko club.

Jeanne explained the cartel guys pulled up front, blocked her car, and sent guys in both the front and back doors. After sending Lisa and Jamie to the back of the house, she was able to shoot the men as they entered the home. She then told the team she used Lisa's SUV to escape with them, but an SUV of Manio's men had been waiting in the alley. Jeanne worried about the traffic congestion in the city and decided to take Lisa and Jamie to Jeremiah's. Jeanne told them the only safe place she could think of for Jamie and Lisa to hide was Jeremiah's tunnel. The men were close behind them and there was no time to spare. Jeanne described the men hunting them from the grasses. She heard Pablo and Thor arrive, then saw one of the men shoot Pablo.

Ray listened with a look of terror on his face. "This is why I don't do field shit. This right here! Geeks live longer!" Everyone chuckled.

Simon explained that Core's wife and daughter had already been moved to a secret location for safety, but the National Guard was still securing the perimeter of the field office for effect.

John's phone rang. It was Tourey. John signaled to Roger to step away from the group so they could talk.

John said, "Tourey's at the country house. Patterson was shot. Looks professional. Tourey left the house, hid his car, and is down the road a piece so he can watch the driveway. He doesn't think anyone knows Patterson is dead yet."

The first thought that went through Roger's mind was Core. Roger looked at the group and told them about Tourey's call. Paul offered, "If Tourey has any recording equipment, maybe we can bait the scene and see what happens." The team discussed a couple of other ideas. Roger went back to Paul's.

"I like Paul's idea best. They are expecting deliveries of kids, and I would bet at least one of them will go out there to make sure the house is ready. Probably the Senator. I would like to see how he reacts to Patterson being dead. He may have done it. Regardless, somebody has to get rid of that body." The decision was made. Tourey would wire the place up and send the feed to Ray at the Star Ship.

Roger explained some information from the communication sting and part of his plan to get the cartels. He told the team he was not at liberty to talk about a portion of what had been found out. Roger handed Ray a slip of paper. "We have a serious security problem. Mathew Core used this code to access our witness protection program. He said he can get into anything he wants with it. It has been 'hard programmed' in. I want to test this. Do you have a site you have trouble getting into?"

Ray looked at Roger, "Lots of them. Most of CIA for one. I can only go to level eight, and I get stopped. Want me to try?"

Roger nodded. They all watched Ray key in the code and then the CIA web address. Ray entered a couple of keystrokes. He was in. He kept entering search keywords and finding new file sites. Each entry he made he would lean in closer to his monitor and type faster.

Finally he turned to look at Roger, "I can get anything I ask for. That should not have happened."

Roger said, "Try ATF and DEA." Again, Ray had no problem. He was getting any information he wanted.

Simon was pacing, "Core's computer hack Sims is behind this. How many people have this code?"

Roger shrugged, "I have no idea. Ray, give this code to the CIA gurus working on this stuff. See if they can't tear it down, plug it, whatever you guys do. Tell them OSI stumbled on it." John frowned at Roger. Roger shrugged.

Paul was flipping through the banking data from French Quarter Bank. "Has anyone had a chance to skim through here looking for names we know?" Simon volunteered he was getting ready to do that. Roger asked Ray to send the sicko club names to all field offices. The focus would have to be keeping eyes on the children, but the field offices had to know the perpetrators too.

Roger leaned against the wall and watched the team with admiration. He knew they were the best of the best and silently thanked Ellen. He was sure she had arranged for it to work out this way. Jeanne looked over and Roger signaled her to join him upstairs. She knew he was going to order her to take some time away from the case. She had been dreading this moment. Jeanne looked to Thor, he looked away.

Once in the kitchen, Roger closed the door and invited Jeanne to take a seat. He smiled a weak smile and shook his head. "You are a remarkable agent, a remarkable person. You have to be exhausted and troubled by the events of yesterday and today." Roger waited for her response.

Jeanne focused on Roger, and he momentarily pulled back from the intensity of her eyes. "I understand why you believe I should feel those things. Maybe I should, but I don't." Jeanne leaned forward, "I know your specialty is behavioral science. Maybe you can explain it to me, but this is how I feel. The men I killed today and killing Devon yesterday, needed to be done. They were prepared to harm innocent people. I don't feel any remorse. I feel a sense of urgency because we are not done. When I am in these situations, it's like something takes over me, like an automatic reflex. When it's over, I feel the same satisfaction I have from finishing my laundry."

Roger was somewhat stunned by her analogy. He had talked to combat personnel who had admitted they didn't consider the enemy 'real people'. He had never heard killing nine men compared to completing a household task. Roger looked in Jeanne's eyes. "Do me a favor and think of something beautiful, peaceful." Jeanne's expression immediately softened. Roger swore her eye color changed. Roger's phone rang. It was Kim. Roger excused himself to stand on the other side of the room and take the call. "Yes?"

Kim exhaled, "Well, I'm not at all sure why Ellen wants me to tell you this, but you can bet I will bring it up later when we talk. You are looking into the eyes of a very special woman. According to Ellen, in the Voodoo culture, she borders on spiritual. You should trust her to do the right thing. Ellen says her beauty masks her power."

Roger cleared his throat, "Uh, thanks. Yes, I'll talk to you later."

Roger sat down across from Jeanne. The intensity had returned to her eyes. His mind flashed back to the absolute precision of her kill shot to Devon. He remembered Jeanne said her month with Mambo had helped her regain her center. Jeanne's rigid posture was that of a warrior, and she certainly had honed the skills.

Roger folded his hands in his lap and leaned back in his chair. He had to trust Ellen. "What do you need from me?"

Jeanne smiled, "I need you to trust me. I'm okay. I want to stay on this case."

Roger nodded, "Done."

CHAPTER SEVEN

Mathew Core dialed Juan Zelez, head of the Zelez cartel. His call was immediately answered.

"I have been expecting your call. Are we still set for tomorrow?" Juan Zelez was fully aware of the trouble in New Orleans today and suspected he had been set up. Mathew Core had brokered the deal. As far as Zelez was concerned, Core was a dead man. Zelez waved the other men from his office and walked out to his veranda. From here he could see his beautiful gardens peppered with his security men.

Core answered, "Martial law has been declared in New Orleans and your thirty ton shipment has been confiscated. My contact is still good, but some other problem led the Feds right into my shipment, but I'm sure you already know this. I also had a deal with Manio for sixty tons and enough coke to supply the east coast for a month. The Feds have it all."

Zelez considered what Core was telling him. "Are there really ninety tons of weapons at the port?"

Core answered, "Yes. Straight from Algiers. All the good stuff. Lots of ammo. Right now they are in the secured Navy yard. My source says it is all being moved to secure sites by train on Monday."

Zelez was quiet. "Then we take the train. When can you have more information?"

Core answered, "SSA Roger Dance of the FBI is holding my wife and daughter for my cooperation in relaying messages to both you and Manio. He wants you both. I am telling you what he asked me to tell you."

Zelez was puzzled. "I ask you again, not what Dance told you to tell me, but truth if you value the lives of your wife and daughter. Are there really ninety tons of weapons at the Naval Yard?"

"Yes."

"Then the train is a trap. He wants me to take it."

"Probably."

"What did he tell you to say to Manio?"

"Exactly what I just told you. Including the fact that the weapons and drugs will be moved by train on Monday."

Zelez laughed, "Is he a fool? He invites two drug cartels to take his bait and tells us ahead of time where they are?"

Core answered, "Don't underestimate Dance. When is the last time you heard of martial law being declared? Check him out. This is free from me to you: it is important that you not open any accounts at French Quarter Bank between now and tomorrow night at midnight. You probably should close any accounts you might have there. Ignore anything you hear about that bank. You will thank me."

Zelez was quiet for a minute and said, "You, my friend, still owe me. I think maybe you can help me find a way to get those guns. You check around for me. If they are using trains, I might have a name for you."

Zelez continued, "Dance is expecting me or Manio to move on these guns. He doesn't care who or when. If I decided to sit this one out and let him get Manio, what's in it for me?"

Core answered, "New Orleans. Dance goes home, job done."

Zelez asked, "What is Dance promising Manio?"

"Same thing he is promising you. To take out whoever shows up."

Zelez paused, "Why did you warn me about the bank? Did you warn Manio?"

Core said, "Manio sent eight men to kidnap my wife and daughter. I will encourage Manio to use the bank if I get an opportunity. I have every confidence in Dance."

"Interesting."

* * *

Core made an identical call to Jessie Manio, leaving out the information about French Quarter Bank. Manio expressed regrets for his poor judgment going after Core's wife and daughter. Core listened with tempered anger. Manio, too, suggested to Core that while the train was an obvious trap, the guns might still be available for the taking.

Manio had ended his conversation with Core by saying, "I am not a man you want against you, Mr. Mathew Core. I have killed men for far less. I will contact you when I have more information."

Core smiled. He knew he would extract his revenge on Manio when the time was right.

Core hung up and called Roger.

Roger had accomplished his initial goal to buy time, but at what cost?

Mary and I met Teresa and Linda at Senator Kenny's city house. The Senator was pulling out of the driveway as we arrived. Mary looked at Linda and said, "I don't think the judge had anything on his computer about how the children are being taken. He had some videos I copied and a few e-mails, but that was about it."

Teresa chimed in, "Ditto for Andre Baton and Theodore Chain. I'm thinking since Patterson is new to the group the real leader has to be the Senator."

We went into the Senator's house and snooped around until we found a laptop computer hidden in a mahogany bookcase. Teresa sat at the desk and declared, "I think I remember him messing with this middle drawer after Patterson left that day. Remember he told Patterson to go home and pack. The Senator offered to hide him at the country house and have Patterson's house torched? I think he got a phone number from some little book he had down here. He got the arsonist's number from that little book." Teresa started feeling around the bottom of the center drawer. I noticed a tall statute in the corner that looked like an armored man from the Knights of the Round Table. I went over and peeked in the mask. Nothing. Then I went inside to see if I could move it.

Teresa squealed, "Look! A little black book!" She started taking pictures of the pages and came across one with a checkmark next to a name and next to the checkmark was the word 'delivery'. The name was Manuel Cotton and there was a phone number. "This has to be important for him to hide it in a secret drawer." Teresa bent down and looked in the drawer again. She pulled out a tiny yellow envelope, opened it, and a key fell on the desk.

I waved at everyone with my tin arm, but they ignored me. Mary rolled her eyes and shook her head. I think a little comic relief is a good thing. It doesn't take four of us to look in a stupid drawer.

Besides, Ellen said I had to practice moving things. I tried to do a little soft shoe but someone had welded the suit to an iron post. Shucks. I figured I better pay attention to business, so I moved over to the others.

Mary asked, "Should we send Ellen what we have so far in case this really is important? It might give Roger a head start." Linda thought that was a good idea. Teresa downloaded all of our watches to hers and sent it all to Ellen. We hope.

Mary sighed, "Well, checking out Patterson at the country house is the last thing on our list. We are going to have to get some kind of a bright idea. Ellen is counting on us." Oh the pressure of some jobs.

We took off for the country house humming Linda's 'Hall of the Mountain King'. We were convinced that song gave us inspiration. We sure needed some now. The flaw in this whole plan is while we still think like mortals, we think like 'nice' mortals. Not pedophiles and murderers. I stopped midflight and yelled, "WAIT!"

Linda, Mary and Teresa came back to where I was and in unison asked, "What?"

"We need to think like bad guys. We're thinking like four nice old ladies!" Mary frowned at me, but I pushed on. "That's why we can't figure this out! We need to read the minds of some pedophiles, murderers, and slimy types to see how they think. How they plan stuff."

Mary stared at me and then looked at Linda, "I hate to say this, but she's right. The guys we need to catch are in New Orleans now and they are planning now. If we are going to catch them, we have to look for really sicko auras and read their minds."

Teresa and Linda were nodding. "Yup. We're going have to get our hands dirty. Real dirty." Teresa was rubbing her hands together and nodding. "Right after we go to the country house, we are going to do some ugly aura shopping!"

What woman doesn't enjoy a spontaneous shopping trip?

Roger called Frank Mass at the NO field office and had him send Agent Phillips to the French Quarter Bank. The bank manager needed help getting the information together they needed and there was no way Roger was going to make Ray do that. Roger warned Mass that the bank manager was a nice enough fellow but extremely slow. Being with him might push Agent Phillips to the end of his patience. Mass laughed and said he would instruct Phillips not to shoot the guy.

In the basement of the Star Ship, Roger drew a chart on a big white board. The rest of the team called out dollar amounts and dates from banking papers handed out by Simon. Roger wanted to establish a flow chart of the transactions posted to Core, Patterson, and Devon's bank accounts.

Simon stated Mathew Core used his corporate account like a clearing account for his clients. Global Corporation's account had money coming in primarily from two offshore accounts. One was in Patterson's alias, Bernard Jacobs, and one was in Devon's alias, Mike Parker. Three hundred million had come into Core's corporate account in one hour. From that money, Core had sent three wires of fifty million each to three offshore accounts in non-cooperative banking countries. Simon stated it would be nearly impossible to get identifications on those accounts.

Roger tapped on the white board next to those transactions. "Core moved this money right after Paul and I met with him this afternoon."

Simon offered, "I have Patterson making a ten million dollar payment to, drum roll please, retired Senator Rolland Kenny yesterday morning."

Roger smiled, "Probably payment to the Senator to hide Patterson at the country house." Roger drew a line from Patterson's account and wrote the name Kenny.

Paul volunteered, "That will be a tough one for the Senator to explain." Everyone in the room smiled.

Jeanne looked at Simon and asked, "Did you ever get names on the two accounts Core put money *in* late yesterday?"

Simon went to his computer and spoke as he keyed in a search code, "Didn't see names in this first batch. Wait a minute, read those numbers off again." Jeanne read the account numbers and

Simon pushed his chair back. "Roger, one of these is our Deputy Director, William C. Thornton. I don't recognize the other name."

John offered, "Thomas Fenley?"

Simon pulled his head back, "How did you know that?"

Thor asked, "Who the hell is he?"

CHAPTER EIGHT

Spicey and Sasha hung on to each other for support as Spicey unlocked her apartment door at the Voodoo shop. Sasha gave one wave goodbye to Willie and Wilma. Willie had announced he was going to take Wilma for an ice cream. The mention of food made Sasha start to gag. Willie's car burped as it turned the corner followed by a whiff of fried chicken, a barking collie, and a wiener dog.

Sasha collapsed into Spicey's overstuffed chair and declared, "My first day as a spy ain't goin' exactly like I planned." She shuddered and pulled a colorful blanket from the couch up under her chin. "Tourey gonna need to know 'bout this." Sasha frowned, "You think maybe Tourey a real spy? He knows a lot a stuff he don't need to be knowin'. He told you to stay away from that country house and sure 'nuff we got issues out there."

Sasha shuddered again. "Somebody made real sure that dude was dead." Sasha hiccupped again. "Dang hiccups! Makin' my boobs hurt."

Spicey sat on the couch looking at her phone. "I wondered 'bout Tourey bein' more 'an he claims to be. Mambo said he was in danger, and she gave him an amulet. That there makes him a good guy." Spicey started twirling her long necklace, "I'm thinkin' Tourey'd like to know Abram and some guy was out there in the prison barn." Sasha and Spicey both shuddered at the mention of the barn.

Sasha got a determined look on her face, "You know what I do if'in we catch whoever hurtin' kids? I take their man part, cut it right off, string it up, and hang it out at Mambo's on a strap of leather. Decorate one of them little trees of hers. That's what I'd do!"

Spicey looked at Sasha, "I think I saw one of them at Mambo's when we were there. Man part on a strap. Figured some dog got caught off the porch." They both chuckled and then got serious again. Spicey tried to dial Tourey, but he didn't answer. She left him a message saying there was something important he had to know about the country house.

Spicey looked at Sasha, "I'm gonna take me a nap 'til Tourey calls back. You goin' home or stayin' here?"

Sasha didn't hesitate two seconds, "I'm stayin' here. I'll take me a nap in this chair."

Spicey offered a weak smile, "Nappin' in a chair didn't work out so well for that guy at the country house, did it?"

Neither Spicey nor Sasha even closed their eyes as they laid covered in blankets waiting for Tourey's call. Spicey jumped every time Sasha hiccupped.

✳ ✳ ✳

William C. Thornton nervously sat on the bench in Lincoln Park, DC, waiting on Thomas Fenley. Not only had recent events guaranteed Fenley would be sporting a foul mood, but Fenley did not like being summoned for anything. He always called the shots. William was actually looking forward to this meet though. He had perhaps the best news Thomas could imagine. A safe money haven in the U.S. and they already had accounts established. Thornton knew the members of LUCY would be pleased.

Thornton saw Fenley approaching. Fenley's facial expression was exactly what William expected. Sour. Fenley sat heavily on the bench and glared at William. "You wanted to talk. Talk."

William squirmed a little. "OSI and CIA did this martial law thing. Roger Dance slipped into it and turned it into a communication sting. Including secure government bands. The sting started at 8:45 last night, ends tomorrow midnight."

Fenley's facial expression changed to fear, "They have our calls from last night?"

William put his hands up to motion for Fenley to relax. "There was a computer glitch between the government communication bands and the federal banking wire system. They lost all of the early calls and created a huge mess at the Fed. I spoke with Franklin Morris at the Fed. Every existing account at French Quarter Bank has been issued an exempt Fed banking number. They are going to renumber 'real' Fed accounts and then work on changing back these problem accounts. Estimate is two years before they can finish. In the meantime, all history on these accounts will be untraceable."

"What do you mean 'exempt' Fed banking numbers? Exempt from what?"

William couldn't contain his excitement, "Everything! All tracking, all regulation! And everywhere these accounts move, they erase the old activity record. We have two years, at least, of safe money haven!"

Thomas's expression softened, "Isn't that where Core opened accounts for us?"

"Yes. The entire history of how those accounts came to be has been erased."

Thomas Fenley stood and looked down at William. "You didn't even know there was going to be a martial law operation in your own agency. I'm supposed to believe you have good information on this?"

William stood, "A few guys at the Fed and the National Security Council are the only ones that know. Check it out. Dance is the one who screwed this up. By the way, his only goal is to take out Zelez. Should we rethink our plan?"

"What about Manio?"

William shrugged, "Dance is focused on Zelez. Probably sees it as more glory for less work."

That made sense. Thomas nodded, "Don't call again until this is over. If I need you, I'll call you. For now, tell Core to back off Dance and Casey."

Thomas turned and walked back to the waiting BMW.

Across the park two OSI Agents packed up their listening devices and video cameras. Taking down the big guys was fun. These guys were huge.

✳ ✳ ✳

"Can I have Zack back?"

Roger listened to Core and glanced at Paul. Paul could tell something had taken Roger by surprise. "You know who he is?"

"Of course, ATF, I've always known. I also think he and I can work the docks better than you can. Especially since Zelez just called me with the name of a man in charge of trains." Roger told Core he would call right back.

Roger had moved away from the team to take the call, and now motioned for John to join him and Paul in the corner. Roger relayed Core's request, looked at them both and said, "My gut says we can trust Core to a certain extent. This does bring him much deeper into this operation. What do you guys think?"

John offered, "Short of Ellen popping up and saying don't do it, I think it sounds good. Those two are known at the docks. He is right about them getting a lot more than we could. I think we need him."

Paul pushed his chin out in his nervous twitch, "ATF might not feel the same way. I heard Zack got somebody at the agency in real trouble for leaving him out to dry."

John said, "That was me. Guess I was in the mood for some shit kickin'. I can smooth it out with a call or two. Tell Core we need to be kept posted often. This is really going to move now that he has contacted both cartels."

Roger called Zack first. Zack was good with the plan as long as he only had to report to Roger. Zack still felt a little burned by the ATF.

Roger called Core back. "Just got word someone shot Patterson out at the country house."

Core paused and then said, "Might have been a pissed off parent."

Roger felt a cold chill run down his spine. He knew from the tone of Core's voice he was talking to Patterson's murderer. "Might have been. Zack said to call. I want you reporting to me, Core.

Often. I can't have a loose cannon out there. My team's safety is at stake."

"Zack and I will work the ports all night if we have to. By the way, I live across the street now, over the jewelry store. Keep your phone on." The line went dead.

Thor came down the stairs to join the team. His hair was wet from his shower, and he had fresh clothes on. He looked at Simon, "Hey, I grabbed one of your shirts until that laundry guy brings our shit back. Hope you don't mind."

Simon shook his head, "No problem. Where's the bloody clothes you took off? He'll do a pickup when he gets here."

Thor moved to point and popped two buttons on Simon's shirt. "Shit!"

Simon laughed, "I don't wear size 'bull', Mr. Muscle. You better find something that will stretch."

Thor left the room cursing and came back in a shirt that fit. "I think this belongs to Core. Found it in Ray's closet."

Ray looked over, "Sure as hell isn't mine."

Roger asked for his team's attention. He told them about his interview with Core, Core helping them, Zack working with Core, and how Core and Zack were working the ports for information tonight.

Roger added, almost as an afterthought, "I told Core to tell both cartels the drugs and guns would be on a train Monday heading for Kansas underground storage."

Thor stood and his voice boomed. "Do you just think this shit up?" Thor looked at Paul, "Who does this shit?" Thor looked back at Roger, "How are we going to protect a train full of guns and drugs from two cartels that we *invited* to play?"

Roger chuckled, "I haven't really worked that out yet."

* * *

"I'm goin' *tonight*. Don't care what your skinny ass wants to do." Toby put one end of the leather strap between his teeth and tied a knot to the end of the dead turkey's foot and pulled it tight. He left about five foot of slack and then cut the strap from the roll. "I figure I need about three more turkeys for bait. You ridin' with me into Slidell or not? Don't matter no way." Toby was only seventeen years old, but he was a big boy. Stood taller than most men and had hands the size of pig hams.

Junior was the same age, but on the skinny side. Kind of tall and lanky. They had been friends since they started school. Toby had got it in his head they could get a picture of the Rugaru on his cell phone and sell it to make a bunch of money. Tonight was supposed to be a full moon, and he was dead set on goin'. Junior had talked it up good 'til Toby actually picked a day. He wasn't so sure he really wanted to go into the swamps at night. Especially since everyone in town been talkin' that cops were findin' people bones out there.

Toby said the people bones were proof the Rugaru was back. "Pa's boat's already out to the crab shack waitin' on us. I figure we put on those body waders he's got in the shack, boat down to where they been findin' them bones, and walk in from the back. We get deep enough in from shore, string up our bait, get up in the trees, and wait for our money picture. *RUGARU!*" Toby threw his fist into the air.

Junior didn't want Toby tellin' everybody at school he was too chicken to go. "How long you figure we have to wait? I get home too late and Momma's gonna ground me again. I want to go to the dance 'morrow night. You sure Rugaru don't climb trees?"

Toby laughed, "Rugaru is part wolf. How many wolves you know climb trees?"

"He's also part man. That part might climb trees! I don't want to be out there in the swamp at night no longer than I have to."

Toby shrugged, "Kind of hard to get much information on feedin' times for the Rugaru since most people don't believe. I 'spect they eat dinner like everyone else, when it gets dark. We get there right at dark, should be goin' home in a couple hours. You in?"

Junior rubbed on his amulet and shooed a fly away, "Yeah. I bet my ass gettin' grounded again."

＊ ＊ ＊

We arrived at the Senator's country house in time to see Tourey taking a bunch of stuff from the trunk of a car hidden in the brush. Teresa asked, "I wonder what he's doing? Isn't he that undercover CIA guy John Barry knows?"

Mary answered, "I think he's putting a bunch of electronic stuff in his pockets."

Tourey closed the trunk lid and made his way toward the mansion walking down the edge of the tree line. Linda said, "He's trying to be sneaky, or he would be walking up the driveway. Maybe he thinks someone might be coming out here." Tourey sprinted across the lawn and walked in the front door.

We followed him in. He stopped right in the foyer and started placing a camera to point at the front door. We sort of floated around watching him awhile when Mary mentioned there sure were a lot of flies in the house. That should have been my clue.

Teresa screamed from the other room. Linda and I looked at each other. That was not a good scream. With a look of terror on her face, Mary came flying out of the room Teresa was in screaming

"DEAD GUY!" She flew right past us, right through Tourey, and back outside. I grabbed Linda's shirt sleeve, and we inched our way through the wall to where Teresa was. She was staring at a chair that was pointed away from Linda and me.

Teresa pointed, "I think we found Patterson."

Eee Gads. Mary was peeking in the window from outside. Tourey had moved into the room we were in.

Linda said, "Do you think he knows there's a dead body in here?"

Teresa rolled her eyes, "Yeah, but I bet he doesn't know a car is pulling up in the driveway!" Her voice had gotten louder and faster as she watched past us through the front window.

Mary burst through the wall, "The Senator is here! Tourey doesn't know! He has to hide!"

Linda yelled, "Mary and I will stall the Senator. You guys hide Tourey!" Linda and Mary flew through the front wall to the driveway.

Teresa and I just starred at each other. "How do we hide Tourey?" I figured we just had to draw his attention to the front window, so he could see the Senator's car. I turned myself into a monkey and started screaming as loud as I could as I swung from the front window curtain rod.

Tourey and Teresa both whipped their heads around and gaped at me. Teresa put her hands over her head and yelled "Not a monkey!" I went back to being invisible and zapped Tourey's memory. When he shook his head, he saw the Senator's car, gathered his equipment, and ran toward the back of the house. Linda and Mary had the Senator's car horn honking and car alarm screaming.

Linda and Mary flew into the room. Mary was gasping, "He's trying to fix his car. Is Tourey hidden?" Teresa and I both nodded our heads. Linda floated up to the ceiling on the far side of the room. She had a look of pure disgust on her face from looking at the body of Patterson in the chair. I joined her.

"I was a monkey."

"Of course you were."

CHAPTER NINE

Thomas Fenley pulled his BMW over to place a call to London. Donavan Luntz, the sitting chairman for the oil consortium in LUCY, answered. OSI traced and recorded the call. Donavan Luntz was a name that so far had escaped the radar of the OSI and CIA. The agents recording the call were very much interested in what Donavan and Fenley had to say to each other. Ellen sat on Fenley's passenger seat in the BMW. She wanted to read Fenley's mind.

Donavan barked, "Bring me up to date." Fenley repeated everything Thornton had told him.

Donavan told Fenley that Manio had called and informed him an emergency shipment of coke and weed needed to be brought in to New Orleans and distributed tonight. Martial law or no martial law. Manio was using Donavan's facility and needed Donavan's staff available for transport. With

New Orleans dry, Manio figured he could raise the price of this supply and actually make money as a result of the sting.

Donavan laughed, "Manio is making more money on his dope because of this raid. Wouldn't it be ironic if the FBI gives us what we want by accident, too? A money safe haven in the United States. I'll check this out and call you back. Manio's using the rig again tonight. Make sure we are left alone at the port, Thomas."

Fenley couldn't believe their luck either. He started making notes in a small notebook of the accounts that needed to be moved to French Quarter Bank if this was true. He would wait until Donavan confirmed before he called Manio about the money. One screw up was enough on this deal. It was bad enough Manio wasn't getting his guns.

The OSI agents transcribed the call and forwarded it to their Director. A whale had just entered the pond. Donavan Luntz. It was becoming clear that Donavan, Fenley, Manio, and probably Thornton were all members of LUCY.

Ellen memorized the account numbers Fenley wrote down and headed for Roger. She knew what the gals were doing and decided to leave them be. She laughed to herself, a monkey?

Abram pointed down a side street as the car crawled through the traffic nightmare caused by the National Guard jeeps. "Down the end of that street, there's where that Voodoo lady, Ms. Spicey, has her place." Abram rubbed his chin as he looked in the rearview mirror to see if any cops were following them. "I got myself enough trouble tryin' to figure out my new job. Don't need the likes of her lookin' over my every move."

Jackson was silent as he took in the sights of the city. It had been five very long years in prison for just stoppin' to say hey to the wrong dudes at the wrong time. It suddenly struck him that he had no money and nowhere to live. Jackson turned to face Abram, "I'm needin' to find a place to stay. You know 'bout anything?"

Abram honked his horn at a lady walking five dogs of various sizes all colored bright rainbow colors. She had started walking into the path of their car, and Abram yelled out the window. "Crazy bitch! Move them damn dogs!" She flipped him off. Abram commented if he had more time he would go back and shoot her.

Jackson looked out his window. This is not the life he had planned for himself. He wondered if his Momma was still alive and livin' over on Desiree Street. She was the only family he had left. His momma being crippled and with no car, he hadn't seen her since the day they took him to jail. Once he got settled he'd go see if she was all right.

Abram told Jackson to start payin' attention to where they were. They were almost at the gang house. Abram started slowing down and rolled the car to a stop in front of a large white stucco building covered in graffiti.

"We need to go inside, so I can give you your orders. Then you can be on your way. Whole operation is a mess with Manuel gettin' killed an' all." Abram looked at him, "You bein' just out of jail, I'm gonna give you some money 'head of time. Got a new cargo van you be drivin' to snatch these kids. You best keep mindful of cops. City be crawlin' with 'em. Ain't the best time for all this shit to be goin' down, but we need the money, ya know?"

Jackson nodded and followed Abram into the building through a large heavy steel door. A group of six young men were hanging out obviously waiting for Abram. They all started shouting questions at him at once. Abram shot his gun at the ceiling to shut them up.

"You dogs gonna wait your turn. I ain't Manuel. I talk to you one at a time, and right now my man Jackson here got my ear. Go outside and decide who gets my ear next." The group slowly moved from the building mumbling and looking back towards Abram.

Jackson asked, "How'd you get this job anyway? No offense, but you seem a little more…. 'together' than those other guys."

Abram answered, "Manuel always be my best friend. These dudes think I was number two in the chain, ya know? Just cuz I always be by his side. Really? Don't know crap 'bout what I supposed to do now."

Jackson was surprised by Abram's confession and offered, "I'm thinkin' you best be a fast learner."

Mambo was troubled. She paced the large room of her hut and then went outside toward the swamp's edge. She closed her eyes and listened to the swamp's whispers. At a decibel level too low for mortal ears, she heard a low moan, weeping, and whispers of terror from tortured souls. Mambo rubbed her amulet and asked the Spirits to free their voices. Let them be loud and clear, so she could understand. The normal sounds of the swamp ceased and the mist thickened. Dark swirls churned in the mist. Screams and pleadings from hoarse voices assaulted the air. A child's voice urgently whispered, "Please hurry." Mambo would need to call on all of her Spirits. There was trouble coming.

Senator Kenny finally got his car alarm to stop. He walked up the front steps of the mansion making a mental note to call his auto mechanic. The door began to open as he put his key in the lock. Patterson must have been outside and forgot to lock up. He walked into the foyer and immediately was met by a swarm of flies. What the hell? He swatted his arms around and looked to the drawing room on the right. The flies were so thick in there it looked like a black cloud hanging low in the room. His nostrils flared at the sour stench assaulting his nose.

Rolland yelled, "Bernard? You here?" He saw the feet protruding from the end of the chair. He bent his arm to cover his nose as he inched closer. Patterson's bloody body was sprawled across the recliner and covered with crawling flies laying their piles of glossy white eggs. He saw the bullet holes everywhere. He started to gag and ran back out of the room to the fresh air outdoors. Good Lord, what was he going to do?

Tourey heard the Senator's car squeal away down the drive, and he went back to the job of installing his video and listening equipment. He used his phone to call Ray to test the computer feed and noticed he had a message from Spicey. After he and Ray made some minor adjustments, Tourey walked back to his car and listened to his message. Tourey frowned. Spicey said she had some information about the country house. He bet she came out here after he told her not to. This was a complication he didn't need. He decided he would stop in and see her in person instead of returning her call.

Tourey called John Barry and told him the Senator had discovered the body but left in a rush. Probably wasn't him who shot Patterson.

It was six o'clock at the Star Ship and promised to be a long night. There had been no progress figuring out which kids were to be abducted. They also had no idea who had been hired to do the kidnapping. If they could arrest the sicko club soon, maybe one of them would talk or have the information somewhere. Reading the missing children statistics from Tourey had everyone in a sour mood. Roger rested his head in his hands as he sat at the kitchen table at the Star Ship.

Paul walked up from the basement. "I'm thinking maybe we should tell the team to break until we call them? Been a long day, and we're probably going to have some fun tonight when the sicko club finds out about Patterson."

Roger looked up, "I was just thinking the same thing. I think I'll volunteer to stay and watch the feed. We can't miss that coming over. I can't remember the last time Ray even left this place." Roger stood and turned to go to the basement.

He glanced back to Paul. Paul shrugged, he knew Roger was second guessing himself.

When Roger reached the basement he volunteered to watch the computer. Simon and Ray told him to leave. They were perfectly fine staying. Scotty, the bartender, was bringing them Cajun food from across the street. When Roger got back upstairs, Paul was on his phone and looking out the window to the street.

Paul put his phone back in his pocket and said, "Frank just called. The LA boys said two guys on the LA list of the sicko club died today. One was in a car accident, other appears to be a suicide. Swallowed a barrel. Said he also got an update from New York that a guy on their list was shot in a mugging. Broad daylight in the financial district. Chicago had one jump from his condominium balcony." Paul pushed his chin forward in his nervous twitch. "Appears to be a bad day for sickos."

Roger exhaled, "Yes it does. Want to grab some dinner?"

✳ ✳ ✳

Jackson was petrified. Here he was driving this brand new van. Cops everywhere. He hadn't driven in five years, and he didn't have a driver's license anymore. Suddenly he started laughing. It occurred to him he should be worried about getting caught snatchin' kids a little more than being stopped for no license. Abram told him to find a place to stay for the night, get some dinner, and come back. By then maybe Abram would have found the names of the kids Jackson was supposed to snatch. He also needed the name of his contact, so they could set up the switch.

With so much money involved, Jackson couldn't believe how disorganized this was. When Manuel got shot today, no one even questioned if Abram was the new boss. Abram said he didn't realize it 'til people started asking him what they should do. Crazy.

Jackson drove down Desiree Street and found the little house where his Momma had lived. He parked and walked up on the porch. It was falling down so badly he had to shift his weight as he stood at the door so as not to fall to the side. He knocked and waited.

He heard a shuffling sound on the other side of the door, and the door slowly started to open. His momma was hanging on to a metal walker and asked, "Who be there?"

Jackson couldn't believe she didn't recognize him, and then he noticed the gray blue of her eyes. She had cataracts so bad, she couldn't see anymore. Jackson could feel a lump growing in his throat, "It's me, Momma. Jackson."

She looked straight ahead, her bottom lip quivered, "What be the name of your first dog?"

Jackson laughed, "PeeWee."

A big smile erupted on her face and tears flowed from the corners of her eyes. "My baby. You come home."

Abram called Judge Williams. "Look, you want this here done you got to send me all the info again! I'm tellin' ya, Manuel got killed today, and I don't know his computer password!"

Judge Williams closed his eyes and rocked in his chair. Jesus Christ! How hard is it to find reliable people? Abram had assured him he understood everything that was supposed to happen. He just couldn't pull up the names and address of the kids. Judge Williams scowled and finally agreed to send the list to Abram's computer. What choice did he have? This was Thursday for God's sake. They only had 'til Monday to get this all done and deliveries made.

Abram said thank you and hung up.

No more than a minute passed, and Judge Williams's phone rang again. "Now what?"

It was Rolland. "Harold? We have a problem. I don't care what your schedule looks like, be at the country house at eight tonight." The line went dead. Judge Williams scratched his neck. Rolland always had a flair for the dramatic. Probably got some sort of traffic ticket he doesn't want to talk about on the phone. The Judge exhaled loudly. Was he the last intelligent form of life left on this planet?

CHAPTER TEN

Tourey finished wiring up the house and left. We decided to snoop around some. The mansion was really nice. There were no signs of anything sinister there, except of course the bloody body in the living room. We decided to check out the barn. That's when things got interesting again. Linda flew out, her hand over her mouth gagging, followed by Mary and Teresa. I'm thinking it's not always bad to be the last one to get everywhere.

I looked at Linda, "Another body?"

She shook her head and said, "Kennels." Huh?

Mary volunteered, "There is a row of kennels with toilets and beds in them. It must be where they put the children."

What? I didn't need to hear *that*, and I was sure I didn't need to see it.

Teresa was fuming. "Let's go find those dark auras. I am beyond motivated to kick some sicko butt!" Pretty much said it all for the whole group. I suspect we are the meanest looking bunch of sour faced angels right now that heaven has ever seen.

Just then Ellen popped in to join us. "Okay, let's just take a few deep breaths and talk this out. I got an attitude alarm on you gals."

Really? An attitude alarm?

Actually, mortals could really use those.

Teresa looked at me. "Mortals have them. They're called horns."

Ellen cleared her throat and smiled, "I know this is extremely difficult for all of you because you still have many mortal thoughts and emotions. You need to focus on the fact that you are angels. You must not harm mortals. Any mortals. Are we clear?" We all nodded.

I'm thinking, define *harm*. Long term permanent harm, or you deserve this in your face right now harm? Ellen frowned at me, "All harm. What is your next plan then?"

Teresa explained we thought we would go looking for bad auras and do some mind reading. Let our mortal thinking go to the dark side. Try to find the bad guys before they got a chance to hurt any kids. Ellen liked it. A lot.

"Do you remember the Saint you met at Mambo's? She contacted me. Mambo is calling for all Saints to meet her at midnight. I think we should be there too. If I don't see you before then, I'll meet you at midnight at Mambo's."

Mary asked, "Is this like a party? Should we dress up?"

Oooooooooooo, too cool!

Ellen laughed, "Hardly. It means Mambo is asking for help." And she was gone.

I still think I'll wear a party dress. Maybe red.

* * *

At the field office, John Barry straightened a pile of brochures and pamphlets and placed them in a large envelope. He wanted to give Jerome some material to look at and keep Jerome focused on doing something good with his life. Mass walked over to where John stood. "I see you are cleaning out our recruitment crap for us. Are we that shorthanded on this case?"

John chuckled, "Remember the woman who was rescued out at Mambo's? Adele Brown? Her son, Jerome, thinks he might want to grow up to be a cop."

Mass shook his head as he walked out the door, "Sounds like a fool idea to me."

John went to his car and noticed the National Guard was having a change of shifts. He looked at his watch and was surprised it was already six o'clock. Time was flying. His stomach growled, and he realized he needed some food. John made his way through the Quarter to the address of Adele's tailor shop. Jerome was sitting on a side stoop talking to another kid. John smiled to himself. Jerome was a smart boy. Adele had done a good job raising him under difficult circumstances.

John parked and walked over to the boys. Jerome jumped up and ran to meet him. "Mr. Barry! Meet my friend Donny." Jerome waved for Donny to come over and join them. John put his hand out to shake hands. He could tell Donny didn't know what to do. Jerome leaned in, "You're supposed to shake his hand." Donny got a big smile on his face and shook John's hand.

John reached over and gave Jerome a big bear hug. "Here's the package of material I promised you. Have you been looking after your Mom?"

With a big grin, Jerome took the envelope, and nodded his head. "I pretty much know where she is all the time. She's still cryin' some, I can tell, but she's happy to be home again. She made a real pretty shirt for Ms. Spicey. I'm going to take it over after dinner."

John was happy to hear Adele and Spicey were developing a friendship. Adele opened the side door. "John? I just made a big pan of Jambalaya if you're hungry?" Adele's big smile made her look even more beautiful than John had remembered.

"I'm starved."

✳ ✳ ✳

Thor, Nelson, and Jeanne decided to walk to the little diner where they had eaten the night before. Dusty had been right. It did look like a dive, but the food was great. Jeanne walked ahead of the guys and placed a call to Pablo in the hospital. She was laughing at his assessment of his condition. He claimed every time a good looking nurse came in his room he had a setback. Pablo told Jeanne his recovery might take a while. Jeanne caught a troubling reflection from a glass store front across the street and told Pablo she would talk to him later.

Jeanne dialed Thor, "We picked up a fan club. Two behind you, and two across the street."

Thor said thanks and told Nelson. They continued walking toward the diner that was now within sight. Jeanne was now walking with Thor and Nelson. She asked Thor, "We still eating?"

Thor scowled, "Hell yes."

They opened the door of the diner and took a table near the front window. Their fan club had gathered across the street and were standing behind the alley dumpster. Jeanne saw one of the men walk down the alley and disappear. Three men stood smoking, talking, and glancing toward the diner. She looked at Nelson, "You know what sucks? Nobody has a good ol' shit kicker anymore. They always want to bring guns. It really takes all of the fun out of it."

Nelson looked at Thor, who just shrugged as he grabbed one of the crab legs from his plate. Nelson said, "Mass has been getting calls all day from the local PD that the muggings are through the roof. Seems what dope is still on the streets is pretty pricey." He leaned forward to look at the group by the dumpster, "These guys look the part."

Thor looked at Jeanne, "Maybe you'll get lucky and they'll still be there when we finish."

Jeanne smiled, "I really hope so." Nelson and Thor realized she was serious.

Their empty plates were removed. Nelson announced he was picking up the tab. "Give me a minute to check out before you start any Rambo crap without me."

Thor held the door open for Jeanne as he stuck a toothpick in the corner of his mouth. He looked her in the eyes and said, "I think they stayed to play."

Jeanne smiled.

Thor chuckled and shook his head. He leaned against the brick wall of the adjacent building, crossed his arms, and said, "Have at it."

Jeanne walked ahead and looked into the diner window watching the reflection of the three men walking toward her. She guessed their ages as early twenties, full of hormones and probably short of dope money. She turned to them at the last moment. "Something on your minds?"

The largest of the three men stopped and said, "We're thinkin' you might be willin' to pay us some money to protect you in the streets. Pretty lady like you should be careful in Nawlens."

"How much money?"

One of the men glanced at Thor who was still leaning against the building about fifty feet away. Jeanne asked again, "How much?"

Big guy answered, "A hundred bucks gets you out of the neighborhood safe."

Jeanne nodded her head, reached into her jeans and counted off two hundred dollars and laid it on the window sill behind her. "Let's make it two. I have to tell you, it's cheaper to go to the gym. I also have to tell you I am FBI and trained. If you get physical with me, I might hurt you. I have a witness that you were warned." Jeanne pointed toward Thor. "If you still want to threaten me for money, there are two rules."

Big guy looked startled at her claim of being FBI. That made this all the better. It was the damn FBI who killed his cousin this morning in the raid. "You guys killed my cousin this morning!" He glanced at Thor again, and then back to Jeanne. "What rules you talking about?" He kept looking at the money on the window sill.

Jeanne said, "First, that man over there gets to frisk you. If I win, you don't get the money. If you win, you get the money and don't get arrested for robbery. Last chance to change your mind."

The three men walked over to Thor who patted them down. Thor removed two guns and three knives. The men walked back to Jeanne. The big guy smiled, "Ain't your friend there gonna help? Don't seem fair."

Jeanne looked at Thor, "Should I give them a minute to call some friends and make it fair?"

Big guy got a menacing look on his face, "You got some mouth on you bitch." He lunged at her.

Nelson came out of the diner, looked at Thor leaning against the brick wall, arms crossed at his chest, legs crossed at his ankles. Nelson saw the pile of weapons on the sidewalk, and then saw Jeanne squared across from three big guys. Nelson raised an eyebrow, and Thor removed his toothpick from his mouth. "She wants this."

The people sitting in the diner had one good show. The entire fight lasted less than five minutes, and all three men were on the sidewalk in various contorted positions. Jeanne had martial arts training and was extremely fast. These guys had just been hit by a train. Jeanne reached over to the window sill and pocketed her money. "You lost. We can call the local PD now to come get you, or maybe you can get a name for us?"

The big guy was trying to stand, but still had one knee on the sidewalk. "Damn, lady! What name you want?"

Jeanne asked, "What name comes to mind if I was looking to hire somebody to snatch up a kid?"

The big guy finally made it to a standing position. The two other guys looked at each other and remained silent. Jeanne tilted her head, "You two get out of here." Now Thor and Nelson walked over.

Thor had his phone out and looked at Jeanne, "Am I calling PD?"

Jeanne reached back in her jeans and took out the two hundred dollars. "I don't think so."

The big guy reached for the money. Jeanne pulled it back and said, "Name."

"Up 'til this mornin' would have been Manuel Cotton. You done killed him. New dude's name Abram."

"Abram what?"

Big guy was holding his shoulder and grimacing, "I don't know a last name."

Jeanne handed him the money and Thor pointed to the pile of weapons, "We're keeping those." Big guy hobbled across the street and disappeared into the alley.

Jeanne turned to face Thor and Nelson and gave them each a big bear hug. "I can't tell you how great that felt! I'm going home now to take a shower and a nap."

Nelson and Thor watched her turn and walk toward her house. They decided to follow at a distance to make sure she got there okay. Thor called Roger with the names.

Nelson laughed, "I don't think she even broke a sweat. Damn."

Jeanne turned after a short while and yelled back, "I've got two big recliners, beer in the fridge, and a wide screen TV."

Nelson yelled back, "Right behind ya."

Thor made a mental note, again, not to piss her off.

CHAPTER ELEVEN

Roger and Paul had decided if they wanted any dinner they had better get it now. Simon had suggested a couple of famous Cajun restaurants within walking distance. As they walked, it was impossible not to feel the magnetism of the French Quarter. It was beautiful, strange, vile, and tempting in each breath. The sounds of music seeped from each doorway and melted into the streets that were packed with people. After six in the evening, traffic was restricted, and streets like Bourbon were for people only.

Paul slowed down to look into the bar they were passing. People appeared to be in costume and having some sort of contest. He looked at Roger, "I wonder how many of these tourists realize how dangerous it is here right now?" Just then a six foot bearded man with huge breasts, dressed in a pink ball gown, carried out a guy by his collar and belt and threw him in the middle of the street. He straightened his dress straps, smoothed the fabric around his hips and went back into the bar.

Roger moved out of the way. "Some of them have a clue."

Paul chuckled, "You remember the gal that bartends at our hotel? Jill?" Paul had a twinkle in his eye that Roger recognized.

"Yes."

"Seems likely we might go tour the Quarter later tonight if this case cooperates." Paul raised his eyebrows a couple of times. "You're welcome to come with. I can see if she has a friend."

"Thanks anyway. My goal is to make it back to the hotel and spend some time on the phone with Kim." Roger offered a small smile.

Paul gave him a punch in the arm. "I knew it! It's only been over a friggin' year you two have been dating! Congrats there buddy. You got yourself a keeper."

Roger laughed, "Sometimes it takes me a while."

Paul started laughing. "Boy will you have the mother-in-law stories!"

✳ ✳ ✳

Rolland called each of the remaining New Orleans club members and told them to meet him at the country house at eight tonight. He was debating with himself about telling them Bernard was really William Patterson. Rolland was sure the 'spook' type guy Patterson told him about was the one who shot him. The cops wouldn't have shot him like that or left him there.

Different scenarios kept running through his head. If he called the cops and reported it, then they would turn the country house into a crime scene. They would see the barn! He had to explain to the club who Patterson was, or they wouldn't understand who probably shot him. All he needed was for Andre to go all 'girly' on them and freak out thinking they were all in danger.

Rolland watched the video of the art contest again and kept replaying the segment with his chosen winner. He turned off his computer and stood up. He would tell the club the whole story, and as a group, they would get rid of the body. Rolland dug around in his desk drawer looking for the keys to the gardener's pick-up truck. He went upstairs to change into some old clothes and then loaded the truck up with tarps and shovels. This promised to be a very long night.

Tourey knocked loudly on Spicey's side door and heard a crash and some cussing from inside. Spicey opened the door looking very unkempt for her. She motioned him inside, and Tourey saw Sasha picking up the remnants of a broken lamp.

"You two fightin'?" Tourey glanced around the room.

Spicey answered, "We be nappin' when you pounded on that door. Scared the bejesus out of us."

Tourey walked around the large chunks of pottery shards and sat at the end of the couch. He looked at Spicey, "You either found a way to fry chicken in your sleep or been out ridin' with Willie in his chicken car." Tourey flared his nostrils for effect.

Sasha's eyes got real big, "There be anythin' you don't know?"

Tourey looked at them both. "Start at the beginning."

Toby and Junior bought three more dead turkeys from Otis in town. Toby dropped off Junior at his house. "I'll be by around eight. Should be gettin' pretty dark by then. You best bring a flashlight and some kind of bug spray."

Junior had been growing more nervous by the minute at the prospect of their adventure and now flipped out. "You seriously believe bug spray gonna stop the RUGARU from eatin' us?"

Toby stopped the truck, "You fool! Bug spray for the dang bugs. We don't need no weapons if we stay in the trees."

Junior frowned and stared at Toby, "Might not need 'em, but sure feel better havin' somethin' just in case. Don't your daddy keep a pistol at the crab shack?"

Toby shrugged. "Don't know there be any bullets. Don't know for sure there be any pistol. I 'spose I could check out his truck and take his good gun, just for tonight."

Junior felt a little better hearing that. At least they could die with some dignity. Junior looked back at Toby as he headed to the door of his house, "I'm not wantin' my obituary sayin' 'Fool fought the RUGARU with bug spray!'"

Jackson had made a quick trip to the corner store and bought some groceries for his mom and him. While the sausage was browning on the stove, he started doing a good clean up job in the kitchen. His mom had always been a good housekeeper but he could tell she couldn't see very well anymore. When he finished, the kitchen had a strange smell of Lysol and sausage. One thing prison had taught him was how to clean up.

Jackson told his mom he had to take care of some business, and he would be back. His mom grabbed his arm gently with her wrinkled, boney fingers. "I know you never did no wrong, boy. I prayed the Lord see that and send you home."

Jackson backed the van out of her driveway and was hit with a heavy feeling of dread. He knew Abram was waitin' on him. His momma could sure use that money. Hell, he could use it. As the van slowly crawled down the street, Jackson turned to where Abram had said that Voodoo lady had her shop. He had a feelin' he might better check his future 'fore he messed up too bad. Abram thought this lady was the real thing.

Jackson parked a ways down the street and saw the Voodoo shop sign. He went in. A young boy was sitting at the counter reading brochures. Jackson walked up to him, "Where's the Voodoo lady?"

Jerome looked up, "She's with somebody now. Should be done soon though. She knows I'm waitin' on her."

Jackson looked surprised, "Ain't you a little young to be worried 'bout your future?"

Jerome laughed. "I brought her a new shirt my mom made. Ms. Spicey is a friend of mine." Then Jerome looked serious, "I ain't worried about my future. I'm going to be an FBI man." Jerome passed one of the brochures over to Jackson. "I have a friend that brought me these. He's a very important man. He is going to help me keep my life straight."

Jackson was startled at the resolve this young kid had. Where had his resolve gone? Jackson asked, "How old are you?"

Jerome answered, "I'll be eleven in December." Jerome looked at Jackson, "You worried about your future?"

Jackson shuffled his feet some and looked back at Jerome, "Got a decision I gotta make."

Jerome held up a brochure, "Friend who gave me these told me the right decisions usually the hard ones to do. If that helps." Jerome shrugged and went back to reading.

Jackson remembered when he was eleven. His momma worked two jobs to pay the bills. Never knew his Daddy. Sounds like this boy had people in his life who cared. He couldn't believe an eleven year old boy had his life together better than he did. "What's your friend's name? He here in New Orleans?"

Jerome smiled, "He just left my house, had dinner with my mom and me. His name's John Barry. I got his card if you want some materials too?" Jerome pulled out the already worn card of John Barry. There was no title or official agency mentioned. Just the name and a phone number. Jackson noticed that all of the materials Jerome had in his stack were FBI.

Jackson took a pen from his pocket and said, "You got a piece of paper? I might write his number down. Case I decide I need some pamphlets."

Spicey came to the front of the shop and frowned at Jackson. She placed her body between Jerome and Jackson, "What can I do for you?"

Jackson thought she could work on her customer service some, but said, "I want my future told if it don't take too long." Spicey looked at Jerome who smiled and said he would wait. He had a lot of readin' to do from Mr. Barry.

Spicey led Jackson past the heavy red curtain to a small table in a dark corner. A big crystal ball sat on the table alongside a deck of Tarot cards.

Spicey clicked on a small light under the table and looked at Jackson, "It'll be forty dollars up front. Case you don't like your future, I still get paid." She finally smiled and Jackson realized how beautiful she was. Damn.

Spicey noticed Jackson paid her from a crisp roll of twenties and appeared to be wearing new clothes. Except the shoes. Them looked like prison shoes. Prison hair cut too. No tats she could see. Spicey asked Jackson, "Is there someone in your life you want to know about first?"

Jackson thought a minute, "Yeah. My momma. She's lookin' a might frail."

Spicey was touched he was worried about his momma. Seemed to her he was actin' like this was news, his momma bein' frail. Prison shoes, new money, new concerns about his momma, and he was definitely worried about his future.

Spicey looked in her crystal ball and held Jackson's hand. "You've been away from your momma a long time and she needed you. Seems you come into a money opportunity got you worried. Maybe you worried about repeatin' mistakes, and havin' to go away again?"

Jackson pulled his hand back. "How you know all that?"

Spicey smoothed the hair on the side of her head and said, "I know because I talk to the Spirits."

Jackson shook his head, "Abram said you be good."

Spicey sat up straight and shuffled her tarot cards. She flipped a few over and pretended to get a message from one. "You talkin' about Abram Davis?"

Jackson slapped his hand on the table. "Damn, woman!"

Spicey started turning cards over and frowning. Her first thought was that Jackson might have been the guy with Abram at the country house. Jackson leaned in closer, "What else you see?"

Spicey started shaking her head, "I see children. I think I see a barn." Spicey raised an eyebrow and glanced up at Jackson.

Jackson was pale. He felt the room spin. He whispered and pointed to the cards, "What's happening to the children?"

Spicey flipped a card and looked straight in Jackson's eyes, "It's horrible. You have to save the children."

Jackson stood. "I knew it! Damn. I knew I be the one needin' to save 'em." Jackson sat back down. "How I supposed to do this?"

Spicey smiled, "There are people that can help you. Tell the spirits your name. Maybe you will get a sign." Jackson had his hand in his pocket and rubbed the piece of paper with John Barry's phone number on it.

Jackson swallowed, "My name is Jackson Moore."

Simon and Ray started getting the evening wire instruction transmissions from the French Quarter Bank. The Fed had installed a software program for reassigning numbers. Ray simply had to forward the wire transmissions through the new software program before he sent them on. Roger had warned them he expected at least a few transactions would be ordered just to test the 'cover story' about the accounts. The numbers being assigned would 'appear' to overwrite all previous account numbers and activity. In reality the information was still accumulating, just not viewable. It had taken all day for the CIA computer gurus to perfect the program and add the clearing info to a trailer from the Fed. The trailer, also invisible, allowed the transactions to move freely through any clearing house in the world.

The first batch of wire instructions looked similar to others done earlier in the week. Simon stated these were probably some of the business accounts of the bank simply reconciling accounts. Then they noticed a few $100K transfers to off-shore clearing houses. About thirty minutes later the same $100K wires came back. Half an hour later the $100K went to a different clearing house. Then came back. Then another wait.

Ray looked at Simon. "Why the wait? They can see these are going through."

Simon answered, "They are checking what history is showing on the new account numbers and what tracking info is attached. I think they are buying this. If I am right, this is going to go on all night on a few accounts, and run through several international clearing houses. Tomorrow all hell is going to cut loose."

Ray made a face. "God, I love my job."

Simon chuckled and dialed Roger to tell him his plan was working. Roger told Simon to let the automatic systems take over and get some rest. If Roger needed him later he would call.

CHAPTER TWELVE

Abram had a group of men waiting outside for him when Jackson arrived at the gang house. One of the men asked him, "You're Jackson, aren't you? Abram said when you got here to send you straight in."

Jackson opened the door and strained to see across the large dark room. There was a faint blue glow in the corner, and Jackson could tell that Abram was sitting at a computer. Jackson walked over and pulled a chair out to sit next to Abram. Jackson cleared his throat and Abram glanced over. "Hey. You know much about computers?"

Jackson answered he worked in the prison library, because he knew enough about computers to keep that one running. He had also spent his five years taking whatever classes were offered at the jail. Abram pushed his chair back and looked at Jackson. "I need help man. I can't tell what all

Manuel been messing in, all these damn files to sort through. Finally found his password an hour ago. Who uses the word 'jailtime' for a password? Especially if you be a crook?" Abram was frowning.

Jackson mustered all of his courage and asked, "Do you have that list of kid names?" Abram shoved a piece of paper toward him. Jackson continued, "Where am I supposed to meet up and switch these kids for the ones that go in that barn?"

Abram looked at him, "It's all on the paper I just gave you. You best get going on it too. Not a lot of time." Abram was frowning at the computer screen and started pulling on his hair. "See this shit right here? What this mean?"

Jackson looked at the screen directing Abram to open a secured file. "It means you click on this here to see the next step."

Abram clicked and an organization chart appeared. They both starred at it. Abram used his finger to trace where Manuel had been on the chart. Then his finger slowly traveled up the chart to other names and the activities they were responsible for. Jackson saw drugs, guns, human trafficking, money laundering, and cartel names. Abram looked at Jackson. "Holy shit!"

Jackson thought this might be a good time to mention Ms. Spicey. Jackson could sense that Abram wasn't ready for his new job. "I stopped at that Voodoo lady place."

Abram pulled his head back, "What you do that for?"

Jackson took a deep breath and answered, "Cuz. I'm not feeling right 'bout this shit you want me to do."

Abram looked angry. He had been hoping Jackson could be groomed to be his second man. Abram needed him. Now it sounded like Jackson wanted out. "What Ms. Spicey tell you?"

Jackson leaned in and lowered his voice, "She told me my future showed kids being hurt. In a barn. No shit! She knew I just got out of prison and came into some new money." Jackson thumped his index finger on the desk. "She said your name."

Abram whispered, "My name?"

Jackson nodded his head, "If we do this thing, we *ain't* gettin' away with it."

※ ※ ※

Core called Thornton and told him he was out of the New Orleans area far enough for the call to be safe. Thornton appreciated the call. "Fenley said for now to lay off Dance and Casey. They may be useful. What does Dance have you doing?"

Core answered, "Nothing. I think Dance just wanted me to pass messages to Zelez and Manio and get lost. He doesn't trust me. He doesn't seem to have a very tight grip on this shit yet."

Thornton chuckled. "Dance has your wife and kid. Seems to me, he would be holding that over you."

"I know he has them. He told me. Between us, after what Lisa went through today I don't think she cares what happens to me now."

Thornton didn't even pretend to care, "You're surprised? Why would anyone in your profession have a family anyway?"

Core answered through clenched teeth, "Seemed like a good idea at the time. Look, I need you to find out what Dance is planning for the weapons. Maybe we can still keep Manio happy and let Dance take the fall."

Thornton didn't know how much he could trust Core anymore. "Dance isn't sharing his plans with anyone."

Core laughed. He knew that would piss off Thornton. He also knew Thornton and Fenley would suspect he flipped to Roger's side. He had to be sure he sounded like his old self. "So you are saying you are at the end of your usefulness? Wouldn't let that get out."

Thornton was pissed. "I meant whatever Dance is doing shouldn't influence any plans we come up with."

Core asked, "Can you arrange for the drugs and guns to be moved? I can't touch them at the Navy yard. You guys have screwed the pooch on this and left me out to dry."

Thornton answered, "Call me back. Give me a few hours." Thornton hung up. It struck him Core might be right. He might be at the end of his usefulness.

Core looked at Zack. "Thornton has been challenged now. He will try something to prove his value."

Zack scratched his chin, "How did you know I was ATF? I was careful."

Core smiled, "You are good. That's why I want you now. I was told you were being assigned and to keep you in the dark."

Zack asked, "Does Roger know that?"

"I don't know."

Zack figured whatever was going on would be resolved with people much higher in the food chain than he was. All he knew right now was that Mathew Core had been given the name of a 'train man' by Zelez. He also knew that Roger had baited both the Zelez Cartel and the Manio Cartel with a Monday train filled with drugs and ninety tons of weapons.

The logical place the drugs and weapons would be sent to was to Kansas underground storage. Most federally confiscated items were stored there until they were distributed or destroyed. A train heading for Kansas left a lot of opportunity for problems.

Zack asked Core, "Which cartel will make a grab for the train?"

Core answered, "Whoever's more greedy than smart. Let's check out the train man."

✳ ✳ ✳

Roger was back at his hotel room. He turned the television on to listen to the news and rest his eyes. An hour later his phone woke him. Mass was calling, "Roger? Bad news. We have four kids missing from LA, two from Chicago, and one from Topeka."

Roger rubbed his eyes and stood, "What happened?"

Mass answered, "I think we just got the heads up too late for these kids. There may be more. I'm still waiting on some of the other field offices. Are you making any progress on this?"

"We think we will have the New Orleans branch of this club in a compromising situation tonight. We may get something out of them. Thanks for the call." Roger disconnected from the call and paced the small room. He felt guilty. He had actually lost an hour to a nap.

Roger's phone rang again. "Roger? John Barry. We just got lucky. I have two guys headed for the field office who say they were hired to snatch kids for Judge Harold Williams."

Roger exhaled, "Thank God! I'll get Paul and meet you there."

Rolland watched as Judge Williams's car pulled up the driveway. He knew Harold would be the first to arrive. He always was. Harold noticed Rolland waiting outside by the front door. As Harold got out of his car, he heard motors behind him. Theodore Chain and Andre Baton were also heading up the drive. Obviously Rolland had called a full club meeting. The only person missing was Bernard. Harold assumed he would arrive shortly.

Theodore pouted as he acknowledged the others. "This better be important. I have a gallery showing I'm already late for." Rolland grimaced. He had forgotten to tell them to wear old clothes.

Andre walked up the steps to the front door, "What's up? Is there a problem?"

Rolland answered, "Go see for yourself, in the living room." He watched them all inch through the foyer, walk reluctantly toward the living room, swatting flies, and covering their noses.

Andre sputtered, "Jesus! What the hell smells dead?"

Rolland followed them in. "Bernard."

Ray started yelling, "Simon! Get down here. We have company at the country house." Simon took the stairs two at a time and sat next to Ray.

Simon pointed at the screen, "Let's see if we can figure out who each of these guys are. Turn up the volume." Ray clicked the volume as high as it would go just in time to hear Andre puke all over the rug. Simon laughed as he dialed Roger, "We have four guys at the country house. I'll let you know what they decide to do."

Rolland had just told everyone that Bernard was really escaped felon William Patterson, and the FBI and some crazy spook guy had found him in New Orleans. Rolland told the group Patterson had donated one million dollars to their club, so he could hide at the country house for a while. Rolland figured it didn't make any real difference now that Patterson had actually given him ten million dollars. After all, he should be compensated for this new mess.

Judge Harold Williams sat on the couch and put his head in his hands. "William Patterson? THE William Patterson? Did you know this Rolland?"

Rolland assured them all he had found out just yesterday. He was as shocked as they were.

Harold shrugged, "Well, we can't call the cops. We have to get rid of the body."

Andre went nuts. "If you think I'm touching that, you're crazy. There are maggots!" He started gagging again and went to the corner to puke.

Theodore looked at Rolland. "How long have you known he was dead? Do you have a plan for this?"

Rolland answered, "I found the body a couple of hours ago. I brought my gardener's truck, some tarps, and some shovels. I figured we'd bury him."

Harold looked up, "Where? If you bury him here, he is tied to us forever. Don't you ever watch crime shows? Some damn animal is always digging up old bodies." Harold got up and walked to face the chair Patterson's body was in. His face was contorted with disgust. "I say we dump the chair, the rug, and his body in the middle of the swamp. Not right off the edge like your friends do, Rolland. You know how many bodies the FBI found over there yesterday? At least six! One was a kid!" Harold's eyebrows went up, and Rolland dropped his head.

Rolland didn't realize that Harold knew about the swamp dumping site. That was actually how Rolland met Patterson. They were both there at the same time getting rid of bodies. That was quite a night.

Theodore was studying the body. "Should we leave it all in one piece?" Andre ran for the corner again. He held onto the fireplace mantel as he dry heaved. Rolland proclaimed he didn't know anyone with a boat he could trust to go into the swamp at night. From the far side of the room, Andre announced he wasn't going into the swamp.

Harold whipped around and pointed his finger at Andre, "You will do everything the rest of us do. We are all going to be equally guilty in this. It's our only protection." Harold could tell he was going to have to take charge. These idiots had no clue what to do.

"Look, we can't involve other people in this thing. Not one soul. Andre, you run out to Pete's, rent a shrimp boat, and take it down to Dicky's place. He'll be in jail for another thirty days. You know what? Go back to Pete's and rent a swamp boat too. Somebody said once you have to be careful not to have too much weight on those boats. Pete knows I could have him in jail anytime I want. He won't say anything to anybody."

"Dock the boats, walk back to Pete's for your car, and get back here fast to help us get this piece of shit ready to transport. At dark we can leave from Dicky's, make it clean out into the middle of the bayou." Harold frowned at Patterson's body. "He'll never be found." Harold rubbed his chin, "I don't know what to do with the chair and rug."

Theodore offered, "There's that junky spot where the gator hunters launch their boats. Out toward Slidell. Lot of people dump old furniture over there."

Rolland piped in, "There's a difference between old furniture and a chair covered in blood and bullet holes. I say we chop these up and burn 'em out back right here. Let's get rid of the chair and rug first, so when we're done in the swamp, we're done."

Harold shook his head, "Be our luck, someone would see the fire out here and call the fire department. Let's just clean this blood off the chair and dump it in Slidell."

They had a plan.

CHAPTER THIRTEEN

Simon called Roger to tell him what was happening at the country house. Ray reminded them that Tourey had placed a GPS locator deep in one of Patterson's bullet wounds, his throat, and also in the anal cavity. Depending on how they chopped Patterson up, they might have a clear trace. Roger told Simon he was just walking into the field office and would be there a while. They were about to get a big break on the kidnapped kids.

Roger wanted to catch the club actually disposing of the body. Since the sicko club mentioned the swamp, Roger wanted Simon to line up both Jeremiah and Dusty's boats for tonight. Frank Mass could call Dusty, and hopefully someone had a number for Alan, Jeremiah's nephew. Whatever plan the sicko club came up with, Roger wanted to make sure his team would be ready and wouldn't be seen. He prayed Tourey's equipment held up.

✳ ✳ ✳

Dusty and Alan were still at Mickey's bar. It was eight o'clock. They'd been there since four. They really hadn't had much to drink. They were actually a good team and had made three hundred dollars from playing pool with tourists. Alan looked at his watch, "I'm in deep shit with the wife about now. Looks like she called me a couple of times. Damn good thing I can cross her palm with some money. I best get goin'."

Dusty laughed, "All I got waitin' at home is some damn cat thinks he lives with me. If I be too slow gettin' in my door, he just runs in." Dusty started laughing to himself, "Did I tell you 'bout the time that damn cat jumped in my bed…." Dusty's phone rang. He looked at the caller ID and grabbed Alan's arm. "You've got to be shittin' me! It's the FBI callin' again!"

Alan was laughing, "You better answer man. Not like they don't know how to find ya."

Dusty answered, frowning at Alan the whole time. Alan heard Dusty say, "I don't suppose I have a choice?" A few moments of silence and Dusty shrugged and said, "You guys lookin' to fund my retirement all in one week? Oh, crazy me. Ain't gonna be no retirement is there? You got your head set on gettin' me killed! You look out a window? It happens to be dark out at night."

Alan realized they wanted Dusty to go into the swamp again. Alan's phone rang. He looked at the caller ID. FBI. "Shit!" Dusty hung up his call and stood by his bar stool looking at Alan.

"Best you answer that. Not like they don't know how to find ya." Dusty had his hands on his hips, smirking.

Alan answered. It was Agent Simon Frost calling. Alan listened a while and finally said, "Sure. Need to get your guys to Jeremiah's." Alan hung up and frowned at Dusty. "I gotta go too. Seems they want two boats. Must be some bad shit gonna go down tonight."

Scotty, who had been listening, asked, "One last beer?"

Simon called Thor and told him boats had been arranged to take them into the swamp. Roger wanted two agents on each boat and two agents on the streets. It sounded like the sicko club was heading for the swamp in about an hour or so. Roger had told Simon he and Paul had a huge break they were following up on. Thor would be in charge of the swamp plan.

Thor laughed, "Sounds like you're finally going to get a swamp tour. Have Mass and one of his guys take the streets. Jeanne and I will go in Jeremiah's boat with Alan. You and Nelson can have Dusty." Thor paused a moment and said, "Bring all the ammo you can carry. The swamp at night will not be fun."

Jeanne and Nelson had been listening to Thor on the phone. Jeanne had just gotten up from a nap, and Nelson looked like he had been asleep in her recliner. Nelson spoke first, "How did I know the sicko club would get rid of the body in the swamp? Why can't we just grab 'em as they unload from their car? On good ol' terra firma?"

Thor shrugged, "That's probably the plan, and we're just backup. We need to swing by the field office, get some night vision crap, and decent guns. Simon is bringing a video camera, so I guess we are making a movie. Make sure your GPS is working. Patterson has been plugged with three locators in case they cut him up. I'm guessing it's the only way we will find these guys in the swamp."

Thor started walking toward the door. He stopped and looked at Jeanne. "What's wrong?" Jeanne's facial expression looked concerned.

Jeanne answered, "You don't realize how creepy the swamp is at night."

Nelson tilted his head toward Thor, "I'm not real happy to hear it scares *her*."

Thor looked to the ceiling. "And again, our fearless leader is chasing down some big lead. Can this guy plan or what?"

We decided to start our hunt for dark auras at the docks. All the stories I ever read talked about the shady dealings at the docks. Flying around we came across Mathew Core and Zack walking behind some buildings and knocking on the door of a little shack by the train control center. We swooshed in and decided to watch.

Teresa said, "I'm kind of surprised Mathew Core isn't showing a dark aura. Just kind of greyish."

A short bald man opened the door, and Core and Zack went in. We followed. Core started the conversation with, "I was told you could tell me about a very special train."

The bald guy looked at them both and then said, "That's not public information."

Core sighed, "I'm not public, and I don't have all night."

The bald man laughed, "Yeah, looking at the muscles on you two I suspect you'll be unloadin' that shipment here shortly too. Got word the subs started arriving at the rig about half an hour ago with the second batch."

Core nodded. He had no clue what the guy was talking about, but he was going to find out. "So what is the deal on the train? Has anyone started this yet? Are we loaded?"

The bald guy leaned forward and looked around as if someone might be watching. "I hear the Navy will load up eleven cars tomorrow and the train will leave here Monday at eight a.m. Headin' for Kansas."

Core asked, "What kind of security?"

The bald guy shrugged, "I was told there might be a couple of Navy guys assigned to transport, but just our regular people. Seems they don't want to draw attention to it."

Core handed the guy a card. "Call me if anything changes. You understand who I'm working for, right?"

The bald guy stood up. "Hell yes! Manio. You think I tell just anybody this shit?"

Core nodded. Actually it was Zelez that had given him this guy's name. Interesting.

Zack asked, "Where do you suggest we wait for the shipment?"

The bald guy frowned, "You two must be new." He reached in a drawer and pulled out two ID tags. "This here was a real rush job. Go right to your regular dock. We have all the lights down being fixed. Trucks are waitin' in building four." He winked.

When Core took his card, he recognized the oil company insignia. "Thanks."

Core and Zack walked down the dirt road next to the railcars toward the loading docks. We were flying close enough to just listen to them talk. Mind reading actually gives us headaches. Go figure.

Core looked at Zack, "These are oil company passes. This makes for a beautiful plan. Think about it. Nobody checks their boats or buildings. They're above reproach, with their own security people. I bet there are dope subs in the gulf unloading product to a cargo boat under a rig station. These have to be Lanitol Oil cargo boats to get access to this dock. Did you note that our train man is working both cartels? Zelez gave me this guy's name, but he assumed we were Manio men coming for the same information."

Zack said, "I missed that. I can't believe we have a serious shipment coming in already. Coast Guard governs surface vessels, but Department of Interior governs drilling operations. Sounds like a perfect regulatory overlap to create some enforcement loopholes. How the hell do we figure out which rig the subs are using?"

Mathew Core shrugged and said, "We play it by ear and hope we get lucky."

Teresa looked at us, "I know how to figure out which one. All we have to do is fly out to each oil rig and see which one has submarines at it."

I cleared my throat. I see a teeny flaw in this plan. "Submarines are underwater. I can't swim."

We all looked at each other. None of us could swim.

Mary said, "Just pretend it's wet air."

Right. That will take some pretending.

Linda put her finger in the air to signal an idea, "Let's go out in the gulf as a group and just *try* swimming. Mary may be right and we really can swim now. At least we're there to help each other."

Nobody drowning is going to want *my* help. On the other hand, if we are good, we could do some of those water ballet things where everyone lifts their legs and sticks their butts in the air, and...

Teresa made a face, "Stop it."

Fine.

Ellen popped up next to Mary. "You guys are a stitch! I'll go with you. You can all swim now, like fish! Mary is right. It is sort of like wet air. You'll love it!" Ellen laughed, "I'll also help you search. There are over six thousand active oil rigs and over eight hundred that are fully manned. Just in the Gulf."

"Six thousand?" We all looked at each other. That's a long first swimming lesson. Wet air.

Ellen motioned for us to follow her to the first oil platform. She was going to show us how to find the submarines. She said Roger was going to need any information we could get as soon as possible. She told us to take pictures of any subs, both inside and out.

The platform for the oil rig looked like it was on big stilts. It was open on two of the four sides for boats to dock under the structure. The platform where Ellen brought us was the size of a small city on stilts. We all floated near the top of the pilings as Ellen showed us how to dive down in the center space under the platform, next to the narrow docks.

Ellen said, "You will see one sub docked below to your left here. These are robotic subs used for making repairs. This is not the type of sub we are looking for. Ours will be a little larger and have a bump on the top for pressure exchange. The bad subs will have one human onboard."

We all took turns diving down and looking at the sub. Ellen was right. It was easy and fun. I'm going to make a mental note. When we are done with this assignment, to come back and turn into the Loch Ness Monster. Cool.

Ellen tapped my shoulder, "No, you're not."

Roger, Paul, and John just spent an hour interviewing Jackson and Abram. Abram brought the laptop with Manuel's business records on it and whatever items he could find at the clubhouse. If he was going clean, it was going to be squeaky clean. Except for the two hundred thousand dollars he took home from the gang house safe.

Jackson told them everything that had happened to him since Abram picked him up at the jail this morning. He stated more than once he hoped he didn't have to go back to jail. Jackson and Abram now waited in an interview room together.

Abram rubbed his hair as he looked at Jackson, "I be worried what the street gonna do to us. If it gets out we snitched, we be dead."

Jackson shrugged, "Most the streets just now findin' out Manuel dead. Don't know shit about you. Hell, you didn't know you be the new boss. Just play dumb. We did the right thing man. The street can go to hell."

Abram looked at him, "You're right. The street can go to hell. Besides, we got the Spirits on our side now." Abram dangled his amulet in front of his shirt.

The door to the interview room opened, and Roger came in and sat across from them. John and Paul watched from the observation room. Computer techs downloaded Manuel's computer and forwarded all the information to the FBI organized crime unit.

Roger folded his hands on the file he had brought into the room, "As a law enforcement officer, and as a citizen, I want to personally thank you both for coming forward. I will do everything in my power to protect you. In my mind right now, you are heroes. Innocent children are being harmed. I need your help."

Roger leaned forward, "We got word a while ago that seven children, at least, have already been abducted. You said you were expecting five for a switch and didn't know where they were coming from. Right?" Jackson and Abram both nodded. "Think hard guys. Any names you might know. Other people must be in charge of picking up these kids. Someone has to know the whole network and coordinate the plan. Maybe you know someone, who may know someone? We need to intercept these switches."

Jackson looked worried, "Only people I know anymore are in jail."

Abram snapped his fingers and looked at Jackson, "Weren't Chiclet name up by prostitution on that chart?"

Roger pulled a print out of the chart from his folder and turned it around for Abram to see again. "Chiclet?"

Abram was studying the chart, "Yeah right here. Ramon Daily. Call him Chiclet cuz he got a new tooth with a big diamond in it, 'cept the new tooth way bigger than the rest of 'em. You know, looks like that there gum. Chiclet."

John and Paul both chuckled in the observation room. Paul looked at John, "Took me years to figure out how Roger can be so effective in interviews."

John asked, "So what's the secret?"

"He called them heroes. He means what he tells them. He just tells it straight."

John nodded, "Famous quote from Otto Von Bismarck, 'When you want to fool the world, tell the truth'."

Paul was surprised at John's quote. "There's more to you than just a pretty face."

John smiled as they both looked back to the interrogation room.

Roger asked Abram, "Do you know Chiclet well enough to get some information out of him? Maybe tell him your guy is unreliable and get us some names?"

Jackson looked offended, but Roger smiled at him. Abram was getting into the mood. "I know him real good. Married my sister, twice. Can't fix stupid. He be stupid. I can get information from him today and tell him tomorrow I decided not to take the job. That boy'll never get two plus two to come out four. You want I call him or go over to his crib?"

Roger answered, "Let's see what he'll give you by phone. Then I need a big favor."

Abram and Jackson looked at each other and then to Roger. Jackson swallowed, "What favor?"

"I need you to take this computer back and act like nothing has happened. We need more names, and I need to know how this group works. There isn't enough here to help us."

Abram felt a wash of pride at the prospect of working for the good guys. Suddenly he gushed, "I stole a whole bunch of money from the gang tonight. 'Bout two hundred grand."

Jackson's eyes looked like they were going to pop from their sockets. "What the *hell?* You don't know that be a sure way to get killed? Somebody be comin' by for that money, and you best have it!"

Roger looked at Abram who now looked terrified. "I think Jackson is right. I can't tell you what to do, but I would take it back. Real fast."

Abram nodded. He knew it had been too easy. Him havin' that kind of money. Why is it the rewards for doin' the right thing is never money?

CHAPTER FOURTEEN

Core and Zack walked down to the Lanitol Oil secured yard and showed their passes to the guard leaning against the chain link gate. He frowned at them, hit a button and the gate buzzed open. The guard was a big guy, looked them over and asked, "Where you goin'?"

Core raised his ID and pushed it within inches of the guy's face, "Building four." The guard pulled his neck back, flipped some pages on a clipboard and frowned. "My sheet says everybody's already here."

Zack took a step toward the guard, "Then somethin' is wrong with your sheet. I didn't bust my ass to get here for a 'special' to argue with your ass."

The guard knew this had been a last minute deal. "You got any names you can toss around?"

Core had a fifty-fifty chance of being right. "Manio a name?"

The guard's eyebrows went up, and he shrugged, "That be the right name. Last building on the left."

Core noted the guard wore a Lanitol Oil work uniform. Under his name tag it said he was Third Mate, cargo operations.

As Zack and Core approached the building, Core made a quick call to Roger. "Zack and I are at the Lanitol Oil dock building number four. We are going to try to blend in with this crew. The train man slipped up and told us a drug shipment is expected here shortly. Big one coming on Lanitol Oil cargo boat."

Roger's head was spinning, "How in the world did they get the drugs into the port now? With martial law?"

Core answered, "We think they have sent a fleet of one man drug subs and are unloading at one of the rigs. I'll update you when I can, but they are ready to load these into waiting trucks right now. Building four, Lanitol Oil."

The line went dead and Roger repeated what Core had said to Paul and John. Roger shook his head and said he was going to bring the Director up-to-date.

John looked at Paul, "We are going to have a very busy night.

At the docks, Core turned to Zack, "I'm going in the service door. If I can blend in as a mainte-nance or dock worker, I will. You wait ten minutes before you come in and do the same. I'll tell them there should be another guy coming shortly."

Zack asked, "How will I know if it goes bad?"

"You'll hear gunfire."

* * *

On the way to the Star Ship, Jeanne was giving Thor and Nelson a quick lesson on swamps at night. The more she talked, the slower Nelson and Thor walked. Finally Thor asked, "Why haven't you said anything about alligators? Do they hide at night or something?"

Jeanne answered, "I was leaving the best for last. Alligators are nocturnal. They hunt and feed at night."

Nelson stopped walking, "That doesn't sound good."

Jeanne continued, "They rest semi-submersed in the water and wait for their prey. Sometimes as little as two inches will be exposed on an eight foot gator."

Now Thor stopped walking. "I thought you and Jeremiah said we were the last thing they wanted for dinner."

Jeanne looked serious, "During the day! They have vertical eye pupils like cats, excellent night vision, and are hyper sensitive to threats during feeding hours. Their eyes reflect reddish orange at night. The alligators will be a threat during feeding time."

Nelson smiled, "Let me guess when dinner time is. Now."

Jeanne walked ahead of them and yelled back, "You haven't asked about the Rugaru."

Thor looked at Nelson, "The what?"

Spicey finally convinced Sasha to go home. She gave her an extra amulet, a courage potion and locked the apartment door as Sasha left. Tourey never said exactly how he fit in this picture, but Spicey was sure he was one of the good guys. He wasn't too happy with her right now.

Spicey walked over to her couch, turned on the TV, and pulled the blanket up to her chin. The blouse Adele had made for her hung on a hook by the door. It was beautiful. Spicey smiled at the thought of Jerome. He was going to grow up good. Be somebody.

Spicey's eyelids started to droop. The sound of the television became distant and blurred. Spicey felt a hand on her shoulder. She looked up. A vision of a Saint was standing next to her.

The Saint said, "Do not be afraid. Mambo needs you tonight at midnight. You must come."

Spicey wasn't afraid. She felt strong, almost invincible. "I'll be there." The Saint left.

Spicey dialed Sasha, "Get back here!"

Sasha protested, "I just walked in my door. You just kicked me out!"

"Things have changed. Please?"

Sasha looked at her phone. Spicey never said please. Sasha reluctantly said okay and hung up. Huh. Maybe Spicey just afraid to be alone tonight.

Spicey dialed Dusty to see if he would take her to Mambo's. She told him it was important she be at Mambo's at midnight. Dusty started screamin' at her so loud she had to hold the phone away from her ear. Some shit about the whole world wantin' to kill him, too many damn conventions in the swamp, and how he already had a date for tonight. That boy better back away from them drugs soon.

She had to find her a boat. Spicey called Willie to give her and Sasha a ride to Pete's, the swamp boat rental place. She asked Willie if he knew anyone who could guide their boat to Mambo's.

Willie sounded puzzled, "You talkin' going tonight? In the swamp? You want to be at Mambo's at midnight?"

Spicey sighed, "I don't want this Willie. The Spirits have told me to be there. I ain't got a choice. How long it gonna take to get to Mambo's from Pete's place?"

"That be clear the other side of Honey Island. I'd say at least a couple of hours. Can't use a motorboat. Have to use a flat bottom boat to get over there. Assumin' you don't get lost." Spicey looked at her watch, it was already nine-thirty.

"I best be going soon then. Will you take me?"

Willie paused, "I ain't lettin' you go in the swamp at night with no stranger. I think I 'member how to get to Mambo's. I'll be at your place as soon as I find my gun."

Sasha knocked on the door, Spicey opened it. Sasha could tell from Spicey's facial expression that something was wrong. "You best not want me to find any more dead bodies today."

Spicey tried to smile, "We've been invited to a party. Sort of. Maybe more like a meetin'. I have to go. The Spirits have told me. You believe now I really do see 'em right?"

Sasha nodded her head. She would never forget Mambo confirming the Spirits had talked to Spicey. Sasha asked, "Where this party be?"

Spicey cringed and answered, "Mambo's at midnight."

Sasha slowly nodded. Her stomach had just fallen to her knees and her head began to throb. She knew she couldn't let Spicey go alone. "How we gettin' there?"

Spicey answered. "Willie."

Sasha exhaled. Seemed to her the Spirits wouldn't ask Spicey to do something that would get her killed. "Okay, I'll go. You best be givin' me a raise. This here is employee harassment." Sasha muttered, "Just hope he ain't takin' us on a chicken boat."

Sasha's voice rose to a shrill, "What about them snakes?"

Spicey answered, "Don't got to worry 'bout snakes at nighttime."

Sasha relaxed.

Spicey mumbled, "It be the gators at night."

Abram and Jackson left the field office in a rush. Roger assumed they were going to return the money Abram had stolen from the gang house before the theft was discovered. Roger, Paul, and John sat in a small room at the field office going over the answers Chiclet had given Abram on the phone. Chiclet knew of two other switch places and the names of the kids getting snatched. Abram told Chiclet he needed the names and phone numbers of the kidnappers so his guy could coordinate the switch. The children Chiclet said would be switched matched the missing children on Roger's list.

Roger said, "I think we need Ellen's help now." John and Paul agreed and Roger's phone rang. It was Kim.

Roger answered, "Hello again."

Kim laughed, "Hi to you, too. Ellen is in my ear somehow and just said for you to ask your questions. She would give me her answers. Oh, before you start, Ellen said to tell you she was looking for the rig. She also said she knows about the abducted children."

Kim made a noise, "You have a terrible job! Ellen says she can find them if you have any names."

Roger gave her the names Chiclet knew and asked, "Are the children that are missing okay so far?"

Kim answered, "Ellen says, yes. She is going to get you the submarine information first, so you can deal with the drug delivery. Then she will work on helping you save the children."

Roger said, "Tell Ellen thank you for us."

Kim offered, "You know it doesn't sound like you are having a very good day. Don't worry about calling me later."

Roger laughed, "It might be late, but I *definitely* will call."

John and Paul looked at Roger. He had actually forgotten they were sitting there. Roger was a little embarrassed but shrugged it off. It was too late now anyway.

Paul chuckled and elbowed John, "See? I told you he was human. Notice how sweet he talks to her?"

Roger made arrangements with the field office closest to Jackson's switch location, to be on standby. The logistics were still unknown on the information from Chiclet. He only knew the scheduled switch for Jackson's trip was somewhere in Kansas.

Ray and the FBI Crime Unit were searching for more information on the names Chiclet had given Abram. Roger was hoping the cell phone numbers would lead them to the kidnappers.

Paul pointed at the list of New Orleans kids, "Did you notice Mathew Core's kid was one of the kids Jackson was supposed to grab?"

"Yeah, you know what really gets me? Nobody even asked Jackson what his plan was for snatching these kids. Just gave him a list of names. He was totally clueless. Doesn't this all sound a little sloppy?"

John shrugged, "I'm always amazed at the sloppy planning on these things. Based on the number of missing kids every year, it's amazing how successful they are."

Roger shook his head, "I think we are all guilty of thinking this shit only happens to the other guy. We're all so wrapped up in the little details of our lives, the big threats just sort of flash in and take us by surprise."

Paul leaned back in his chair and pushed his chin forward in his nervous tick, "Going back to Core, sounds like Core and Zack walked into more than we expected. We got another drug bust tonight?"

John offered, "Why not? That ought to really piss Manio off. You notice we brought an oil company into it now? Lanitol Oil is the largest oil company working the gulf."

Roger nodded, "Yep. Didn't really want to hear that yet. We can't pull this off ourselves in time. I want the Director involved on this drug raid. He will have to line up serious help, fast."

We found the right oil platform just as the last submarine was unloaded by some men on a narrow dock under the pilings of the platform station. The boat they were loading was a Lanitol Oil cargo boat. All of the logos and marine signs were openly displayed. We counted two hundred bundles unloaded which Ellen said were kilos of cocaine. That was just one sub! We went into the cargo boat and counted how many kilos had already been loaded.

There must have been five subs. We counted one thousand kilos of cocaine. According to Roger, each kilo was worth about thirty five thousand dollars on the street. That's thirty five million dollars' worth of cocaine to be unloaded tonight. Yikes!

Linda asked Ellen, "How did they get so much of this here so fast?"

Ellen shrugged and answered, "I expect after the drug seizure last night a lot of pressure was applied to replace what was taken. Some important people had to pave the way for this to happen this fast. The supply will always be there, as long as there is a demand."

Teresa shook her head, "Mortals are frying their brains with this stuff. It's scary."

Ellen nodded, "Very. Okay, we're done here. I'm getting this information to Roger, and you guys start chasing down those names Abram gave Roger."

Back to ugly aura shopping.

CHAPTER
FIFTEEN

Andre followed his GPS to find Pete's Swamp Boat Rentals. It wasn't exactly the kind of place he would normally go. The narrow, winding bayou roads were perilous at night, and he had to wait twice for alligators to cross the road. His car lights reflected from slime covered tree trunks that looked like milky white, ghostly figures jumping from the road's edge. This couldn't be a worse night if his mind had dreamed it in a drunken, drug induced nightmare.

Andre thought about what the others were probably doing. He was sure they would cut up Patterson's body to make it easier to move. At least he didn't have to see that. He finally came to a sign that said Pete's Swamp Boats. An arrow pointed down a narrow dirt drive. Wooden signs declaring the rental fees and business hours were nailed to trees. Branches draped with gray moss bent low and brushed his windshield. He had thought the bayou road was spooky. This was downright terrifying.

His window was lowered about an inch. The stench of the swamp seeped in to mix with his air conditioning. The further he drove, the louder the sounds of the swamp. An owl screeched nearby, and Andre slammed on his breaks. Was that a scream? He knew he would shortly be walking this road to get the second boat. Andre pressed his fingers to his forehead. He was getting a headache. He looked at his reflection in the rearview mirror. Could be the last time he ever saw his reflection.

He parked near the porch of a run-down shack and took a deep breath. At least someone was here. An old pickup was parked right up to the building, and a light was streaming from the window. Andre walked up the steps to the porch. A tin sign, hanging from a hook on the wall, said to walk in.

A man, Andre assumed was Pete, sat in a tattered chair with his feet up on the desk. "You be Andre?"

Andre nodded.

"Told the judge he ain't wantin' no shrimp boat to go in the bayou at night. Them's for deep water." Pete laughed. "I 'spect you boys have no clue what you doing, but hey? Do I care?" Pete laughed some more. Then he asked, "Do you know where in the swamp you will be goin'?" Andre shook his head, he wasn't saying shit about anything. Pete got a serious look on his face, "You have guns, right? You ain't thinkin' bout takin' this little adventure with no protection?"

Andre didn't feel like a lengthy chat with this filthy swamp man, "I just want to rent two boats, okay? Talk to the judge if you want his full agenda."

Pete snarled as he stood up, "Ain't no reason to get all persnickety. I'm tryin' to give your ass some good advice. But you know what? I really don't give a shit what happens to ya as long as I get my boats back. Just pick two of them flat bottom jobs and grab two poles."

Andre frowned, "Where are the keys?"

Pete laughed, "For what? You wantin' my truck too or somethin'?"

Andre sighed, "To start the boat engines."

Pete shook his head, "You be in bad trouble boy. These boats ain't got motors. You take a long pole there, and find just the right spot in the muck to get you some traction without disturbin' the gators." Pete pulled his big feet from the desk top and stood. "Get goin' now. You dock one and walk that spooky road back here for the other. I'm willin' to bet this here entire rental fee, I never see your pansy ass again." Pete slapped his desk hard. "Nobody see your ass again!" Pete sat back down, laughing hysterically. "What's on your feet? Them must be five hundred dollar alligator shoes! Who puts on their Sunday best to go in the swamp?" Pete was dabbing his eyes as he laughed.

Andre slammed the door as he left the building to find the damn poles. Andre vowed to find some reason to sue this guy someday. If he lived.

Roger called the Director and explained the situation at the docks. The Director agreed the Coast Guard could seize the Lanitol Oil cargo boat and maybe a few of the subs leaving the rig. That plan would alert Lanitol Oil that the authorities were wise to them and maybe keep future drugs from arriving at the dock. Their hope was the already short supply of drugs, and confiscating this shipment, might push Manio to an even more daring plan.

The Director sighed, "You remember Thornton calling Franklin Morris at the Fed? I have confirmation that Thomas Fenley called a member of the National Security Council regarding the banking issues at French Quarter Bank. You were right. He didn't take Thornton's word for it. Our guys monitored the call and the story was relayed as we wished. Thornton has a legitimate reason to feel comfortable calling Morris. Thomas Fenley is outside of official channels. For him to make this call personally to someone at the National Security Council in itself is troubling. The Security Council member Fenley called is now the number one suspect as being a mole for LUCY. I can't tell you who it is at this time but I will tell you LUCY has infiltrated our National Security at the highest level. No wonder they do anything they choose."

Roger wasn't surprised, "We keep uncovering security problems under every rock we kick. What has been done about the computer code we passed on to the CIA today? The one Mathew Core gave me."

The Director's voice sounded troubled, "That little line of code has caused quite a stir. I'm hearing noises that a few people very deep in this LUCY case had it programmed for covert purposes. I certainly can understand the guys working on LUCY not knowing who they could trust. Especially with what I know now! That code was a way for them to get whatever information they needed without asking for it. I'm told Jason Sims was asked to design and implement it before he 'retired'. The question becomes how many people *really* know about it and why. CIA programmers are attaching a reverse snooper to the code line to identify anyone using it. I confess my understanding of the technology we use is limited. I suppose it is fair to say that LUCY is no longer a secret among agencies. Something will have to be done now, before the wrong people find out how much we know."

Roger said, "Mathew Core told me Jason Sims was a good guy. Ellen confirmed."

The Director answered, "That's what I've been told too. My understanding on Jason is that we are now protecting him from LUCY. The powers that be are sure the LUCY members will try to eliminate Jason to protect the codes he has installed. When Ray saw Jason making programing changes in that 'cloud', it was Jason trying to block the few LUCY backdoors that were still open. He had to leave them some access to look legitimate. Back to our money sting, I understand tomorrow may be a very busy day at French Quarter Bank."

"Yes, it does look that way. Let's hope this works. It appears to be our only leverage. Every illegal activity they do is for money. If they can't clean it, they can't use it. I'm betting on their greed. If this works, it will expose their cleaning methods for the last five years. Not to mention the actual loss of their money."

The Director said, "We only get one shot at this. Heaven help us."

Roger dialed Core to tell him the Coast Guard was taking over the cocaine delivery between Manio and Lanitol Oil, and to get out of there. Core didn't answer.

Zack waited ten minutes. He hadn't heard any gunshots. He walked to the service door of building four and grabbed the door handle just as his phone rang. It was Roger. Zack answered and explained Core was already inside the building and exposed. They would ride it out. Unlike the dock area which was pitch black, the lights inside the building were glaring. Zack saw a group of guys huddled by the back of a truck.

Core moved away from the group and motioned him over. Evidently he had managed to blend in. When Zack moved next to the group, Core put his arm on the shoulders of the guy next to him. "Zack, meet Jimmy. He and I did a nickel together in Dade County."

Jimmy slapped Core's back and laughed. "I stayed close to this bad ass. Only thing that kept me alive."

Core looked at Zack, "We timed this perfectly. One truck is already loaded. Just waitin' on one more, and we can call it a night." Zack smiled, which had always been their cue they needed to talk. Core looked at Jimmy, "Zack and I got plans for later. You interested in joinin?"

Jimmy shrugged, "Sure."

Core signaled for Jimmy and Zack to walk away from the group. Mathew waited until they were on the other side of the room and asked, "What's up?"

Zack looked at Core and then Jimmy.

Jimmy whispered, "CIA."

Zack told them about Roger's call.

Jimmy said, "Don't know as we have time to wait for the Coast Guard. That loaded truck is leaving as soon as the driver gets out of the bathroom."

Core looked down and pretended to be laughing. Some of the other guys had started watching them. Under his breath he said, "No, it's not."

CHAPTER
SIXTEEN

Dusty was waiting at his brother's dock for the FBI agents. He had brought a large lantern, a sack full of bug spray, and three poor boy sandwiches from Mickey's bar. He took a broom from the dock and swept the empty cartridge shells from the boats deck into the murky water. He couldn't believe how many bullets these guys had shot yesterday in the swamp. He finished sweeping and sat on an old bucket in the center of the boat.

The noises coming from the swamp sounded like some kind of musical mix of normal and mystical. He could hear crickets, gator growls, cicadas, and owl screeches. He could also hear what sounded like wails and moans. Bullfrogs croaked in the mist and animal screams preceded sounds of surface water thrashing. Each scream provided a few moments of absolute silence. The sounds of the swamp recoiled with each threat and then resumed after each kill.

Dusty was acutely aware living things were dying as he sat there. Things he could only hear. He strained to see beyond the first bend in the bayou. The thick swamp mist only hinted of forms moving in the grasses. Dusty shuddered. There was no good reason he was there. This had to be that damn karma everybody always talkin' about. He tried to remember the last time he did something wrong. It must have been a doosey.

"You ready?" Simon's booming voice startled him and he clutched his chest.

Nelson walked down the dock and gently dropped a small leather bag containing the video camera onto the deck of the boat. Nelson nodded hello to Dusty, "Feel like I have to yell, it's so loud out here."

Dusty was grateful for human voices of any volume. "You guys have one sick boss send you to the swamp at night. That's why I work for myself."

Simon stated the obvious. "You're here too."

Dusty frowned.

Simon asked, "You know where a guy by the name of Dicky lives out here?"

Dusty answered, "Only one Dicky I know. Heard he was in jail."

Nelson offered, "That's the one. We need to get near his place and stay out of sight."

Dusty pulled the long pole from the edge of the boat and gave the dock a push. They started gliding toward the south when Dusty said, "It ain't like goin' to Mambo's clean on the other side of Honey Island. Dicky's place is just down the way a piece. Not too far from the swamp boat rentals." Dusty raised his eyebrows. "You know you could have rented a damn boat and left me at the bar."

Willie, Spicey, and Sasha pulled into the Swamp Boat rental parking area just as Pete was locking up the door to the shack. Pete walked over to the car as they all got out. Willie asked, "Any way we can rent a flat bottom boat tonight?"

Pete answered, "Only got that blue one over there left, Willie. This other boat here already been rented. Just waitin' on pickup." Pete was more than a little curious what everyone was doin' in the swamp tonight. He looked at Willie, "Pert near worse idea I ever heard for a date. You takin' these two beautiful ladies in the swamp at night. What you be thinkin'?"

Willie chuckled and Spicey answered for him, "We got a date all right, but it be with the Spirits. We need to be at Mambo's by midnight."

Pete straightened up, "Mambo's? She be clear on the other side of Honey Island." Pete looked at his watch, "I'm thinkin' you ain't got time to go the regular way."

Sasha rolled her eyes as she chewed on the inside of her bottom lip. Can't nothin' be easy?

Willie said, "I ain't gone by way of ol' Jeremiah's in years. Don't know the swamp still open that far down."

Pete nodded his head, "Oh hell yes. Especially lately. Been FBI and all kinds of shit down by Mambo's. 'Bout halfway from here to there is where the FBI been findin' all them bodies."

Spicey and Sasha looked at each other. Terror was etched on their faces.

Sasha grabbed her amulet and started rocking. Spicey dabbed her forehead and cheeks with a hankie.

Willie asked Pete, "You been down that way lately? Still got that blue glow over there?"

"Glows like a witch's candle. Actually, easier to find at night 'cause of it. You cut a full hour off your trip you go that way. Once ya get past Jeremiah's, just keep bearin' to the left, follow the blue light."

Willie looked at Spicey, "I think we'll take the short cut. Just a few more gators is all."

Spicey rubbed her amulet and nodded.

Sasha put her head in her hands and moaned.

Jeanne and Thor loaded Jeremiah's boat with the extra guns and ammunition while Alan said goodbye to Jeremiah at the house. Thor sat on an old box seat at the back of the boat and looked at Jeanne. Even in the middle of a swamp she was stunning.

Jeanne turned to look at Thor. He had a strength she couldn't define, a presence. "I bet Mass and his guys catch this bunch on land before they even get in the swamp."

Thor had turned on his GPS tracker and said, "Hope you're right. No sign of anyone yet."

Jeanne took a few deep breaths. Thor could taste the stench of the swamp. "How can you do that? Breath in this crappy air like that?"

Jeanne laughed, "I guess you get used to it. Remember, I lived out here for a month."

Thor shuddered. He didn't want to admit it, but he was spooked out here at night. Everything looked different. It felt like a thousand eyes were watching them. "It's so damn noisy."

Jeanne said, "That's a good thing. When it gets quiet, danger is near. Have you heard of silent crickets?"

Thor shook his head. Jeanne continued, "Many cultures use caged crickets as a sort of alarm system. When a male cricket is frightened, it stops chirping. Quite a few insects do that actually. In the marsh when there is a threat nearby, the swamp goes silent."

Great, Thor thought to himself. Now I have to listen for what I don't hear.

Alan joined them and pushed the boat from the shore. They headed opposite of how they would go to Mambo's, and toward where they had found Becky and Amy the day before. Jeremiah's place was about half way between the two locations. Dicky's was just past where the bones had been found according to Jeremiah.

Alan said, "I like this side of the bayou better than over by Mambo's. A little deeper water. Not as many inlets and islands to mess you up. Still pretty easy to get lost though."

Thor hadn't even thought about them getting lost. He thought about it now.

Toby and Junior had taken Toby's dad's crab boat to the far north shore of Honey Island. They finally made it to shore when Toby gave his dad's gun to Junior to carry. Toby had the four dead turkeys to bait the Rugaru hanging over his shoulder. They put on the chest waders at the crab shack. If they were going to climb into trees, the chest waders had to go.

Junior complained, "I can't even turn around in this damn getup. How I goin' to climb a tree?"

Toby answered, "We just get this boat up in the grasses, cross over to where they been findin' those bodies, and take the waders off. Leave 'em at the bottom of the trees, hang our bait, and wait for the Rugaru."

Junior stepped off the boat and sunk knee deep into the murky water. He let out a yelp. "Damn it all! I got your dad's gun wet."

Toby had his own struggle going on trying to pull the boat up on the grass while holding four dead turkeys. "Hush your mouth! Can't be out here screamin' and shit. Ain't no matter 'bout the gun. Probably waterproof. Get up here and help me. Damn boat weighs a ton."

Junior could hardly move through the muck. It took all of his strength to inch forward. "I think I'm in quicksand Toby! Can't lift my feet to move none."

Toby knew there were a lot of pockets of quicksand in the swamp. Heard tell of whole people just disappearin'. "Damn it all Junior!" Toby threw his dead turkeys a few yards into the grasses and waded back to Junior, "Grab my hand and let me pull ya."

Junior threw the gun past Toby into the grasses and grabbed Toby's hand with both of his. Toby yanked and Junior screamed, "You're bustin' my arm!"

"Will you quit screamin'? Take off them waders. Drop your straps and put your arms around my neck. I'll walk you out." Junior knew Toby was strong, but this still sounded like a bad plan. He dropped his straps, Toby backed up, and knelt down some so Junior could grab on to him. Toby grunted his way to the grasses, turned, and dumped Junior on shore. Toby dropped down to sit next to him.

Toby saw his daddy's gun, grabbed it, and shook the water from the barrel. "I'm thinkin' it's still okay."

Junior started to crawl backwards as he pointed to a large water moccasin swimming toward them. "Hope so! You gotta shoot that!"

Toby's eyes opened wide and he aimed. The first time he pulled the trigger the gun just clicked. Junior froze in fear. Toby pulled the trigger again. He was shocked when the gun fired and actually hit the snake. They both stood, hanging on to each other, as they tried to regain some composure.

Toby took his waders off and threw them in the boat. "The sooner we get to some trees the better. Your cell phone workin'?"

They both checked their phones, which were fine. Toby picked up the four dead turkeys and put his daddy's gun in his waistband. Junior was feelin' sick to his stomach. Too bad. Toby was already walking deep into the marsh land and yelled back, "Best be movin' it little buddy."

Yup, Junior was pretty sure he'd be gettin' grounded after tonight.

✳ ✳ ✳

Simon, Nelson, and Dusty all stopped talking. They were nearly to Dicky's when they heard a gunshot. Simon called Thor. "You just shoot something?"

194

Thor answered, "No. I was just going to call you. Guess we're not alone out here."

Simon kept his voice low, "How far are you from Dicky's?"

Thor asked Alan. "Alan isn't sure. We're almost at the spot where the bodies were found. Sounded like the shot wasn't too far from us. We don't have GPS activity yet. Maybe we'll just hang around here for a few."

Simon agreed that was probably a good idea. Dusty was happy to hear that they weren't going to chase down whoever was doing the shooting. Dusty dug around in his sack and lifted out a sandwich. "You guys hungry? I brought poor boy sandwiches."

Nelson was about to say he already ate when a large alligator head rose out of the water next to Dusty and opened its jaws. Dusty threw his sandwich at it. The alligator grabbed the sandwich and disappeared under the water without making a noise.

"SHIT!" Dusty fumbled in the bag for the other two sandwiches and threw them to Nelson and Simon.

Nelson caught it and said, "What you expect me to do with this?"

Dusty yelled, "Give it to the next one, man. Better 'an them eatin' us!"

Simon laughed as he tossed the sandwich away from the boat. "They smell your sandwiches. That is why they are here. You baited our boat." Nelson threw his as far as he could and chuckled.

"We need to be quiet. You got anything else in that bag?"

Dusty reached in and brought out a can of bug spray they all passed around. Dusty moved to the center of the boat and whispered, "You see those eyes? Blood red them were. Damn."

Simon shuddered. He didn't want to admit, it had scared the crap out of him too.

Nelson looked at Simon, "This is probably just the beginning. *Jeanne* is afraid of the swamps at night." Nelson looked at Dusty, "Do you know what a Rugaru is?"

Dusty fell off the bucket he was sitting on. "Is that why we're out here? You crazy fools want to arrest the RUGARU?"

✳ ✳ ✳

Willie, Spicey and Sasha stopped talking. Sasha hiccupped. Willie looked at Spicey, "That be a gunshot."

Spicey had a trace of courage because the Saints had invited her. She moved the wooden box she was sitting on to the center of the boat and began a low, soft chant. She occasionally waved her arms above her head and swayed to her own music.

Sasha's hiccups were back in full force, and they were loud.

Willie frowned, "Animals attracted to noise, ya know. Best you two quiet down if we're to make it clean across this swamp."

Spicey swallowed her last chant and looked at Sasha who shrugged, "Hic!"

CHAPTER
SEVENTEEN

Roger and Paul walked to the Star Ship from Canal street where Mass had dropped them off. Even though it was early evening the heat blasted up from the concrete and cobblestone sidewalks. A sour stench filled the air and crowds of tourists pushed quickly from one air-conditioned store to the next. Beggars and musicians sat on wooden boxes and lined the brick walls of buildings as far as the eye could see.

Ray was in the basement still monitoring the wire transfers at French Quarter Bank. Roger wiped the back of his neck. "What are you still doing working? You can put those on automatic until morning." Roger was worried his team was becoming as obsessed with this case as he was.

Ray answered, "I know. I'll probably stop soon. It is kind of like watching a video game. You get involved in it. Some serious money is starting to move now. We have gone from a few hundred thousand on each wire to in the millions. Simon thinks they're testing for threshold triggers."

Roger just shook his head. "I admire anyone that can follow this money shit. Simon is one of the best."

Ray spun his chair to face his second computer. "You have an email here from the Los Angeles office."

Roger walked over and opened the email. The children already verified missing were four from LA, two from Chicago, and one from Topeka from an earlier report. Update: add two more children from Dallas and three from Orlando. Also of note: Six more members of the sicko club have been reported dead today. Shot. Death total: Ten.

Roger closed the email and looked at Paul, "This looks to be more than just a bad day for sickos."

Paul pushed his chin out in his nervous twitch. "I'm thinking about the three transfers Core made to offshore accounts earlier."

Roger nodded, "Yeah. Me too."

Ray looked over, "What's happening?"

"It's possible that Core paid three individuals to kill the members of the sicko club."

Ray swung his chair around to face his computer, "I hope they finish, and we never figure this out."

Roger's phone rang, it was the Director, "Yes Sir."

"Department of Interior is trying to block the Coast Guard from seizing Lanitol Oil's cargo ships and dock storage. They threatened to call the Governor on this. We're trying to stop drugs from coming into the port, but all they can talk about is the nearly two billion dollars in taxes the oil companies pay into the state coffers every year."

Roger could tell the Director was angry. "We have two men in that facility right now."

The Director responded, "Three. CIA has a guy undercover from what I'm being told. The bad part is when this goes down the Coast Guard won't know the difference. We can't risk exposing their cover. You know what this is starting to sound like? Lanitol Oil and Manio cartel could be LUCY players."

Roger asked the obvious, "Are they getting a pass on this, or are we taking the drugs?"

The Director answered, "No pass. Thank goodness for this martial law order. It took some heavy lifting, but I gave the Guard the go ahead about ten minutes ago. You better warn your guys to get out of there fast."

Thomas Fenley was reading his evening paper when his private line rang. The caller ID said it was London. Thomas answered, "Yes?"

Donavan Luntz was on the other end. "What are we paying you for? Do you realize the Coast Guard has just been given orders from the FBI to seize one of our rigs, our cargo boat, and our dock facility? Do you fully understand the implications of the U.S. government associating Lanitol Oil with drug smuggling? You better think of something fast!"

Thomas threw his newspaper on the floor. He just read a headline about the Zelez Cartel being accused of seizing shrimp boats for smuggling in the Gulf. It gave Thomas an idea. "Dump the people. When you get official notification of this, just say these were *not* your employees. You're a victim. Someone captured your rig and boat. Blame Zelez."

There was silence on the other end. After a pause, "That might work. Manio was using a rig that has been dormant for some time. Fix this shit in New Orleans, Thomas. I do not appreciate this kind of news. Manio is losing another 2000 kilos of cocaine tonight. You explain it to him."

Thomas paced his spacious sitting room and called Thornton. When Thornton answered Thomas said, "What the hell are you guys doing over there?"

Thornton sputtered, "What are you talking about?"

Fenley sighed, "Don't tell me you didn't know about this raid either?"

* * *

Roger dialed Mathew Core. "Can you talk?"

"No."

"Can you listen?"

"Yes."

"Coast Guard should be there any minute. Get out of there."

"Will do."

Core looked at Jimmy, "Time to leave. Let's get ugly and have Zack take us outside."

Jimmy smiled and landed a fist against the side of Core's head. Core shook his head and smiled. Zack started yelling for them to take it outside. Zack grabbed both of their shirt collars and acted like he was breaking up a fight. Core landed a punch on Jimmy and teased him to the door. "Come on! You think you want some of this?" The crowd of guys across the room started to walk over.

Jimmy pushed past Zack and went out the door. Core and Zack followed. The minute the door shut behind them they ran for the chain gate. Core punched the guard as Zack hit the buzzer. The three of them jumped between the railcars and ran towards the back buildings. They heard the motors of the Coast Guard jeeps and trucks enter the dock area. From the side of a railcar they saw dozens of guardsmen begin to circle building four.

Core looked at Zack, "Should we buy Jimmy a beer at Colby's?"

"Sure."

Core dialed Roger. "We're out."

Roger said, "Call Manio. I want him to know you have good information."

Manio listened to Mathew Core describe the raid on Lanitol Oil's dock building, the seizure of the cargo boat, and the seizure of the rig. Two thousand kilos, gone. If authorities discovered this method of supplying his product, it would be devastating to his delivery network. He had invested a fortune in the submarines alone. There could be no connection between his drugs and Lanitol Oil.

Manio asked Core who set up the raid. Core answered he didn't know, but he found out from a train man who assumed he was part of Manio's dock crew. Core informed Manio the security guys at the docks needed to be replaced. Core had walked in, been told of the drug delivery, and infiltrated Manio's men with one line of bullshit.

Manio thanked Core for the call and hung up. The weak link in all of their goals was the deteriorating quality of their own workforce. The influences of their own drug business made it difficult to find valuable people. Many had serious drug habits. Most were uneducated, unreliable, and sloppy.

Manio wanted to see how long it would be before Thomas Fenley called him about this new problem. A full hour passed and Manio's phone rang. It was Donavan.

Donavan was surprised Fenley hadn't called Manio yet. He explained he was going to claim his facilities had obviously been compromised by some drug ring, most likely Zelez, and Lanitol Oil was a victim. Manio listened as Donavan explained he had called Fenley before the raid and told him it was going to happen. Donavan's contact at the Interior Department would help spin the story that Lanitol Oil was an unsuspecting victim.

Donavan expressed his regrets that this episode was costing Manio over fifty men and two thousand kilos of cocaine. Surely Manio understood it was more important to protect the integrity of Lanitol Oil. Especially since they had plans for unlimited future business. Manio thanked Donavan for the information and sat rocking in his chair. He waited for Fenley's call. Half of his supply could have left the docks before this raid, if they had been warned.

Manio looked at his watch when his phone rang. It was Fenley. Manio was sure Donavan had warned Fenley he'd better call. "I assume since you are the third person to call me, you will have the most information."

Fenley's mind raced. Third? "I'm still trying to discover what has happened, and who's responsible. For now, we have to spin this."

Manio tapped his pen on his desk. "So I've been told." Manio started to sketch a picture of a stick man being shot. "Remind me why we pay you?"

Thornton sat at his laptop searching for any authorization notices he might have missed. Nothing. He couldn't call anyone and ask what was going on without explaining how he knew. He couldn't call Core because the government lines were still being monitored. Thornton rubbed his neck and slammed his fist on his desk. Damn it all! Another raid? He didn't even know a shipment was coming in. He knew damn well who was going to be blamed for this though. Core's suggestion he was at the end of his usefulness gnawed at his thoughts. This had to be Dance. But how?

The Director sent an email to Roger: *Coast Guard has seized everything. Lanitol Oil claiming they have been infiltrated and victimized by the Zelez Cartel.*

Roger emailed back: *Can we leak this to the press exactly that way?*

The Director responded: *No problem.*

Roger sat next to Ray at the computer station and turned on the television on the far wall to Headline News. He expected it would only take a short while for this news to hit the air. Roger was startled when Ray yelled, "Look who's back? Thought you had a good gig going at the hospital?"

Roger turned and saw Pablo with a big smile on his face walking down the stairs. "I couldn't stay away."

Pablo looked at Roger, "I thought Ray and I could compare scars while you do the hard stuff."

Roger chuckled, "I can't imagine your doctor thinks it is okay for you to leave the hospital. You just had surgery six hours ago."

Pablo sat heavily in a chair. He did look tired. He pointed to a couch against the wall, "I'll probably crash there for tonight instead of going to Jeanne's. I don't feel like walking six blocks."

Roger said, "You didn't answer my question. Is it alright that you are here?"

Pablo nodded his head. "Doc said to take it easy and stop in tomorrow sometime for a peek. He doesn't want me in the field or driving any heavy equipment." Pablo smiled, "Have I missed anything?"

Ray laughed. "You've been gone since this morning. What do you think?"

Roger pointed to the television showing Breaking News along the bottom. He turned up the volume. Both Pablo and Ray looked stunned at what they were hearing.

Ray asked, "We did another raid? Tonight?"

Pablo smirked at Ray, "Seems you missed something too."

CHAPTER
EIGHTEEN

Andre had docked the first boat at Dicky's, walked down the swamp road, and was now nearly at the end of the creepy drive to the rental shack. His phone rang. It was Harold screaming at him, "Where the hell are you? We're waiting here."

Andre explained he had to walk back from Dicky's to the boat rental place. He was just now getting the second boat, and had to walk back again to get his car. Andre reminded Harold that it was at Harold's insistence they have two boats to ensure they wouldn't sink.

Harold sounded exasperated. "Just take your car to Dicky's. Don't bother comin' back here. We'll load this without you. We should be there in about thirty minutes." The line went dead. Andre kept telling himself this was all worth it.

He had wanted to tell Harold these boats didn't have motors. Oh well. Andre noticed Pete's truck was gone. An old Cadillac sat in its place. The shack was dark, and the sign on the door said closed. Andre walked over to the Cadillac and looked inside. It was empty and clean. Maybe someone left with Pete. As Andre walked over to the shack to get a pole for the second boat, he could have sworn he smelled fried chicken. Something scurried behind him. He whipped around to see green eyes staring at him from the brush. He could hear throaty breathing. He ran to the dock.

Andre tossed the rope from the dock into the boat, climbed in, and pushed off with the pole. He barely cleared the end of the dock when he heard a gunshot. The sounds of the swamp went silent. Andre held his breath. He looked around, but the mist was so heavy he couldn't see anything. His heart was pounding, and his palms were sweaty. Like a boiling pot the low groans and cricket chirps rose from the grasses, and met with the screeches of the owls. The shot sounded like it had come from some distance away. People hunted in the swamps all the time, he told himself. Something thrashed in the water behind him. Snakes slithered from the shore and dropped into the murky water. Andre reached in his pocket and retrieved his inhaler.

Andre pushed on the pole to turn the boat towards Dicky's and stopped to listen. He could have sworn he heard a woman's voice chanting. He shuddered. Creepy, damn place. A river rat crawled up the bank near him and hissed. Red eyes glared at him from the water. This certainly was visiting hell. He pushed on down the shoreline until he saw Dicky's dock. Once there, he tied his rope to the dock and started his final walk back to Pete's. Damn old swamp fart. Said he wouldn't make it back for the second boat. He was right about the shoes though. These were going in the trash tonight.

Toby hung all four turkeys from low branches while Junior fought to climb his tree. "Be quiet! What is wrong with you?" Toby hissed at Junior.

Junior whispered back, "The trees are slimy! It's hard to climb up here."

Toby shook his head. Junior was turning out to be more of a problem than a helper. Toby surveyed his work. The turkeys looked fine. They all hung about six feet from the ground. Toby shimmied back along the branch to rest in the crotch of the tree. He whispered over to Junior, "From now on send me a text. We shouldn't be talkin'." Toby heard a thump on the ground next to Junior's tree.

He texted Junior: What was that?
Junior answered: I dropped the bug spray.

* * *

Alan had been pushing their boat slowly since Thor didn't want to make any noise. Alan still didn't know why these guys wanted to stake out Dicky's. Last he heard, Dicky was in jail for moonshinin' and poachin'. FBI wouldn't care about that. Their boat inched around a peninsula when Thor put his hand up for Alan to stop. Jeanne looked back at Thor.

Thor whispered, "I swear I saw a blue light up in the trees over there." He was pointing across the narrow inlet.

Jeanne frowned as she tried to focus. Jeanne walked over to Thor and whispered as she pointed, "We got a turkey hanging from the tree over there."

"What?"

Jeanne started walking to the edge of the boat. She looked at Alan and whispered, "Get me closer to that shore."

Thor tapped her shoulder, "I'm lead on this case. You stay here, and I'll go." He looked at her again, "What am I looking for?"

Jeanne smiled, "I think someone hung the turkey for bait. They might be in the trees."

Thor looked at Alan who shrugged. Thor had to wonder what kind of prey required a whole turkey for bait. Six foot high yet.

Thor mumbled as he stepped on the shore, "Miserable place. Maybe the turkey just committed suicide."

Thor inched his way toward the bait and tripped on a cypress log covered in moss. He let out a loud moan as he fell to the ground. A bullet passed his face from above. He rolled to his side, pulled his gun, and yelled, "FBI."

Toby screamed, "Don't shoot! I thought you were the Rugaru!"

Thor yelled, "Drop your weapon." A gun thunked on the ground about fifteen feet from where Thor was now standing. "Get down here. What's your name?"

Toby yelled, "Toby"

A voice a couple of trees down yelled, "And Junior."

Rolland frowned at Theodore, "I thought you quit smoking."

Theodore frowned back, brushed a maggot from his sleeve and said, "Sometimes I have a weak moment if I'm stressed."

Harold returned to the room with a large bucket of water and some cleaning spray. He threw Theodore and Rolland each a pair of rubber gloves. "Hurry up and clean the blood off from this chair. We can't take all night getting this done."

They had rolled Patterson's body in the blood stained rug and carried it to the back of Rolland's garden truck. Harold covered it with a tarp and pushed it to the side to make room for the chair. It was apparent to him that Rolland and Theodore were not only pansy cowards, but out of shape as well. Harold made sure his daily agenda included exercise and eating healthy. He shook his head as he thought about how lost these guys would be without him. Now he had to hurry them along, like lazy kids.

Harold bellowed, "For God's sake Theodore, put that damn cigarette down, and get to scrubbing. This isn't a cocktail party."

Theodore threw his cigarette into the bucket of water and put on the rubber gloves. "You know Harold, you might show a little compassion for those of us that don't spend every day of our working lives dealing with murder and bodies."

Rolland cringed. Confronting Harold was never a good idea.

Harold sighed and apologized. Rolland was stunned. Harold said, "Legally we haven't done anything wrong. Yet. We didn't shoot him. Once we move this body…."

Rolland interrupted, "If I have to go down for something, I would much rather it be murder than what we really do!"

Harold continued, "I was going to say, once we move this body to the swamp we should be okay. Every minute this body is here we're in trouble. In fact, I want to just take the chair to the swamp too. We don't have time to go to Slidell to dump it. I'd like to wash these maggots off me."

Rolland threw his gloves down. "Why bother washing the chair? Let's just get the hell out of here."

The three of them moved the chair from the room and to the truck. Theodore and Harold decided to drive their own vehicles to Dicky's.

Rolland got in the truck and looked around to the bed. The big blue tarp had been anchored with the bloody chair. The arm of the chair was exposed, and displayed a bullet hole in the middle of a red-black splotch. Rolland turned his head forward and began driving. If someone had told him tonight he would be driving a dead body, he would have thought them mad. He was a retired Senator for God's sake. Rolland took a deep breath. William Patterson was in the back of his truck. Dead. He looked at his reflection in the rearview mirror. He had to admit; tonight he looked like a criminal.

✳ ✳ ✳

Ray's chair squeaked as he leaned back and looked over at Pablo. Pablo, stretched out on the couch, opened one eye, "What?"

Ray said, "I didn't want to wake you. Our sicko club loaded the body, and is heading for the swamp."

Pablo rolled over, "Wake me up when we catch 'em. I want to hear how they explain this."

Ray called Agent Mass to make sure his GPS was picking up Tourey's equipment. Mass answered his signal was coming through fine. They were stationed at Dicky's, waiting for the club members to arrive.

Ray switched his screen to watch the money transfers from French Quarter Bank. He had told Roger it was like watching a video game. Actually it was better than a video game. He was watching some very large rats race to get in the trap.

The numbers were growing with every hour. It wasn't even midnight yet, and the transactions now being moved were in excess of a billion dollars each. There were hundreds of them. Ray couldn't help but let out a soft chuckle.

Pablo didn't move but asked, "What's so funny?"

Ray answered, "Roger's money sting is going to hit like an atomic bomb."

Pablo moaned and held his shoulder as he rolled over to face Ray, "What money sting?"

✳ ✳ ✳

Simon called Thor, "Was that another shot?"

Thor answered, "Yeah. Couple of punks out here thought I was the Rugaru. Tried to shoot me. They're out here wanting to get its picture so they can sell it."

Jeanne could hear Simon laughing through the phone from where she was standing. Toby and Junior sat at the bottom of the tree. Their heads rested against the trunk as they exchanged worried glances.

Thor asked, "What should I do with these guys? They got here by boat. One of them has a dad with a crab shack down the way."

Simon still laughing answered, "Well, they did try to shoot a federal officer. Other than that, there's no law against being stupid. Why don't you write down their ID information and have them turn themselves in to the local cops. Let them decide if any charges are needed."

Thor grunted okay and hung up. He looked at them both, "Which one of you had this idea in the first place?"

They pointed at each other. Thor frowned. Toby offered, "Might have been my idea to get a picture of the Rugaru, but Junior's the one needs money."

Thor looked at Junior, "What do you need the money for?"

Junior answered, "I wanna go to college next year."

Thor turned around and looked at Jeanne who was smiling. He turned his palms up and shrugged to indicate he hadn't expected college to be the answer.

Jeanne's expression instantly changed, "Freeze."

Thor froze, and Jeanne threw her knife at the tree trunk over Toby and Junior's heads. A water moccasin dangled from her knife two feet above them, and then fell in two pieces to rest on their shoulders. They both jumped up screaming.

Thor walked over, retrieved Jeanne's knife for her, and looked at the boys. "You get used to it. Look, I'm sending you back to town. Quit screaming! Turn yourselves in to the local cops. If you want my help explaining what happened out here, call the number on the card I gave you. Remember, you both promised to take a gun safety class and not to hunt the Rugaru anymore, right?"

Both kids were nodding.

Thor said, "Get out of here, and get out of this swamp."

Spicey looked at Willie. "That be another gunshot! I think I heard people screamin' too."

Willie tilted his head, "Heard the gunshot. It did sound closer than before. Best we just stay calm and keep movin'."

Sasha fisted her shawl under her chin, "Hic!"

✳ ✳ ✳

Toby and Junior practically ran back to their boat. Thor and Jeanne chuckled about what the boy's parents would do. Alan said, "Those boys not much older than mine at home. I guess I better have a talk with mine 'bout not huntin' in the swamp at night. I know Toby's dad. He's not gonna be too pleased about this."

Thor noticed his GPS tracker alert was flashing. He looked at Jeanne, "They're coming."

Alan's posture straightened, "Who's comin'?" Alan realized nobody was going to answer him. "Sure would be nice to know who's comin'." Especially since he was in the middle of it all.

Thor said, "We can move in faster now. I want to be as close to Dicky's dock as we can and still stay out of sight."

Alan gave a hefty push. Jeanne pointed for Thor to look in the water. Three sets of red eyes peeked from the black water and watched as they floated by.

Jeanne was watching both the shores and the water for dangers. She noticed Alan looking around. "You're lost."

Thor frowned. Of course.

Alan answered, "How'd you know?"

"This is the second time we passed that cypress trunk with all the skulls nailed on it."

Thor's head whipped around. "Who nails skulls to tree trunks?"

Jeanne answered, "Hoodoo."

Thor asked, "Don't you mean Voodoo?"

Jeanne shook her head, "Think of Hoodoo as the black magic sister of Voodoo."

Thor stared at her. She was serious. Holy crap.

Jeanne said, "Turn left up here through that little inlet."

Alan did as Jeanne suggested, and the inlet opened to a wider waterway. Alan said, "This looks right now."

Jeanne put her hand up for quiet. They heard it at the same time. A loud, high pitched chirp. It cut through the other sounds of the swamp. It wasn't a normal swamp sound. They listened and heard it again, this time louder. The swamp sounds silenced. Jeanne glanced at Thor, and they both raised their weapons.

Their boat edged around a peninsula and practically ran into the boat with Willie, Sasha and Spicey on board. Sasha and Spicey screamed. Willie crossed himself and kissed his amulet.

Thor yelled, "FBI. Identify yourselves." Jeanne had her gun pointed at them, and Alan had thrown himself on the bottom of the boat.

Thor looked at Spicey, "Aren't you that Voodoo lady?"

Spicey had her hands in the air, "Yes sir."

Jeanne and Thor holstered their guns. Thor asked, "What are you doing out here?"

Spicey answered, "The Spirits want me at a meetin' at Mambo's at midnight."

Thor looked at Jeanne. This Mambo shit was her expertise. Jeanne looked at Willie, "Are you sure you know how to get there?"

Willie nodded his head. Thor asked, "Are you armed?"

Spicey, Sasha and Willie all raised pistols. "Crap! Just answer the question. Don't pull guns out when a cop is talking to you!" Thor shook his head. Everybody in this city was packin' and crazy.

Jeanne looked at Spicey, "Why did Mambo call a meeting?"

Spicey shook her head, "All I know is a Spirit came to me today and said Mambo wanted me there at midnight. Willie here just makin' sure we get there alright."

Jeanne handed Spicey a card. "I'm a friend of Mambo's too. If you need me, please call."

Sasha hiccupped. Jeanne smiled at Thor. That was the sound.

Thor exhaled, "You better get going."

Jeanne looked at Willie, "Watch out for the river rats. I've been seeing them tonight all along the banks. They move fast, swim, and they have a vicious bite. When you get to Mambo's you had better shoot them. They won't be afraid of you, and might attack. Depends how hungry they are. Some look about ten pounds and they are blending in with the shore. I think I heard they feed at night. They have the bright yellow eyes."

Spicey gasped. She had been so busy looking for gators she forgot about the river rats.

Willie pushed his pole in the muck, said thanks, and maneuvered their boat to pass by. Spicey rubbed her amulet and she rocked on her crate seat, and Sasha hiccupped as they disappeared into the mist.

Alan stood up and grabbed the pole to get them moving again. "You sure 'bout them river rats? I ain't seen any."

Jeanne pointed, "There's one on the bank looking at you now."

Alan whipped around. The ugly varmint hissed at them, long rodent fangs exposed, bright yellow eyes reflecting the moonlight like lasers. Alan yelped.

As their boat glided along towards Dicky's, Alan said, "I never realized how busy the swamp was at night."

Thor muttered, "Party's not even 'til midnight."

Thor sat on a crate and watched blood red eyes in the black water follow them. The swamp noises were deafening. Jeanne was standing at the front of the boat. Her pose reminded him of some warrior statue in a park. It was her perfect posture, and she held her chin a little high. She was right about the swamp. It was a creepy place at night. Thor slapped a mosquito on his neck and exhaled. He checked his GPS. They needed to hurry.

CHAPTER
NINETEEN

Ellen asked us to concentrate on finding Chiclet's building. She said that Abram had told Roger the names of the other kidnappers were probably in Chiclet's computer. Roger needed those names to locate the children that had been abducted so they could be saved.

Linda and Teresa were studying their locators on their watches. Linda said, "Well, I can't find anything under Chiclet, I'm going to try Ramon Daily. Wasn't that his real name?"

I said, "I can't believe we are looking for some guy named Chiclet. What was his mom thinking?" There have been many studies about the influence our names will have on our lives.

I was shaking my head at the obvious curse this guy's mom had put on him, when Mary said, "You really need a hearing aid. Linda just said, his real name is Ramon Daily. Chiclet is a nickname."

Oh. That makes more sense.

Teresa was looking at her watch locator, looked around, and said, "I think I've found him. He is in a building not too far from here."

All I could think of was that barn with kennels. I didn't want to trigger that attitude alarm again, but I started to get that angry feeling. Chiclet was the real boss in charge of kidnapping these kids. I think when we find him I am going to put that tooth….

Teresa looked at me and said, "I'm with ya sister. These guys should be taught a lesson."

We were nearly at the building when Linda said, "Wait." She pointed to an old blind man sitting on the sidewalk a couple of buildings down the street. "Something is telling me to check on him. Let's make sure he's okay."

The old man's cane leaned against the building, and he had a hat on the sidewalk between his feet. His thin, white hair looked damp from perspiration and there was tape holding the soles on his shoes. He was kindly, and said "Evenin'" to the few people who walked by. None of whom dropped any money in his hat.

Linda stared at him and said, "Remember the old man we found in that basement in South Bend? Couldn't we give this man some new clothes and maybe some food? I bet his life has been really hard."

Mary said, "I remember we got into trouble for that."

Teresa frowned, "If we were mortal you know each one of us would give him some money or do something."

I'm with Teresa on this. Heaven knew there were risks with us still having mortal thoughts. "I vote we help him and deal with Heaven later."

Yikes! That didn't sound right even to me.

Mary looked at me, "You would." Then she got a decisive look on her face, "Let's do it!"

Linda took matters into her own hands and 'poof' the old man had all new clothes on and a bag of food next to him. A golden retriever puppy was sitting in his hat.

Teresa asked, "A puppy?"

Mary offered, "I did that. It could grow up to be a seeing-eye dog. At least he has a buddy to love him." The puppy walked out of the hat and peed on the sidewalk next to the old man. Oops.

The old man felt his new clothes and looked up. "I see angels. Thank you kindly."

We looked at each other. He can see us?

The puppy crawled up the old man's chest and started licking his face. The old man slowly rose to a standing position. He carefully touched the puppy's face and tears streamed from his blind eyes. He whispered in the puppy's ear, "You be needin' someone to love? You be needin' to be looked after? I do my best, but I understand if you leave."

He slowly bent down, and picked up his hat. He cradled the puppy in one arm and felt for the money that wasn't in his hat. He placed his hat on his head and wiped his eyes. He held the puppy's face in front of his own and said, "Big cities be brutal. Take unsuspectin' souls and eat 'em alive. Nawlens, don't even chew." His chin quivered, and we lost it.

The raw despair on his face brought us to tears. I couldn't even look at him. I just wailed into my arm against the building. Linda was patting my back trying to be comforting, but I could hear her sobbing behind me. Teresa and Mary were blowing their noses and wiping their eyes. It was just a pitiful vision. Now we made it worse! How is he going to take care of a puppy?

Ellen popped up. Uh oh.

Ellen looked at us and sighed, "You gals are emotionally all over the place. Your mortal settings must be extra sensitive because we are dealing with saving children." She looked at the blind man holding the puppy, and then looked at us. "Why don't we really give him something nice?"

We all stopped crying. Huh, I don't think we're in trouble. Mary had handed us each really pretty little hankies. She is so thoughtful.

Ellen smiled and whispered something in the old man's ear. Then she put her hand on his head and a glow spread to his whole body. When she lifted her hand, he slowly lowered his head and prayed.

When he opened his eyes, he whispered, "Thank you Lord." He cradled the puppy in his arms, "We best name you Angel." He nuzzled the puppy, raised his arm in a wave, and walked away.

Ellen said, "I told him there was a winning lottery ticket for tonight in his pocket. Not a big one, but enough." She smiled.

Teresa said, "He's forgetting his cane!"

Ellen said, "Now he can see."

Whoa.

Ellen looked at us, "That wasn't me. I asked for a favor."

Ellen pointed to the building Chiclet was in. "Now. Let's kick some dark aura butt."

That comment would have sounded more natural coming from one of us. I wondered if we were a bad influence on Ellen.

Inside the building, all of the auras looked dark above the men standing around. One man sitting at a computer yelled, "You two still here? I told you we have a deadline. That money ain't gonna jump into my safe. Start with Manuel's gang. New guy's named Abram. He be my brother-in-law, so don't mess with him none. Get my money, and see how much product he be needin' for the weekend."

The phone rang next to the man yelling. He smiled wide exposing a huge front tooth with a diamond in it. Chiclet! He was sweet talking some girl on the phone, and we were cracking up at that tooth.

Suddenly everyone in the building was frozen in position. Ellen said, "I did that. I can freeze them in time for longer periods than you can. Two of you go outside and make sure no one comes in this building. If someone comes to the door, you can follow them in and freeze time around them. The other two can help me find the information Roger needs. There is a small filing cabinet here and a safe you can check out. I'll download the computer and send it to Roger."

I looked over and Linda, Mary, and Teresa were doing rock, paper, and scissors. Hmmmm.

Agent Mass called Thor. "We're positioned in the brush at Dicky's place. We can see the lights of the cars coming down the drive now. Get ready."

Thor called Simon, "Cars arriving. Move in close and get your camera ready. We're almost there."

Simon looked at Nelson, "They're here."

Dusty's eyes flew wide open, "Who's here?"

Nelson told him to be quiet as he removed the camera from the case and tossed it to Simon. Nelson checked his gun as quietly as he could, but it still made a metal clacking sound. Simon flinched and checked his gun also. Even with the noises of the swamp that metal sound stood out. Simon motioned for Dusty to get them closer.

As Dusty slowly pushed them closer, Nelson whispered, "Got one on the dock."

SSA Mass and Agent Grimley waited in the brush at the end of the drive near the dock. They saw a pickup truck pull in and park within twenty feet of where they were hiding. Two more cars pulled in and parked nearby. Their voices carried and Mass heard someone say, "Get this chair out of here first, so we have some room."

The men struggled with what looked like a recliner chair then started pulling a long bundle from the bed of the truck. They carried the bundle to the dock. Mass was ready to move in when a voice to his right said, "Hurry up! Let's get this over with." Mass looked over and a man was standing on one of the boats.

Mass whispered into his phone, "Move in."

Thor and Jeanne stood in assault stance. Their boat came into view of the dock. Alan was pushing them through the mist at record speed without a sound.

Nelson looked at Dusty and whispered, "Get me to that dock fast." Nelson had his weapon aimed, and Simon was running the video.

Dusty was terrified. He pushed with everything he had, and they practically rammed the boat

Andre was standing in. Andre hadn't seen them emerge from the reeds. Rolland, Theodore and Harold had just dumped the body on Andre's boat.

Thor yelled, "FBI. Freeze."

It looked as if they thought of turning to run when Frank Mass yelled from behind them, "Don't move."

Andre fainted and fell into the swamp. Thor cursed, tossed his gun on the floor of the boat, and stepped into the murky water. He yanked Andre from the water by his hair and the collar of his shirt. Thor grabbed Andre's belt and tossed him onto the deck of the swamp boat, next to the rolled up rug. Alan was surprised at Thor's strength. Dusty had his hands over his ears expecting gunfire. Andre opened his eyes and looked at the rolled up body next to him. He yelped and jumped to his feet. His hands went in the air, "I want a lawyer."

Nelson chuckled, "I imagine you do."

Harold sputtered, "Officers, I'm a judge. There's a perfectly logical explanation."

Mass roughly snapped cuffs on Harold, "I'm listening. Rest of you listening?"

Simon was now on Andre's boat filming the rolled up rug and the men's faces on the dock. "Why don't we see what these guys were bringing to the swamp?"

Rolland cringed as Thor and Nelson each grabbed an edge of the rug and gave it a tug. William Patterson's body rolled out, covered in maggots with the eyes open. Mass looked at Harold. "You were sayin'?"

Dusty leaned forward. That sure looked like a body. He fainted. Thor shook his head, "Crap. At least he didn't fall in the swamp."

The wails of approaching sirens competed with the noises of the swamp to create a bizarre audio blend of nature and mankind. Alan moved over to help Dusty and whispered, "You know what I'm havin' when we get these guys back in town?"

Dusty's eyelids fluttered, but he was coming to. "A lot of beer."

Linda and Mary were outside guarding Chiclet's building to keep anyone from coming in. When Ellen froze time, Chiclet had frozen with his mouth open. I tried to get close to see how that diamond was stuck in that big tooth.

Teresa had moved over by Ellen and was flipping through some papers on a table. "You could help us instead of looking in that nasty mouth."

Ellen yelled, "I've got it! Get Linda and Mary in here!"

Ellen handed Teresa a piece of paper and also handed Mary one. "Here are the identifying numbers on the vehicles. The kidnapped children are in them. Here are the names of the drivers. It will be easiest the find them by their names. Use the locators on your watches and find them. Then call me."

We looked at our watches and entered the information. Teresa looked at me, "You and I will take the one in Texas, Mary and Linda will take the one in Kansas." I looked around to say goodbye to Ellen. She was already gone.

Teresa yelled, "Move it!"

Man! She really flies fast! I was seeing signs saying welcome to Dallas before I could hum 'Hall of the Mountain King' for the second time!

CHAPTER
TWENTY

Roger received the call from Mass confirming the arrest of the sicko club. All four remaining members of the New Orleans branch were in transport to the field office for processing. Then off to jail to await arraignment. Mass predicted they would all lawyer up. He bragged Simon had captured the entire thing on video. Roger's team was on their way back to their vehicles.

Roger called Thor and thanked him for a job well done. Thor hung up and relayed the message to Jeanne. Jeanne smiled, stared at Thor a minute, and then turned to look away.

Thor looked at Alan, "You in a big hurry to get home?"

Jeanne looked back at Thor. There was no mistaking the eagerness of her expression.

Alan answered, "If you need me, I'm yours. Just need to call the wife."

Thor looked at Jeanne but was talking to Alan, "I'll pay you extra to take us to Mambo's. Ms. Jeanne here wants to know what's going on."

Jeanne smiled.

Alan called Dusty, "Gotta pass on that beer. Guess our boat's goin' to Mambo's for a meetin'."

Thor could hear Dusty yell, "Now?"

Dusty put his phone away and looked at Nelson, "Just curious. Do you guys ever sleep?"

After about ten minutes heading towards Mambo's, Jeanne pointed. "See that?"

Thor looked, "See what?"

"The turkeys are gone."

Thor stared and saw a few leather straps hanging from the branches. The shrubs and grasses under the straps had been stomped out flat. No turkeys.

Holy crap.

Roger's phone rang again. This time it was Kim.

"Ellen says she has located vehicle information for two of the children's kidnappers. She says Mom, Teresa, Mary, and Linda are on their way to try to find them now. Ellen is sending you an email of the vehicle identifications. She will call again when she has the exact locations. Shouldn't be long now. One is in the Wichita, Kansas, area and one is in the Dallas, Texas, area if you need to get ready."

Roger answered, "I do. I still plan on calling you later." He chuckled, "It's already 11:00. What time is too late for you?"

"Are you kidding? Talk to you later. Get those kids!"

Roger called Paul, "Have you started your date with Jill yet?"

Paul answered, "I'm standing right behind you on the stairs."

Roger turned around to see Paul and John both smiling. John said, "I wanted to check with Ray and watch the sicko club movie."

Paul shrugged, "I told Jill tomorrow night might be better."

Ray waved to the guys. Pablo continued to snore on the couch. Paul lowered his voice, "When did he get here?"

Roger whispered, "A while ago. Ellen identified the vehicles of the kidnappers and has a general location for them. There are two. I'm just getting ready to start the rescue effort."

Paul and John looked at each other and smiled. John gave Paul a twenty dollar bill.

Paul smiled at Roger, "I bet him the night wasn't over."

Roger contacted the FBI field offices in both Wichita and Dallas and passed on the vehicle information and the tip that kidnapped children were being transported in these vehicles.

Linda and Mary were flying around Kansas trying to follow their locator on Mary's watch. Linda asked, "What city are we near?"

Mary answered, "I think we are heading north on Interstate 135 from Wichita, and it looks like our locator says to go east on Interstate 70 towards Topeka."

Linda looked down at the miles of traffic, "Is there a way we can narrow this down? Does our locator say what color vehicle we are looking for?"

Mary answered, "Nope, just a license number. I think this dot gets bigger the closer we are to the right vehicle though."

About three minutes passed and Mary pointed down, "I think our guy is probably in one of those big trucks. Let's just fly down and check the plate numbers on all of them."

It was tricky to match the speed of the trucks while trying to read the plate numbers. At first Mary was flying too fast. Once she was at the truck's level, she just flew through them all. She circled back and did that about three times before she hit the right speed.

Linda had decided to just land on a truck and climb down the back to look at the plate number. They located the truck in the middle of the pack. It was a large eighteen wheeler with very few markings. Mary called Ellen with their location.

Kim called Roger, "Wow, I didn't think I would be involved in this. Ellen said Mary and Linda are flying with one of the trucks that have the kids. They are on Interstate 70 in Kansas heading east towards Topeka!"

Roger had to be careful about what he said to Kim. Ray and Pablo were within hearing distance. "Is everything okay?"

Kim assumed Roger was asking about the children. "Ellen said Mary is inside the truck with the kids trying to make them feel safe, and Linda is riding on top of the truck." Roger shook his head. What a vision he was getting.

Kim continued, "Ellen says they are coming up to mile maker 110. She says Linda can try to make the driver think he needs a rest stop. I guess there is one up ahead." Roger told Kim that sounded good and hung up.

Roger asked Ray to put out a felony stop APB on the vehicles and to let the Kansas State Troopers and U.S. Marshals know one vehicle had been spotted near mile marker 110 on Interstate 70. It may have entered a rest stop. He prayed no one asked them who had supplied the tip.

Roger told Ray, "Be sure to alert them that kidnapped children are in these trucks."

Ray was busy with the bulletin and John and Paul had started calling the respective offices of the U.S. Marshals.

John yelled out to the room, "U.S. Marshals have people on Interstate 70 now, they are turning back to find our truck. They sound close."

Linda got a message from Ellen to 'help' the driver turn into the rest stop. Linda messaged back asking how. No answer. Linda flew inside the truck to talk to Mary.

"You know how to drive an eighteen wheeler?" Mary shook her head. "I can drive farm trucks."

Linda said, "Close enough. Ellen wants us to get this guy to turn into the rest stop ahead! I see the exit coming up fast!"

Mary looked at the children sniffling in the truck. "We can do this!"

Linda and Mary flew into the truck cab. Mary sat on the driver's lap and surveyed the dash board. Linda watched her and said, "Just tell me when you're ready."

Mary looked at her, "This guy stinks. I don't have a clue what to do." Just then she saw the turning signal and lifted it up to signal a right turn. The driver frowned and put it back down. Mary put it back up. Traffic was starting to honk at them.

Linda reached over and pulled the air horn. The driver's eyes flew open. He tried to stop it. Linda kept pulling on the horn, and Mary kept turning the signal on.

The driver cursed and looked in his rear view mirror. He assumed something was wrong with his truck and moved to the exit lane for the rest area. Mary had windshield wipers on high speed and was pushing all his radio stations buttons.

Linda and Mary smiled at each other and left the cab. They sat on top of the truck and could see police vehicles rapidly approaching further down the highway. They concentrated hard hoping the Marshals would see the truck going into the rest area. They did!

By the time the driver had parked the truck, a steady parade of police vehicles was entering the rest area. Mary and Linda went back in the cab and pushed the driver out the door into the waiting arms of the US Marshals.

Paul held a phone to his ear and yelled, "We got 'em!"

Roger smiled, "One more to go."

Linda and Mary stayed a while and watched the children being loaded into ambulances so they could be checked out. Linda overheard one of the Marshals reporting on his phone, the children were all in good shape and it appeared none of them had been physically harmed. Linda and Mary both listened as the families of the children were told of the rescue. They could hear the cheers of joy from the parents over the phones, and they watched the broad smiles and high-fives of the officers.

Teresa and I got lucky. Our guy was driving a van, and had parked at a restaurant off the toll road near Dallas. We waited in the van with the children until the State Troopers arrived. They had arrested the driver in the restaurant. It seemed like only minutes before the entire parking lot was filled with police vehicles and ambulances for the children. None of the children were hurt, but all of them were crying and wanting to go home.

Teresa sniffled, "Thank God we found them!"

I decided to sit in the cop car with the truck driver. If you really concentrate, you can pull twenty single hairs from a human's head per minute. I timed it.

Teresa made me leave.

Ellen called for us to head to Mambo's. We were late.

Shoot! I haven't decided on a party dress yet!

* * *

Willie stayed in the boat while Spicey and Sasha made their way along the narrow dirt path to Mambo's hut. Spicey pointed to a shrub, "Right there. Don't that look like a man part to you?"

Sasha frowned, "Pretty dinky. I think it be dryin' up." She giggled.

Spicey looked back to where Willie was waiting in the boat. "You know girl, it be a good friend that bring you out in the swamp at midnight."

Sasha fluffed her hair, "I think it be a *better* friend that comes along with y'all for no good reason."

Spicey nodded and put her hand around Sasha's shoulder. "I'm not too proud to tell you I'm scared 'bout what might happen in there." Spicey was pointing at Mambo's hut. "It be one thing to tell people you talk to Spirits. It be a whole 'nother deal to have it come true."

Sasha was carefully scanning the dirt path as they walked and asked, "Why did this happen? What made Spirits start talkin' to you?"

Spicey stopped walking when she heard a rustle in the grasses next to the path. "Girl, I have no idea. 'Member that expression, "Careful what ya wish for"?"

Sasha started running toward Mambo's hut, "I be wishing we get inside 'fore a bunch of rats eats us!" Spicey was right behind her.

Spicey and Sasha quietly knocked on Mambo's door. They were about five minutes early. Mambo was seated in the center of the room in front of her open fire pit. Mambo waved them over and told them to be seated. Sasha and Spicey tried to calm themselves down. Their chests were still heaving and Sasha felt dizzy.

Mambo looked at Sasha, "You will see everything that happens here tonight. That is a privilege for mortals. The Spirits have chosen Spicey to help them."

Mambo looked at Spicey, "We are asking for the Spirits help with the messages coming from the tortured souls in this swamp. I can only determine a sense of urgency. I do not know what they want."

Spicey swallowed. Tortured souls? In the swamp? This must mean dead people.

Sasha had the same thought. She cleared her throat, "Ms. Mambo? I got no problem being kicked out of this here meetin' 'fore it even starts. I promise I just do anything Ms. Spicey asks me to."

Mambo smiled, "You may leave."

Spicey started to protest, but Sasha frowned at her and hiccupped. Spicey decided it might be better lettin' her go. Sasha ran from the hut.

Mambo raised her arms. "Let us begin."

Suddenly the room filled with Spirits. They all showed themselves in somewhat human form, dressed in various period clothing. Mambo threw a powder on the fire that sent a sweet fragrance through the air and a flash of blue light. Mambo said, "We will be joined by angels."

Spicey was stunned as she looked around the room. Was this really happening? She bit her tongue and definitely felt the pain.

Mambo leaned on a cane and raised her old body. She raised her arms in the air. "Voices of the mist speak now."

A low rumble sounded from the walls. The hut filled with mist. Spicey could hear words escaping through the rumbles. Heavy breathing. Distant screams that seemed to be coming closer. It sounded like crowds of people, some far away and some very close. Spicey could only make out partial sentences and some cries for help. Then very clearly she heard a voice plead, "They must be saved."

Mambo looked at the Spirit wearing a white gown and asked, "Do you hear the warnings of the tortured souls?"

The Spirit looked very serious, "Yes, I do. I will need the help of the angels."

A vision of a small boy stood in a blue haze. He walked out of the mist, "I need to go home."

Spicey realized she was weeping. The anguish in the voices pulled at her heart, and her mind was swimming with questions. Where were the angels?

Alan, Thor, and Jeanne arrived at Mambo's to find Willie and Sasha waiting in their boat. Thor pointed to Mambo's hut. An intense blue light shone up through the chimney of the hut.

Jeanne looked at Thor, "The Spirits are with her now."

Thor was totally creeped out. He was no scientist, but that was no natural light.

Sasha said, "I'm thinkin' you best wait 'fore you go bargin' in." Jeanne nodded agreement.

Alan looked at Willie, "I hear you got your Cadillac to run on chicken fat. How's that workin' out?"

Willie answered, "Save me a bunch of gas money, but I spend a lot of time taking dogs back home. Keep follerin' me."

Thor kept staring at the blue light coming from Mambo's chimney. He listened to Alan and Willie making small talk about a chicken fat car. Doesn't anything rattle these people?

Jeanne went over to sit next to Sasha. "How long has Spicey been able to talk to Spirits?"

Sasha answered, "This be real new. She's mighty worried what they want her to do."

Thor had been looking around and mentioned he didn't see any alligators or river rats.

Willie offered, "They be far gone from this here spot right now, with the meetin' an all. Got more sense than we do."

We arrived at Mambo's at the same time. Mary and I were the only ones that remembered to wear party dresses. Ellen introduced us to the Spirits. Spicey was squinting. Ellen said, "Spicey can hear the Spirits talking to us, but she can't see or hear us. We are of another dimension."

We are? Huh.

The Spirit in the white gown looked at Ellen and said, "There are many souls that were held prisoner in the mortal city and murdered here in the swamp. The souls say another group of people will be brought here soon and killed. This is done whenever a new group of prisoners is being delivered. The souls are saying there is not much time."

Ellen told the Spirit we would help.

Mambo had her hand on the blue spirit boy as she spoke to Ellen, "This boy needs to go home."

Ellen knelt down and held his hands. She looked at him and said, "I promise you will go home soon."

Ellen asked Mambo, "What is Spicey going to do?"

Mambo answered, "The Spirits have replaced all of her potions. Spicey will communicate with mortals as the Spirits need her. The Spirits believe she will be of great help."

Spicey heard that and her eyes opened wide. "I don't know nothin' 'bout how to use *real* potions!"

Mambo chuckled. The Spirit in the white gown produced a tattered book and gave it to Spicey. "You will find what you need in here. Be warned.

There are Hoodoo influences that may challenge you once they discover your power."

Spicey took the book and swallowed. Suddenly the entire hut was empty except for Mambo and Spicey.

Mambo looked at Spicey, "You may leave. Use wisdom in your choices."

Spicey bowed as she backed out of the hut and ran to the boat. She said a soft, token hi to Alan, Jeanne, and Thor, sat next to Sasha, and then screamed, "Holy SHIT take me home!"

✳ ✳ ✳

Ellen told us this would be a good time to visit with our families for a while. She would call us when we were needed. We didn't have to be told twice.

✳ ✳ ✳

Jeanne looked at Thor, "Our turn now."

Thor looked at Alan and then back at Jeanne. "What do you mean 'our turn'? You're the one that believes this Mambo stuff, not me."

"Please? How often do you get a chance to meet a Mambo?"

"Truthfully, it's not even on my bucket list. Desire zero."

Thor watched Willie's boat disappear in the mist. He knew he couldn't say no to Jeanne. Damn it. He looked back at her, "Let's get this over with."

Mambo invited Thor and Jeanne to sit with her at the fire. Mambo told them what the Spirits had said. Thor looked at Jeanne. "Sounds like a human trafficking ring."

Mambo nodded. She looked at Jeanne and said, "I wish to speak to Valtare alone."

Jeanne looked at Thor with one eyebrow raised. Thor looked back at Mambo. He couldn't believe she had said that. "No one knows my name is Valtare."

Mambo smiled, "Valtare Daniel Thor. You have much to learn."

Jeanne rose and said she would wait with Alan. Thor was afraid to be left alone with Mambo. How did she know his real name? Mambo leaned forward and held out an amulet attached to a thin leather strap. She motioned for Thor to lower his head so she could place the amulet around his neck. Thor leaned forward, watched the amulet pass his eyes and hang from his neck. He felt Mambo's frail hand on his forehead. She began to chant. Her hand felt hot. A strange peace crept through his body.

Mambo sat up straight, "There is much for you to learn. Jeanne is a messenger of Erzulie Dantor, the Black Madonna. She has only recently begun to understand her destiny." Mambo waited for Thor's reaction to her statement. He had a quizzical expression on his face, but he did not speak. Mambo continued, "She is more than mortal and has unique burdens. You have Nordic spirit in your blood. You were destined to meet her again. She will choose you. She will consume you."

Thor sat up straight, "No disrespect Ms. Mambo, but I don't believe in this mumbo jumbo. I'm here doing a job. No woman is going to *consume* me. I just met her four days ago!" Thor was visibly distressed. This creepy old lady was getting to him.

Mambo smiled, "Your souls have known each other for centuries. It is important you not force your will on her. She will not tolerate it. The same way you do not tolerate the ordinary. Your life has left you disappointed and angry. You have known something essential was missing. It was her. When you saw her, she seemed familiar to you. You have thought of nothing since." Mambo paused with one eyebrow raised. She continued, "Together you will accomplish great things. Go. You have many problems to solve, and you are needed by others."

Thor stood and looked around the room. None of this seemed real, and yet it all seemed strangely familiar.

Mambo made a motion of shooing a fly away and said, "You have many things to do and very little time.'

Thor backed out of the room and walked toward Jeremiah's boat where Jeanne and Alan waited for him. Damn. He was going to end up as crazy as the rest of them. When he was settled, Jeanne asked, "You were with Mambo a long time. What did she say to you?"

Thor looked off into the swamp, "She said we have a lot of work to do and not much time." Jeanne nodded. Thor noticed Jeanne's eyes reflected the moonlight in an eerie way. He swallowed and looked away.

Alan said, "We better get goin' then. Jeremiah said Mambo never wrong 'bout nothin'."

Thor was silent as the boat glided through the tall marsh grasses toward the open water and wondered what happened when someone *consumed* you.

Jeanne watched him rub his amulet. He was different somehow. Stronger.

CHAPTER
TWENTY ONE

Roger called everyone on the team and told them about the rescue of the children. Thor told Roger what Mambo said about human trafficking. Roger couldn't believe Thor had gone to Mambo's after the arrests. He looked at his watch. It was one o'clock in the morning. Roger had told the team he didn't expect to see any of them until later tomorrow. They needed rest.

After speaking with the team Roger sent an email to the Director detailing the arrest of the sicko club and the rescue of the children. He finally arrived at his hotel, showered, and watched some of the news footage of the children being rescued. These moments were why they all did this job.

Roger dialed Kim who answered on the first ring. He could tell she was crying. "What's wrong?"

"Nothing! I am so proud of you! These children are going to be with their parents soon. Ugh…. how do you handle this stress?"

Roger smiled, "I have you."

Spicey woke with her arms clutching an old tattered book. Her sheets were tangled with amulets and beads, and her Bible stared at her from her pillow. She lay with her eyes open glancing around her room. She sat up and looked at the tattered book. It had the words Truth Seeker on the cover. She opened the book and yelped! It was in some kind of strange language. She couldn't read it!

Spicey threw her sheets back and got out of bed. What was she going to do? She walked around the room holding the book. She looked inside again. Now she could read it. She tossed the book onto her bed as if it was on fire. Sweet Jesus! What had just happened?

✷ ✷ ✷

The next morning Tourey turned on his television to CNN and watched the news reports on the rescued children. Few details of the case were being released, but the FBI was credited for solving the case.

The story about the children was immediately followed by the investigation of the Zelez Cartel infiltrating the security of Lanitol Oil Company and using the oil company facilities to smuggle cartel drugs into the ports of New Orleans. Reportedly over 2000 kilos of cocaine had been seized at the port.

Aw SHIT! Tourey rubbed his temples and conceded that he and John were going to be knee deep in LUCY real soon. Probably today.

The news journalist smiled as he introduced the big headline of the morning. Four prominent men of New Orleans were arrested last night for attempting to dispose of the body of escaped murderer and pedophile, William Patterson. Among those arrested were a retired Senator and a sitting judge.

Tourey carried his coffee mug to the kitchen sink, rinsed it out before putting it in the dishwasher, and leaned against his counter. Tourey could still see his television. John was right about Dance and his team. They had no qualms about kicking a hornet's nest just to see how many came out.

✳ ✳ ✳

Simon purchased a box of beignets for the guys at the Star Ship. He wiped the powdered sugar from his mouth with a napkin as he and Thor talked about being in the swamp last night. Ray was mesmerized hearing about the gunshots, alligators, hanging turkeys, and the meeting at Mambo's.

Thor asked Simon, "Do you know what 'silent crickets' means?"

Simon nodded his head. "It means you have a serious threat nearby. Along those same lines, you can count the number of times a male cricket chirps in fourteen seconds, add forty, and get the Fahrenheit temperature of outdoors. Dolbears Law."

Thor looked at Ray, "Who knows this crap?"

Thor looked back to Simon, "Okay Mr. Wizard, what the heck is a Rugaru?"

Simon laughed, "Evidently, an FBI Agent!"

Thor frowned.

Ray had Googled Rugaru. "Says it's a fabled half wolf, half man, said to wander the swamps of Louisiana. Oh hey, and he eats humans." Ray leaned back and smiled at Thor. "We should add turkeys."

Thor looked at Ray's screen. "Google Black Madonna."

Simon raised an eyebrow.

Ray read a minute and then tried to pronounce a name, "Says otherwise known as Erzulie Dantor, woman warrior of the Spirits. She's supposed to have messengers that protect women and children." Ray looked at Thor, "Says messengers of Erzulie Dantor are believed to be rare blue eyed Haitian women."

Jeanne started coming down the stairs, Ray quickly hit a button to clear his screen. Simon stared at Thor before saying, "Damn."

✳ ✳ ✳

Mathew Core stood in the jewelry store apartment staring across the street at his old building as he sipped tea. He looked at his watch, nine a.m.. It might still be too early. He knew Roger had a late night last night.

He turned his attention back to the news. Yesterday had been a good day for the FBI, and a bad day for pedophiles. Today could be a very bad day for everybody.

✳ ✳ ✳

Paul locked his hotel room door and headed to the elevator to get some breakfast downstairs. Three men boarded the elevator next to his. As Paul rested against the wall of his elevator, he had a bad feeling. He watched the lights above the door count down. Something about the three guys getting in the other elevator hadn't been right. Did they avoid looking at him? Did they really get in the elevator?

Paul dialed Roger as he pressed the elevator stop button. No answer. He cursed at how slow the door was to open. He bolted out of the elevator and ran for the stairs.

Roger realized he must have overslept. He had been exhausted. He looked around the hotel room and then looked at his watch. It was already after nine. He threw his blanket back, just as Ellen jumped on his bed and made a wild hissing sound as she pointed toward the door. Roger grabbed his gun and stood at the edge of the bathroom wall. He could hear the soft swiping sound of someone at his key lock.

Suddenly Ellen leaped from the floor with a bloodcurdling screech. A man stumbled sideways and screamed in agony. Roger lunged forward in time to see Ellen scratching at a man's face and neck. Two other men had guns drawn and were making their way into the room. Roger fired; one man fell to the floor. Roger yelled, "FBI, drop your weapon." The second man took aim, and Roger shot him. Ellen continued biting and clawing until Roger pushed the barrel of his gun in the man's back.

"Drop your weapon."

Ellen dropped to the floor and hopped over to the credenza where she licked her paws casually and watched through narrowed eyes.

Roger pressed the man's face against the wall with his forearm and began searching him. He had a knife in addition to the Glock he had dropped. Paul burst through the partially opened door, and Roger asked, "You got cuffs?"

Paul nodded and cuffed the man as Roger unloaded the man's gun and glanced at Ellen. Roger said thanks to Ellen and Paul answered, "No problem. Saw these guys by the elevator. Decided to circle back. Didn't like their looks."

Roger was in his boxer shorts. Not exactly his normal attire for interrogations. A crowd was forming in the hall. Roger stated FBI and slammed his door shut. He looked at the man as Paul pushed him into a chair.

Paul had his weapon aimed at the man. "Who are you?"

The man tightened his lips and turned his head. Roger flipped through the man's thin wallet. There was no ID anywhere. Roger lifted his phone, took a picture, and sent it to Mathew Core with a question, "Know this guy?"

After about three minutes Roger's phone rang. It was Core. "Rafael Ortiz. Manio man. Thinks he's a bad ass. Done some enforcement work for Manio. Where is he?"

"In my hotel room with two dead buddies."

Core paused, "Seems Manio has eyes on you. Probably wants you gone. When you have a minute, I need to talk to you."

Roger looked at Paul, "I'm going to take my shower. Call local PD to have this guy picked up. Name is Rafael Ortiz. Manio man."

Paul answered, "No problem."

Ellen stretched, then curled herself into a black ball with her green eyes peeking through slits above her fur. The man glanced at her, and she raised her chin to hiss at him.

He looked at Paul, "That's one *mean* cat." The man's face and neck were lined with deep scratches, bite marks, and trails of blood.

Paul controlled his urge to chuckle. "Evidently."

Kim felt like jogging. She put on her running shoes, a big hockey jersey and headed down the block towards town. She figured she might stop in the bookstore and see what new releases might be out. She wasn't even a block away from the house when I saw her. Ellen had told us to spend a little time with family this morning before we started our next job.

I was so excited about the children's rescue I just started jogging next to Kim.

"Was that cool or what?"

Kim looked over, "The kids? It was fabulous! Since when do you jog?" She was smiling. I knew she was happy to see me.

"I have to jog now because you are. Feel free to stop if you are worried about your tired old mom though."

Kim glanced at me and laughed. "Nice try. What's up?"

"Getting ready to bust a human trafficking ring, I guess. Hey, I just heard three guys broke into Roger's hotel room this morning with guns."

Kim stopped, "What the heck? Was he hurt?"

I could tell she was upset, "Noooooo. That's why I just told you kind of casual like, so you wouldn't freak out. Seems that didn't work."

Kim kept running. People were watching her run by, talking to herself, but I didn't want to point that out either. Finally she stopped in the middle of the sidewalk, "You know what? Let's make a deal. You quit telling me shit about child molesters, murderers, and people trying to kill Roger, and I won't jog when you are here."

Touchy, touchy. "Are you having a bad day or something?"

Kim started crying, still jogging in place, "It's murder, murder, murder, and worse! Kids! I never realized how sick some people are. Roger deals with this every day. "

People were walking past us on the sidewalk and staring at Kim. I didn't want to say anything, but she really needed to calm down.

I patted her hair with my hand, "Roger really cares about you. You need to trust that he can do his job and stay safe. He knows his job sucks. He has to retire sometime! Besides, what can go wrong? He has angels helping him!" I smiled. Kim smiled back.

A police car pulled alongside of us and an officer got out. Kim was jogging in place. The officer said, "Are you okay, ma'am? We got a call you were acting…. strangely. Talking about murder?"

Kim looked at me, "Oh, this isn't funny. Fix it."

I looked at her, "What do you want me to do? He can't see or hear me."

Kim scrunched her mouth.

The mom in me took over, "You're going to make wrinkles." Kim gave me 'the look'.

The officer touched Kim's elbow, "Why don't you come with me for a while and we'll try to straighten this out."

Kim pulled her arm away, "Officer I'm fine. I just talk to myself when I'm running."

The officer had a concerned look on his face, "It's okay. It's okay. Hey, I sing in the shower."

The officer escorted Kim to the back of the patrol car and pulled away. Kim turned her head and looked at me as they turned the corner. Uh oh.

CHAPTER
TWENTY TWO

Abram and Jackson left the FBI field office the night before and returned the money Abram had stolen to the gang house. This morning Abram had called Jackson and asked him to be at the gang's building early, so they could start working on their undercover assignment. When Abram arrived, there were already nine guys at the building waiting for him.

Abram was immediately barraged with questions from the guys inside. He yelled for everyone to shut up, just as Jackson entered the building. Abram motioned for Jackson to sit in a chair over by Abram's computer. It was a hundred degrees in the building already, and it stunk of body odor and beer.

One burly guy walked over to stand in front of Abram, "We need some product. Can't make no money, can't go nowhere but peoples yellin' at us."

Just then two guys from Chiclet's gang walked in the building. "Who be Abram?"

Abram swallowed and glanced at Jackson. Abram stood, "Who are you?"

The larger of the two put his fist in the air to greet Abram and said, "We come for Chiclet's money and to see what ya need for the street."

Jackson had been searching Manuel's computer for some idea of how much product Manuel was moving and how much money he had to pay for it. Jackson asked, "How much money is Chiclet expecting you to bring back? We're still diggin' through all of Manuel's notes."

Abram was grateful Jackson had asked the question. He was just going to hand over the two hundred thousand he had taken from the safe the night before.

The burly guy called Chiclet. "How much we 'sposed to be pickin' up? With Manuel dead everyone learnin' the job, ya know?" He listened a while and disconnected from the call. "Chiclet said you owe him fifty grand for yesterday and whatever you want to buy for today. Today be pricey. No product out there to compete. He sez you get the brother-in-law special. Only twice as much today for you."

Abram winced, "So you want fifty grand for yesterday and a hundred grand for today?"

The burly guy rubbed his chin. "That's sounds right. Got your product outside. You want us to bring it in?"

Abram nodded. He looked at Jackson and shrugged. Jackson felt a sinking feeling. He and Abram were clueless. They were bound to make some kind of huge mistake by lunch time.

The Director of the FBI read the emails that Roger had sent him the night before, and placed a call to him. The Director told him Ellen had determined eight ports in the United States had Lanitol Oil dock buildings with large quantities of cocaine. The long standing relationship between the government and the oil companies at the ports was based on history and an economy of resources. The oil companies could well afford their own security and were beyond reproach. Or so everyone was led to believe.

Roger agreed with the Director that since Lanitol Oil claimed they had been victims of a drug cartel, the logical law enforcement move would be to investigate all ports. Not just New Orleans. The fact the original offense was discovered in a martial law zone might give them expanded authority if later challenged.

The Director told Roger he was going to request the National Security Council issue the order to the Coast Guard as soon as Ellen identified who was the weak link in the Interior Department. The Director didn't want Lanitol Oil warned they were coming like they had been in last night's raid.

Roger thought it would be best to wait until they had a full day of money transfers before issuing the raid on the other ports. Perhaps timing the raids to start a few hours before the martial law order expired would be best. The Director agreed.

Roger told the Director about the three men at his hotel and that Core had identified them as Manio men. The Director enjoyed the part of the story about Ellen.

The Director sighed, "These relationships we are discovering have been honed for years. Our actions now with LUCY will be taken as threats and will come with severe repercussions."

Roger answered, "We are twisting their melody. Listen to Bolero. The orchestra wins over the drums. To me, the orchestra is all that is right and just."

The Director hung up his phone and laughed. You never knew what Roger might say, but this seemed strange even for him. The Director searched his computer for Bolero, found it, and hit play. He leaned his chair back and closed his eyes. At the end of the piece he laughed. He saw what Roger meant.

The Director answered a knock on his office door. "Come in." His smile quickly faded.

William C. Thornton walked in and sat in the seat across from the Director's desk. "Morning. Anything new?"

Roger had called Ray at the Star Ship and told him what had happened at the hotel. He asked Ray to check for information on Rafael Ortiz. Then Roger called the local PD to arrest Ortiz and get the coroner to clear his hotel room. The hotel manager arranged a different room for Roger. The manager was mortified and promised to get Roger answers on how these men had obtained the key to Roger's room.

We had heard from Ellen what happened in Roger's room, and decided to come back and see for ourselves. On the way there I remember thinking how cool it was Ellen could just hang out with mortals, because she was a cat. I think I might have let my imagination take over at that point. When we arrived in Roger's room we were all kittens. Ooops. Teresa glared at me and sent me her thoughts. "Now what?" Mortals were in the room. I just shrugged. Ellen hissed at us.

Thor had heard about the problem at Roger's hotel and made his way through the people in the hall to Roger's door. He knocked quickly on the door as he entered. Roger and Paul looked fine and were talking to the coroner. Thor glanced over and noticed Roger's cat sitting by its carrier with four kittens nearby.

Thor asked, "How the hell did your cat have kittens?"

Roger and Paul both whipped around to see four little black kittens sitting in a row next to Ellen. Paul stuttered, "They're not hers."

Roger looked at Paul and then to Thor, "One of the hotel staff brought these here hoping Ellen would nurse them."

Thor starred at Ellen, and then said, "Something is wrong with these kittens. You ever see kittens just sit still like that?"

Roger shrugged. He couldn't believe he had to deal with this now. I took Thor's comment as our cue to act like kittens. I bounced straight up at least a foot, spread out all four legs and belly flopped onto Linda.

Mary bit my head and Teresa started pushing her legs into all of our stomachs. This was actually a ton of fun. We were a ball of fur and legs in no time. Linda jumped straight up and landed on Teresa and Mary grabbed me and rolled me over. Someone was biting my tail!

Then Thor asked, "Well, is she nursing them?"

I stopped biting Mary's ear and looked at Ellen. Maybe it's lunch time. Ellen sat up and hissed at us. Guess not.

Roger thanked Thor for coming over but said they were headed for the Star Ship soon. Thor said he'd meet them there. He looked back at Ellen and said, "You might talk to that gal that owns the kittens and tell her this isn't looking good."

Roger asked Ellen before he shut the hotel room door, "Are these your angels?"

Ellen winked.

Roger closed the door and looked at Paul, "Nice save."

Behind the closed door Ellen frowned at us. We had changed back to look like our old selves. I raised my hand, Ellen nodded at me.

"It was my fault. I just thought it would be fun for mortals to be able to see us." Figured I might as well confess. She probably knew it was my fault anyway.

Ellen said, "The decision was made to give you the skill. I don't see how we can get mad at you for using it." Ellen smiled.

You are kidding? I'm going to do this all the time! That was too much fun. Now everyone was frowning at me.

I threw my arms up in the air, "Okay, from now on we'll take a vote." Shucks.

Paul and Roger decided to walk to the Star Ship and see what was happening with the French Quarter Bank wire activity. Today was Friday and hopefully the day LUCY would die.

Paul looked around as they walked the three blocks to the Star Ship, "Guess we need to be more alert. I didn't expect a nine a.m. hit in your hotel room."

Roger nodded. "Core thinks they've been watching. Probably knew we had a late night, and waited for you to leave the hotel floor."

Paul asked, "Has Core ever said any more about Fenley's hit on us?"

Roger chuckled, "Sorry, I forgot to tell you. Yeah, that's been cancelled."

Paul laughed, "Just slipped your mind?"

Roger stopped walking, "Shoot. Core wanted to talk to me about something."

Roger dialed Core, "Sorry it took so long to get back to you. What did you want?"

Mathew Core set his tea cup down and took a deep breath. He hoped that Roger would accommodate him, "I want a phone number to talk to Lisa."

✳ ✳ ✳

Spicey had dressed for the day, made herself a cup of herbal tea and sat at her small dinette set staring at the book the Spirits had given her. Truth Seeker. Huh. After a few moments she pushed her cup aside, pulled the book toward her, and began reading. Hours passed, and Spicey was stunned back into reality by a banging on her apartment door.

She went to the door and Sasha came in. "Why you not open yet? You sick?" Sasha set her purse down on the table and saw the open book. "You be studyin' that new potion book?"

Spicey nodded and said, "I hope I get more instruction than this. It don't make sense to me yet. What time is it anyway?"

Spicey turned around and looked at the wall clock. "Dang! It's almost noon and I ain't even opened the shop yet."

Sasha mumbled, "That's what I been sayin'."

Spicey ran out into the shop, flipped the Voodoo sign to ON, and Sasha took her seat by the register. Sasha said, "Look here at all these jars on this back shelf."

Spicey walked over and saw at least ten narrow shelves lined with small jars of powders and liquids. Each little jar had a label with strange writing on it. Spicey threw her arms up in the air, "I can't read what these mean. How I supposed to know what I'm doing?"

Sasha picked up a jar and gave Spicey a worried look, "What so hard 'bout this? Says 'crow beak' right on it."

Spicey's mouth flew open. She could read the labels now. She looked at Sasha, "I'm tellin' ya this Spirit stuff is spooky. Strange things been happenin' already."

Sasha asked, "What you think 'crow beak' be for?" She shook the powder in the jar and held it up to the light. "You look in your ball yet?"

Spicey froze. "Nope."

* * *

Carol and Cindy had known Spicey back in Michigan when she went by her given name of Sadie Corbin. That was before she decided to be a Voodoo lady. They all worked at The Tavern in Niles, Michigan, where Teresa, Mary, Linda, and Vicki would go for lunch before they died in their accident. Carol and Cindy had been friends outside of work for years and had saved to take a vacation together. Knowing Sadie had a Voodoo shop in New Orleans made the French Quarter their logical choice. That, and the fact they were both somewhat 'colorful' characters in their own right. The French Quarter in New Orleans was an irresistible destination.

Cindy found them a travel package on the internet that promised their room at the Inn would have them in the heart of the French Quarter. When the taxi pulled up in front of a bright orange building with teal window trim and a tattoo shop at street level, Carol said, "This doesn't look like the website picture."

The cabby started laughing. "You see the one with the big wrap around balcony and all the red flower pots hangin'?"

Cindy answered, "Yeah! That's the one."

The cabby laughed, "Half the Inns use that same picture. This here be where you're staying. Ain't a bad place really. You still be in the safe part of the Quarter."

Cindy exhaled loudly. "Well, we're here. Should we check it out?"

Carol laughed, "We don't care anyway! We're not staying in our room. We're here to party!" Cindy agreed. They paid the cabby and hauled their suitcases into the tattoo shop. The owner of the tattoo shop had them sign in.

He looked at them both, "How long you stayin'?"

Cindy answered, "We'll be here five nights." She and Carol elbowed each other and giggled. This was just so exciting.

"My name's Ernie. You gonna have to pay in advance."

Cindy asked, "How come we have to pay in advance? Didn't say that on your website. That doesn't seem right." She and Carol emptied their purses on his counter and started digging for their hidden money.

The tattoo owner smiled, "You ladies be pretty fine lookin'. You'd be surprised how many ladies come up missin'. We just started chargin' up front for the pretty ones. Just in case."

Cindy and Carol looked at each other. That didn't sound real good. Carol pulled out a slip of paper from her purse, "We have a friend owns this Voodoo shop. Do you know how far this address is?"

The guy drew them a little map and said, "Most them Voodoo shops don't open 'til afternoon. Go late into the night some of 'em. Tourists, you know." He pointed to a narrow staircase and said, "You be the first room on the left there. Got two big queen size beds and our best bathroom. *Welcome to Nawlens!*"He placed a long beaded necklace on each of them and handed them their keys.

Carol was getting in the mood and kept repeating 'Welcome to Nawlens" until she felt she had the accent just right. Cindy was shaking her head as she dragged her luggage up the steep stairs.

Roger gave Core the phone number for Lisa. It would be up to Lisa to decide if Mathew was going to stay in their lives. Some people within the government considered Core a victim. Roger was fully aware that often people with his skill set were used up and discarded when no longer needed or trusted. Core had taken what the government had taught him and built his own retirement fund. Not only was this known, but some very important people had assisted him. Lisa would have to come to her own conclusions.

Roger and Paul had just reached the Star Ship when his phone rang again, "Yes? Yes this is SSA Roger Dance." He listened a while. Paul could tell whatever the conversation was, Roger didn't like it.

Roger took a deep breath and rolled his eyes, "Trust me. You have made a mistake. She is fine. Probably more sane than the rest of us. Let her go home." He listened a while longer and then said, "I understand, it was a perfectly normal misunderstanding. Of course you have to follow procedure." Roger disconnected and looked at Paul, "Kim was detained by the local cops."

Paul looked serious, "What for?"

Roger started laughing, "Public nuisance. She was jogging and talking to herself. The police detained her for her own safety."

Paul leaned against the building laughing.

Roger added, "Bet she wasn't talking to herself."

"Bet she hated to give them a number to call you."

"Yep."

Paul opened the door to the stairwell, "Well, you calling Kim?"

Roger shook his head. "Not yet."

They went inside and heard voices from the basement. It sounded like the team had decided to show up early. Roger and Paul went down the stairs to find Simon, Ray, Thor and Jeanne huddled around Ray's computer screen. Pablo was sitting on the couch drinking coffee.

Roger asked Pablo, "How are you feeling this morning?"

Pablo nodded, swallowed, and answered, "Other than a bunch of pain, and this sling, I wouldn't know anything happened."

Ray said, "French Quarter Bank is having a big day already. Simon thinks we'll hit a trillion dollars' worth of activity by lunch." Paul whistled.

Simon volunteered, "I talked to Mass's guy Phillips a few minutes ago. He says the Branch Manager is just ignoring the whole thing. Figures it doesn't have anything to do with him. That probably is a good thing."

Roger told the team about Manio's men coming to his hotel room. He asked them to be extra alert since obviously Manio was feeling threatened. "Since you guys are all here, I might as well give you the scoop on how the drug raid came about last night." Everyone listened to Roger recap how Zack and Core found out about the cocaine delivery by accident and how the Director arranged for the Coast Guard to do the seizure.

Simon asked, "Lanitol Oil has a relationship with the Manio Cartel to smuggle dope in on cartel subs, unload at vacant rigs, and bring the dope into oil protected docks. Is that what I'm hearing?"

Roger answered, "Yes."

Simon continued, "After the raid, Lanitol Oil claimed to be victims of the Zelez Cartel to cover this up?"

"Yes."

Thor rubbed the back of his neck. "Just think about how long this has been going on. We don't even check the cargo boats of the oil companies do we?"

John had come down the stairs and answered Thor's question. "We will now."

John whispered something to Roger, and Roger looked at the team. "OSI has authorized John to share some information with you. It seems this team is getting involved in another set of problems that was discovered in our communication sting."

Thor coughed, "Oh goody."

When John finished explaining the history of LUCY, the group was silent. Before they could ask any questions Roger informed them the Coast Guard was prepared to raid eight more ports that will disclose large shipments of cocaine in Lanitol Oil storage buildings. They planned to delay that raid until later tonight. The money sting would be jeopardized if they moved on the drug raid sooner, given they were dealing with the same players.

Simon asked, "How will Lanitol Oil maintain their victim status once drugs are discovered in eight more ports?"

Paul answered, "That will be a tough one."

Roger pointed out Manio was the one feeling the true squeeze right now. Manio was out the drugs and associated income. Lanitol Oil had yet to suffer. Roger was hoping the additional raids would push Manio or Lanitol Oil into doing something stupid.

Simon commented, "I'm still wrapping my mind around cocaine being brought into the gulf in subs. Unloaded at protected oil rigs, to protected cargo boats and simply unloaded again at protected docks. No wonder we are losing this drug war."

Roger shrugged, "Don't forget we still have the Zelez Cartel sniffing around. If we get lucky, we can dent their operation too. However, Zelez is playing this smart. He's staying in the background." Roger sat down and let out a small chuckle, "We seem to have come a long way, considering a year ago, we were called to South Bend, Indiana, to help catch a serial killer."

Ray said, "I can't believe everything that has happened since we got to New Orleans. The Big Easy ain't been so easy."

Roger stated Thor had some news. "Why don't you tell the group what Mambo said to you?"

Thor straightened up. What the hell? He wasn't going to tell *anyone* what Mambo said to him. How did Roger even know?

Roger continued, "You know, the human trafficking."

Thor relaxed. Oh that.

Dusty couldn't believe he was awake. Last night in the swamp, he promised himself if he lived, he could sleep 'til noon. Nope. Wide awake. He looked at the check Agent Mass had given him last night after they arrested all of those dudes. Another one thousand dollars. He still had the last check for a thousand and five hundred from when he and Alan took that Voodoo lady to Mambos. Alan told Dusty he was paying off the last of his mortgage. Dusty figured he best open himself a bank account.

He went into his bathroom to shower and shave. He looked in the mirror and wondered if he was turnin' all establishment or somethin'. All this time he'd been spendin' with cops. Now he needed a bank account? Hadn't had one of them since college. He turned on the shower and stepped in. He could still smell the swamp. Weren't 'nough showers in the world to get rid of that smell. Never did hear who that dead guy was. FBI ain't like the local cops. FBI don't say shit.

He figured he would open an account, save out about a hundred cash and go over to Jackson Park for a while and do some portraits. Sooner or later Nawlens had to go back to normal.

The French Quarter Bank branch manager walked over to Amy and asked, "You sure you want to work today? You can take as much time as you want after your ordeal."

Amy looked at him and smiled softly, "Home is too quiet right now. I'd rather stay busy. I'll be okay."

The branch manager walked over to Agent Phillips, "She's one of the girls that murderer kidnapped and took to the swamp to die."

Agent Phillips looked over. Amy looked very professional and was seated at the customer service desk. Phillips looked at the branch manager, "People deal with stress in different ways. If she says she's okay I would leave it alone." The manager nodded and sauntered back to his office where Phillips knew a game of solitaire was open on the computer.

CHAPTER
TWENTY THREE

Abram watched as one of Chiclet's guys moved in six kilos of cocaine. One guy looked at Abram and said, "Chiclet called back and said to give you one extree. Since you be related or somethin'. 'Member you paid double for this shit. Your guys gotta charge double or you be loosin' money for the boss. That there ain't a good retirement plan."

Six of the guys standing around got busy dividing up the dope, weighing it and putting it in small bags. Jackson walked over and held up a tiny plastic bag, "What be the street cost of this here size bag?"

The one guy looked up and said, "Normal be twenty. Guess now it be forty." Jackson watched them for a while longer and motioned for Abram to step over by him. Jackson was doing some math on a piece of paper.

"Looks to me you be making about two hundred and fifty grand *profit* from that."

Abram's eyes got wide. "Shit."

Jackson raised an eyebrow and Abram frowned, "I know."

A big guy with a pencil mustache leaned against the far wall and said, "We got fourteen people just been loaded up from a Mississippi boat in Baton Rouge. They be on their way here. Only take a few hours to get here. Got no place to put 'em, 'less we make room like last year."

Jackson hair went up on his arm. What was this guy talkin' 'bout?

Abram had a small notebook in his hand and looked at the guy that just spoke. "Keep in mind this all new to me. I got to fix all these messes. What's your name?"

The guy stood up straight and crossed his arms on his chest. "Daryl Cotton. Manuel used to be my cousin."

Abram shook his head, "Hey man. That be some bad shit 'bout him dyin' and all. What are you talking about boat people?"

Daryl frowned. "Man you got no clue what all Manuel's job be. Manuel stores the prostitution people for Manio. We got a dozen or so fresh ones coming to replace who's here now."

Abram asked, "Where this storage place be?"

Daryl didn't answer right off. Abram frowned at him, "You want I call Manio and tell him you won't give me information I need?" Abram had no clue how to reach Manio. Jackson was shaking his head trying to look bad.

Daryl shuffled his feet some and decided he didn't care one way or another. "Our buildin' over on Commerce Street. Manuel called it the flea market there in that computer."

Abram gave Jackson the signal to look it up in the computer. Jackson found a file named flea market. It indicated there were fourteen people there now, and fourteen new ones expected today. Manio was paying fifty thousand dollars for their delivery and some kind of percentage calculation for their storage. Jackson signaled Abram to come look, and Jackson pointed to the pertinent information.

Abram asked, "How did you make room last year?"

Daryl looked around, "Ain't talkin' 'bout that with these dogs here."

Abram yelled for everyone but Jackson to leave the building. When everyone was gone Daryl said, "We load 'em up in a van, drive 'em up to a special spot at the swamp, and make 'em cross over to a little island out there. Then we target practice. Not that big a deal really. Two of us can do it."

Abram rubbed his face and told Daryl to wait outside with the others while he made a couple of calls. Damn.

Jackson looked at Abram, "I think I'm gonna be sick, man."

✳ ✳ ✳

Donavan called Manio at ten a.m. Friday morning. Manio had decided to visit New Orleans during this time of trouble and tighten the leash on his men. After a night at the casino he wasn't in the mood for any more bad news from London. Manio knew Donavan was the acting head of LUCY but Donavan's personality had never impressed him.

Manio answered, "I trust you will start my day well."

Donavan answered, "I'll do you better than that and start your day great. The martial law operation caused a computer problem at the French Quarter Bank. What I am about to tell you has been veri-fied with the highest sources. We have tested this information with the best computer people in the world for over twenty- four hours. I did not want to bring you bad information."

Donavan proceeded to explain how the French Quarter Bank was now virtually a safe haven for all of their money. Existing and new accounts opened today were being issued special federal account numbers. Transactions moved freely without re-porting tags and effectively erased all previous banking activity records. Even the international clearing houses reported the transactions moved through with absolutely no information tags.

Manio listened with great interest. He finally said, "I have accounts there now. If I move money from these accounts to offshore and return with larger balances, my money has been laundered by the United States Federal Reserve? This is hard to believe."

Donavan cleared his throat, "I have tested this. Seven hundred billion dollars of Lanitol Oil money has been moved since yesterday afteri oon. I did this before telling you. We will save billions of dollars not having to launder this money any longer. I understand this opportunity will expire at midnight tonight."

Manio smiled, "This certainly is surprising news. I thank you for the information." Manio disconnected the call and picked up his elderly cat to cradle in his arm. As he stroked its fur, he muttered, "Foolish men create opportunities for their enemies. I am not convinced Roger Dance is a foolish man."

Carol sat cross-legged on her bed surrounded by maps and brochures. She yelled to Cindy who was changing clothes in the bathroom, "Where do you want to go first?" Carol wore costumes often in her day to day life. Just for fun. So bringing a wardrobe suitable for her vision of New Orleans had been no problem at all. She had decided that today she would wear her long, blue, old lady dress with the oversized boobs and fake big butt. Instead of her wig though, she chose a wide brimmed hat with twinkle lights around the brim.

Cindy came out of the bathroom in a cute walking short set with a twinkle necklace dangling. "The guy downstairs said the Voodoo shops open later, so why don't we just walk around some? We can do a little shoppin', grab lunch, and then go see Sadie."

Carol corrected her by holding up her index finger, "You mean Spicey, remember? We promised."

Cindy chuckled, "Right." Carol stuffed her coin purse and room key inside one of the fake boobs and declared she was ready. Cindy grabbed her purse and one of the maps from Carol's bed.

Carol said, "I already packed a map and some extra money in my fake butt. Case we get robbed."

They locked their door and made their way down to the tattoo shop. Carol's big fake boobs made it hard to see to walk down the narrow steps. The owner of the shop was bent over some fat guy's arm doing a tattoo of a big spider. Cindy and Carol leaned over to see what he was doing, and he raised an eyebrow at them. He stared at Carol's huge boobs and fake butt and laughed. "You gals gonna love Nawlens!"

When they stepped outside the door, a kid on a unicycle nearly ran them over. Carol squealed. "Oh, how cool is that?" She started running after the kid on the bike. "Wait! Wait! I want to learn how to ride that thing!"

Cindy watched them both turn the corner. Carol's gigantic fake boobs and butt bouncing, and the kid's terrified face looking back at her as she chased him.

At least four times Spicey paced by the table holding her crystal ball before she had the courage to sit down. She put the book the Spirits had given her on the shelf next to the table. Her hands were clasped tight. She unclasped them, wiggled her fingers, and placed her palms against the ball. With one eye closed she peeked deep inside. Huh. It looked like it always did.

Spicey relaxed, opened her other eye and asked, "Is there something I'm supposed to be doin'?"

Her ball started getting a bluish tint in the center and suddenly the face of a small boy said, "I want to go home." Spicey fainted. Her head dropped on the table and sent her ball rolling. It dropped on the floor, rolled under the curtain and out into the main store. Sasha was ringing up a lady's purchase of some beads as the ball rolled by. The lady tourist watched the ball stop next to a display cabinet.

She asked Sasha, "Do you need to get that?"

Sasha shook her head and said, "I ain't touchin' that no how. It be fine right where it landed."

The lady left and Sasha poked her head around the curtain just as Spicey walked through the doorway. Spicey's hair was all tussled and she was breathing hard. "This ain't goin' so good." Spicey walked over, picked up the ball, and frowned. With a look of determination she said, "You come for me in 'bout ten minutes if I ain't back out here." Sasha nodded. This gonna be a steep learnin' curve by the looks of it.

Sasha swiveled in her chair, staring at the small jars of potions. She decided to memorize the labels in case Spicey needed her help. Some were easy. Herbs and roots. Some sounded very strange. All had the same caption: Caution.

Roger and Paul took one of the SUVs and went to the field office. Frank Mass met them in the lobby area. "Uh oh. Trouble follows you two. I just heard you had company for breakfast."

Roger said, "Core identified them as Manio men. I suspect we're getting in their way."

Mass chuckled, "You think? I'm glad you're here. I have to put together a package for the prosecutor on this sicko club. He says all we have on them is disposing of a body. I don't know what you guys have proving they are pedophiles. He's not sure we have legal grounds for the video stuff. Our CSI says those kennels in the barn are pristine. They could make bail on disposing of a body. Especially considering who they are."

Roger's eyebrows went up. "I'm going to involve the Attorney General on this and ask for a special prosecutor. We have a retired Senator and a judge. These boys have deep ties here. I want them charged with everything. Pedophilia, murder, harboring an escaped felon, kidnapping, unlawful imprisonment, disposing of a body, everything. We have a lot more evidence than the videos. I'll pull every thread I see hanging to unravel this bunch. We may even throw in trespassing for Dicky."

Roger walked away to find a private office for his calls, and Paul looked at Frank. "You really think they could get bail?"

Mass watched Roger's demeanor while on the phone in the far office. "Not if he has anything to say about it." Mass started walking toward his office and motioned for Paul to follow. When they were seated, Mass said, "Our field offices are reporting forty-six of the one hundred and thirty two members of this club have died in less than two days. I'm being asked some rather pointed questions about who has Roger's list."

Paul pushed his chin out in his nervous twitch, "I bet you are."

Roger walked into Mass's office about ten minutes later. Roger sat down and said, "Let's get everything we have and send it to the U.S. Attorney General's office. The local prosecutor is being told he does not have this case. Our prisoners will be transported to Federal prison immediately following their arraignment later this morning. There will be no bail."

Mass said, "That was fast."

"Occasionally, things go our way. Frank, I would appreciate it if you could hold a press conference and provide the media with a very small taste of the charges we intend to prosecute."

Mass nodded, "Public trial first."

Roger smiled, "Absolutely."

William C. Thornton sat across from the Director waiting for an answer. He had asked what was new. He was hoping to find out about the drug raid the Coast Guard had made on Lanitol Oil last night. He also needed to get some kind of idea what Dance was up to.

The Director finally just shrugged and said, "I have a ton of emails I haven't read yet today. As far as I know, nothing's new. The martial law period ends tonight. I think we have probably done all we can."

Thornton smiled, "What about Dance taking down the entire Zelez Cartel? We just let him say 'oops'? Or is there some grand plan I haven't heard about?" Thornton was wearing his arrogant sneer.

The Director fought the urge to punch him. "Roger may have overstated what was achievable."

The Director's intercom buzzed, he answered, and a voice said, "Turn on CNN."

The Director raised the remote to his TV, and he and Thornton turned to see Frank Mass in the middle of a press conference. The Director turned up the volume. Mass was detailing the arrest of four local prominent citizens who had been arrested for a yet undefined list of offenses. He gave the full credit of the arrest to the FBI and specifically the team of agents supervised by SSA Roger Dance.

The Director clicked the TV off. "Well, now we know what Roger has been doing. Maybe now he can concentrate on Zelez."

Thornton asked, "What's the plan for the weapons and drugs we have sitting at the Navy yard?"

"What's your idea?" Here it is, the Director thought.

Thornton answered, "Seems Dance is out of his league if he steps outside of pedophiles. I better secure this contraband, or we could end up on the wrong side of a press conference."

The Director nodded. He wanted Thornton to believe he was giving the suggestion serious consideration. "I think it's safe where it is until the martial law expires tonight. Come to me later today with a plan, and we'll talk."

Thornton could hardly contain his glee. "I'll get back to you before five."

CHAPTER
TWENTY FOUR

Abram sat at a long table helping six guys bag up dope so it could be sold. Abram wanted these guys out of the building as soon as possible, so he and Jackson could leave.

Abram told Jackson to send everything he could get from the computer to Roger. Jackson copied the entire file on the Flea Market and sent it to Roger's email address. A surprising amount of detail about the operation was in the file. The accounting history went back four years and included many names and transactions. The file used some kind of code system only known to Manuel. Jackson hoped the FBI could figure it out. The computer at the gang house was an old desktop, with different files than the laptop Roger had copied the night before.

Jackson found and forwarded the email Judge Williams had sent Abram listing the kids to be kidnapped. He knew that was important. He also found an email notifying Manuel that fourteen new people would be arriving today.

Finally Jackson found the file he had hoped to find. He was sure it was the kidnapping lists for the Judge and Senator Kenny going back over several years. He sent that file to Roger too. Jackson was getting sick to his stomach again. That barn.

Abram shouted for the guys in the building to leave. "Your shit be ready. Now get out of here. You supposed to be out selling this crap. You remember the price change, or it come from your pocket." The door to the building slammed shut.

Abram walked over to Jackson. "I'm thinking we got about an hour or two 'fore people start figurin' out we don't know what we be doin'."

Jackson swallowed, "Probably not that long. Daryl plannin' on shootin' them people real soon."

Abram nodded, "You think we just go over an' tell Daryl we decided we gonna do it and take 'em?"

Jackson said, "I got that big new van. After we get 'em, we just call the cops."

Abram nodded his head, "Know what? I ain't never even shot a gun on purpose. Shot my leg one time tryin' to look all bad and shit. Can we look convincin'?"

Jackson stood and dangled the van keys. "Guess we gonna find out." Jackson pulled an amulet from under his shirt. "That Voodoo lady sold me this. Said it was protection."

Abram frowned, "We best stop by there real quick and get me one too."

Tourey placed a call to George Fetter at the Gallery. George answered, "Damn! Have you seen the news? The FBI arrested Theodore!"

Tourey was smiling, "I called to thank you for your help, George."

George's voice was barely a whisper, "I got you that video of the art contest. Am I going to have to testify or anything?"

Tourey answered, "What video?" He could picture George's relief that he wasn't going to have to be involved.

There was a brief silence. George asked, "What are you really? You sure as hell aren't a retired inventor who's going to write a book."

Tourey answered, "Oh, I'll probably write a book someday, and I can be very inventive. Stay cool, George. Be seein' ya around."

Tourey decided to hang around the docks this morning and catch some gossip. The raid on the Lanitol Oil docks last night would be big news.

Roger and Paul were preparing to leave the field office, standing in the lobby, when Roger's phone rang. It was Kim. Roger answered, "Hi. You okay?"

Kim paused before answering, "I have a bruised ego, and I'm embarrassed."

"Are you going to get mad if I tell you I laughed my ass off after the cops called me?"

Kim burst out laughing, "I've been laughing too! Thanks for helping." Kim continued, "Ellen asked me to call and tell you Abram and Jackson sent you an important email."

Roger thanked her for the message, hung up, and told Paul.

"I can pull it up for you on my phone."

"Thanks. How do you figure out these gadgets anyway?"

Paul laughed, "Don't worry about it. It's just not your thing. Here you go. Just scroll down to read more." He handed the phone to Roger.

Roger squinted and frowned. "There are seventeen pages attached. Let me run back in Mass's office and print it off."

Roger went back to Mass's office. Mass leaned back in his chair and watched as Roger started flipping through the pages coming off the printer. Roger looked up and motioned for Paul and Mass to start reading.

Roger finished the last page and asked Mass, "Can you mark this location for me on a map? Paul, can you do that computer thing where we have a live street view from the satellite? We should be able to tap naval satellites right now. We still have them."

Roger placed a call to the U.S. Attorney General, "How would you like an email from Judge Harold Williams to the kidnappers listing the kids' names, where they were to be delivered, and the amount of payment to be made?" There was a brief silence and Roger said, "I'm not kidding. Yes, he was that stupid. Give me your email address and I'll forward it right now."

Mass returned with a map, and Paul had the Navy on the phone honing in on the address. They would have live feed momentarily.

Mass pointed on the map, "One of the worst areas in the city. I don't think local PD goes in. Least not with only one car. Your basic kill zone. Simon and Nelson had that shootout in this neighborhood. The gangs know the people and cars that belong there. When that satellite comes up, check out the surrounding buildings. I bet you will see guards, open drugs, weapons, and not even a hint this was once a residential area." Mass frowned at Roger, "I hope you don't plan to go in this building."

Roger smiled.

"Shit. I should have locked my door when you left my office earlier. I remember thinking to myself, huh, nothing happened."

✳ ✳ ✳

Sasha looked at her watch for the tenth time. Yup, ten minutes had gone by now. She carefully pulled the red curtain back and peeked toward the corner where the table with the crystal ball sat. Spicey had her hands on the ball with her nose practically touching it. Balls of tissue lay on the table and floor, and Spicey's new potion book was open.

Spicey's head stayed where it was, but her eyes rose to meet Sasha's gaze. Spicey pulled her hands from the ball, sat up straight, and rubbed her amulet. She looked at Sasha and said, "I'm figuring this out. Spirits can talk to me normal through this ball. I just listened to this little boy's story."

Spicey pushed her chair back and stood. She looked at her reflection in the mirror and gasped. "Lordy! What have I done to my hair?"

Sasha nodded, "Gotta agree with ya girl. You ain't lookin' real fine right now." Sasha said, "Let me fix your hair, and you tell me the little boy's story."

Spicey and Sasha heard the bells tinkle announcing a customer in the store. Sasha ran out to the front and then poked her head back through the curtain. "You best come out here."

Spicey pulled the curtain back and saw Jackson and Abram standing at the counter. Abram said, "You gotta sell me an amulet like you did Jackson. We doin' what you told Jackson he supposed to do. We be gettin' ready to go save some people, and we need all the help we can get. We need to be fast!"

Spicey looked at Sasha, "Shut off that sign, lock the door, make me some hot water! We be needin' some kind of tea!" Spicey headed behind the curtain, "You two follow me. We need the Spirit's blessin' on this quick."

Abram and Jackson took seats at the little table with the crystal ball, as Spicey thumbed through an old tattered book, mumbling. Suddenly she looked up. "I be new to this part, so I be apologizin' right now case I turn you into toads or somethin'." She looked back down and kept thumbing through the book.

Jackson and Abram looked at each other.

Sasha came in the room with two cups of hot water. Spicey told her to find the toorue root and the black egg powder. Sasha returned in record time and asked, "Now what?"

Spicey flipped to the back of the book and read slowly, "To protect from danger, pinch each, and slap down."

Sasha reached over and pinched both Jackson and Abram and then began slapping them. Spicey's eyes flew open wide, "Girl! Stop it! It mean a pinch of each potion in the hot water. Slap it down means drink it! Lordy."

Jackson had raised his arms to protect himself from Sasha who was now laughing.

"Oh, that be too funny."

Abram looked at his watch, "Hurry, Ms. Spicey."

Spicey put her hands on the ball and asked, "Spirits please help me protect Abram and Jackson on this dangerous mission to save these people."

The ball instantly clouded inside. Abram and Jackson watched as they slapped down their tea and made faces.

Abram shook his head, "This here shit ain't gonna catch on."

Spicey stared into the ball. The face of the Spirit in the white gown let Spicey know Abram and Jackson were protected now.

Spicey looked at them both, "Spirit said you be okay now. Go save them people fast!"

Abram asked, "What we owe ya?"

Spicey answered, "Nothin'. I'm just glad you ain't toads."

* * *

Dusty had trouble manipulating his easel, chair, pad, and box of pencils through the double doors of the French Quarter Bank. Finally, a man was leaving and held the door for him. Dusty looked around the lobby and didn't like the looks of it at all. He was supposed to leave his money with these people? Look at all the fancy shit they spent somebody's money on. What if they wouldn't give him his money back?

Dusty had just about decided to leave when a pretty girl sitting at a desk called over. "Anything I can help you with?" She had a great smile. Dusty saw a chair by her, so he walked over.

Dusty said, "I was thinkin' 'bout openin' a savings account." He leaned his easel and chair against the wall. The pretty girl gestured for him to sit.

"Well, my name is Amy, and that's what I do here. Customer service. Have you had accounts with us in the past?"

Dusty explained he hadn't had a savings account since college. He kept thinking he knew her from somewhere. He was good at faces since that's how he made his living. He suddenly remembered and whispered, "Are you one of the girls that was in the swamp?"

Amy nodded yes.

Dusty said, "I was pushing the boat that brought you back. You probably don't 'member. You were mighty tired."

Amy ran around the desk and gave Dusty a big hug. "You are one of the men that saved us! You're a hero! Thank you, thank you, thank you!"

Dusty smiled and looked around to see who might be watchin' them. "I ain't no hero. I didn't want to be there. The FBI hired me is all."

Amy shook her head, "I don't care why you were there. You're a hero." They talked about ten minutes. Then Amy opened an account for Dusty and explained to him how it all worked. When she was done, she thanked him again.

Dusty offered, "You ever be in Jackson Park I'll do your portrait for ya. You have nice face bones."

Amy smiled.

Outdoors again, Dusty dragged his easel toward the park. Nice face bones? Who says that? Could've said a pretty face. Geesh. At least that would sound like he had a brain in his head. It's no wonder he never had any dates.

Dusty set up his easel under his favorite shade tree, arranged his pad and his box of pencils, and began to sketch Amy's face from memory. He could feel the bank book in his back pocket. It felt kind of good. Proof he had some security in his life. Like he was a real adult or something. If he could do a few extra portraits every day, he could put a little more money in his account every week and see Amy. Dusty smiled. She seemed real nice, and she smiled at him a lot. Nice face bones.

CHAPTER
TWENTY FIVE

At the field office, Roger, Paul, and Mass watched the live satellite feed on the building identified in Jackson's email. Mass was right. The neighborhood was bad. An armed man leaned against the building by a back door. They watched a man walk up to him, give him some money, and walk in.

Paul said, "There went a John."

Mass answered, "Yep."

Paul said, "We have split screen available and we can use the mouse to travel." He glanced at Roger and just went ahead and changed the screen view.

Roger smiled, "You looking to take Ray's job?"

Paul shook his head, "Only you would think that qualifies as geeky."

Paul manipulated the satellite camera to surround the building on two screen views and allow them to search the neighborhood with the other two. Mass wrote down descriptions of the people they were seeing at the building to try to get a count.

A large white van pulled up in front of the building. Two men got out.

Roger pointed, "That's Jackson and Abram." Roger dialed Abram, and he answered. Roger saw him hanging around the front of the van talking on his phone.

"Abram, I have you on satellite. What are you doing there?"

Abram looked to the sky and motioned for Jackson to come over. Roger heard Abram tell Jackson the FBI had a camera on them.

Roger shouted into his phone, "Abram! Shut up!"

Roger watched two men walk out of the building. "You have company walking over. What are you doing?"

The two men were now standing next to Abram. It looked like he nodded at them.

Abram answered, "Yes, sir, Mr. Manio. I be takin' care of them people right now. We be expecting your new ones any time." Abram disconnected the call, and Roger watched him bump fists with the guys from the building.

Paul looked at Mass. "How long to get to that neighborhood?"

Mass answered, "With sirens, twenty minutes in this traffic."

Roger shook his head, "Let's see if these guys can pull this off. They stand a better chance getting these people out alive than we do."

It was like watching a horror movie. Roger wanted the team to know what was happening. He called Ray and had him bring up the satellite on his computer at the Star Ship for the team to watch. Jackson moved the van to the back door. Roger, Paul, and Mass watched as person after person was practically carried from the back door into the van. Paul counted fourteen people.

Abram and Jackson bumped fists with the man at the back door and got in the van. They pulled away from the building and headed down the road.

Roger called Abram back, "I can't believe you guys just did that!"

Abram was shouting, "We're scared shitless! No goin' back to the hood after this. Should we take these people to the hospital? They don't look so good."

Roger answered, "Yes. We have troopers on their way to escort you. How many men are in that building now?"

Abram and Jackson had some discussion about that. Abram finally answered, "I saw six, but Jackson said one of the guys said they be expecting a drug delivery from Manio. They usually send three guys. It's not just that building though, whole neighborhood crawlin'."

Roger instructed Abram to come back to the field office when they were done at the hospital. He wanted them to fill out a witness statement. He also wanted to know what they needed for their security.

Abram saw the flashing lights of cop cars in his rearview mirror. One state trooper car passed him and continued just in front of him clearing traffic with his lights and siren. Abram saw at least three more cop cars pull in behind them.

Abram looked at Jackson, "This be the first time I saw a lit up cop car from the back."

Jackson watched the police cars behind them through the side mirror and said, "It's just hittin' me what we did, man." He looked at Abram, "We did the right thing. Some kid just told me, right decision always be the hard one." Jackson frowned at Abram, "You didn't take no money, did ya?"

Abram exhaled loudly, "Can't claim I didn't think 'bout it, but the answer be no."

Now two patrol cars cruised in front of them, and three in the back. They turned into the hospital trauma entrance where a sea of people in blue scrubs waited for them. The minute the van stopped, the back doors were popped open, people were put on gurneys, and then were wheeled through the large double doors.

Abram and Jackson got out of the van. A state trooper came over to them and put his hand out. "I would like to shake your hands and thank you for what you have done. That took some real courage."

Jackson could feel his chest swell with pride. He looked at Abram who casually swiped a tear from his cheek.

The trooper said, "I'll be giving you an escort back to the FBI office when you're ready."

Abram studied the trooper's face. Suddenly his eyes opened wide, "I think I know you."

The trooper smiled, "Yeah you do. We'll be forgettin' all that."

＊ ＊ ＊

Roger said, "We need to secure that building for evidence. National Guard still has jeeps in the area. Let's have them patrol the neighborhood, so we only have to worry about this building."

Paul was holding the email from Abram, "The main guy at this place is Daryl Cotton. I'll pull the mug shot."

Roger dialed Thor, "You guys want to come here to the field office and suit up? I have the Guard handling the neighborhood. I'd like to secure this building before any more of them show up for work."

Thor hung up from his call with Roger and everyone was staring at him. He almost laughed at their eager faces. This team just never stopped. "Yes, we're taking over this building. Got to suit up."

Pablo stood up from the couch. Thor frowned at him, "Don't even think about it."

Pablo smiled, "I was going to the head." He lifted his sling, "I don't expect I could do much more than hold the door open for you." Everyone laughed.

Jeanne was already on the stairs and looked back smiling, "Did Roger mean today?"

Thor shook his head. Did she have to be first at everything?

Daryl sent two of the new guys into the holding room to hose down the floors into the center drain and check that all the beds had working handcuffs and not too many bugs. Nobody liked that job, but it had to be done. If people got too sick to perform, it cost Manio money.

Daryl dialed the number he had for the driver bringing the new shipment of people from Baton Rouge. No answer. He dialed again. No answer. He wanted an estimated time of arrival, so he could plan his day.

Daryl dialed Chiclet, "Hey man. Check that number you gave me for the prostitute delivery. My number must be wrong. There ain't no answer."

Chiclet repeated the number, and it was the same. They didn't know the U.S. Marshals had located the vehicle, done a felony stop, and were loading the people into ambulances about an hour outside of town. The driver was in police custody.

Daryl exhaled, "I guess I wait then. Abram took the old ones, so we're 'bout ready."

Chiclet was surprised, "Abram took the old ones? That don't sound right."

He hung up and dialed Abram's number. No answer. Chiclet shrugged. Seems nobody wantin' to talk to nobody. Make no difference to him no how. It be lunch time.

Carol and Cindy stood outside Spicey's Voodoo shop. The sign out front said 'Closed'. Cindy peeked in the big picture window, "Lots of really cool stuff in here."

Carol pressed her nose against the glass. It was tricky getting in close because her fake boobs were in the way. "Don't see anybody inside. Dang it." She leaned back and said, "That park we wanted to see is just a few blocks down. Jackson Park."

Cindy asked, "Is that the one with the statue of the guy on a horse?"

Carol nodded as she adjusted her big fake boobs. "The brochure said local artists and musicians hang out there. Sounds good to me. If it keeps getting hotter out here, these boobs might have to go. At least one of 'em."

They walked to the park looking in every storefront along the way. Voodoo shops everywhere. Carol said, "Man. Spicey's got some competition here. Must be everybody in New Orleans has a Voodoo shop."

They made it to the park and found some musicians with a pet monkey holding a tip hat. At first it was cute the way the little monkey would grab Carol's hand and try to take her purse. Cindy knew the time would come when it would be an out and out war over the purse between the monkey and Carol. Cindy talked Carol into walking away just as it started getting nasty. Carol and the monkey were sticking their tongues out at each other. They walked the length of the iron fence. A portrait artist sat at an easel drawing. They walked behind him to see what he was drawing.

Cindy asked, "Who is that woman you're drawing? She's beautiful."

Dusty smiled, "I just met her. Only know her first name is Amy." He smiled again.

Carol rubbed her big boobs against the back of his shoulders and said, "He's in love!"

Dusty leaned forward, shook his shoulders, and laughed. "My name's Dusty. You gals visitin' Nawlens for long?"

Cindy answered, "Five days. We're from Michigan, but we have a friend who owns a Voodoo shop here. We're just waitin' on her to open."

Dusty asked, "What's your friend's name? Might be I know her."

Carol and Cindy answered in unison, "Spicey."

Dusty's eyes opened wide, "I know her! Took her and her little friend out to see Mambo yesterday. I heard she was back out there last night for some kind of Spirit meetin'. Hope she made it back okay. Place scared the piss out of me last night, and I was with the FBI. We found a dead guy and arrested a bunch of guys 'bout that same time. There be gunshots out there too last night!"

Carol asked, "Who's Mambo?"

Dusty crooked his index finger at them. Carol and Cindy leaned in close. Dusty whispered, "Mambo is the Voodoo Queen. She's like three hundred years old or somethin'. Lives in a creepy hut on the back end of Honey Island, smack dab in the middle of the swamp. Spooky blue lights all 'round her place. Little blue flames poofin' out of the water. Eyeballs be lookin' at ya from every bush. Mean soundin' noises *everywhere*. Little skulls hangin' from the trees." Dusty shuddered.

Cindy and Carol were frozen with their mouths open.

Cindy asked, "You sure we talkin' about the same Spicey?"

Dusty described her and added, "She got this little friend named Sasha who works with her too."

Carol yelled, "She told me about Sasha!" Carol looked at Cindy, "What if she didn't make it home last night, and she's lost in the swamp?"

Cindy straightened up, "Then I would say she has a problem. Don't even think you're getting me to go in the swamp."

Dusty said, "I got a friend was out there last night told me about her there. You want I call and see if he knows she got back?"

Carol and Cindy nodded and watched as Dusty dialed Alan, "Hey, did that Spicey Voodoo lady leave okay last night? Couple friends of hers worried 'cause she not open yet." Dusty listened a while and said, "Thanks man."

Dusty said, "Alan said they left before he did, and he didn't see 'em anywhere. They probably got back okay. They were with Willie. He knows the swamp good."

Carol looked at Cindy, "How 'bout we have Dusty do our picture then go back to Spicey's?" Carol looked at Dusty, "How much do you charge for a picture of us together?"

Dusty answered, "It'll be less if I don't have to draw them boobs."

Carol reached in and took her boobs out. "Now how much?"

Dusty told them twenty dollars each. Carol and Cindy sat on the rock wall next to the sidewalk and Dusty guarded Carol's boobs under his easel. She told him her money was hidden in there. When he finished, they squealed with delight.

Cindy clapped her hands, "This is terrific! You are really good," Dusty beamed. Carol put her boobs back in her dress. Cindy asked, "Where should we eat lunch? There are a million places to choose from, but we want to make our money last."

Dusty stood and pointed, "You see that place with the blue siding way down there? Got good food, and the price is right. Looks like a dive but decent inside. Fact, went there with Spicey and Sasha couple days ago. Don't you walk past there though. Neighborhood gets real bad, mighty fast."

Cindy and Carol waved goodbye and made their way to the diner. As they passed the musicians again, the monkey stuck his tongue out and screeched at them. Carol mimicked the monkey right back.

Cindy shook her head, "You already pissed off a monkey and scared a cyclist half to death on our first day." They both laughed. This would be a vacation to remember.

Ellen sent us all a message on our watches to go to Spicey's shop for a surprise. Personally, I have seldom been happy with surprises. My life usually required time to prepare. Just sayin'. Teresa, Linda, and Mary were hanging outside on the sidewalk watching the tourists go by, and waiting for the Voodoo shop's sign to say open.

Linda said, "Bob and the boys finally finished putting the new floor down in my living room. It looks fantastic." She smiled, "It was nice just being around them for a while. They seem to be doing okay. Bob moved our favorite picture over to the nightstand." Linda brushed a tear. "Still having some mortal feelings makes these home visits touchy."

Teresa was nodding, "I visited every single one of my relatives. I thought the same thing when I was with Mom. I know she is missing me a lot, and I wish I could let her know I'm okay." Teresa smiled, "Actually, I did. I left her a note."

Mary added, "I did that, too. I left a note saying I'm fine on the refrigerator at my sister's house."

Linda looked at me, "How's Kim?"

I just started laughing, "She got arrested for talking to herself, but she's okay now." I knew I was the lucky one. Since Ellen chose to use Kim to communicate with angels, I get to talk to her all the time, and she can see us.

Teresa asked, "I wonder what the surprise is?"

Linda pointed, "I don't believe it! Look who's walking this way!"

Walking toward us were Carol and Cindy from our favorite bar in Niles, Michigan. The four of us met at the bar before we left for the airport and ended up in our fatal accident. Carol and Cindy arranged the wake for us at the bar, too.

Teresa was laughing, "Look at the getup Carol has on!"

Mary said, "That's her old lady outfit minus the wig."

Linda laughed, "It must be hot 'cause she's carrying her boobs. I bet they are on vacation and coming here to see Sadie."

I cleared my throat, "You mean Spicey."

Carol and Cindy walked up to the door and rattled it. "Dang! Still closed."

Spicey poked her head from behind the curtain and let out a squeal. She ran to the door and unlocked it. Sasha followed and squealed too, even though she didn't know what was going on.

Spicey was jumping up and down, "I can't believe you guys are here! Wait 'til you hear what's goin' on!"

Ellen sent us all a signal and address on our watches with a 911 tag. EEKS. Never got that before. Teresa took the lead, and we ended up at a building about six blocks from Spicey's. We saw Roger and his team arriving.

Roger, Paul, and Frank rode in one SUV. Thor, Jeanne, Simon, and Nelson rode in another. Roger confirmed the National Guard was posted at the end of each street, in the neighborhood, and visible.

Roger gave Thor's team the signal to go in the back. Roger, Paul and Frank went in the front. Roger was the first in the building and yelled, "FBI. Freeze." Daryl Cotton was sitting at a table and reached for his gun. Roger shot Daryl's hand. He needed Daryl taken alive. Roger yelled,

"Freeze" again. Roger removed Daryl's gun from the table as Daryl cradled his hand to his chest and screamed.

The men in the building had no intentions of just surrendering to the FBI. The way they saw it, they had the home base advantage and superior gun power. Bullets began flying everywhere. Suddenly Ellen froze time on everyone but Roger and Paul.

Roger's phone rang.

Paul was panting and looked over, "You're kidding me?"

Roger answered as he looked at the surreal scene. Kim's voice said, "Ellen said to take their weapons and force their arms up in the air. You can't remove the bullets that are in the air but you can move the people to get them out of the way. She says you have to be fast. She can't hold this freeze long. She is going to zap their memories and interrupt the satellite before she is done. Mom, Teresa, Linda and Mary are there helping too. Don't forget the guys that are outside."

Roger yelled Ellen's message to Paul as they disarmed the frozen men and threw the weapons in a pile. Moving their arms was difficult. They moved like robots. In all, ten men were in the building, two outside the front door coming in armed, and three coming toward the back door. Roger and Paul followed the bullet trajectories and moved people the best they could.

Paul went out the front door and Roger ran to the back. We helped take weapons and moved people's arms up. Paul kept jumping as the frozen men somehow robotically moved their arms. Paul yelled to Roger, "This is beyond weird. I think we have helpers."

Ray watched the satellite feed at the Star Ship. He took a big bite of an apple and stopped chewing. "Pablo, look at this. What the heck is going on?"

Pablo walked over to see the four split screens. Everyone but Paul and Roger appeared to be frozen. Roger and Paul took weapons and raised the arms of the suspects. Pablo looked at Ray, "What the heck? These guys look like they're frozen or something. I would say the feed is frozen but Roger and Paul are still moving. They are taking weapons."

Ray pointed to another screen where Simon, Nelson, and Jeanne were in assault stance in the back of the building, and three men stood frozen with their weapons aimed directly at them. They watched Roger come out the back door, disarm the men, and raise their hands. Roger ran back into the building. The satellite feed went dead.

Ray and Pablo looked at each other and didn't speak. Ray pushed his chair from the computer and spit out his apple into his hand and threw it in the basket. He looked at Pablo, "Tell me what you think you saw."

The freeze ended and Paul and Mass instructed the remaining six men to stand against the wall. Paul cuffed them as Mass held them at gunpoint. Nelson came through from the back and walked over to help pat down the men against the wall.

Thor and Jeanne led three cuffed men from the back into the main room. Simon had stayed in the back to guard that door.

Thor caught a glimpse of a man through the window. He had a weapon, and he was focused on Jeanne.

Thor yelled, "Look out!" He leaped to his right pushing Jeanne to the floor as the man's gun went off. Roger turned and shot the man at the same instant Nelson and Paul shot him. Roger looked over to where Thor lay motionless on the concrete floor. His heart sank. Jeanne crawled over to Thor and lifted his head. Her heart was pounding.

Thor's eyes opened tiny slits. "Son of a bitch. That hurt."

Roger couldn't believe his eyes when Thor began to sit up. Thor reached in his shirt and pulled out the amulet hanging from a leather strap around his neck. The bullet was crushed and imbedded in the center of the amulet.

Roger looked at the amulet and looked at Thor. "I can't believe this. You're okay?"

Thor opened his shirt and showed them the bullet never even hit his vest. The amulet stopped it completely. Thor stood and looked at Jeanne. "You alright? Sorry about that." Jeanne nodded and turned away. She walked to the back to help Simon guard the back door until the local PD came to take the men. Slowly her heart rate returned to normal. She took a few deep breaths. The vision of Thor lying motionless on the concrete floor was etched in her mind.

Simon asked, "What happened in there?"

Jeanne shook her head, "Guy took a shot at me, Thor pushed me and took it in the chest. His amulet stopped the bullet."

Simon whistled, "Gotta get me one of them."

Ellen had us do memory gaps on everyone but Roger and Paul. She told us to get over to the Star Ship and place memory gaps on Pablo and Ray. We would have to zap them each multiple times. They had way more than three thoughts that had to disappear.

At the naval satellite computer control center an officer turned from his screen and asked, "Was anyone besides me watching that New Orleans feed just now?" Everyone shook their heads, and the officer turned back to his screen. He had thought at first the satellite feed had frozen. Then he saw a man walking around disarming other men and putting their hands up. It looked as if everyone outside of the building had frozen in place except one man in the front of the building and one in the back. Then suddenly everyone in the picture was moving. The satellite feed went dead. Moments later the feed had been restored. He watched as a parade of handcuffed men were led to waiting patrol cars. He rubbed his face. He knew what he saw.

Nine months until retirement. He wasn't going to say shit.

✳ ✳ ✳

CHAPTER
TWENTY SIX

William C. Thornton placed a call to Fenley.

Thomas Fenley answered on the second ring. "Yes?"

Thornton scowled. Fenley always sounded so abrupt. "The Director has asked me to come to him later today with a plan for transporting the confiscated drugs and weapons to secured storage. That gives us Texas or Kansas. He is finally seeing Dance as the screw up he is. If you contact Manio for a suggestion, we might be able to make up for some of this mess."

Fenley slammed his palm against his steering wheel. This better be a secure line since Thornton just tied him to Manio and the guns. Thornton was getting way too sloppy. It was going to cost them all. Fenley decided when this New Orleans mess was over a decision would have to be made about Thornton. The risks to LUCY clearly outweighed the benefits.

Fenley answered, "You must have dialed wrong. I have no idea what you are talking about or who you are." Fenley hung up.

Thornton's neck and face became red as he sat looking at his silent phone. Fenley was too paranoid; he was becoming impossible to deal with. Thornton vowed when this New Orleans crap with Dance finally gets done, he was going to have to talk to Donavan. It seems Fenley needs to be reminded who has official standing and who doesn't. LUCY could always find another Fenley type.

Two OSI agents removed their headphones and fist bumped each other. They couldn't have scripted a more damaging message than the one Thornton just gave Fenley. The Director of OSI had instructed them to forward all communications to the Director of the FBI as soon as they came in. Which they did.

The Director of the FBI listened to the call on his computer and smiled. Roger had said that Thornton would risk everything to stay in the good graces of LUCY. Thornton was asking for Manio to design the plan that Thornton would present to the Director later today as his own. Arrogance of power. That was the phrase Roger said they could count on.

The Director hit play on his computer and listened to the snare drums begin their march in

Bolero. This was quickly becoming his favorite classical piece.

Fenley pulled his BMW over and gathered his thoughts. He couldn't undo that call from Thornton. He might as well try to salvage what he could with Manio. Fenley opened his phone and dialed.

Manio answered, "Yes?"

Fenley didn't like Manio's soft spoken demeanor. Everyone knew what he really was, a ruthless, cold-blooded lunatic. Fenley said, "I have been told that the Director of the FBI is looking for an alternative plan for moving the confiscated drugs and guns from New Orleans to either Texas or Kansas underground storage. This plan needs to be presented later this afternoon and your input is being invited."

Manio set his cat down gently on the floor before he stood and answered, "Are you telling me that Mr. Dance's plan to move these by train on Monday is being circumvented by his own boss?"

Fenley chuckled, "Dance is proving to be a colossal screw up. His career won't survive the mess at French Quarter Bank. I'm told the Director is willing to consider an alternative, more secure plan to minimize the risk of anything more going wrong in New Orleans."

Manio paused, "You mention the bank again. Do those transactions still appear safe?"

Fenley answered, "Donavan says that forty trillion dollars will have been scrubbed by the time the Federal Reserve closes today. When the Reserve opens again on Monday, more than half of our cash assets are invisible. You have taken advantage of this, haven't you?"

Manio cleared his throat, "Donavan's confidence level is impressive. Forty trillion dollars represents a substantial amount of faith."

Fenley noted that Manio had not answered his question. "Call me if you decide to offer a suggestion regarding a new plan. I will see that it gets to the right ears." Their call ended, and Manio walked to his window at the Casino. He had come to New Orleans to see for himself what Roger Dance was spending his time on.

The news reports on the television and newspaper indicated that the FBI team led by Roger Dance had been preoccupied with some national pedophile club. Mr. Dance may have overextended himself. After all, he was only human.

Manio called his financial man and instructed him to move over twenty billion dollars to French Quarter Bank immediately. While that was a lot of money, it represented only a fraction of his worth. His advisor assured him the transaction would clear within the hour.

Manio sat at his desk and began tapping his pen. Now to form a plan for the guns. Manio's cat jumped back on his lap and Manio stroked its fur lovingly. "Perhaps Mr. Dance is a fool. Pity. I had hopes of a worthy opponent."

Roger and the team arrived at the field office to return the assault gear and have a quick briefing. Roger found a vacant office and called the Baton Rouge agents that had intercepted the delivery of new victims for the human trafficking ring. The driver of the vehicle and a man helping him were in interrogation now. The people that had been saved were identified and that list was being forwarded to Roger. In general, they were in good health, but all complained of being injected with drugs for several days.

Roger hung up from the call and checked on the condition of the people Jackson and Abram had taken to the hospital. They were not as lucky. Many were in deplorable physical condition and some near death. Most had yet to be identified.

Paul walked in with two cups of coffee and sat across from Roger. Paul slid one coffee over to Roger. Neither spoke. Roger passed the papers over to Paul with the information he had just received. Paul read them, sipped his coffee, and placed his mug on the desk. "We will never stop all of this. I don't know what would stop all of this." Paul rubbed his hair and grunted, "Ughhhh."

Roger nodded.

"Don't say it."

Roger smiled, "Don't say what?"

"We're not done yet." Paul pushed his chin out in his nervous twitch. "Well, today is Friday. Last of the martial law and the money sting ends today. When do our LUCY guys find out they've been had?"

Roger's eyebrows twitched, "Monday morning when the Fed opens unless we tell them sooner."

Roger's phone rang, it was Core. "Yes."

"Zack and I are at the docks. Word is Manio is in town and staying at the Casino. He likes to gamble, but word is he's brought his best people to town to clean things up. Heads up, you're part of the dirt needin' cleanin'. At least two of Manio's men involved in the dock raid last night are dead. Manio feels they failed him."

Roger asked Core, "When Manio comes to the Casino, how does he travel?"

Core answered, "The Casino has a private helipad for Manio on the roof. They wouldn't tell you that, but it is the one that is always roped off as being under repair."

Roger thanked Core for the update and looked at Paul, "Manio's in town. He's staying at the Casino. Core says he's brought some trusted men with him. Core thinks he's here for some hands on management and trash removal. We're part of the trash." Roger smiled.

"Cute."

"Let's line up our ducks on Manio. If he is in town, this is an opportunity I don't want to miss. You interview Daryl Cotton as soon as the hospital is done with him and I'll see if we have enough from Abram's files to get us an arrest warrant on Manio for trafficking. The Baton Rouge field office may be able to apply some leverage with the driver they are interrogating to tie this even tighter. This guy was caught driving fourteen people that had been kidnapped and drugged for the purpose of prostitution. He might talk to make a deal. Men like Manio may be clever, but they are forced to use common thugs to do their dirty work. I think if we play this right we can go after him under RICO."

Paul stood to leave and then said, "Mass mentioned earlier he was getting some pointed questions from the other field offices on our sicko club list. Seems the sickos are dropping like flies. It's raising some eyebrows."

Roger stretched back in his chair, "What are we up to?"

"Forty six dead out of a total of one hundred thirty two." Paul looked at his watch, "In exactly twenty four hours. Three cities."

Three cities made sense. They suspected three hit men were hired by Core.

Roger stood, "Nobody has come to me directly on this yet. Should we have the remaining members warned? It may be interesting to see how many are willing to trade acknowledgment that they are in a sicko club for protection."

Paul shook his head, "They'd rather die than admit that. Did you see some of the names on that list?"

Roger nodded, "At least we can say we warned them. We certainly don't have the manpower to afford them any security. We have a legal obligation to warn them even if we only have suspicions they may be in danger."

Paul smiled. "I'll give the order for the notifications."

Lockers were slamming in the back room at the field office as everyone replaced their vests and gear in the proper storage units. Simon and Nelson had mentioned they were starving and heading for Mickey's. Simon looked across the room to where Thor and Jeanne were. Jeanne was looking at her phone and Thor started walking over.

Thor said, "I could eat some lunch." He looked back at Jeanne, "You coming?"

Jeanne shook her head, "I missed a call from Spicey. I'm just going to go over there."

Thor asked, "That Voodoo lady at the swamp last night?"

Jeanne nodded and walked up close to Thor, "You saved my life back there. Saying thank you doesn't seem to cover it." Jeanne stood on her toes and kissed Thor's cheek. Her eyes were glistening, and she whispered, "Thank you." Jeanne left the room. Thor's cheek was warm from her lips. He realized he was holding his breath. He felt as if he had been shot again.

Simon walked over, "Let me see that amulet thing again. You're one lucky bastard." Simon raised his eyebrows a couple of times.

Thor knew he wasn't referring to the amulet.

Now that the bad guys had been caught, Ellen told us we could go back and visit Carol and Cindy. Ellen pointed her finger at us, "Behave!" Then she disappeared. Recess! We flew into Spicey's shop so fast I got tangled in the tinkle bells at the door. Teresa frowned at me and went "Shhhhh." Like I did it on purpose?

Cindy, Carol, Sasha and Spicey were all talking at the same time standing around the counter. Spicey was telling Carol and Cindy about how the real Spirits were talking to her now. Sasha was telling them about being in the swamp last night at Mambo's. Carol and Cindy told them what Dusty had said about a dead guy, the FBI and a bunch of bad guys in the swamp. Finally Spicey asked, "So what else is new with you guys?"

Carol and Cindy looked at each other and Carol answered, "Not too much I guess."

I got an idea.

Teresa looked at me and smiled. "You better ask Linda and Mary first."

Linda asked, "Ask us what?" Mary had that look of suspicion on her face.

"I want Kim to call Carol and tell her we are here!"

Mary frowned, "We can do that?"

This is going to be easy. "Sure."

Mary tilted her head, "Let me rephrase. Are we supposed to do that?" That's the question I didn't want to hear.

Teresa saved me. "They gave us the ability to communicate. Why would they do that and not let us use it?" Silence. I was sure one of these skeptics would say something. Nope. Alright then!

Carols phone rang, "Hello?"

Kim said, "Hey Carol. This is Kim. Vicki's daughter."

Carol got a big smile and punched Cindy. "It's Kim! What's up, girl? Guess what? Cindy and I are in *Naaaawlens*! We're standing here with Sadie right now. I mean Spicey." Carol shrugged as she glanced at Spicey.

Kim said, "I figured that out. I want you to listen carefully. Mom, Teresa, Linda and Mary are there with you now. They are angels, sort of. They want to visit with you and Cindy but they have rules they can't break. They can only talk to humans through me. I feel like I should apologize to you and Cindy. Well, you know Mom. Mom says when their boss tells them to leave, you might not remember this happened."

Carol was listening to Kim and looking around. "I don't see them."

Sasha had been listening and started looking around. "See who?"

That's our cue! I grabbed Spicey's ouija board from the shelf and laid it on the counter.

Sasha fainted.

I looked at Mary, "You're going to have to do this. You spell the best and these things creep me out."

Mary laughed, "It creeps you out that Spirits might really use ouija boards? Really? What are we?"

Hmmm, when she put it that way. I grabbed the little wooden pointer on the board and spelled 'Hi'.

Carol looked at Spicey her mouth open, "Did you do that?"

Spicey shook her head.

Carol looked at Cindy, "It's just the gals! Ask 'em something."

Cindy looked out into the room, "Do you like being angels?"

Mary moved the pointer to yes. Sasha fainted again.

Carol said, "We have to find another way to do this, Sasha isn't going to make it."

Spicey said, "Don't expect me to have any answers. Maybe they can talk through the crystal ball!"

Teresa looked at Linda, "Can we do that?"

Linda answered, "Well, remember the Spirits can understand us now, and the crystal ball is how they communicate. We could try."

Mary used the ouija board to say we would try. Spicey, Sasha , Cindy and Carol all huddled around the ball. Spicey asked, "Can Cindy and Carol's friends hear me?"

Spicey's eyes got wide as all four of us crammed together so we could talk to her. She understood us and relayed messages back and forth until Ellen called us to join her. We had to say goodbye.

After we had left, Spicey said, "Well, that's one Nawlens experience you won't forget. I think I have an idea for another one."

Cindy and Carol both said "oooo." At the same time. The tinkle bells at the front of the shop were ringing. Sasha walked out to take care of the customer and walked back after a few minutes.

"That FBI woman is here. Said you called her."

Spicey looked at Carol and Cindy, "I don't want to make you mad but I need to talk to her alone. Can you come back in about an hour?"

Carol and Cindy said no problem and left through the apartment door.

Spicey walked out to the front where Jeanne was waiting.

"You called me?" Jeanne had taken a small notebook and pen from her pocket.

Spicey leaned forward and whispered, "Please believe me. A young boy spirit has come to me and given me information. He wants to go home."

Jeanne nodded, "How did he come to you?"

Spicey answered. "Last night at Mambo's, the Spirits told me they needed me to communicate information for them. Today, I saw the little boy spirit in my crystal ball." Even Spicey worried this sounded crazy. Here she was telling this to an FBI agent. Sasha was rocking on her heels, obviously very nervous.

Sasha blurted, "Spicey ain't no fake. Well, not anymore. Weird stuff been happenin' for two days." Sasha was nodding.

Jeanne looked at Spicey, "Tell me everything the little boy told you."

Spicey asked, "Can we go in the back and sit for this? I think my knees be a little weak today."

Jeanne and Spicey sat at her small dinette table as Spicey told the little boy's story. His name was Michael Summers. He was six years old and had lived in Cleveland, Ohio. Last year he had been abducted from a children's birthday party at a restaurant. His abductor had given him some kind of drug. When he woke, he was at a strange man's house.

The boy said an angel had come and stayed with him the whole time he was at the man's house. The angel kept putting his mind to sleep and singing him little songs. After he was dead the angel told him the man's name and showed him where the man had hidden his Winnie the Pooh sweater.

The angel told the boy that someday another angel would come and take him home.

Spicey said the little boy wants his remains sent to his mom so she can stop crying. And he wants the bad man to be punished so he can't hurt anyone else. Spicey finished the story and realized she was crying.

Jeanne wiped a tear from her cheek also. "What was the man's name?"

Spicey tried to control her anger but she was shaking and her voice was laced with disgust. "Senator Rolland Kenny. Michael's sweater is in a secret closet behind the Senator's bookcase at his city house. Michael told me his bones had been taken from the swamp by the FBI, and that is why he has the courage now to tell his story. He said an angel told him at Mambo's she would take him home soon."

Jeanne closed her notebook. "Spicey, I believe you have been chosen to help the Spirits. I will take this information and make sure Michael returns home." Jeanne stood. "You have a great responsibility now."

Spicey nodded. She felt a strange bond with Jeanne. "Will the Spirits keep talking to me, or was I only supposed to help Michael?"

Jeanne smiled, "Only the Spirits can answer that."

Sasha had been listening and asked, "What if you just be a 'friend' of a chosen person?"

Jeanne chuckled, "I'd say you are a very special friend. You have been allowed to witness." The three of them started walking back to the store front. Jeanne noticed the small table with the crystal ball.

"Would you mind giving me a moment alone with your crystal ball? I'm curious about something."

Spicey shrugged, "Sure. We'll just wait in the other room."

Jeanne waited until they had left the room. She sat at the table and stared at the ball. This was something she had always wanted to do, but had been afraid to try. She placed her palms around it and felt a tingling on the surface of the glass. It felt very warm. Jeanne concentrated on blocking out everything around her. Mambo had said she would soon understand her destiny. Jeanne stared in the ball and asked the Spirits to explain.

At first she saw nothing. Maybe the questions she had would remain unanswered. Suddenly, tiny images formed in the center of the ball and began to tell a story. Her mind flooded with a wave of images and hundreds of soft voices. She had been transported to another world, another dimension. It felt familiar and real.

In the storefront room, Spicey and Sasha stared at the red velvet curtain covering the doorway. They watched as a dim blue light peeked from behind the folds of the curtain and grew in intensity. A gust of wind rushed from the backroom, forcing the curtain to wave, as if a blast had occurred. The smaller items on the shelves vibrated and tumbled to the floor. The tinkle bells at both doors rang as if caught in a hurricane. Then silence.

Jeanne walked out from the backroom, thanked Spicey and Sasha, and left.

Sasha and Spicey stood motionless and watched her walk out the front door.

Spicey looked at Sasha, "Damn."

Jeanne sat outside in the car and wept. She now understood why she was so driven, and had always felt as if she didn't fit. Her soul finally belonged to her now. She felt a peace and a strength that comes from understanding yourself. Jeanne composed herself and rubbed her amulet as she gave thanks. She wiped the tears from her face, put the car in gear, and dialed Roger. Michael needed to go home. She was going to get him there.

Roger looked at his watch and then to Paul. "If I hurry I can make the arraignment." The arraignment would be the first time Senator

Kenny, Judge Williams, Theodore Chain and Andre Baton would hear the charges they were facing. Roger had arranged for the U.S. Attorney General's office to take the case and appoint a special prosecutor. The trials would take months if not years, but today he would see their faces.

Roger said, "I want to be there. I want to represent those kids and their families."

CHAPTER
TWENTY SEVEN

Roger leaned against the wall of the large marble hall of the courthouse. He stood off in a corner to stay away from the press people that flooded the entire rotunda. The noise was deafening. Mass's press conference had been like giving a starving man a sniff of fried chicken, and telling him dinner was in an hour.

The presiding judge for the arraignment had just been given the amended list of charges for the case. The judge paced in his chambers. These were four of New Orleans most prestigious citizens. He was friends with Judge Williams and Senator Kenny. Kennels? My God, what kind of monsters were they? The judge looked at the filing papers of the U.S. Attorney General's office. This was serious shit. He noticed they had appointed a special prosecutor and flipped the page to read the name. Holy crap!

The U.S. Attorney General's office had sent their best litigator. His nickname was "Catahoula". A reference to a dog breed, a Louisiana leopard dog. The Catahoula was known for fierce fighting abilities, ice blue eyes and cunning attack skills. Roger watched Catahoula walk toward him as he gave last minute instructions to Jeanne on searching Senator Kenny's city home.

Catahoula walked up close to Roger and nodded, "Where's the bow? This little present you gave us has everything but the bow." Catahoula snickered.

Roger answered, "I think we are getting that for you right now. A confidential informant has given us the name of a murdered child, whose remains we found in the swamp a few days ago. A secret closet at Senator Kenny's house should reveal a Winnie the Pooh sweater with the little boy's DNA. My team is going there now."

Catahoula shook his head, "How do you do it? I have bank transfers linking these guys to William Patterson. I have them disposing of his body on film! I have a country house with a barn full of kiddie kennels. I have a national pedophile club I can tie them all to. I have recent kidnapping victims that can testify and kidnappers willing to turn state's evidence."

Roger smiled, "Don't forget the trespassing charges."

The bailiff walked out the double doors and motioned the judge was ready for their case.

Catahoula glanced at Roger, "Why don't you sit at our table on this. You'll get a better view."

The courtroom was packed. To the surprise of everyone, the judge allowed as many press in the room as could fit. Roger knew that was a bad sign for the defense. About five minutes passed and a far door to the courtroom opened and retired Senator Rolland Kenny, Judge Harold Williams, Andre Baton and Theodore Chain walked single file to the defendants' table. They were dressed in the same clothes they had on in the swamp the night before. All four actually turned to the press and smiled as the cameras flashed.

Rolland was actually telling a reporter it was all a silly mistake. Everything would be fine, just wait. Roger watched their body language. For the circumstances, they appeared confident and relaxed. Andre kept smoothing his hair and Judge Williams was in quiet conversation with their attorney.

Catahoula leaned over and whispered to Roger, "Watch this. They haven't seen the charges yet. They're trying to figure out who I am." Catahoula had a fist full of briefs in his hand. He walked over to the defense attorney, whispered in his ear and greeted the defendants with a smile, and, "Gentlemen." He walked back over and took his seat next to Roger.

The arraignment Judge entered the courtroom from his chambers and the bailiff called out "All rise."

Roger whispered to Catahoula, "What did you say to the defense attorney?"

"Run."

Roger glanced over at the defense table and saw they were in a tight huddle. The judge banged his gavel and brought the courtroom to silence. You could hear the sounds of the traffic outside bleeding through the courtroom window glass.

The judge openly scowled at the defendants. "Are we ready for the reading of charges?"

Catahoula walked to a podium that faced the judge. "The United States of America, represented by the United States Attorney General's office, hereby charge multiple infractions of each charge of murder, kidnapping, sexual assault on a minor, illegal disposition of a body,….."

The rumble in the room erupted to a roar from gasps, the clicking of cameras and shouts from the press. Any other arraignment, the judge would have cleared the court. The judge allowed the outbreaks to continue and motioned for Catahoula to raise his voice. Catahoula not only raised his voice, he walked to stand within three feet of the shocked defendants and started reading the charges from the beginning. He articulated each charge a little louder than the last.

When Catahoula finished reading the charges, all four men at the defendants' table looked sick. The judge banged his gavel again to bring order. The cameras kept clicking as Andre dropped his head on the table. The defense attorney had neatly stacked the papers Catahoula had given him and slid them over to Rolland.

Catahoula reached the podium again and turned back to the defendant's table. "My apologies to the Court, I forgot to read the last charge. Trespassing." He glanced at Roger and smiled.

The Judge banged his gavel once and asked, "Do the defendants wish to plead?"

The defense attorney stood, "The defendants plead not guilty your honor. We would request the court grant bail…"

The Judge banged his gavel again. "Thank God I'm retiring next month. Bail denied." The Judge rose from his seat and turned toward the door to his chambers. He was clearly heard when he said, "May you all rot in hell."

There were a lot of people in Jackson Park. When the weather was nice people would picnic there, read books in the shade of the big trees, or visit the vendors lined up around the perimeter iron fence. Dusty looked back to his picture of Amy on the easel as he twirled his pencil. Something was missing. Dusty finished some shading under Amy's cheek bones. Maybe he needed to work on her smile some more. He wasn't capturing it quite right. Dusty looked up and Amy was sitting on the stone wall watching him.

Amy smiled, "Is that me?"

Dusty nodded.

Amy opened a brown paper sack and held up a sandwich, "I decided to walk to the park for lunch and see your work. You want half of this?"

Dusty was so excited he nearly toppled his easel as he reached for the sandwich. Amy giggled. Dusty yelled, "Freeze! That's the smile I want!" He laid his half of the sandwich on his lap and quickly began sketching over Amy's mouth on his picture.

Paul met Jeanne at Senator Kenny's city house to help her look for the secret closet. The CSI team was still there and the house had been searched earlier by Mass's FBI team. Paul was a little concerned that this confidential informant might be on the wrong track. Paul lifted the search warrant papers to show Jeanne.

"Had these amended to included items concealed in the property structure."

Jeanne nodded, "It's in a bookcase somewhere."

Paul followed her into the house and asked, "Who is this informant anyway?"

"A Voodoo lady."

Paul burst out laughing and Jeanne frowned. Paul put his hands up, "I'm sorry. I know you're into that stuff. Trust me, I am beyond surprise with this case." Paul hoped they didn't have to disclose the identity of their informant in the future.

Jeanne walked ahead and Paul stopped to talk to the CSI agent in charge. Jeanne's voice yelled from the other side of the house. "I think I found it."

Paul shook his head. Two teams of law enforcement had combed this house for a full day and she's been here ten minutes. Paul walked into what looked like a library to find Jeanne teetering on a chair, running her fingers down a row of books.

"There are hinge screws for European style hinges behind this trim. There should be a pressure button somewhere." She had no sooner finished the statement and it looked as if the entire wall was falling into another room. Paul grabbed Jeanne's waist and lifted her to the floor. They watched as the entire wall of books opened to a small room.

Paul handed Jeanne a pair of rubber gloves as he put his on. He stepped into the ten by ten foot area and felt for a light switch. The room illuminated and looked like a well-stocked child's closet. Paul saw a stack of shelves holding folded sweaters and immediately found the Winnie the Pooh. Jeanne was across the room. She slid hangers on the rods. Paul heard her softly sniffle. They both knew each piece of clothing represented a horrific nightmare forced on an innocent child.

Jeanne crossed herself, wiped a tear, and started bagging the clothes.

Paul touched her shoulder. He was holding a bag with the Winnie the Pooh sweater.

"We only need this. Let's go. CSI will get the rest."

Roger and Catahoula walked out of the Courthouse building together and stood on the wide marble staircase. They discussed how the case would most likely proceed. People bumped around them balancing briefcases, coffee cups and cell phones. This was a very busy court and the expansive wide staircase looked as if at least a hundred people were either coming or going. Roger squeezed toward Catahoula to allow room for a group of men to pass by.

A horizontal row of marble chips jumped from the step in front of them. Another horizontal line of marble chips exploded in front of them, crossing from the opposite direction. Roger felt the sting of the chips hitting his face and neck and heard the unmistakable popping of an automatic rifle. Roger saw a flash from the weapon. It protruded from the passenger window of a black Explorer stopped in the street, dead center of the staircase.

Roger's training kicked in before his mind even fully registered what was happening. He leaned his body into Catahoula and pushed him over the stair railing into the overgrown shrubs. Roger yelled to the crowd on the stairs, "FBI, get down." He drew his weapon and fired at the passenger window and the front tire.

He pushed two ladies to the ground that were standing, frozen in fear. Roger advanced in a sprint toward the Explorer, taking the courthouse steps three and four at a time, practically sliding down the steel stair rail. Flying papers from fallen people rained down on the scene obstructing his view. Some people crouched along the exposed staircase covering their heads and screaming. Roger had to jump over a couple of them.

His weapon was nearly empty. The passenger's weapon dropped to the street. Roger shot the rear tire and adjusted his course to attack the driver. The driver had opened his door, and began to sprint away. Roger stopped, aimed, and yelled, "FBI! FREEZE!" The runner stopped and put his hands up.

Two New Orleans patrol officers ran up and cuffed the driver. Roger walked over, still panting. He grabbed the front of the driver's shirt in his fist and using the driver's chin for leverage pushed up and back. The driver's head slammed into the Explorer door frame. Roger heard the mashing sound of skull to metal. This wasn't a kid. This was a hardened thug, about Roger's age.

Roger had his face inches from the driver. "Who sent you?" Roger saw into the cab of the truck. His picture was clipped to the visor, the passenger was dead. Roger glared into the driver's eyes.

The driver answered, "I tell you, I'm dead."

Roger yanked the driver away from the SUV and spun him around, "Look around you!" There were police everywhere, and more coming. Sirens blared from all four directions. Roger pushed the man against the car again, "You tried to kill a cop. Me. Who sent you?"

Catahoula was limping, but had made his way over to Roger. Catahoula had been close enough to hear what Roger was asking the driver.

The driver looked around. Roger yelled over to the patrol officers, "Come get this piece of shit. Tell everyone in lock up he killed a kid. After he molested him." Roger turned to walk away.

The driver yelled, "I want a deal."

Catahoula snickered and held up his card, "U.S. Attorney General's office. Name first. Deal later."

The driver leaned forward to read the card, then looked at Catahoula. "You'll never get him. The name's Manio."

Catahoula stuffed his card in the driver's shirt pocket, "You give me proof. Or no deal."

Patrol officers shoved the driver into a patrol car and headed for the police station.

Roger looked at Catahoula. "You're bleeding and limping."

Catahoula chuckled, "That's because a bullet went through my leg just before you threw me into the thorn bushes. By the way, that was an eight foot drop. You're bleeding, too." He pointed to Roger's neck, head, and arm.

Roger felt his head and neck and brought his bloody hand out to where he could see it. A patrol officer asked if they wanted ambulances. Roger shook his head and looked at Catahoula, who also declined. Roger looked back at the carnage on the courthouse steps.

The patrolman stated, "We have one dead, one serious, and about ten wounded." He looked at Roger, "I've never seen anyone charge an automatic weapon with a handgun."

Catahoula answered, "Beats a knife."

Roger looked at his watch, "Want a ride to the hospital? I don't have all day."

In the car, Catahoula asked, "I know you don't have all day, but you want to tell me the story on how you managed to get yourself on a hit list with the Manio Cartel while you were chasing pedophiles?"

Roger finished telling Catahoula what he could of the story. Roger ended by saying, "Actually, I wasn't expecting Manio to be really mad at me until tomorrow."

Catahoula reared his head back and laughed, and then yelped, "Damn. This leg hurts. I would love to nail Manio." Catahoula had a determined look on his face that projected authority and competence.

Roger smiled, "I wouldn't think of asking for anyone else. We're putting together your present."

Roger turned the car into the hospital ER parking lot and helped Catahoula walk in. They were both covered in blood, and immediately swarmed by hospital staff. Roger called Paul as nurses and doctors worked on him. "Don't want you hearing this on the news. I got shot at the courthouse a couple of times. Just flesh wounds. Getting patched up now."

CHAPTER
TWENTY EIGHT

A bram and Jackson pulled into the FBI field office parking lot. Abram looked at Jackson, "Ain't no how I ever 'spect I be comin' here on purpose."

Jackson opened the passenger door and smoothed out his shirt as he prepared to walk in with Abram. "Feels good man." Jackson nodded his head and looked at the mid-day sun in the sky. "We did real good today."

They reached the door to the building and Abram held it open for Jackson. Mass saw them coming in from his open office door and rose to greet them. He walked over, introduced himself and asked them to join him in his office.

When they were all seated, Mass said, "You two are heroes. I need you to give full statements to one of our agents. First, I have some news."

Jackson didn't always get good news. 'Specially from cops.

Mass smiled, "Five of the kidnapped people that were being transported here from Baton Rouge had families and communities offering rewards for their return. Roger Dance put in his official report that both of you are to receive those rewards." Mass leaned back and smiled.

Jackson and Abram looked at each other. Did he mean money?

Mass chuckled at their facial expressions. "You should each be getting about one hundred and fifty thousand dollars. You'll have to pay taxes on it."

Abram and Jackson both jumped up. Jackson asked, "You sure about this? We're gonna get a hundred and a half each?"

Mass nodded, "Pretty soon too. Next couple of days. I need you both to sit down and listen a minute."

Abram and Jackson sat back down. Jackson couldn't sit still. This was more money than he had ever had.

Mass said, "We are worried about your safety. This money is enough that you can start your lives somewhere new. Or we can put you in witness protection."

Abram shook his head, "Nawlens my home man. You give that Dance dude another week there won't be no more bad dudes in Nawlens."

Jackson nodded. The first thing he would do is buy his momma a new house, then get her eyes fixed. Jackson said, "I know where to stay away from. I'm with Abram. Most dudes that even know me is dead now or in jail."

Simon, Thor, and Nelson paid for their lunch at Mickey's and grabbed Ray's to-go order. The juke box was playing one of Simon's favorite songs, 'Summertime.' Simon started singing along.

Nelson shook his head, "You know Pablo is a jazz singer? You two should talk about getting a gig while we're here."

Thor said, "See if Ray knows how to sing or play the piano. He really needs to get out more. He's missing all the joys of New Orleans."

Simon stopped singing and said, "We won't be here much longer."

Simon looked at his watch. It was already two in the afternoon. He knew Roger would be shutting down the money sting before long. They had the two cartels Roger planned something with, but now that the sicko club was in custody, they might be nearing the end of their time in New Orleans.

Outside the bar, Simon handed Nelson Ray's food. He told Nelson that he and Thor would be there shortly.

Thor's toothpick wiggled in the corner of his mouth. "What's up?"

"Thought I'd tell you a story."

Thor raised an eyebrow. "Have at it."

Simon exhaled, "I love my wife. Still, even though we divorced. We're still close, and as soon as I retire, I know we will be together again." Simon's gaze softened. "Years ago, before I met my wife, I met the most amazing woman in the world. My world anyway. I think I knew I was in love with her the first moment I saw her."

Thor rubbed his forehead, "Is there going to be a point to this story?" It was over a hundred degrees outside, and the afternoon stench of the streets was starting to rise.

Simon frowned, "Shut up and listen. I think she felt the same about me. There was magnetism. I met her when on assignment, so there was never any time to see where it might really go. I let the moment pass. I should have stayed. To this day my heart aches to see her again. I think she was my goose."

Thor frowned, "Your goose? What the hell do you mean by that?"

"Geese mate for life. They mutually choose each other at first sight. I used to hunt until I read that somewhere. Couldn't bring myself to shoot them after that. She was my goose."

Thor asked, "Why didn't you go back and find her?"

Simon shook his head, "I did about six months later. She had died in an auto accident. I visit her grave at least once a year. In some strange way I feel connected to her when I am there. I leave her a goose feather." Simon's voice had cracked.

He took a deep breath and tapped Thor's shoulder with his index finger. "Every man has one big regret in his life. She is mine. Just wanted to tell you my story. Never told anyone before." Simon turned and started walking across the street to the Star Ship. He yelled back, "I think this case wraps up in another day or so."

Thor watched Simon walk away. What the hell was that about?

Jason Sims had been deep undercover for the CIA on the LUCY project for over five years. He was one of a dozen programmer's worldwide working for LUCY. Jason Sims not only had to program to the specifications of LUCY, he had to simultaneously program protection triggers for the CIA. These triggers would have to be undetectable to the other programmers on both sides. Jason was a genius, but he was also a realist. He hoped he had not made any mistakes. In cyber warfare there was always someone younger and brighter moving up the ranks.

Jason now looked at the faces of the men at the conference table. The Senior Advisors of the National Security Council of the United States. It didn't get any more important than this. These men had approved the martial law order for New

Orleans because the CIA had Jason make it appear LUCY was beginning an attack. Actually, the CIA and LUCY Task force had been waiting for an opportunity to launch an attack of their own. The deception was necessary because the CIA suspected a LUCY mole in the National Security Council.

Roger's idea of a communication sting on the weapons transaction fit perfectly. Claiming a money wire mess had resulted from the communication sting provided another perfect cover. Of the entire National Security Council, only the Chairman knew French Quarter Bank was a LUCY trap. Everyone else only knew that the communication sting had identified some suspected LUCY players. Only the Chairman knew that Thornton, Fenley and Donavan had been exposed in the communication sting, and were being set up in the money sting.

Ellen was in the room flying over everyone and reading their thoughts. She knew that someone in this room was involved with LUCY and was actually a traitor. This person would have a plan to keep Jason from stopping the cyber threats should LUCY choose to implement them. Jason was no longer an asset to LUCY, but a threat.

The Chairman of the Council asked Jason a second time, "Are you confident that adequate protections have been programmed so we may proceed?"

Jason knew he was being used as bait. Jason's answer had to sound as if he needed to physically implement his controls. "I designed the software they will use against us. I have hard programed "imploding" keys I intend to activate. I have run a 'test' attack of my own from each of their centers and stopped them. I think we are as ready as we'll ever be."

The Chairman nodded. "Mr. Sims, this country owes you our deepest gratitude. My understanding is that any attempts to trigger these cyber threats will immediately identify the actual person initiating it. Is that correct?"

Jason answered, "Yes. We will also be able to capture all subsequent transmissions from that computer address. That may actually tell us more. We will see who is expecting reports."

The Chairman looked at the others members of the Council and said, "Gentlemen, I believe we have decided to take down LUCY within the next few hours."

The representative from the International Monetary Fund added, "Criminal charges must be harsh and brought against individuals in addition to the entities that attempt retaliation."

Heads nodded around the table.

The Chairman declared the meeting adjourned and walked over to where Jason Sims waited by the door. "Did you take the precautions we discussed?"

Jason answered, "Yes sir."

The Chairman had a very uneasy feeling. "I am greatly concerned for your safety."

Jason nodded. "I appreciate your concern. I intend on vanishing after tonight. The systems are safe now, even if something happens to me."

Ellen identified who the threat was and called the Director of the FBI. The Director would need help taking this guy down. Then Ellen called us. She told us Jason was in immediate danger.

Jason rode in the back of the car provided for him and dialed Mathew Core.

Mathew answered on the first ring. "Are you alright?"

Jason answered, "Yes. Maybe after tonight I can get my life back."

Core exhaled, "LUCY ends tonight? Not to seem morbid, but is there a plan in place in case something happens to you?"

Jason laughed, "Hell yes! I don't even have to be there now! We're on autopilot."

Core chuckled, "Well, it's been quite a ride......" Core heard what sounded like an explosion blast come through his phone. Core's heart sank. The line was dead. He tried calling back. Nothing.

People were screaming, bleeding from flying glass and fiery metal debris. A burning fuel stench filled the air and flames engulfed the remains of a car in the center of Pennsylvania Avenue. Sirens screamed and flashing blue lights appeared from nowhere.

A man holding his cell phone, recording the blast, threw his cigarette to the sidewalk and spoke into the phone. "Did you get that?"

✳ ✳ ✳

Ellen told us to meet her on Pennsylvania Avenue in Washington D.C. She told us to just stand in the middle of the road and wait for her. This would not have been a good idea in mortal life, but hey? Not long after we got there Ellen showed up. She was studying her watch and said, "When I say 'freeze' I need you guys to help me freeze everything in sight. Got it?" We all nodded.

About one minute later Ellen yelled, "Freeze." We froze everything, cars driving, birds in the air, people on sidewalks, everything. Ellen flew down to a black Lincoln Town car. "This is the one. Help me move the driver and the guy in the back seat over to that bench by the corner. This is Jason Sims."

Teresa asked, "Mathew Core's computer guy?"

Ellen answered, "Yup. Let's hurry, this car is going to blow up. They are not going to under-stand how they got out of this car and we can't do anything about that. This is one of those things mortals will just have to accept as unexplainable. Hurry, this is going to blow!"

Shit!

We got the car door open and Teresa and Mary moved the driver, and Linda and I moved Jason. Ellen kept doing something with her watch and went under the car. When Jason and the driver were safe, Ellen said, "Now follow me."

She went about a half block and stopped next to a man that was holding a cell phone out in front of him. Ellen said, "We are going to unfreeze now and I am going to trace that phone call. After the explosion, I am going to call the FBI Director and tell him what happened. He will have someone come to pick up Jason. You gals stay with Jason to make sure he stays safe. Got it?"

Whoa! There's going to be an explosion, and a rescue, and we get to stand guard and ….

A huge roar and rumble thundered into a deafening blast. Flames exploded from the car and sent traffic veering in all directions. The sounds of metal crunching metal and people screaming filled the air! The car was a ball of fire in the middle of the street.

Jason and the driver watched in horror as the car exploded just yards from them. They looked at each other.

The driver was clearly shaken, "How the hell did we get here?"

Jason shook his head and looked for his phone. It must still be in the car. He wasn't comfortable using the driver's phone. Something told him to just stay put a minute.

Jason answered, "I think someone just tried to kill me."

"You mean, us."

✳ ✳ ✳

The medical examiner looked at the note his assistant had passed him. The remains of the child found in the swamp were suspected to be those of Michael Summers, Cleveland, Ohio. The assistant had retrieved the remains from the steel unit housing them and was arranging them for the examiner on the table.

The medical examiner placed a call to the FBI forensics lab to give the DNA sample they had provided priority. He also asked them to compare the results with the DNA they had on file for young Michael.

The medical examiner stood over Michael's remains and sighed, "We're going to get you home now young man."

Thor walked into the Star Ship and heard the voices of the team rising up from the basement. He decided to take a quick shower. He could smell the sulfur on him from their raid on the trafficking building earlier. Wearing the assault gear had made him sweat in the humidity. He just wanted to feel clean again. Thor walked into the room he had been using as his and removed his shirt.

Thor heard a quiet knock on the door and said, "Come in." He turned to see Jeanne standing in the doorway. She moved her eyes from him and said, "I'm sorry, I didn't realize you were going to shower."

Thor shrugged, "It's okay. What's up?"

Jeanne looked back to him. "Simon wanted me to tell you Roger is on his way here. He doesn't want anyone to leave." Jeanne noticed Thor's amulet resting in his chest hair. Thor's physique was beautiful. He was a very strong, handsome man.

Thor's voice startled her back to the moment, "I'll be down in a minute."

Jeanne closed the door and went downstairs to join the others. She had to force herself to focus on the conversations around her. This was a problem.

Paul turned on the news and the team watched the coverage of the arraignment of the sicko club and the subsequent shooting on the courthouse steps. Ray spun his chair around to address Paul when the news started repeating itself. "So how many 'flesh wounds' does Roger have now? I count one at the church during the neighborhood sweep thing, and three today?"

Roger came down the stairs, "Five today."

Everyone turned to look at him. Now both sides of his neck had bandages, a small one behind one ear, a small one on his forehead and one on each arm. Roger walked over, sat on the couch next to Pablo, and smiled.

Pablo looked over, "Trying to steal my sympathy card?" Pablo still sported his sling from having been shot in the shoulder at Jeremiah's.

Roger chuckled and then moaned, "These didn't hurt when it happened." He gingerly leaned back on the sofa and winced.

Paul asked, "Didn't they give you anything for pain?"

Roger frowned and said, "The Security Council just voted to shut down LUCY. Jason Sims has assured the Council that the world's targeted security and utility computer systems are protected. The money LUCY members thought they permanently laundered will be seized any minute." Roger looked at Ray, "How much are we up to?"

Ray smiled ear to ear, "I've checked it a couple of times to be sure, lots of zeros, eighty five TRILLION dollars."

Roger knew there would be a high sum of money involved, but he was stunned.

Pablo's voice broke the silence, "Oh shit!"

Simon volunteered, "That's only about half of what is estimated to be out there as laundered money."

Roger continued, "The Director of the FBI is going to leak the money seizure information to William C. Thornton."

Simon interrupted, "They want to see who he runs to, right?"

Roger nodded, "Right. He can't win on this. He's made his own trap. If he warns them, we have him. If he doesn't warn them, they will assume he knew. It will be interesting to see what he decides to do. Our other issue is Manio. We have enough to arrest him and I want to do that tonight. He came to town to secure that shipment of guns and drugs. He is providing us the opportunity to arrest him, I think we should take it."

Paul chuckled, "Don't forget Manio plans to take out the trash. That means getting rid of us. Manio had Roger shot today."

Thor had walked downstairs, fresh from his shower and said, "How do you know Manio ordered the hit today?"

Roger answered, "Our shooter also shot Catahoula of the US. Attorney General's office. Catahoula has already started to deal with the shooter."

Simon raised his eyebrows, "Will Catahoula prosecute Manio after we arrest him?"

Roger answered yes and Simon let out a yelp. "Finally! Manio just might go down."

Roger looked at his watch. It was already four in the afternoon and he wanted to arrest Manio about eight this evening. The Coast Guard needed time to make their raids on the other eight Lanitol Oil docks. Roger looked at the team and said, "Why don't we meet up at the field office about 7:30 and head to the Casino to pick up Manio. That will give us all a couple of hours down time."

Thor asked, "I'm not complaining there isn't enough to do, but did you ever figure out a plan for the two cartels coming for Monday's gun train?"

Roger chuckled, "I sent the train out yesterday. It's already been unloaded in the Kansas underground storage. The plan now is to watch who robs an empty train. If we arrest Manio, it only leaves Zelez."

Simon looked at Thor, "Like I said, we're just about done here."

Jeanne felt herself stop breathing for a moment. She looked at Simon and asked, "Are you leaving New Orleans after we arrest Manio tonight?"

Simon answered, "The minute Roger says we're done. I'm getting the hell out of here and going home." There were a few chuckles.

Pablo looked at Simon, "Don't forget me, man. You said I could follow you around."

Jeanne grabbed her bottle of water and quickly made her way up the stairs.

Ray shook his head and looked at Thor.

Thor put his palms out and shrugged, "What?"

CHAPTER
TWENTY NINE

Carol asked, "What is Spicey cooking? Smells yummy." Carol and Cindy had walked up and down Bourbon Street checking out the shops. They each had a dozen bags from their shopping, and were now plopped on Spicey's couch taking off their shoes.

Sasha smiled, "Got a big pot of gumbo started. I think she be wantin' you two stayin' for dinner."

Spicey came from the back and after hugs said, "I have an idea for you two to have a Nawlens experience to remember. How 'bout a swamp tour? Not the kind tourists get but a real one. " Carol and Cindy started to squeal and Spicey interrupted them. "You want to meet a real Voodoo Queen?"

Carol clutched her chest, grabbed Cindy and started shaking her. "A real Voodoo Queen! In the swamp! Can you believe it?"

Cindy frowned and looked at Spicey, "Gee. Thanks."

Spicey laughed and said, "I called my friend Willie to pick us up and take us out there. You two dressed mighty cute for a swamp. You want to change clothes 'fore we go?"

Cindy said, "I'm not walking all the way back to our hotel room."

Carol smiled and tilted her head, "We're all about the same size." She was leaning back winking at Spicey.

Spicey threw her hands in the air, "Okay! You can get in my closet but I ain't wantin' to see any of my church clothes headin' for the swamp." Spicey pointed the way to her bedroom and shook her head. Cindy and Carol disappeared behind the colorful blanket that adorned Spicey's bedroom doorway.

Seconds later Carol squealed and peeked her head out, "Can we wear your jewelry too?"

Spicey answered yes as she stirred the gumbo.

Sasha asked, "I'm hopin' I get to stay here and mind the shop?"

Spicey answered, "That'll work. Can we take your gun?"

William C. Thornton buzzed the Director of the FBI. Manio had called Fenley with an alternate plan for moving the drugs and guns that had been seized Wednesday night at the port. Fenley had already made a few calls to make sure Manio's people could be substituted in key security jobs. Now all that had to happen was for Thornton to get the Director's approval for the new plan.

The Director had finished a phone call with Roger and had reluctantly agreed to allow Thornton one more day of freedom. Roger had pointed out that they had plenty of evidence on Thornton. Maybe leaving Thornton free would produce even more evidence on the other players. The Director was itching to let Thornton know he had been found out.

Instead he answered the buzzer, "Sure, come in."

Thornton entered the Director's office and sat. "I have a new plan for moving the drugs and guns from Wednesday night's fiasco to Kansas. I think instead of sending out a train, which by the way would risk every civilian between New Orleans and Kansas, we'll put it on a boat and send it to Texas."

The Director nodded. He loved Thornton's description of the martial law raid as a fiasco. He couldn't wait to see Thornton's reaction to his next statement. The Director slid the plan over and put it in his top drawer. This would be even more proof that Thornton had worked this out with Fenley and Manio.

The Director cleared his throat and said, "I owe you an apology."

Thornton asked, "For what?"

The Director leaned his chair back, "I lied to you about French Quarter Bank. We had a sting planned and I wanted to keep our people out of it."

Thornton's posture went rigid. "I don't understand."

The Director smiled, "Of course you don't. I haven't explained it yet. We haven't lost any communications from the martial law communication sting. The CIA and OSI are going over each one as we speak. They put out the rumor that there had been a problem with the accounts at French Quarter Bank, so that certain entities would then identify themselves by moving money through there."

Thornton went pale. The Director continued, "My understanding is that there is eighty five trillion dollars that was seized about an hour ago. That number will multiply to include all accounts that can be linked internationally."

Thornton stood and began pacing. "Are you saying that the United States Federal government is going to freeze the accounts at French Quarter Bank? How could this happen and I not have been told?"

The Director shook his head, "I didn't say the accounts were going to freeze. I said we were *seizing* them under the RICO Act. These guys will never get their money back. I was protecting you by not telling you. What's it to you anyway? This is a CIA project. It doesn't have anything to do with any cases we are working on." The Director pointed to his center drawer where he had just placed the plan Thornton had given him. "Oh, I don't really need another plan on the guns, but I'll look it over. I guess Dance had those moved Thursday. The weapons and drugs are already in Kansas."

Thornton sat heavily in the chair opposite the Director's desk. His mind wasn't even processing what the Director was saying. His eyes locked on the Director, "Are you telling me that the Federal Reserve never changed account numbers or anything at that bank? That this has been a sting?"

The Director laughed, "Oh they changed account numbers and added some computer codes, but just so it would be faster to sort out the bad guys. This way these accounts clearly build the RICO case on their own. No sorting the good guys from the bad. They have their own special numbers. It was beautiful really. They voluntarily put on ID tags saying they were the bad guys." The Director actually laughed at Thornton's expression. "We should hear by tomorrow who they are."

Thornton's voice rose, "I can't believe I didn't know this. This isn't right." Thornton leaned forward. A look of fresh awareness cloaked his face, "How much of this has been Roger Dance?"

The Director tried to look puzzled. The whole time he was enjoying every single moment. "Dance? You're the one that thinks he's an incompetent buffoon. What makes you think he's involved?"

Thornton rubbed his face with his hands and answered, "I don't know. I'm going home. Seems to me my job has been redefined by this office without as much as an email to me."

Thornton scowled at the Director and slammed the door on his way out.

The Director hit play on his computer, leaned back, and smiled while he listened to Bolero. He still wanted to slug the son of a bitch.

Thornton pulled onto the highway. He wasn't even sure where he was driving to. What was he going to do? He couldn't warn Fenley and Donavan about the sting. It was probably too late now anyway. Maybe he could just act surprised. The Director said that the communication sting did not lose any calls. That meant eventually his role would be discovered anyway. Thornton slammed his fists against the steering wheel. *Damn it all!*

Thornton's mind raced. There was nowhere to go. Thornton's cell phone rang. He lifted it and saw that Fenley was calling him. He pitched the phone against the passenger window. A mile ahead the concrete supports of the overpass came into focus. He had always wondered what made people do this sort of thing. He unsnapped his seat belt, and clenched the steering wheel with both hands.

Traffic was heavy all around him, he didn't care. He stood on the accelerator and recklessly thrust his way through the traffic. At the very last minute he twisted the wheel and veered straight into the bridge.

Roger and Paul walked back to the hotel. Paul declared he was going to the sidewalk bar to chat with Jill, the bartender. Roger took the elevator to his room. The CIA had placed security personnel at the hotel for both Roger and Paul. Roger nodded at the agent in the hall as he unlocked the door to his room. The Director had insisted on the security after the shooting at the courthouse. He had also insisted that the security come from the CIA, since Manio was the threat. Roger agreed the CIA had a better handle on Manio and his affiliates than the FBI.

Roger draped his jacket on a chair and headed for the bathroom. He turned the water on for a shower and winced as he removed the bandages that peppered his face and neck. The bleeding had stopped, but long red grooves promised to be reminders for quite a while. Roger realized how close he had come to death today.

When his shower was finished he called Lisa Core. After some small talk about how she and

Jamie were doing, Roger offered to answer questions about Mathew. They spoke for about twenty minutes. By the nature of Lisa's questions, Roger knew Lisa and Mathew were talking about Mathew's history with the government. Lisa seemed to be a person of character and made decisions carefully. If Mathew was going to get his family back, he would have to be honest with her.

Roger made a cup of tea and watched the news. He had almost drifted off to sleep when the Director called.

"The funds at French Quarter Bank are now seized. The Coast Guard has recovered cocaine at two port storage buildings belonging to Lanitol Oil. They are moving in on the remaining six."

Roger answered, "What kind of retaliation are we expecting from LUCY initially?"

The Director answered, "I wish I knew. LUCY had a mole in the National Security Council. Ellen is with me now and has shown me a 'video' of the Secretary of Defense ordering the car bombing of Jason Sims. She also has a captured video call back to the Secretary from the bomber, showing him the explosion as it happened minutes ago."

Roger sat up straight, "The Secretary of Defense was a LUCY mole? They killed Jason Sims? That means LUCY can take down everything. Soon." Roger's chest tightened. He could feel his heart pounding. My God he hoped he hadn't set everyone on a path to destruction.

The Director spoke in a calm voice, "Ellen and her angels saved Jason and alerted me what happened. Jason and his driver were moved to safety and the CIA picked them up. OSI is watching the Secretary of Defense and his bomber friend. There isn't much we can do without real evidence."

Roger knew the Director meant they couldn't use what Ellen had given him. Roger was still alarmed, "Are the computer programs at risk? Can Jason get to them in time?"

The Director explained that Jason had built in safeguards for precisely this risk. The programs were secure to the best of anyone's knowledge. He added, "LUCY players believe Jason flipped to our side. Their attempt to kill Jason only proves they believe their programs can still cause harm. Once they discover their money is gone and their programs blocked, LUCY will have to retreat and start over."

The Director continued, "I told Thornton about the money sting. As far as we can tell he didn't make any calls. He drove his car into a bridge support five miles from here. He caused a ten car pile-up, the bastard. He's dead."

Roger rubbed his forehead and remained silent.

The Director sighed, "I wanted to prosecute that son of a bitch. Hell, I wanted to slug him first! Now I have to go to his funeral. Our publicity people are reporting it an accident. What's your next move?"

Roger answered, "I plan to arrest Manio at eight o'clock tonight for human trafficking and attempted murder of an officer. He's staying at the Casino here in New Orleans. I want to tie his activity to this RICO case on LUCY."

"Timing sounds tight on this. He may or may not know about the money sting and the drug raids by the time you get to him."

Roger said, "I thought about that. He still thinks there are ninety tons of weapons he can steal at the dock. Not to mention a lot of coke. I'm betting on his greed and ego. I don't see him running home empty handed."

The Director asked Roger to hold the line. When he came back on the phone he said, "OSI and CIA are monitoring a lot of chatter. Donavan Luntz represents the oil side of LUCY and he seems to be arranging a conference call of some very influential people. Ellen has left to monitor that and get us transcripts. I think we are about to find the other players. Good luck with Manio. I'll keep you posted."

Roger said, "Thank you, sir."

Roger's mind started replaying everything that had happened in the last year and a half. From his phone call to go to South Bend and help catch a serial killer, to now. Within hours he would be arresting Manio, and LUCY would be stripped of their power. The most amazing part of it all was Ellen and the angels.

Roger looked at his watch, he still had some time. He dialed Kim, "You working, home, or what?"

Kim answered, "Home. Just walked in the door. What's up?" Kim kicked off her shoes and plopped in her chair. Roger was in a good mood but sounded tired.

"I want to *do* something. Go somewhere. This case is almost done. Can you get some vacation time?"

Kim was silent. "Did you get shot or something? You never have time to do *anything*."

Roger laughed, "Actually, I did get shot. No big deal, just flesh wounds."

He was still laughing when Kim said, "I have a lot of vacation time. Where can we go where people won't try to kill you?"

Roger answered, "I have some business in Hawaii I need to wrap up."

Kim shouted, "You want to go to Hawaii?"

Roger chuckled, "Only if you go with me. Well?"

Jeanne had been aimlessly driving around. The case was almost over. She would have to decide to stay in New Orleans or return to New York. This team would be splitting up soon. She may never see any of them again. She started thinking of Thor. Jeanne looked at her watch. It had only been twenty minutes ago she left the Star Ship. It seemed a lifetime ago.

Jeanne told herself to focus on the things she should be doing. She pulled over and called the medical examiner's office. He reported to her that the DNA for Michael Summers had been a match and that he was preparing the shipment of Michael's remains for transport. Jeanne called Spicey and told her that Michael was on his way home.

Jeanne saw a grocery store to her right and decided to pick up a few items for Jeremiah. She hadn't talked to him since before Pablo had been shot. Jeanne drove down the length of Jeremiah's driveway and parked nearly on the swamp's edge. She saw Jeremiah sitting on his favorite stump skinning minks.

Jeremiah tilted his head so his one good eye could see her. "You all done shootin' folks?"

Jeanne sat on a stump next to him, retrieved her knife from her boot, and started helping him. The mink and alligator skins were Jeremiah's only source of income. He was in his seventies and slowing down. He couldn't do this forever. Jeanne looked at him, "You ever think of selling some of your land and retiring?"

Jeremiah raised an eyebrow. "Retire from what? I never had no job. Just livin' off the land. Lived here all my life."

Jeanne nodded and kept skinning. "You ever hear of a life estate?"

Jeremiah nodded much to Jeanne's surprise. "Old lady Nelson sold her place to her boy and kept a life estate. Meant she got money for sellin' and didn't have to move, I think."

Jeanne nodded, "That's right. What if Alan bought your place so you would have some extra money to do what you want? You could still live here and the property would stay in the family. You wouldn't have to work as hard."

Jeremiah laughed, "You get hit in the head in that shoot out or somethin'? Ain't no bank gonna lend on this place. Ain't even got 'lectricity the normal way."

Jeanne asked, "What if I lent the money to Alan?" Jeanne was really hoping Jeremiah would consider the offer. She cared about him and she worried about him trying to live off the land in his senior years.

Jeremiah stopped skinning the minks, "That there sits on me like a charity thing. Don't like the sounds of it."

Jeanne said, "I have money at the bank they are only paying me one percent on. If I lent it to Alan at two percent, I would double my interest. You would actually be helping me." That was her last good argument. She stared at Jeremiah.

Jeremiah shook his head and looked sideways at her, "There not enough lipstick in the world for that pig. Only got one eye, but I be seein' through you."

Jeanne asked, "Can I mention it to Alan and see what he thinks?"

Jeremiah smiled, "You always get what you want?"

"Actually no."

Jeremiah tossed a dead mink at her. "Here. You want to help me, get to work." Jeanne smiled and started skinning the mink.

* * *

Willie, Spicey, Cindy and Carol arrived at Pete's swamp boat rentals just as Pete was leaving for the day. Willie yelled over to Pete, "We be takin' a swamp boat if it be okay."

Pete laughed, "Where you keep findin' all these beautiful women? Dang! Then you be bringin' 'em out to the swamp at all hours? Guess ya gotta go with what works for ya. Leave the money in the box by the door." Pete waved, pulled his heavy frame into his pickup truck and took off down the drive leaving a dust cloud behind him.

Spicey and Willie walked over to the dock and climbed in a flat bottom boat. Cindy and Carol were close behind. Cindy flared her nostrils. "Sure smells bad out here."

Spicey frowned, "It's a swamp."

Carol smacked Cindy's arm, "It's a swamp!"

Cindy noticed a bucket filled with hammers sitting on the dock. "How good is this boat put together? I don't like the looks of a bucket full of hammers sitting right here."

Willie laughed, "Those for the tourists. You take a swamp tour they tell ya to grab a hammer case you gotta thump a gator head. These flat bottom boats got no motor. No noise to scare gators off. They can get a little nosey, sometimes get too close."

Cindy reached in the bucket and grabbed three hammers. Carol got back out of the boat, grabbed the whole bucket, and sat back down on her crate. She looked at Willie who was frowning at her. "Case we have to throw some."

Willie told everyone to sit down on a crate while he pushed off from the dock. Willie looked at Carol and Cindy. "Spicey said she wanted you girls to have a real swamp tour. To my thinkin' that means you need to learn about what lives out here. You girls heard of the Rugaru?"

Cindy and Carol both shook their heads. Spicey rubbed her amulet and started softly chanting. She figured it would add to the story. The swamp boat slowly glided away from the docks and turned into the dark waters of the narrow bayou. Spanish moss hanging from cypress branches tickled their heads as they silently passed. Strange noises rose from the shore as grasses rustled and snapped. Under the umbrella of the cypress branches it quickly became dark.

Willie whispered, "Them noises you hear be your security alarm. What you don't want, if you be in the middle of the swamp, is *silent* crickets. Means danger real close."

Spicey thought Willie might be doing too good a job. She was getting creeped out already and it would be a whole hour or more 'fore they got to Mambo's.

Chapter Thirty

Roger had ordered room service for his dinner. He had a lot of calls to make before leaving to arrest Manio. He called Catahoula and told him what evidence he had on Manio for a RICO charge. Catahoula agreed there was enough for an arrest warrant and said he would have one prepared and sent to the field office shortly. He wished Roger luck and complained his leg hurt like hell.

Roger chuckled, "I took mine in the face. Looks like I lost a bar fight."

Catahoula's voice was somber, "You be careful tonight. Manio is ruthless, and his men are devoted. Last time he was arrested his men attacked the transport convoy. Manio never even stepped inside the jail. It was a massacre."

Roger had forgotten about that. But it gave him an idea. "What if I deliver him to the Navy? They're right down the coast from the Casino. That way we could arrange a military transport."

Catahoula laughed, "How the hell are you going to get the Navy to do this for you?"

Roger smiled as he answered, "I have a martial law order good 'til midnight."

"Yes, you do." Catahoula hung up and Roger dialed Mathew Core.

Core answered on the first ring, "Yeah."

Roger and Core spoke about Manio's arrest for a few minutes. Roger wanted Core's help and some advice. Roger asked what the news was at the docks.

Core answered, "You know Zack and I have a buddy we call Jimmy with us, right?"

Roger knew there was a CIA undercover that had been with Core and Zack at the raid last night. "Yes, he's CIA, right?"

Core answered, "Right. He is being told something bad is being put together. We don't know what. We do know where."

Roger asked, "The port?"

Core answered, "Worse. The guys being brought in have high level military skills specializing in explosives. They also have engineering and drilling training. They are only used for extreme missions. An entire force of them were used in the Gulf War to protect oil interests. Their legacy lives on. All specialized outside contractors. Bad dudes."

Roger asked, "Can you guys identify these men when they arrive and find out the plan?"

Core answered, "Depends who they send. Last I knew, most of them were from the States. Right here on the gulf. Won't take them long to put a team on this port. Could be tonight. Jimmy and I haven't been invisible for the last ten years. We know some bad folks. We won't be able to get very close if they recognize us. And they won't be slumming around the bars when they get here. We are going to need a lot of luck to figure out what they are planning, and where they might go."

Roger told Core to keep him posted and hung up. Roger was processing all of the new information. The Director had said the chatter Ellen was going to investigate had just started. CIA put Jimmy on alert. The people Jimmy was told were coming wouldn't have anything to do with the money seizure. LUCY had a plan B.

Roger called the Director with his suspicions. The Director was furious that the CIA wasn't sharing all of the information they were getting. The Director and Roger agreed that without Ellen the paranoia of the agencies would tangle any plan to the point of uselessness.

The Director wished Roger luck on his arrest of Manio and added, "Since we are going with RICO on this, I want Fenley and Donavan arrested, too. I think we will wait for all of the chatter to end. See what this plan B might harvest."

Roger paced his hotel room waiting for Paul. There was one flaw in his plan for tonight he had to fix. He had to get Manio on the roof.

Tourey leaned against the brick wall of the alley behind the diner and watched Core, Zack, and Jimmy leave Colby's bar. Zack and Jimmy walked to the back of Colby's, presumably headed for the dock storage buildings. Mathew Core walked straight toward Tourey.

Tourey was impressed. Core was good. Core nodded to Tourey as he took a position on the wall next to him. Core pulled a piece of paper from his pocket and said, "I was hopin' you would come snoopin' around. I have a Christmas list for you. I'm hoping you're Santa."

Tourey took the paper and read through the items. Tourey chuckled, "You sure you want me to be Santa? Ain't I supposed to know who's been naughty?"

Core chuckled, "Can you get them in two hours?"

Tourey's eyebrows went up. "I have to pass this by my boss first."

Core turned to face Tourey. "Roger Dance is going to have a big problem tonight. None of us are sure how bad it might get. I'm trying to be prepared for a worse case. If it turns out I need this shit, it will be too late to ask."

Tourey knew that John was using Core as an asset and that LUCY was coming down tonight. The items Core wanted pointed to a fear that LUCY had a plan B. Core was right. Neither John nor Roger would approve Core having this stuff without more information.

Tourey stood up straight and said, "You realize what you are asking me?"

Core said, "If I don't have to use this shit, no foul. If I do have to use it, you helped save the day. Just you and I will know where it came from. That I promise you."

Tourey exhaled loudly, "My gut says I have a friggin' Christmas list to fill."

Core smiled and walked away.

Thor walked down to Jeanne's house and knocked on the door. No answer. He sat on the porch swing and gave it a small push. The moaning of the rusted chain against the hook filled the air and he stopped the swing. He made a mental note he would fix that for her when the case was done. He saw the deep grooves in the trim along the front door and noticed they had initials next to them. He chuckled to himself as he pictured Pablo and Jeanne measuring who was growing the fastest. He was sure Jeanne was angry every time Pablo was taller.

Thor stood. What was he doing here anyway? They had a huge arrest tonight he needed to rest up for. Simon's voice was in his head. *This case is over in a day or so. I'm heading home the minute Roger says we're done. Every man has one big regret in his life. She was my goose.*

Mambo's voice took over. *Your souls have known each other for centuries. She has chosen you. She will consume you.*

Thor stepped off the porch and walked toward the noise of the city. Mambo had been right about one thing. He did know something essential was missing in his life.

John Barry hung up his phone and looked at his watch. He was going to help Roger with the Manio arrest in one hour. John dialed Adele, "You and Jerome want to catch a quick ice cream? I only have about an hour."

John stood and put his suit jacket on. Adele had been thrilled at the offer, and said Jerome was sitting on the stoop, memorizing the brochures John had left him. John grabbed a fistful of new materials from the recruiting rack as he left.

Thomas Fenley turned on the news only to hear that the Federal Government had seized the assets of an unnamed organization that had infiltrated the French Quarter Bank. The reporter bragged it was the largest government seizure of money in history. Fenley changed the channel to another news station. Breaking news. Same story. Fenley called Donavan.

Donavan answered, "Yes, I have seen your news."

Fenley asked, "Is it true? Is it us?"

"Damn right, it's true. It was a trap. A damn good one. They haven't frozen our assets, they seized them. Eighty four *trillion* dollars, Thomas. You hear that number loud and clear? I ordered the Washington D.C electrical grid to go down in ten minutes."

Fenley was going to puke. "They will release our money when their grids go down. Have you talked to Thornton?"

Donavan answered, "Thornton? He drove his car into a concrete bridge. He's dead! Explain to me how I know everything before you do?"

Fenley hung up and ran for the bathroom.

The team started arriving at the field office to put on their assault gear. Pablo had come just to feel a part of it. This was probably the biggest arrest that would ever happen in his career. He cursed the wound in his shoulder. It wasn't fair. Simon walked into the room and opened a locker filled with vests. He started to put one on and looked at Pablo.

"I made a couple of calls this afternoon. After tonight I am going to take a couple of weeks' vacation and report to the Indy office. I left the door open for you to come too."

Pablo nodded, "I just want to drain your brain as long as I can. Sounds fine to me. Why not somewhere warm though? Like Hawaii?"

Simon laughed, "Indy might have an opening."

"Isn't that Thor's post?"

Thor walked in the room, "Who says Indy may have an opening?" He was frowning.

Simon answered, "Let's just say a birdy told me." Simon finished cinching his vest and walked up to

Thor. Simon handed Thor a small white feather and winked. "Put this in your pocket for luck."

Thor stuffed the feather in his shirt pocket and rubbed his hands over his forehead, "This whole team is going crazy."

Jeanne came in and asked, "Who's going crazy?" She frowned at Pablo, "You are, if you think you are going tonight."

Pablo put his hands up in the air, "I'm just here to cheer you on."

Jeanne sat on a long wooden bench and started loading her boots with knives. She had secret slits all over them. She looked up and everyone had stopped what they were doing and watched her.

Jeanne said, "You throw your knife you've lost your weapon. Always need a few spares."

Nelson nodded, "Sometimes you do need to be quiet. Knife works for me, as long as I also have this." He was holding up an assault weapon.

Roger and Paul came in the room and began putting on their gear. John Barry walked in, his shirt covered with brown stains.

Paul asked, "What the hell did you have for dinner? Looks like you're wearing it."

John laughed, "Chocolate ice cream. Lost my scoop."

When everyone was suited up, Roger stood and asked for their attention. He passed out drawings to each of them and said, "Our goal is to get Manio on the roof. I need you to leave his escape route clear. Cover all exits. We can assume he has men with him and they will die to protect him. Mass and his guys will be going in the front and making noise about the arrest. Hopefully, Manio will head for the roof at that time. He has a helicopter there and he will be instructing his pilot to get it ready."

Roger continued, "Do not risk any civilians. If Manio is heading for the roof your job is done. I want you to stay alive. I don't even care about Manio's men. I would like Jeanne and Thor to cover Paul and me from the back. Manio will have men protecting his escape stairway. This is a short, one story stairwell to the roof. Jeanne can take them out with her knives and Thor can pull their bodies out of the way. I don't want Manio hearing shots behind him."

Thor asked, "Who is on the roof besides you and Paul?"

Roger answered, "John Barry, and Nelson until Jeanne and Thor can join us. I have planned a roof top party I will explain to you now."

Thor looked at Simon. "Can't wait to hear this."

Twenty minutes had gone by. Fenley still had power. He went to his laptop and keyed in access for the security sites. They were all still functioning. What was happening? These were supposed to be down. Fenley paced. He wasn't sure he should call

Donavan again. Donavan was in London. Maybe he didn't know the grids were still working.

Fenley dialed Donavan who answered. "Yes."

Fenley practically shouted, "I still have electricity. I can still see our security systems. What is happening?"

Donavan answered, "I have been told our programs are impotent. We have been stopped."

Fenley collapsed in his chair, "Now what?"

Donavan said, "Just keep watching the news. There is always another plan Thomas. Remember that. Remember also that none of us are indispensable." Donavan disconnected the call. Fenley was very clear about the threat Donavan just made to him. He was done. He didn't know when or how, but it was over.

Tourey had located nearly everything on Core's list. He was short a very fast boat and some explosives. There was only one way he knew to get the boat. Steal one. John Barry would get him the explosives, but there would be some explaining to do later.

Tourey called John, "You busy?"

John was climbing in the assault wagon, "You might say so. Getting ready to arrest Manio."

Tourey whistled, "I need some plastic fast. And some blasting binary cylinders. Can you hook me up with the Navy? I'm outside their gate number three now."

John was stunned, "Can you tell me what this is about?"

Tourey answered, "I'm going to ask you to take this on faith. I think you need me to do this or I wouldn't be calling."

John told Tourey he would make a call and someone would meet him at the gate shortly. At the last minute Tourey had asked him for a fast boat, too. John repeated his conversation with Tourey to Roger and asked, "Does this make any sense to you?"

Roger nodded, "Maybe. There is LUCY chatter suggesting some team of black-op military types have been ordered here."

John said, "Sounds like they know we have their money and that their cyber threat didn't work. They have a Plan B."

CHAPTER
THIRTY ONE

Willie pointed ahead of their boat and said, "See that little peninsula there? Mambo's place be just the other side."

Spicey looked at Carol and Cindy's faces. They were so excited it made her giggle. "Told you guys this here be a fun trip."

Willie turned out to be the perfect swamp tour guide. His knowledge of local history and stories of the swamp had been captivating. The critters in the swamp had cooperated, too. Spicey never even had to shoot her gun. Willie's boat turned the corner and they saw that Mambo had company already. A small swamp boat was tied to the shore.

Spicey said, "Dang. Guess we just wait our turn."

Carol and Cindy were pointing to all of the little skulls hanging from the bushes as Willie tied off their boat next to the other one.

Spicey leaned over and looked in the small boat. "Willie come over here. Don't that look like a pile of offerin's?"

Willie leaned over, "It sure do." Willie's face got serious, "I been hearin' tales 'bout people comin' out here and robbin' Mambo. They know folks bring her precious trinkets for potions and shit." Willie looked toward Mambo's hut, "I don't see none heaped at the door neither."

Spicey frowned and pulled out both her and Sasha's guns. "Willie, we be goin' in." Spicey said to Carol and Cindy, "We might have somebody robbin' Mambo. They be in her hut now. You two stay here and Willie and I'll check this out."

Carol jumped up, "I want to come too!" She grabbed a hammer from the bucket. "Cindy and I got your back, girlfriend."

Cindy's eyes flew open wide as she grabbed her hammers. Willie and Spicey ran toward the door of the hut. Cindy and Carol followed, Spicey's borrowed flowing dresses catching and tearing on the briars along the path.

Carol kept whispering, "Shit. Shit," as she unsnarled them. She knew Spicey would not be happy when she saw what was left of her dress. Willie and Spicey had run into Mambo's hut. Carol and Cindy heard shouting and then gunshots. They momentarily froze.

Carol yelled, "Oh shit!"

Cindy raised one of her hammers, "We better see what happened."

Cindy and Carol inched their way to the door, they peeked in to see Spicey holding her guns on two young men. Willie had tied their hands with rope. An old lady sat in front of a fire pit chanting. That must be Mambo.

Spicey saw Carol and Cindy and said, "Go out to this guy's boat and bring back Mambo's stuff. It be that little pile there by the bucket. These two fools out here robbin' her! Couple of low life scum, caught 'em tryin' to take her refrigerator!"

Cindy and Carol ran out to the small boat and returned in minutes, panting. Spicey's dresses were shredded. Spicey looked at her cell phone. "Dang, got no reception out here. That's okay. We gonna take these boys back to Pete's and call the cops to come get 'em."

Spicey frowned at the young men and yelled, "You two sit your ass on the ground there and cross your legs. You just wait 'til we be done. I didn't come all this ways for my friends to meet Mambo and them not get to talk to her."

Spicey handed Willie her guns, "You keep 'em still 'til we be done okay?"

Willie nodded and asked the men, "Why you rob Mambo?"

One of the men answered, "We know people bring her valuable stuff to get protection potions and shit. All she got today is some trinkets and junk. We thought maybe the good stuff in here."

Spicey frowned and looked at Mambo, "Did these guys hurt you?"

Mambo shook her head, "Heavens no. They've been here before. I keep tellin' 'em I ain't got no valuables. This time they wanted that little fridge there." Mambo pointed. "Told 'em I liked that. To leave it be. Didn't want to listen, so I cursed 'em. Then you showed up."

The young men's eyes opened wide. One of them yelled over, "What you mean you cursed us? Ain't no such thing as a curse, crazy ol' woman."

Mambo chuckled, "You might ask Willie to tie your hands in the front. You gonna have a bad itch for about a week. Give you time to think of somethin' productive to do with your hands once your itch goes away. Itch won't start right away, got about an hour or so." Mambo smiled and looked at Carol and Cindy. "So, you be friends of Spicey?"

They chatted for half an hour. Mambo gave them both amulets and potions. Spicey told Mambo about Michael coming to her in her crystal ball. She also told Mambo about Jeanne calling to say he was on his way home. Mambo nodded and said, "The Saints reported that the angels saved the other people, too. The swamp is at peace now."

Spicey stood, "Except for these two. This really ticks me off. You got nothin' better in your life then robbin' some old lady lives in the middle of nowhere?" Spicey stomped over and took the guns from Willie. She pointed them at the two young men. "I got half a mind to just shoot your asses and leave you out here for the gators."

The two men look terrified. Spicey's face was beet red with anger. She looked as if she was on the edge of a very high emotional cliff and ready to jump off.

Cindy cleared her throat, "I would like to lodge an objection to that plan."

Carol nodded, "Me too. What she said."

Willie said, "Let's take these two back to Pete's. Spicey can take their boat and the gals here can hold the guns on our prisoners. How does that sound?"

Everyone agreed that sounded like a plan. Spicey hugged Mambo, and Carol and Cindy shook her hand.

When they were outside the hut, Carol squealed, "Wow, can you plan a swamp tour or what? We even get to arrest pirates!"

Spicey laughed, and waited for everyone to be seated on Willie's boat before she pushed off. "You guys stay close to me. I might need you to shoot something."

Carol and Cindy each held a gun. Neither one of them had ever held a gun before.

Carol looked down the barrel of Sasha's gun, "Dang thing is sure heavy."

Willie suggested they just lay them on the deck of the boat where they could reach 'em quick if they needed. Those two waving those guns didn't sit well with him at all. He was scared to death one of them was going to shoot somebody by accident.

Half way back to Pete's their prisoners started squirming. Mambo's itchin' curse was starting to set in. First, they started rubbing themselves sort of casually and shifting their weight as they sat on the boat's deck. Cindy and Carol glanced at each other and started giggling. Another five minutes and the young men were crossing their legs and covering their faces with their roped hands all the while moaning and squirming.

Willie chuckled, "You be pretty miserable by the end of the week." Willie looked at Spicey. "Didn't Mambo say this itch gonna last these boys a week?"

Spicey yelled over, "You two scumbags be puttin' on quite a show. Believe in curses now?"

Carol looked at Cindy, "Isn't this just the best vacation *ever*?"

Mass and two of his agents went through the front door of the casino and demanded to see the head of security. A few minutes later a man introduced himself as the head of security for the casino. Mass notified him they were there to arrest Manio. The security man read the warrant and looked at Mass.

He spoke into his shoulder radio and said, "Code red: Manio."

The security man looked at Mass, "He'll be warned you're here. I need to protect the rest of our patrons."

Mass answered, "I think we are prepared. Have your men stay out of the way. Where is Manio now?"

The man answered, "High stakes room, top floor."

Mass nodded and said, "Let's try to do this peaceful."

The security man shook his head, "That's not going to happen. He has twenty men here with him."

Mass radioed to Roger with Manio's location. Roger looked at Paul, "I want to chat with Manio for a minute. I want you to wait on the roof."

Paul was stunned, "What part of that makes sense? You *have* lost your mind."

Roger laughed, "I'm going to chat by phone. I want to get him moving to the roof. I need you there."

Paul shook his head but left for the stairwell to the roof.

Roger dialed Manio, "I assume by now you know we have seized the money at French Quarter Bank. You may find it interesting that we have also seized your drugs at eight ports. Our gun train left early, already unloaded in Kansas. I'm coming for *you* now. RICO arrest warrant. I'm in the Casino. I would like you to turn yourself in. Fight this in the courts. No sense making a mess tonight."

Manio spoke, his voice breaking as if he were walking fast. Roger's earpiece told him that was exactly what was happening. Four men were walking with Manio, two were waiting in the hall. Manio said, "I underestimated you, Mr. Dance. You are a worthy opponent. However, I must decline your invitation to join you. You have been misled if you believe I will allow myself to be detained."

The phone went dead. Thor was speaking in Roger's earpiece. "Manio and four guys just went to the roof."

Roger answered, "Keep that stairway clear, I'm on my way now. Don't shoot me."

Thor looked at Jeanne, "Let Manio and four guys through. More Manio guys on the way and Roger is coming, too. Let's back up and take 'em further down the hall."

Thor and Jean positioned themselves where Thor could see who was coming from around the corner. Thor was standing in a room with the door opened so that he could see to his left through the jam and to the right directly down the hall to Jeanne. Manio and two of his immediate guards passed and entered the stairwell. Jeanne could see all of Thor and watched for his hand signals. Thor signaled Jeanne there were two men coming.

Jeanne pulled two knives from her boots and pressed herself in the threshold of a door. She waited to hear the rustle of the men's clothing as they ran down the carpeted hall. There were gunshots coming from the roof, gunshots coming from further down the hall. Jeanne leaped to the center of the hall, and threw her knives directly into the chests of the running men. Thor motioned two more men were coming. There was no time to move the bodies. Jeanne reached down and grabbed two more knives from her boots. She stood in the center of the hall and slowly walked toward Thor. She needed to be closer to her targets. Thor's mind was screaming, *What the hell is she doing? She needs to take cover and shoot them!* Thor prepared to shoot from his position.

As if Jeanne read his mind she raised her arm and shook her head. Thor realized she didn't want to shoot them, she was going to try her knives again. HOLY CRAP! The men turned the corner. Thor signaled they were in sight. Jeanne ran forward twenty feet and stopped. The instant the men turned the corner she threw her knives. Both landed in the center of the men's chests. One man started to rise and Jeanne kicked his head, removed her knife from his chest and slit his throat.

Roger turned the corner and Thor signaled to Jeanne, Roger was coming. There was still gunfire on the roof. Roger glanced quickly at the fallen men and ran past Jeanne and through the stairwell to the roof. Thor and Jeanne now took positions at the end of the hall to keep anyone else from entering the stairwell to the roof.

Thor looked at Jeanne. She was in a different zone. She wasn't even breathing hard. They heard footsteps coming from the adjacent hall. It was Simon and Nelson.

Simon said, "All clear below. Just need to secure the roof." The four of them ran for the roof stairwell. They arrived just in time to see the helicopter lifting from the pad and making a sharp turn to the south.

Simon raised his gun to fire, Roger yelled. "Hold your fire, we have him."

Simon shook his head, "It really worked?"

Roger nodded. Nelson looked around at the bodies on the roof. He counted at least five men down. A couple seemed to be injured, not dead. John Barry and Paul had them at gunpoint. Sirens screamed from all directions converging on the casino.

In the helicopter Manio shouted to the pilot, "Thank God, it's you. When my pilot got shot, I thought I was done."

Mathew Core turned around and smiled, "You are. I work for the good guys now."

The co-pilot turned around, pointed a gun at Manio, and removed his helmet.

Zack smiled and yelled to be heard above the rotors of the copter, "You are under arrest. You're being delivered to the United States Navy. Want to have me read you your rights now or later?"

Manio looked out the side of the copter. The waters of the gulf looked black and foreboding. Core watched Manio in his mirror. He yelled at Zack, "Take over."

Core turned to face Manio, "Remember giving the order to kidnap my wife and daughter?"

Manio went pale.

Core continued, "A sharp turn here and you just happen to fall in the gulf. Saves Dance a lot of paperwork."

Manio scowled at Core, "Dance would never have approved that."

Core clenched his teeth. The temptation to push Manio out was almost overwhelming. "You are probably right." He shot Manio in the arm. "He won't mind that though."

* * *

The team was back at the field office. Roger called Catahoula after it was confirmed that Manio was in the custody of the Navy. Catahoula snickered. "Are you done in New Orleans now? Can't be much left."

Roger answered, "I'm afraid something is in the works, but I don't have any details. It's these other members of what we call LUCY. I understand there is a lot of chatter that points to some kind of retaliation."

Catahoula sighed, "There are always going to be bad guys, Roger. Do yourself a favor and take a break. Life's too short."

Roger walked into the locker room at the field office where his team was replacing the equipment. The adrenaline was pumping as everyone shared their stories from the night. Roger felt a lump in his throat. He hated to say goodbye to this team. Every single one of them was special. Every single one of them would have laid down their lives for each other. Roger shook his head. He didn't know if he could do it.

Paul looked over and knew exactly what Roger was feeling, but the time was now. Paul walked over to Roger and said, "You going to cut these guys loose? You managed not to kill them."

Roger looked at Paul and nodded. That was the plus side of sending them home. They were safe.

Roger cleared his throat. "Could I have your attention for a minute?"

Everyone stopped talking and faced Roger. Roger smiled at them all. He hoped his voice didn't crack when he began speaking again.

"This is tough for me." Roger cleared his throat. "It has been an honor working with each of you. This team will be legendary in the agency. Actually, I think you already are. I am proud to have been a part of it all with you." Roger swallowed. Looking at their faces he realized how important each of them had become to him. "I wish you all a safe and healthy future."

Roger wasn't much for goodbyes and he wanted-ed the team gone before any of them got wind of the LUCY problem. They would want to help, and Roger didn't want to risk them with some unknown LUCY plan. It was better to keep it short and send them home.

Thor asked, "You going somewhere?"

Roger chuckled, "No. You are. We are officially done in New Orleans."

The room was silent for a minute and Nelson finally exclaimed, "I am going to be bored *shitless* for the rest of my career!" Laughter broke the awkward silence.

Roger and Paul stood at the door as each team member left the room. The handshakes were both a celebration of a job well done, and the sadness of leaving good friends. Simon stopped in the doorway, "Not that I haven't had fun, but I made plane reservations for an hour from now. Mind if I take a company car to the airport?"

Roger and Paul started laughing. Roger smiled, "Do whatever you want. Are you going to keep an eye on Pablo?"

Simon nodded, "It appears I don't have a choice. The asshole is flying out with me tonight. Like trying to shake a puppy."

After everyone left, John Barry walked over. "We have some more LUCY chatter to talk about."

CHAPTER
THIRTY TWO

Thor had walked back to Jeanne's house again. He didn't know what he would say when she came home. He knew he didn't want to spend the rest of his life thinking he had let the moment pass. He felt in his pocket and pulled out the feather Simon had given him. Damn it all. What if she was his goose? What if he was wrong?

He leaned back in the porch chair, pushed his chin up and closed his eyes. What was he going to do? Now that the case was done, his mind was flooded with thoughts of her. The hot, sticky air made the skin on his arm shine from the porch light. He looked around, the shadows the porch light cast on the old swing almost camouflaged the potted dead plant. He could imagine her sitting there. He stretched his legs out in front of him, the muscles of his thighs pulled at the seams of his jeans, and he gave the swing a short kick. Thor listened to the rhythmic moan of the heavy chain against the support hook. He felt a cool breeze pass through and closed his eyes again.

He started to think of her. He could feel his blood flowing faster, his chest stretching the sweat stained t-shirt. He could smell the leather of his shoulder harness and the sulfur from his gun. He was drowning in his thoughts of her. He ached. Each pore of his body was acutely aware of his tension. His throat was dry and constricted. He pushed himself to sit up straight. Forced his mind to clear, and opened his eyes.

She was standing in front of him.

Jeanne leaned against the porch support. Strands of her black hair were plastered to her neck from sweat. Her chest heaved from having jogged in the thick humid air. Her thoughts had been jumbled by her desire for him. She had fought to regain control. Her punishing run had backfired. She wasn't exhausted, she was *alive*. With each deep breath she felt every muscle and nerve in her body speak to her. Her skin tingled from the beads of sweat that ran down her spine.

He was here.

Their eyes locked, neither of them wanting to be the first to speak. Thor couldn't look at her anymore. He closed his eyes for a moment so he could remind himself to breathe. He felt her touch his hand. He opened his eyes when her hand gently pulled on his. He slowly stood. Jeanne moved toward him a step, lowered her lashes slightly, and

Thor felt a force field pull him to her. He wrapped his arms around her and pulled her to his body. Jeanne raised her chin and her lips met his. Thor drowned in a mad swirl of passion. The porch door slammed shut behind them.

✳ ✳ ✳

Jimmy sat on the boat with Tourey and tried again to call Core. Jimmy glanced at Tourey, "How long have you been with the company?"

Tourey answered, "Lately, I've been thinkin' too long. Goin' on twenty five years. You?"

Jimmy shuffled his body on the hard boat seat, "About ten. Met Core when I first came on. He shot my leg so he could save my life. Long story."

Tourey just nodded. "What's going down tonight?"

Jimmy checked his phone again for missed calls, "Got some bad dudes coming here to blow up something. I'm thinking deep water well. Nobody tells us the whole story, you know how it is." Jimmy looked at what Tourey had brought for Core. He pointed to the items and said, "That's some bad ass shit. I bet Core is going to make sure the backflow preventers are operable, and then set a counter charge to stop the main explosion."

Tourey said, "That's my guess too. I think it sounds ambitious, considering he will be fighting off whoever has been sent. He won't have much time."

Jimmy stood and stretched his legs, "Yeah, this one might be too much."

Jimmy's phone rang, it was Core. "Zack and I will be there in about ten minutes. Did Tourey show up?"

Jimmy answered, "Yes. Before you ask, I haven't heard any more from the company."

Core hung up and looked at Zack. "SUV at two o'clock." Core and Zack were in the shadows at a remote airstrip east of New Orleans. Core had kept Manio's helicopter and landed in the brush a mile away.

Zack pointed in the sky, "There they are."

A small Cessna circled the landing strip and lowered with military precision. Four men walked down the jet's ramp and got into the SUV. Core focused his binoculars to read the plate number on the car. He got a clear vision of the driver. Shit.

Core looked at Zack, "I know the driver. He did some work in Iraq and Afghanistan. Contractor. Him being here tells me everything I need to know about 'what' they plan to do. Now the question is, which one?"

Zack asked, "Which one what?"

Core answered, "They're going to blow a live deep well. Cause a spill. This guy has done it before."

Zack rubbed the back of his neck and followed Core back to the helicopter. Zack asked, "You think the oil company is going to blow their own rig? Isn't that kind of stupid?"

Core laughed, "They don't pay for it! Congress passed a legal cap on how much they can be fined and assessed for cleanup charges. Oil companies make sure there are at least three other companies with some kind of liability to keep it jammed in the courts for years. They can drag out a spill as long as needed. Let that puppy pump. Let's say, as an example, for some crazy reason their bought and paid for politician isn't elected President. The next best thing is to stick the guy they don't like, with a gigantic problem his first months in office. Get him to start seeing things your way as it drags out, and miraculously the spill gets fixed. It takes real skill to blow this just right." Core frowned, "The real beauty? It gives them an excuse to raise oil prices. They actually make money from it all. Record profits. Go figure."

Core dialed Roger, gave him the plate number of the SUV and told him what he was watching. Core ended with, "I need some good Intel fast. We definitely have a problem."

Roger hung up from Core and relayed what was happening to Paul and John. John immediately dialed someone at OSI and Roger called the

Director. Someone had to know something they weren't sharing.

Paul walked down to Frank Mass's office to see if he was still in the building. He was. Paul knocked on the open door, "I'm curious if you have had an update on the members of the sicko club that have met an untimely death lately."

Mass looked at his email. "Here's one. LA office. Number of suspicious deaths on sicko club list at ninety seven. Members warned."

Mass looked at the rest of his emails. "Here's another from Dallas office: Minister willing to trade info for protection. Please provide advice."

Mass looked up at Paul, "Well? What's our advice?" Mass was ready to answer the email.

Paul answered, "Have them call Catahoula. He might not need any more evidence."

Paul turned to rejoin Roger and John, "Catahoula will probably tell this minister to pray."

Ellen finished updating the Director, gave him transcripts from Donavan's conference call, and headed for New Orleans. She called us and told us to meet her at the docks. We had been playing cards waiting for her call. It's hard to cheat when the other players can read your mind! I still tried.

Linda said, "How much you want to bet we're going swimming again."

We looked and Mary had already put on a darling swimsuit. She is one gifted gal.

We flew over the docks and saw Tourey sitting in a boat with the CIA guy named Jimmy. We flew in so we could get an idea what was going on before Ellen got there. We kind of just hovered above them while they talked. I saw a box on the floor that was marked explosives and elbowed Teresa to look.

"Cool!"

Cool?

I also saw some sort of tool box and a canister labeled 'hazardous material, dangerous'. This little job might get ugly.

I looked at Linda, "Do you think Tourey is going to blow something up?"

Ellen popped up, "Not Tourey."

The Director had sent the transcripts of Donavan's conference call to Roger's email. While he waited for Roger's call he dialed the Director of OSI. He was still trying to form an explanation for how he got the transcripts when the OSI Director answered.

"Congratulations on your money sting, the port raids, and I guess arresting Jessie Manio. This has been quite a ride, hasn't it?"

The FBI Director answered, "I'm afraid it's not over. If I send you an email of some transcripts, can you forget where you got them for a few hours? I need your help."

The Director of OSI was surprised by the request. He and the FBI Director had formed a new friendship and trust during the last weeks, but very seldom was information shared in this manner between agencies. "I guess you are looking to avoid our normal channels. The obvious next question would be, who are we worried about?"

The FBI Director answered, "Everybody. LUCY has a Plan B. If they are successful, our bigger worry is who caves in to them, and why. I want you to help me assume the worse and develop a Plan B of our own."

The Director of OSI said, "Send it over. Will this hell ever stop?"

Distant air horns from cargo ships and tankers filled the muggy, hot night air. The normal sounds of the docks masked the motor of the idling jet boat at the pier. The boat's running lights were off, leaving the moonlight that peeked from passing clouds the only risk to the shadowy figures moving along the pier. All four men were wearing wet suits and carrying waterproof bags. Two of the men gingerly handed a large cylinder to the men on the boat. The cylinder was placed in a security harness and cinched tight. The remaining two men boarded, and the boat quietly sped away from the dock.

Roger, Paul, and John poured over the transcripts from the Director's email. John threw his pages down on the table. "Those arrogant sons of bitches!" John was shouting. "Damn, I'm sick of this shit!"

Paul was hoping he was interpreting the transcripts wrong. "They plan to cause an oil spill in the gulf?"

Roger sighed. He was sick to his stomach. An oil spill from a live deep water well would be devastating to the gulf, the wildlife, the area economy. Some communities would never recover. These plans had been set into play hours ago. Core had already seen the blast team arrive. He had warned Roger that it didn't look good.

Roger stood, "We can try to catch these guys before they arrive at the designated well."

John practically shouted, "How? We don't even know which well! There are six thousand wells in the gulf."

Roger looked at the ceiling, "Ellen, we need you."

Ellen appeared as a hologram. "Don't worry. I have frozen everyone else in the building. You need to know which well? It's number 3290 Lanitol deep well. It is the third largest deep well in the gulf and is actively pumping. The regular employees have been told to evacuate the site and are doing so now. They were told there was seismic activity that could compromise the well and their safety."

John was incredulous, "They plan on blaming an earthquake?"

Ellen answered, "Initially. They have staged a malfunction of control equipment to make it look that way. Then they plan to blame the men being evacuated for not arming all of the security and safety features of the well."

Roger asked, "Why isn't all of this in the transcripts?"

Ellen answered, "I just got this from reading the mind of one of the men headed for the well."

Roger asked, "We know where they are? Can we stop them?"

Ellen paused before answering, "The only way to stop them will risk other mortal lives. The gals and I are going to meet these men at the well site and do our best to stop them. We are prohibited from doing them harm. And we can only manipulate mortal environments within certain criteria."

Roger was stunned. It sounded as if even the angels couldn't really help. Roger said, "Thank you Ellen. I appreciate your candor and what you are doing."

Ellen said, "I must leave now, but I suggest you have a Coast Guard boat in the vicinity of the well. Not too close. But just in case. You never know when a miracle might happen." She was gone.

John asked, "What did that mean? A miracle? I thought she said there wasn't anything she could do?"

Roger had his phone out dialing the Coast Guard, "I have no idea but I'm getting the Coast Guard out there. I want to be there, too."

Paul said, "Tell them they have three passengers to load before they take off."

Zack and Core arrived at the pier and met Jimmy. Tourey had left. Core looked over the items Tourey had obtained and smiled. He got his whole Christmas list. Core asked Jimmy, "Any hint where this is happening yet?"

Jimmy shook his head. Core's phone rang, it was Roger. "Yeah."

Roger said, "Our Intel indicates this is out of our control now. It doesn't look as if there is much we can do. I wanted to thank you for everything you *have* done Mathew."

Core answered, "Give me some credit man. What's the well number? I might know something that can be done."

Roger wasn't about to send Core on a suicide mission. "Let it go. Jamie and Lisa are waiting for you." Roger hung up.

Jimmy's phone rang, he listened a minute, hung up, and yelled over to Core, "Well number 3290 Lanitol."

Core walked over and put his arm around Jimmy's shoulder. "Thanks, man." Then he punched Jimmy so hard he was out cold.

Zack glared at Core, "Don't even try that shit on me. I'm going with you. One man can't do this."

Core frowned, "I don't have time to argue. Stay here. This is a one way trip."

Core jumped into the boat, turned the key, and twisted to full throttle. Zack jumped into the boat just in time. "What the hell! You think I'm going to let you get all the glory?"

Core frowned as he yelled over the noise of the engine, "I'm serious. I don't expect to come back."

Zack shook his head and yelled back, "At this rate we're not even going to get there. Move it!"

CHAPTER
THIRTY THREE

The Coast Guard had the boat ready and took off as soon as John, Paul and Roger boarded. Roger told them there had been a seismic warning at 3290 Lanitol Oil and he was concerned about recovery of any employees should there really be a problem. It was impossible to come up with a viable story in such a short time frames. He knew the Coast Guard staff thought he was crazy. Thank God the martial law order was still in effect.

John's phone rang, it was the Director of OSI. John pulled on his neck as he listened and gave worried looks to Roger and Paul.

John hung up. "My Director just got a call from the CIA. The undercover man with Core and Zack passed on the well number to Core. He didn't know not to. Core slugged him and took a boat. Both Core and Zack are headed for the well."

Roger cursed and slammed his fist on the side of the boat. It was a suicide mission. Roger asked for Ellen. Suddenly a black cat was sitting on the rail of the boat. Paul looked around nervously as John tried to shield Ellen from anyone's view.

Roger said, "I'm sure you are very busy." Ellen winked. "We have just found out that Mathew Core and Zack are heading for the well to stop these guys. Can you help them?" Ellen just stared at Roger. John and Paul were getting nervous. Roger felt sick to his stomach. Roger said, "If these guys manage to stop this well from a spill it will save thousands of wildlife habitats and animals. Not to mention the human suffering. If they can't stop them, I am worried they are going to die trying." Roger didn't know what else to say. Then it hit him that Ellen had rules she had to follow and that she had bosses, too.

Roger asked, "Is there a higher power you can ask to intervene?" Ellen winked.

Roger nodded his head. "Thank you, Ellen. I won't take any more of your time. We are going to be near the well in case we are needed." Ellen vanished.

"Where'd she go?" I was looking all over for Ellen. She had left us on a pier under a drilling station, watching four guys in wet suits. These did look like pretty rough dudes. They had what looked like big metal fish with handle bars they had unloaded from their boat onto the pier.

Teresa said, "I've seen those things on TV. They propel people through the water fast. See that fan thing in the back?"

Mary said, "I think that's the front. They ride on top of them." Huh, kind of looks like fun.

The men were putting on oxygen masks and tanks and slipping off the pier into the black water. Mary shouted, "I'm going in. We need to see what they are doing."

Linda yelled after her, "Read their minds while you're down there!" Mary was already gone. "Dang it." Linda jumped into the water and followed Mary down.

Teresa looked at me, "I suppose we should go, too."

"Yup." Sure wish I could think of something else that needed doing. Wet air, here I come.

Teresa and I dove in together and had to swim a long ways, straight down, before we saw Linda and Mary and the four guys. It was like an underground factory down there. The four men had docked their 'fish' things in what looked like bicycle racks alongside a huge iron pipe. We must have been at least a couple of hundred feet under the surface and it was pitch black except for the flashlights on the swimmer's masks. We could see bubbles coming from their tanks.

Two of the men were turning a huge wheel that looked like a hatch in a submarine. The men opened the hatch and swam into what looked like a big control room. We watched them start flipping switches and pushing buttons. Mary was reading their minds.

"These controls are for backflow preventers on the main pipeline. These controls are supposed to keep oil from coming back through the pipe in the event of an explosion or something. These guys are shutting them off!"

Teresa had followed the other two men straight down the side of the huge pipe toward the floor of the gulf. She sent us her thoughts, "These other two guys are taking explosives further down the pipe to blow it where it will cause the largest leak but actually be the easiest repair later. You guys swim down here. You won't believe how far down we are! Man, is it dark!"

I started swimming down to Teresa. Mary and Linda were still at the underwater control room attached to the main pipeline. It was amazingly easy to understand each other considering we were all underwater. I tried to talk with a gurgle just to mess with them. Teresa made me stop.

Mary suddenly screamed, "We have company! It's Mathew Core and Zack!"

Mary and Linda were watching Core and Zack swimming toward the two men in wet suits that had entered the control room.

Teresa and I were about as far down as you could go. The two men we were watching were actually walking on the floor of the gulf. Teresa yelled to Mary and Linda, "These guys down here just set some kind of timer on an explosive canister. They are on their way back up to you."

Linda yelled to all of us, "Core and Zack are here. They are trying to keep the two guys up here away from the backflow preventers. Zack is in the control room fixing what these guys messed up I think. Core is wrestling with both of these bad guys."

Teresa and I swam as fast as we could back up the side of the huge pipe toward Linda and Mary. Suddenly Ellen was next to Mary and told us all, "Start pulling the air hoses of the bad guys. They will head for the surface for air."

Easier said than done. They were screwed in or something. I was twisting and pulling and screaming at the stupid thing to come off. Teresa came over and showed me you pushed in and twist. Like a child proof medicine cap. I hate those, too.

The two guys that had been at the bottom setting the explosive charge were now at our level in the water and pushing on Core and Zack's masks. One guy pulled out a long knife and pulled back to stab Core. Core twisted the guy's arm for what seemed like three minutes, and managed to turn the knife all the way around. Core stabbed the bad guy in the chest. He slowly floated toward the surface leaving a wiggly trail of blood behind him.

Teresa managed to disconnect the air hose of the other guy Core was wrestling and that guy quickly swam for the top. Linda disconnected another guy's hose and he left for the surface too. Core swam over and stabbed the guy attacking Zack. All the bad guys were gone now.

Zack swam behind Core in a race to the gulf's floor to stop the timer on the explosive. Core was carrying his explosives. It was too late. The pressure from the blast shook the earth beneath the water and gushed rocks and debris toward us like a meteorite shower stuck in a tsunami. We could see Core and Zack being forced towards us in a frothy, tumultuous underwater wave. Ellen jumped in front of us and yelled, "Grab them as they get close to you. Take them to the top and hold them out of the water as far from here as you can."

We could see Core and Zack being blasted toward us from the bottom of the gulf. They looked dead, and contorted. Mary and Linda grabbed Core as the force of the blast pushed him toward them. Teresa and I grabbed Zack. I could see Ellen and Granny standing just below us, in the center of a massive swirling tunnel. Their arms were spread wide. They had frozen the wall of debris and water from the blast. Ellen yelled, "Hurry, we can't hold this very long."

On the Coast Guard boat the first sign something was wrong was what sounded like a large burp, then a rumble. It felt as though the oxygen was being sucked out of the air. A tremendous pressure preceded an earth shattering, earsplitting blast! The entire top of the oil platform launched itself in an explosion of flames that shot as high as you could see. Black toxic smoke billowed and mushroomed above the rig. Every few seconds another explosion rocked the air. Finally one huge blast actually blasted the glass out of the windows on the Coast Guard boat.

Roger covered his face to shield it from the flying glass. His arms were bleeding, his heart pounded. He turned to see if Paul and John were okay. Paul had been thrown to the deck floor and John was wiping blood from his neck.

Roger grabbed Paul's arm and helped him up, "You guys okay?"

Paul nodded. He looked at Roger with empty eyes. John said, "We have two men in that hell fire."

Another, smaller blast sent white flames shooting horizontally across the surface of the gulf waters, igniting the fuel on the water's surface. It was a sea of fire. Roger turned his head from the blazing light.

Then there was only the sound of the roaring flames and sirens.

Roger, Paul and John were speechless. The Coast Guard alarm horns were sounding and their rescue lights of blue and red flashed above. The deck hands loaded into the rescue boats in case survivors could be found. The waters were black and the debris had fallen as far from the platform as the Coast Guard boat. It was as if hell had risen out of the center of the gulf.

Roger, Paul and John watched helplessly as the rescue boats raced toward the platform.

At least thirty officers scanned the surface of the water with their high powered night vision binoculars. They were looking for signs of life. Nothing.

✳ ✳ ✳

Tourey had circled back to the pier and found Jimmy nursing his jaw. The explosion lit up the docks like an atom bomb. Ambulances and emergency vehicles swarmed the docks. Everyone was hoping to assist survivors.

Jimmy looked at Tourey, "Core knocked me out. They knew it was a suicide mission."

Tourey had felt the blast ten blocks from the docks. He knew no one could have survived that explosion. Even if they had been able to stop the deep well blast with the backflow preventers, they wouldn't have had time to get out of there in a boat.

Tourey dialed John, "Not lookin' good. LUCY will let this leak 'til they get what they want. Where are you?"

John answered, "I'm with the Coast Guard recovery boat. No luck so far." John had hung up.
Tourey knew that tone in John's voice. He had
heard it before. Like before, it had been LUCY.

Wet air my foot. Geesh! Mary had Mathew Core,
Linda had Zack, Teresa had one of the bad guys,
I had one of the bad guys, and Ellen had a bad
guy in each hand. We were swimming under them
and holding them up for the Coast Guard to see.
We couldn't even see Mary and Linda but they had
told us they had no idea what kind of shape Core
and Zack were in.

A bright light swept across the surface of the
water above me and someone lifted the bad guy
away. Whew. Talk about water sports.

Roger, Paul, and John anxiously identified the
men as they were lifted on board. They were dead.
Roger told the Coast Guard Captain, "These four
are all criminals. Our guys are still out there."

The Captain said something in his radio and
then looked at Roger, "We've got two more!"

Roger asked, "Are they alive?"

"Yes."

Roger moved to the side so Kim could walk down the tunnel first. Once they reached the tarmac the warm Hawaiian breeze blew her hair across his face. He swiped it away and chuckled. "Is this beautiful or what?"

Roger gave Kim a big kiss, picked up their bags and said, "Let's get my business over with right away. Should only take a short while, and then we don't even have to leave the beach if you don't want to."

Kim smiled. It was so nice to see Roger relaxed. He said it was the shirt she made him wear. A big Hawaiian print. They hadn't even talked that much on the flight down. Roger kept dozing off. Then waking up to ask her what she was reading. She answered the same every time, "Same book I was reading when we took off." Roger smiled every time she answered, rubbed her arm, and fell asleep again.

Roger hailed a cab and handed an address to the driver. "When we get there I want you to wait for us and take us on to our hotel if that is okay."

The driver nodded.

Kim asked Roger, "Where are we going?"

Roger answered, "To a hospital. I want you to meet a friend of mine."

Kim left her book in her purse and watched the beautiful Hawaiian scenery flash by their windows. After about fifteen minutes, the driver pulled into a long drive that opened up to a rather small facility. It was only three stories and had garden type grounds.

"This doesn't look like a hospital."

Roger answered, "It's not supposed to. It is for very important patients."

Kim noticed the security personnel everywhere. Wow, must be very important patients.

They walked down a long hall after Roger had cleared them through the main security. Roger knocked on a door and opened it. It was a large, well lit room. A man was in a wheel chair and a little girl was on his lap. A beautiful woman stood at the window, turned and rushed over to hug Roger. She wiped tears as she pulled away and nodded at Kim.

"I'm sorry. Roger is my hero." Lisa wiped tears again and put her hand out to Kim, "Lisa Core."

Kim shook her hand and smiled. She knew who Lisa was from what Roger had told her about the case. Kim pointed, "That must be Jamie?"

Lisa was smiling. "Come meet Mathew."

Roger and Kim visited a while and then said their goodbyes. In the cab Kim asked Roger, "Will they be safe?"

Roger nodded, "Safe and happy from the way it looks."

Kim smiled, "Sounds like a miracle there wasn't an oil spill. The newspaper said a lot of important people have been arrested for plotting it all."

Roger leaned over and kissed Kim's cheek. He had a grin from ear to ear.

✳ ✳ ✳

Mary sipped her tall umbrella drink, wiggled her toes in the sand and said, "Well, we finally made it to Hawaii."

Teresa, Linda, and I took big sips of our drinks and tried to count how many colors we saw in the sunset.

Teresa asked no one in particular, "What do you think happens to us now?"

Suddenly Ellen was sitting in the sand with us and smiled. "What do you think happens now?"

Mary answered, "I'm proud of how we have done on our first assignment. I think it would be a waste of perfectly good skills to stop helping mortals now that we know what we're doing."

We do?

Ellen nodded. "I can tell you all feel the same as Mary. That's good. We have another assignment waiting as soon as your vacation here is over."

Linda asked, "What kind of assignment?"

"Midnight gals. Meet you at Transition College in the park." Ellen was gone.

Wow, that was only six hours away. Heaven isn't big on vacations evidently.

Kim and Roger were on beach chairs behind us, but Linda had promised Kim we wouldn't peek.

We went back to counting the colors in the sunset. They had all changed in that short time.

A tiny surfer was riding a huge wave. We all watched mesmerized by the beauty of it and the skill that it took to stay right in that curl.

Teresa sat up straight and said, "I think that's Ellen!"

The surfer waved at us right at that moment. Huh.

In Memory

During the writing of this last book of the Trilogy, our dear friend, and co-author, Mary Hale, passed unexpectedly. She is now truly an Angel. She will always be a Shallow End Gal, and will remain in our hearts as well as our future books.

Mary Rachel Hale

With us from

10-6-1950 until 02-27-2013

The Shallow End Gals...Book 3

List of Characters

FBI

Supervisory Special Agent Roger Dance, Senior FBI lead on case

Supervisory Special Agent Paul Casey, number 2 FBI Agent on case

Supervisory Special Agent Dan Thor, Indy Senior Agent...involved with Patterson arrest

Special Agent Ray Davis, FBI Computer tech

Special Agent Todd Nelson, arresting officer of William Patterson in Book One, team member Book Two

Supervisory Special Agent Simon Frost, Senior agent team member from book 2

Special Agent Pablo Manigat, team member book 2, brother of Jeanne

Special Agent Jeanne Manigat, sister of Pablo and victim of Devon and Patterson in New Orleans, book 2

Supervisory Special Agent Frank Mass, Senior Agent in New Orleans office

List of friends *not* approved by Mom

William Patterson, convicted embezzler, child molester, escaped...alias Bernard Jacobs (Book 2)

Jesse Manio, Head of the Manio Cartel

Juan Zelez, Head of the Zelez Cartel

Jason Sims, CIA computer genius, mole in LUCY

Thomas Fenley, works within DC inner circles, represents oil interests, works for LUCY

Donavan Luntz, Chairman, oil consortium, London, current head of LUCY

William C. Thornton, Deputy Director FBI, affiliated with LUCY

Senator Rolland Kenny (Retired), friend of Patterson, member of the sicko club

Theodore Chain, Gallery Owner, member of the sicko club

Andre Baton, Loyola University Benefactor, member of the sicko club

Judge Harold Williams, member of the sicko club

Ramon Daily, 'Chiclet', works with crime gangs in New Orleans

Dayrl Cotton, gang member working in human trafficking

Interesting characters

Kim. Angel Vicki's daughter

Mathew Core, the Fixer, does work for CIA and DOD, black op enemy of LUCY

Tourey Waknem, CIA Undercover, native N.O.

Jimmy, CIA undercover, mole in Manio cartel

Zack, ATF undercover helping Roger

Mambo, Voodoo Queen that lives by Honey Island, NOLA

Jeremiah Dumaine, old swamp man

Allan Dumaine, Jeremiah's nephew

Adele Brown, "Other woman", found in swamp by Jeremiah, book 2

Jerome Brown, Adele Brown's son

Abram Davis, new "boss" for crime gang

Jackson Moore, hired by Abram Davis upon jail release

Lisa Core, Mathew Core's wife

Jamie Core, Mathew Core's daughter

"Spicey", Sadie Corbin, self-proclaimed psychic in New Orleans

Sasha, Spicey's friend and co-worker

Cindy Roy, friend of Spicey's on vacation in New Orleans

Carolyn Gale, friend of Spicey's on vacation in New Orleans

Wilma Abrams, cleaning lady for Patterson

George Fetter, works at Gallery owned by Theodore Chain, helped Tourey, Book 2

John Barry, retired CIA, now OSI (Office of Special Investigations)

Dusty, portrait Artist

Scotty, Bartender at Mickey's

Franklin Morris, Federal Reserve Board of Governors

Angels

Ellen, Angel Trainer that looks like Ellen DeGeneres

Betty, Angel Trainer that looks like Betty White

Linda, Mary, Teresa, Vicki...Angels in training